Dark Calling &
HELL'S HEROES

Other titles by
DARREN SHAN

Also available on audio

Dark Calling first published in hardback in Great Britain
by HarperCollins *Children's Books* 2009
Hell's Heroes first published in hardback in Great Britain
by HarperCollins *Children's Books* 2009
Published together in this two-in-one edition in 2011
HarperCollins *Children's Books* is a division of HarperCollins*Publishers* Ltd,
77-85 Fulham Palace Road, Hammersmith, London W6 8JB

The HarperCollins website address is
www.harpercollins.co.uk

Darren Shan presides over the demon universe at
www.darrenshan.com

1

ISBN: 978-0-00-743651-4

Printed and bound in England by
Clays Ltd, St Ives plc

MIX
Paper from
responsible sources
FSC® C007454

FSC is a non-profit international organisation established to promote the
responsible management of the world's forests. Products carrying the FSC
label are independently certified to assure consumers that they come
from forests that are managed to meet the social, economic and
ecological needs of present and future generations.

Find out more about HarperCollins and the environment at
www.harpercollins.co.uk/green

DARREN SHAN
THE DEMONATA VOL. 9 & 10

Dark Calling &
HELL'S HEROES

HarperCollins *Children's Books*

CONTENTS

Dark Calling

TURN AROUND, BRIGHT EYES

→A small, wiry, scorpion-shaped demon with a semi-human face drives its stinger into my right eye. My eyeball pops and gooey streaks flood down my cheek. In complete agony, I scream helplessly, but worse is to come. The demon spits into the empty socket. At first I think it's just phlegm, but then dozens of tiny *things* start to wriggle in the space where my eye once swam. As I fill with confused horror, teeth or claws dig into the bone around my ruined eye. Whatever the mini-monsters are, they're trying to tunnel through to my brain.

Beranabus roars, "*Kernel!*" and tries to g

I wheel away from him as insanity and

I whip around, flailing, shrieking

strikes again and punctures

consumes me. I'm in hell.

it's Lord Loss. I don't

might be

here

13

→A lifetime later.

I've fallen a

Beranabus

know or care. All I can focus on is the blind, hellish pain.

I pull away from the person or demon and run from the madness, but crash into something hard. I fall, moaning and screaming, but not crying — I no longer have eyes to weep with. The creatures which were spat into my eyes are munching on my brain now. I try to scrape them out with my fingers, but that just adds to the torment.

Then magic sears through my ruined sockets. The things in my head burn and drop away. The pain lessens. I sigh blissfully and slump unconscious.

→I dream of the end of the world. Everything comes apart and everyone perishes. The universe warps and twists upon itself. In my dream, I float as a spirit through panels of light. I don't know how I see the lights without eyes, but I do. There are others — Grubbs, Beranabus, a girl. I slot the patches of light together and we sail from one window to another. Peaceful. No pain. I'm at ease. In my element. Master lights.

his is heaven. Constructing and passing ss series of windows. An eternal, show. I'll settle for that. e, blindness and micro-

→Heaven doesn't last. I wasn't dreaming. The destruction was real. The lights fade and I find myself back on Earth. Blind as ever. Pain muted by magic, but hovering, waiting for its chance to kick back in. Turns out the creatures in my eyes were *maggots*.

No time for panic or self-pity. Beranabus drops a bombshell — we've travelled through time. I'm part of a magical weapon, the Kah-Gash. Grubbs is another part. By linking with the third component, the ghost of a dead girl, we took our doomed world into the past to avert demonic conquest. Now we have to fight again or it will all have been for nothing.

→In a cave. Blindly battling Spine, the scorpion demon. I have the horrible beast pinned to a stalagmite. I'm pounding him with my fists, over and over. Without warning he melts away and I'm left standing in a puddle of sticky blood, frowning sightlessly.

I later learn that I've been cheated out of my revenge by a girl called Bec who's returned to life after sixteen hundred years. She drives Lord Loss back to his own foul realm. Job done.

→We return to the universe of the Demonata. Grubbs comes with us, but Bec stays behind. I'm surprised Beranabus leaves her. She's part of the Kah-Gash. By uniting us, he could wield the power of the ancient weapon and destroy the Demonata. But he's afraid. The Kah-Gash made an independent decision to reverse time. Beranabus isn't sure whether that was a conscious act of mercy or a random reaction. He doesn't want to press ahead, worried the weapon might side with the demons next time and wipe out mankind.

I'm stronger in the universe of magic. I numb my pain and set to work on building a new set of eyes. I'm not sure that I can. Magic varies from person to person. We all have different capabilities. Some can restore a missing limb or organ. Others can't. You never know until you try.

Thankfully I'm one of those who can. With only the slightest guidance from Beranabus I construct a pair of sparkling blue eyes. I build them from the rear of my sockets outwards, repairing severed nerve endings, linking them with the growing globes, letting the orbs expand to fill the gaps.

I keep my eyelids shut for a minute when the eyes are complete, afraid I won't be able to see anything when I open them. I hardly breathe, heart beating fast, contemplating a life of darkness, the worst punishment I can imagine.

Then Beranabus stamps on my foot. I yell and my

eyes snap open. I turn on the magician angrily, raising a fist, but stop when I see his cunning smile. I *see* it.

"You looked like an idiot with your eyes shut," Beranabus grunts.

"You're a bully," I pout, then laugh with relief and hug him. He's laughing too, but Grubbs isn't. The teenager glares at us. He's lost his brother and abandoned his uncle and home. He's in no mood to give a stuff about my well-being. But that's fine. Right now I can't sympathise with him either. All I care about is that I can see. I relish my new eyes, drinking in the sights of the demon world.

I'm so happy, it's several hours before I realise I can see more than before, that my new eyes have opened up a wonder of the universe previously hidden from me.

→I've always been able to see patches of light which are invisible to everybody else. For years I thought they were products of my imagination, that I was slightly (*light*ly) crazy. Then I learnt they were part of the realm of magic. I have a unique talent. I can manually slot the patches together and create windows between universes, far faster than anyone else.

I use my talent to help Beranabus save the world from demons. The magician has been around for thousands of years and has spent much of that time patrolling the demon universe, protecting humanity from its savage, nightmarish hordes. Although demons have limitless galaxies of their own, they long to cross over — they love killing humans.

Beranabus stops them. He ensures no tunnels are built between universes, holds the demon armies in check, prevents mass crossings. I assist him. My gift allows us to zip from one part of the demon universe to another and track down just about any demon we want.

I thought I might not be able to see the lights with my new eyes, but they work the same way as my original pair. I can still see the multicoloured patches, and when I think of a specific place, person or thing, some of the lights flash and I can slot them together to create a window. In fact I can do it quicker than before and my powers on Earth are greater than they were. Where I used to struggle to open windows on my own world, now I can do it swiftly and easily.

But now there are other lights. At first I thought they were illusionary specks, that my new eyes weren't working properly. But I soon realised the lights were real and fundamentally different to those I was familiar with. They're smaller, they change shape and their colours mutate. The regular lights never alter in size or shade, but these new patches grow and subside, bleed from one colour to another. A square pink panel can lengthen into a triangular blue patch, then gradually twist into an orange octagon, and so on.

They shimmer too. Their edges flicker like faulty fluorescent tubes. Sometimes creases run through them, like ripples spreading across the face of a pond.

I can't control the new lights. They ignore me when I try to manipulate them. In fact, if I start to get close, they glide away from me.

There aren't many of them, no more than twenty or thirty anywhere I go. But they worry me. There's something deeply unsettling about them. I initially thought that I was nervous of them just because they were new. But several weeks later, as I was trying to coax them nearer and link them up, they whispered to me.

I know it's ridiculous. Lights can't whisper. But I swear I heard a voice calling to me. It sounded like static to begin with, but then it came into focus, a single word repeated over and over. It's the same word the lights have been whispering to me ever since, softly, slyly, seductively.

Come…"

A WORD IN YOUR EAR

→Beranabus unleashes a burst of magic and the gazelle-shaped demon we've been chasing stops in its tracks. The beast turns and snarls at us. It has the head of a human baby. Opening its mouth, it wails. The noise increases sharply and blood trickles from my ears and nose. I use magic to mute the demon's cry. Beranabus and Grubbs do the same and the three of us close in on the mewling monster.

When the demon realises it can't harm us with its harpy-like wailing, it falls silent and its look of hatred changes to one of fear. It knows who we are and what we want.

I hang back while Beranabus tortures the creature. I have a problem with demons that model themselves after babies or young children. I can't bring myself to hurt them, even though I know they've only stolen their human attributes.

I was a lonely child. Driven by unhappiness, I unintentionally tapped into my powers, kidnapped a demon and used magic to make it look like a baby. I convinced myself the changeling was my brother and I maintained the lie for ages. I was shattered when I learnt the truth. Demons like this one make me think of my "brother" Art and I go cold at the thought of harming them. Beranabus understands. He doesn't try to push me.

Grubbs rips off the demon's head. The baby-faced monster squeals with pain and terror, but doesn't die. In this universe of magic almost anything is possible. Physical dismemberment won't necessarily kill a demon. You need to use magic to finish it off.

Grubbs hates this life even more than I do. When I agreed to join Beranabus and devote myself to battling demons, I didn't have a better choice. My parents knew I wasn't normal, and though they loved me, they feared what I might do. I didn't have any friends. It was Beranabus or a life of isolation and loneliness.

Grubbs has an uncle who he loves like a father. He has lots of friends. He could have rejected his destiny. I'm not really sure why he didn't. Maybe it was the call of the Kah-Gash. Perhaps the weapon persuaded him to leave the human world and ride the demonic waves of this universe with Beranabus and me.

"The Shadow," Beranabus snarls, grabbing the baby's head from Grubbs and gouging out one of its snake-shaped eyes. "Tell us all you know and we'll let you go. Otherwise…" He moves his thumb over the creature's other eye.

The Shadow is our latest foe in a long line of monstrous opponents. Beranabus thinks it's our most dangerous enemy yet, but I'm not worried. I've seen all manner of unimaginable demons. In the early days I thought each was invincible. Every time we went up against one, I was sure we were doomed. But we always got the better of the beasts, pinpointed their weak spots, defeated them with cunning if brute force failed.

I know it's dangerous to assume we'll overcome every demon we go up against, but I can't help thinking that way. I'm sure the Shadow will fall to us when we face it, just like all the others. It's simply a matter of time, patience and violence.

Beranabus and Grubbs believe the Shadow is the herald of universal doom. They saw it in the cave when I was blind, a huge beast that seemed to be made from strips of shadow. They say it was deadlier than anything else we've fought. Maybe they're right. If I'd seen it, I might be trembling with fear too. But I don't think so. It's just another demon. We've fought and killed thousands of them since I joined Beranabus. How can this one be any different?

→We're hunting a flock of sheep-like demons. Each

boasts dozens of woolly heads dotted around its body, no eyes or ears, just large mouths full of sharp teeth. Beranabus hopes they know something about the Shadow, but I think he's scraping the bottom of the barrel.

The Shadow is as elusive as the name we've given it suggests. We've learnt almost nothing of the creature in all the time we've been trying to track it. We know it's gathering an army of demons, that it's promised to wipe out mankind and restore the universe to its original condition (whatever that means), but everything else about it is a mystery.

These minor demons — easy pickings for stronger members of the Demonata — won't provide us with any clues. We're wasting our time, as we've wasted it on so many worlds. We'll torture them, kill a few, then move on, no wiser than when we stepped through the window and set off in chase of the howling beasts.

As we close in on the flock, I sense a throbbing in the air nearby and draw to a halt.

"Come on!" Beranabus shouts. "Don't stop now. We—"

"A window's opening," I tell him, and excitement instantly gives way to panic.

"Start opening one of your own," Beranabus commands and steps in front of me, to protect me.

The tall, muscular Grubbs joins him. They think a demon is after us. But I know better. I've come to understand the lights more intimately than ever since I built my new pair of eyes. This is a window of human origin.

"Wait," I tell Beranabus. "It's not a demon. We have company."

Seconds later a window of orange light opens and two of Beranabus's Disciples step through. One's a beautiful, fiery woman called Meera Flame. I know the other one better, and shout his name with unconcealed joy. "Shark!"

"Been a long time, kid," the ex-soldier grins, shaking my hand as Grubbs and Meera hug close by. Beranabus is squinting at the newcomers suspiciously. He doesn't like surprises.

"What are you doing here?" I gasp.

"Came to catch the sun," Shark laughs, then casts his gaze over my bald, caramel-coloured head. "There's something different about your eyes."

"It's a long story." I smile broadly, still clutching him. We've spent long months in this foul universe and Beranabus and Grubbs are poor company. The unwelcome flames of loneliness have been burning hot inside me recently. I'm overjoyed to see my old friend, to escape the dark feelings for a few minutes. I know Shark must be the bearer of bad news, that he and Meera wouldn't have come unless things were serious, but for a few moments I block that out and pretend this is a social visit.

"Hi, Shark," Grubbs says.

Shark frowns. "Do I know you?"

"Grubbs Grady. We…" He pauses. "Dervish told me about you. I'm Grubbs, his nephew."

Shark nods. "I can see a bit of him in you. But you've got more hair. You're a lot taller too — what's Beranabus been feeding you?"

"Enough of the prattle," Beranabus snaps. "What's wrong?"

"We were attacked," Meera says. "I was at Dervish's. We—"

"Was it Lord Loss?" Beranabus barks. "Is Bec all right?"

"She's fine," Shark says.

"But Dervish…" Meera pauses, glancing nervously at Grubbs.

"He was alive when we left," Shark says as Grubbs freezes with fear.

"But in bad shape," Meera adds. "He had a heart attack."

"We have to go back," Grubbs says, darting for the window.

Shark stops him. "Hold on. We didn't come here directly. That leads to another demon world."

"Besides," I chip in, "if the demons are still at the house…"

"We weren't attacked by demons," Meera says. "They were… *Werewolves*."

That throws me. Does she mean werewolf-shaped demons? Then I recall the curse of the Gradys. Lots of teenagers in Grubbs's family turn into mindless, savage, wolf-like beasts.

Grubbs starts to tremble. Without waiting to be told, I turn, flex my fingers and focus, thinking of Dervish. Lights pulse around me — that means the ex-punk is still alive. I begin to open a window that will take us to him. Then, on second thoughts, I focus on Bec instead. As much as I like Dervish, the girl is more important. She's probably with him, but if not she must take priority. Dervish is only human. Bec — like me and Grubbs – is so much more.

→When a window of amber light opens, Beranabus rushes through, swiftly followed by Grubbs. "There are demons," I tell Shark and Meera, sensing their presence in the vibrations of the lights. "Are you guys ready to fight?"

"Always," Shark grins, cracking his knuckles.

Meera gulps, then grinds her teeth together and nods fiercely.

We cross.

I find myself in a hospital ward. Bec is lying on the floor. She looks like any normal girl, a bit smaller than most, but otherwise unremarkable. You would never guess from looking at her that she'd been dead for sixteen hundred years, or that this body wasn't originally hers.

Two demons are backing away from Bec. One is some sort of lizard hybrid. The other looks like an anteater with several snouts. One of its eyes is missing, blood and goo surrounding the empty socket. I suppress a shudder as Beranabus growls at the demons, "What do the pickings look like now?"

They turn and run. Shark bolts after them. Meera and I follow, leaving Beranabus and Grubbs to help Bec back to her feet. I wonder about Dervish, if he's still alive, but I've no time to dwell on that. Another window is open and the hospital has been flooded with magical energy, but I'm still nowhere near as strong here as I am in the demon universe. My power will dwindle. We need to deal with these monsters swiftly, and we have to be cautious. It's much easier to die on this world.

I spot the remains of a few babies as we pursue the demons. My stomach churns and I tear my gaze away from the tiny corpses. Even so, thoughts of Art flash through my mind. I fill with sorrow, then rage. They shouldn't have gone after the newborns. That was too cruel. I'm going to make them pay.

The demons burst out of the maternity ward and scuttle towards the stairs. Shark crouches, then propels himself forward, shooting through the air as if fired from a canon. He knocks the pair of demons aside and they crash into the wall on either side of the staircase. As they yelp with surprise and pain, Meera and I fall upon them. I take the lizard, leaving Meera to deal with the anteater.

It's a slimy little beast. It slithers around and lashes at me with a forked tongue. Drops of poison hit my eyes and sizzle. I use magic to transform the drops into water, then grab the demon's tongue and yank hard. It utters a choked scream. The tongue slips through my fingers. I follow it back into the demon's mouth, jamming my hand halfway down the lizard's throat. Taking a firmer hold of the tongue, I rip it loose and toss it away. Black blood gushes from the demon's mouth and its beady eyes roll wildly.

I let the demon drop, then pin it to the floor with one knee. I start tearing off scales, working my fingertips into the gaps, using magic to torment the demon. For a long time I didn't understand how Beranabus could butcher so nastily. As evil as demons are… as much as I accept the need to kill them… I couldn't condone torture. But my attitude has changed over the years. I've seen too many corpses.

Too many murdered babies. These monsters deserve all the agony we can put them through and a whole lot more on top.

Shark helps Meera finish off the anteater, then studies me as I work on the lizard.

"Need a hand, kid?"

"No," I pant.

The ex-soldier squats beside me and waits for me to look at him. "I know where you're coming from," he says quietly, "but we don't have time. There are others on the loose. They're still killing."

I sigh, then shoot a burst of magic into the lizard. It slumps and I rise. "Sorry."

"No need to apologise," Shark says. "Another time and place, I'd have joined in and we'd have had hours of fun."

"*Fun?*" Meera barks.

"Sure," Shark smiles. "You've got to get a buzz out of fighting. It'd be a hell of a life if you devoted your time to battle and didn't enjoy it."

"Anyone ever tell you you're a sicko?" Meera snorts.

"We're all the same," Shark protests. "I'm just more open about it. Killing demons is noble and necessary, blah blah blah. But it's a blast too. Right, Kernel?"

"Come on," I mutter, not wanting to engage in the debate, afraid I'd come down on Shark's side and not liking what that says about me. "Let's kill the rest of them before they slaughter more babies."

That sobers Shark and saps Meera of her indignation. Turning our backs on the dead demons, we go into killing mode and set off in search of monsters viler and more vicious than ourselves.

→We kill three more demons, then the mage who is keeping their window open. He's a thin, balding, middle-aged man in a cheap suit. He doesn't look evil. Most people who work for the Demonata don't. He shuts his eyes as we close in on him and doesn't cry out when Shark grabs his throat and crushes it. The nearby demons escape through the window to their own universe before it closes. We let them flee and get stuck into those left behind. Demons don't last long once a window shuts. Their bodies fall apart after a few minutes and they crumble away to dust. But they can still kill a lot of people during that time, so we afford them no mercy.

When the hospital's clean, we join the others on the roof. Bec, Dervish and Sharmila are there. Sharmila's legs have been cut off. Beranabus is working hard to patch her up. Dervish is sitting on a trolley, looking close to death. Meera goes to him immediately, to check that he's OK.

"I'll guard the staircase," Shark says. "Make sure we aren't taken by surprise."

"But the demons are gone," I frown.

"We have humans to worry about too," he snorts, then nods at Bec. "She'll tell you all about it."

And she does, swiftly and clearly. It's a disturbing story. First I learn that an old enemy — once a friend — has returned from beyond the grave. Juni Swan, who I first knew as Nadia Moore, has come back to life in a new, mutated form.

I'm always torn when I think of Nadia/Juni. She was a bitter but kind young woman when we first met. She saved my life in Lord Loss's realm when I fell into a river of lava. She told me then to be wary of her if we ever met again, that she served the demon master now and I should think of her as a foe. But I find it hard to hate her. She's a person who lost her way. She didn't seek out evil — she got sucked into it. I pity her as much as I fear and mistrust her.

Bec describes the attack on Dervish's home in Carcery Vale. Werewolves broke in, supported by humans with guns. She tells us she has a curious gift — she can absorb the memories of anyone she touches. One of the werewolves was a Grady. Its parents turned it over to the Lambs — family executioners — to dispose of. But the Lambs kept the beast alive and they or some other group subsequently used it as a weapon.

We discuss this troubling turn of events. Grubbs is

more worked up than the rest of us — he hates the thought of his relatives being manipulated. Bec thinks Lord Loss masterminded the attack, that he knows she's part of the Kah-Gash. Beranabus agrees, then tells me to open a window. Dervish and Sharmila won't last long in this universe. They need magic to survive.

I'm glad to set to work on the window because I need magic too. My eyes are burning. It was bad as soon as I set foot on this world, but since the demons' window closed, the pain has increased sharply and my vision has started to blur. My new eyes are the work of magic. They can't function normally here. As much as I despise the universe of the Demonata, I'm a slave of it now.

As I'm working on the window, I hear the whispers from the mysterious small lights. I glance around and spot several pulsing rapidly. But the whispers don't seem to be directed at me this time. And they're not repeating a single word. There's a steady stream of phrases, none of which I can make sense of.

Behind me, Dervish and Beranabus are arguing. Dervish wants to stay and find out more about the werewolves. Beranabus says we can't waste time on them. Meera sides with Dervish. There have been lots of crossings recently and the Disciples are struggling to cope. She's afraid the werewolves might be used to target members of the secret group. If they killed a large number of the mages, demons could cross freely.

Even though I'm not paying a huge amount of attention to the argument, I find myself pausing. "It might be related," I say.

"Related to what?" Bec asks. Beranabus waves her silent and frowns at me.

"This could be part of the Shadow's plan," I tell him, the words tumbling out by themselves. The whispers from the lights have increased. I have to concentrate hard to drown them out. "It could be trying to create scores of windows so that its army of demons can break through at once. We'll need the Disciples if that's the case — we can't be everywhere at the same time to stop them all."

"Maybe," Beranabus says. "But that doesn't alter the fact that Dervish will last about five minutes if we leave him here."

"I'll be fine," Dervish snarls.

"No," Beranabus says. "Your heart is finished. You'll die within days. That's not a guess," he adds before Dervish can argue. "And you wouldn't be able to do much during that time, apart from wheeze and clutch your chest a lot."

"It's really that bad?" Dervish asks quietly.

Beranabus nods. "In the universe of magic, you might survive. Here, you're a dead man walking."

"Then get him there quick," Grubbs says. "I'll stay."

"Not you too," Beranabus groans. "What did I do to deserve as stubborn and reckless a pair as you?"

"It makes sense," Grubbs insists. "If the attacks were Lord Loss looking to get even, they're irrelevant. But if they're related to the Shadow, we need to know. I can confront the Lambs, find out if they're mixed up with the demon master, stop them if they are."

"Is the Shadow the creature we saw in the cave?" Bec asks.

"Aye," Beranabus says. "We haven't learnt much about it, except that it's put together an army of demons and is working hard to launch them across to our world."

He stares at Grubbs, and as he pauses, the whispers change. They're softer now, almost musical. I feel uneasy, even slightly sick, but I've no idea why.

"You'd operate alone?" Beranabus asks.

"I'd need help," Grubbs replies, and asks for Shark and Meera's assistance. While they discuss that, I focus on the window again. I'm close to opening it. The whispers of the lights have almost died away. I feel worse than ever, as if we're in great danger. But there's no reason to be afraid... is there?

A pale green window opens. Beranabus still hasn't chosen whether or not to let Grubbs stay. "Time to decide," I tell him, and as I say that, the whispers spark up again.

"Very well," Beranabus snaps at Grubbs. "But listen to Shark and Meera, heed their advice and contact me before you go running up against the likes of Lord Loss or the Shadow." He picks up the unconscious Sharmila. "Follow me, Bec," he says and steps through the window.

Bec doesn't leave immediately. She's confused, not sure of what's happening. Dervish is busy saying goodbye to Grubbs and Meera, wishing them luck, cursing the fact that he can't stay and help them. As he finally stumbles through the window, Grubbs has a short chat with Bec. Then she faces me. She looks more lost than I feel. As difficult as it is, I force a smile. "The world moves quickly when Beranabus is around," I tell her, trying to cheer her up.

"What's it like through there?" she asks, staring at the window with quiet terror.

"Bad." My smile slips. "The Shadow's promising the eradication of mankind and a new dawn of demon rule. Others have threatened that before, but it's convinced an army of demons – even powerful masters like Lord Loss – that it can make good on its vow. We could be looking at the end this time." I take a step into the window of light but don't cross fully, straddling two universes at the same time. I wave Bec forward. "Let's go."

She looks back once, then follows me through the

window to an oasis in the demon universe which Beranabus and I are familiar with. We'll be safe here, for a while at least.

But I take no comfort from our security. I'm steady on my feet, maintaining a calm front, but inside my head sirens are blaring, my thoughts a million miles removed from werewolves, the Lambs, Juni Swan and the Shadow. I feel sicker than when I saw the dismembered babies in the hospital.

I've realised why the whispers unnerved me. That final burst of chattering, just before Beranabus made his decision to let Grubbs go, clued me in to what was really happening.

Beranabus should have brought Grubbs along. He's been wary of uniting the pieces of the Kah-Gash, but this was the time to risk it. Our enemies are on the move, trying to kill one of us or get their hands on a piece of the ancient weapon. Beranabus should have kept us all with him, if not to unleash the power of the Kah-Gash, then to protect us. We'd be a lot safer if we stuck together. Leaving Grubbs behind was madness.

Why did someone as experienced as Beranabus make such a slip? And why did the others – myself included – go along with his bad call?

Answer — the lights. The whispers influenced us. Something didn't want us to band together, so it subtly interfered and split us up, making it seem as if it was our own choice. We're being manipulated by the whispers of the lights!

LYING LOW

→I can't tell the others about the lights, the whispers or my suspicion that we are being used. I want to, but whenever I try to share my fears, my lips seize up. I'm unable to speak, or else everyday rubbish spills out and we end up talking about something else. I've tried writing, scribbling a warning in the sand of the oasis, but my fingers clench and turn against me.

When we first stepped through the window, I thought I might have imagined the whispers or the influence they're exerting over us. Now I'm sure I called it right. The lights did – *do* – control us. They must have planted a hidden command inside my brain that makes me clam up whenever I try to share my misgivings.

While I struggle to break through the spell, the others argue about what to do next. Beranabus wants to hunt the Shadow, pick up where we left off. Dervish is against that. He's determined to go after Juni, to settle old scores.

I stay out of the arguments for a couple of days. But when Dervish is pressing his claim for the umpteenth time, trying to sway Beranabus by saying we might be able to torture Juni to find out information about the Shadow, the small, ever-changing lights pulse and the air hums with whispers only I can hear.

"We can't go after Lord Loss directly — he's too powerful," I find myself telling Beranabus, and although I know these aren't my words, that I'm being used like a puppet, I can't stop. "But we can target Juni. Lord Loss didn't show himself at the hospital, but Juni was acting on his behalf. She might have been part of the group in Carcery Vale too. If more assaults on the Disciples are planned, she'll possibly act as the go-between again, conveying Lord Loss's orders to their allies. If we can trap her, we can find out what she knows about the Shadow."

Beranabus thinks that makes sense – or the lights make him think it – so he tells me to focus on Juni, track her movements and let him know when she slips out of Lord Loss's realm.

I want to scream foul and tell them we're being toyed with, but my lips gum up. I throw everything I have at the spell, to no avail. In the end I do as Beranabus bids. I retire to one of the fake trees – the oasis is dotted with trees made of bones and scraps of flesh – and sit in the shade, glumly training my thoughts on Juni Swan.

→As days pass, the others recuperate. Beranabus and Bec fashioned new legs for Sharmila out of the bones and skin of the trees when we arrived, and she adapts to them smoothly. Bec has worked a lot with Dervish, drawing on her healing powers, doing what she can for his faltering heart. Neither he nor Sharmila can live on Earth again, but as long as they stay in this universe of magic they can function almost normally.

The four of them pass a lot of the time duelling, sharpening their reflexes, testing their skills. Magic is all about trial and error. Even after thousands of years, Beranabus is still discovering new aspects of himself, depending on what's thrown at him.

I'd like to join them, but I've been given a task and Beranabus doesn't take it kindly when one of his assistants disobeys a direct order. So I keep to myself, studying the lights and focusing on Juni Swan and her master.

It's difficult because of the whispers. The murmurs come regularly while I'm concentrating, not as strongly as at the hospital, but distracting none the less. I can't stop thinking about the spell they've woven. Is it the work of the Shadow? Unlikely — if the creature could exert such influence, it would turn us against one another.

The Kah-Gash? A weapon that can destroy universes and distort the laws of time would have no difficulty bending a few humans to its will. But the Kah-Gash would surely have wanted me, Grubbs and Bec together, to unite so it could be reassembled.

If not the Shadow or the Kah-Gash, who can be controlling the lights? Are they self-conscious, some new life form? Or maybe I'm imagining them. I've doubted my sanity in the past. Maybe this time I've cracked for real.

Finally, after a week of self-torment and doubt, I sense Juni opening a window and leaving Lord Loss's world.

"She's moving," I tell the others, disrupting their latest duel.

They crowd around me. "Where did she go?" Beranabus asks.

"Earth," I say after a brief pause to confirm her location.

"And Lord Loss?"

"He stayed in his own realm."

"Can you tell where she is exactly?" Dervish asks.

"No. I should be able to, but I can't place it." That worries me more than I reveal.

"Is she close to Grubbs?" Dervish presses.

I do a quick scan and shake my head.

"Well?" Sharmila asks Beranabus.

"Kernel and I will investigate," he says. "The rest of you stay here."

"Nuts to that," Dervish huffs.

"Don't forget about your heart," Beranabus says. "Or Sharmila's legs. You're a pair of wrecks on that world. Let us check the situation and report back. We won't engage her if we can avoid it."

"What about me?" Bec asks. "I can survive there."

"Aye, but I'm asking you to wait. Please. Until we know more about what we're walking into."

I'd like to know more about it too before I cross. But I've lived with Beranabus long enough to know he doesn't hold much faith in the philosophy of look-before-you-leap. Except for his edgy pursuit of the Shadow, I've never seen him act cautiously. He believes it's best to jump in the fire and deal with the flames when they're licking the soles of your feet.

Keeping silent about my fears, I slot patches of light together and open a white window. With my back to the others, I offer up a quick prayer, the kind I used to reel off when I was a fresh apprentice, before I grew hardened to the terrors of the Demonata. Then, sensing Beranabus behind me, I step forward into the unknown.

DEATH WATCH

→We find ourselves on the deck of a massive ship, close to a swimming pool. Deckchairs are strewn about the place. Bodies everywhere, ripped to pieces, stomachs carved open, heads and limbs torn loose. Puddles of blood merge and spread slowly, seeping into the cracks between the planks. The water of the swimming pool is a deep, dead red.

Beranabus ignores the corpses. He's seen worse in his time. I have too. But it still hits me hard whenever I walk into a nightmarish scene like this. It only takes me a few seconds to recover, but Beranabus doesn't even need that. He's instantly alert, looking for threats, sizing up the situation. I see him relax slightly and, once I overcome my initial shock, I realise why. The area is charged with magic. We're on Earth, but it feels like the Demonata's universe. We can operate at full capacity here.

"We're encased," Beranabus says. "The ship's been sealed off by a bubble of magic. They must have a lodestone."

Lodestones are rocks which were filled with magic by beings known as the Old Creatures. They ruled our world in the distant past, holding the demons at bay. They fled many generations ago, but left the charged stones behind. Many have drained of power over the centuries, and Beranabus destroyed most of the others, to stop the Demonata's power-hungry mages from making use of them. But some remain, secreted away, either unknown to him, inaccessible or indestructible. Demons or evil mages sometimes find them and use them to open limited tunnels between universes, allowing the Demonata to spend more time here and wreak maximum havoc.

"Where's Juni?" Beranabus asks.

"Lower down. I thought it would be wiser not to face her until we'd assessed the risk. I don't know if anyone's with her, but there's an open window. It's not very sturdy. Only weak demons could cross through it."

Beranabus thinks about that, then says, "I'm going back for the others." He steps through the window, leaving me with the dead.

The silence is disturbing. I play out crazy scenarios inside my head, imagining the corpses coming back to life and attacking. I've never seen a zombie film. I heard about *Night of the Living Dead* when I was a child, but my parents wouldn't let me watch it.

I don't have any hair — I've always been bald — but if I did, it would be standing on end. I've got a bad case of what my mother used to call the heebie-jeebies. I want to duck through the window after Beranabus. This ship is bad news. We'll wind up dead if we stay, bleeding sacks of flesh and bone.

Before I can bolt, Beranabus returns and the others cross after him. My nerves settle and I laugh away my fears. Zombies — ridiculous! I've seen enough of the universe to know we need never fear the dead, only the living.

The Disciples are nervous. Bec scans the lower decks and says there's only one demon on board with Juni. I tell the others about the open window.

"We should go back," Sharmila says. "Juni has set this up to ensnare us."

"Why would she be expecting us?" Dervish asks.

"Lord Loss may have reasoned that we would target Juni. Perhaps everything — the attacks on Dervish, Juni revealing herself on the roof of the hospital — was designed to lure Beranabus here. The demon master might be poised to cross and finish us off personally."

"Not through that window," I tell Sharmila, certain no demon master could make use of the opening close to Juni.

"Then through another," she says. "We have never been able to explain why Lord Loss can cross when other masters cannot, or how he goes about it."

Beranabus sighs. "You could be right, but we might never get a better shot at Juni. If she's not expecting us, it's the perfect time to strike. If she is and this is a trap, at least we can anticipate the worst. The magic in the air means she'll be dangerous, but it serves us as much as her. If Lord Loss doesn't turn up, we can match her. If he does cross, we'll make a swift getaway."

"Are you sure of that?" Sharmila frowns. "If we have to open a new window…"

"We won't," Beranabus says. "Kernel will stay here and guard our escape route. You'll know if any other windows open, won't you?"

"Yes," I say confidently.

"Then keep this one alive and watch for signs of further activity. If you sense anything, summon us and we'll withdraw. Is everyone satisfied with that?"

Sharmila is still dubious, but she shrugs. I'm not happy either. I don't want to stay by myself, surrounded by corpses. But we need to protect our only way out. Besides, I'll be safer up here than down there. Beranabus is doing me a favour, though I'm sure he's thinking only of his own well-being, not mine.

As they make their way across the deck, I move closer to the window and pat a couple of patches back into place. Windows never remain stable for more than a few minutes, but I have the power to keep them open indefinitely. If demons were able to manipulate the lights like I can, mankind would have been wiped out long ago.

The minutes pass with agonising slowness. The sun is relentless and my mouth is dry. I could easily find something to drink, but I don't want to abandon my post. I'm sure I could open another window if this one blinks out of existence but I don't want to take any chances. I'm not sure how lodestones work. Maybe Juni could use its power to slow me down.

As I'm concentrating, trying not to obsess about the mounds of corpses around me, the smaller, unpredictable patches of light begin to pulse. "Not now," I groan, but the patches ignore me. Moments later come the whispers. Faster, more urgently than before. I tense, expecting to find myself acting against my wishes. Maybe they'll make me close the window or head after the others, to die with them in the ship's hold.

But nothing happens. If the lights are trying to influence me, they're failing. Ignoring them, I focus on the window, holding it in place, keeping the shape.

Something flickers to my left. I turn and see a

group of the small patches click together. They swirl over and around one another, a mini vortex of various hues and shades of light.

More patches are attracted to the cluster. It grows and spins faster, changing shape, pulsing rapidly. The whispers grow louder, become shouts. I don't know what's happening, but it can only be bad news. I wish the others were here, so we could abandon this place immediately.

When almost all of the small lights have joined and are whirling around, they suddenly zip towards me. Yelping, I throw myself aside. I expect them to chase me, but then I see that I was never their target. They were aiming for the window. They slap into it and shimmer across the face of the white panel. As I sit up and stare, the window becomes a multicoloured rip in the air.

The whispers die away. Silence falls. I stand but don't approach the window. I study it cautiously, fearfully. The lights pulse rapidly, then slide towards the centre, all the colours angling to the focal point, drawn to it as if by gravity.

Then — an explosion. A ball of light bursts from the heart of the window and shoots across the ship's swimming pool, circling it in a spiral pattern, like a punctured balloon careening across a room. The window resumes its white colour.

The ball circles the pool a few more times, then drifts towards the deck and comes to a halt three or four feet above it. The ball is rainbow-coloured, about the size of a large dog, though its shape changes constantly. It reminds me of the jellyish substance in a lava lamp, the way it oozes from one form into another, altering all the time.

"What the hell are you?" I gasp, not expecting an answer. But to my astonishment I receive one.

"I have no name."

I've seen a lot of crazy stuff over the last few years that would leave most people's jaws hanging. I thought I was immune to surprise. But this blows me away. All I can do is gawp at the ball of light like a five-year-old who's walked in on Santa Claus.

"You must come with me," the voice says. I don't know where the words are coming from. They seem to be forming inside my head.

"*Come…*" the voice insists.

"Come where?" I croak. "Who are you? *What* are you?"

"There will be time for explanations later. We must depart this world before…" The voice stops and there's a sighing sound. "Too late."

"What do you mean?"

Before the ball of light can answer, my crazy fantasy of a few minutes ago becomes a reality. All around me, the corpses on the deck shudder, twitch, then clamber to their feet. As impossible as it is, the dead have come back to life, and they're focusing their glinting, hungry eyes on *me*.

COME...

→The rising dead terrify me more than any demon ever did. Demons are natural. They obey certain laws. You know what to expect when you face one of them. But the dead aren't supposed to return. When a body perishes, the soul moves on. That's the way it's always been. But someone must have forgotten to mention that to these walking, snarling, slavering corpses.

I stand like a simpleton, watching them advance. I'd heard that zombies in movies walk slowly, stiffly, mechanically. Not these. They don't have the look of living people, but they move like them, fluidly and firmly.

As the dead close in on me, teeth exposed, hands outstretched, the ball of light flits over their heads and flares, causing them to cover their eyes and stumble to a halt. They mewl like newborn calves and lash out at the light.

"*Come...*" the voice repeats. "Cross while they are distracted."

"Where?" I howl, gaze fixed on the zombies.

"*Come…*" is the only response. The ball of light skims over the heads of the walking dead and hovers by the window.

"I can't," I whisper, studying the ranks of animated corpses. "The others…"

"Doomed," the voice says. "You cannot worry about them. They are no longer your concern. *Come…*" It sounds impatient.

A man without a chest – it's been ripped away, exposing the bones of his spine and shoulders – lowers his arms and blinks. Realising he can see again, he sets his sights on me and rushes forward, howling wildly.

My hands, which have been trembling by my sides, shoot up and I unleash a ball of energy. The dead man flies backwards, knocking down those behind him. As others converge, I blast them with magic and back up close to the window.

"Yes," the voice murmurs approvingly.

But I've no intention of going anywhere with this freakish ball of talking light. I ran out on Beranabus once, long ago. Never again.

Taking a firm stand, I construct an invisible barrier, a circle of magic six or seven feet in diameter, through which the dead can't pass. I'm not good at this type of magic. I doubt I could put a barrier in place strong enough to stop a demon. But if these revived corpses are only as strong as they were in life, it should repel them.

My stomach rumbles with fear as the zombies cluster around the barrier. They scrape, punch, kick and spit at it. I hear – imagine – a creaking noise. I reinforce the barrier, sweating desperately, and turn 360 degrees, trying to cover every angle at once, ensuring there are no weak points.

There aren't. The barrier holds. As long as the magic in the air remains, I can keep these wretched zombies at bay.

I've been holding my breath. Letting it out, I bend over and smile raggedly. I even manage a weak laugh. That would have been an awful death. To stand up to one powerful demon after another, only to fall to a pack of alarming but relatively weak zombies... It would have been a shameful way to go.

"You have done well," the voice says, pulsing eagerly by the window. "Now come with me. We must leave this world. We have far to go."

I straighten and study the ball of light. I'm glad of the excuse not to look at the writhing zombies, especially the children, every bit as ravenous as the adults.

"I'm going nowhere without the others," I tell it.

"They do not matter. You are the one we need. *Come...*"

"Who are 'we'?" I challenge the voice. "What do you want? Where—"

The ship lurches. I'm thrown sideways, towards the ranks of living dead. I yell with shock, but the barrier deflects me away from the gnashing, grabbing zombies.

I get to my feet slowly, rubbing my arm where I collided with the barrier. The ship has tilted. The water in the swimming pool is starting to spill out over the lowest edge, and some of the deckchairs are sliding backwards. A few of the zombies slip away from the barrier, but they're back again moments later.

"What's happening?" I ask the ball of light.

"The ship is sinking," it answers. "Beranabus has been killed. Come now, before it is too late."

It takes a few seconds for that to hit. At first I'm just panicked that the ship's going down. Then the full impact of the statement rams home. "*Beranabus?*" I gasp.

"The Shadow killed him."

"No!" I shake my head wildly. Beranabus can't be dead. The world doesn't make sense without him. He's single-handedly held back the hordes of demons for more than a thousand years. I knew he was old and tired, and he often spoke half-heartedly of retiring. But secretly I believed he was invincible, that he'd live forever, reborn like a phoenix when he grew tired of the confines of his old bones.

"There will be no rebirth," the voice says calmly as everything collapses into chaos. "Beranabus is dead. This world will have to struggle on without him. You must come with me. You *must*."

I expect tears, but there aren't any. I'm devastated by the loss of Beranabus, and maybe I'll weep for him later, but for now I'm dry-eyed. When I'm sure I'm not going to cry, I look at the light again. This time I regard it with a hint of loathing.

"You set this up," I snarl. "You led us here. You're in league with Juni Swan."

"No," the voice says. "We do not serve the Demonata."

"You split us from Grubbs," I accuse it. "You forced me to advise Beranabus to focus on Juni. This is your work as much as it's hers."

The ball is silent for a moment. "You were aware of our guiding hand," it says. "Interesting. You see and hear more than we thought."

"Yes." I laugh roughly. "And I see through you now. Beranabus would be alive if we hadn't come here. You manipulated us."

"To an extent," the voice agrees. "We needed a lodestone. I could not make the final push to your world without one. So we influenced you and your foes, and tempted you to this place. It is unfortunate that it resulted in Beranabus's death, but that is an acceptable loss. All that matters is that you come with me. Everything else is immaterial."

"Bull!" I snort.

The ball of light flickers. "I do not understand."

"I'm going nowhere. My friends are here — Bec, Dervish, Sharmila. I'm staying to help them. I promised I'd keep this window open and I will."

"No," the voice says. "We cannot wait. If you fall, all is lost. I do not have the power to reclaim your fragment of the Kah-Gash. It would go to—"

"So that's it!" I yell. "You want the weapon."

"Only your part."

"You can't have it," I sneer, taking a step away from the window.

The ball turns dark blue, before resuming its normal variety of colours. I think it just lost its temper.

"You cannot defy us," the voice says. "You must come with me. It is vital."

I shake my head and back up to within a couple of inches of the barrier. "My friends come first. Always."

The ball pulses for a few seconds. Then the voice says, "Very well."

The light flicks up over my head and cuts through the barrier, vanishing into the crowd of zombies. The deck is rising steadily. The pool is almost empty now. Some of the less sturdy zombies have started to slide down the deck, towards the end dipping into the sea. But most remain pinned to the barrier.

More worrying than the zombies or the disappearance of the ball of light is the fading magic. The bubble around the ship is intact, but the magical energy is dwindling. I can still maintain the barrier, but not for long.

I think about retreating, closing the window behind me, then building a new one, opening it to whatever level of the ship Bec and the others are on. It wouldn't take more than a few minutes. But they might not have even that short time. If they make it to the upper deck, this window offers their fastest route out. If I disable it, they'll have to wait, besieged by zombies, and that might be asking too much of them. Better to linger as long as I can, and only resort to the other plan if the barrier cracks.

As I make up my mind to stay, a man steps through the crowd. Most of his throat has been chewed away. His head's attached to his torso by stray strands of flesh and muscle. He puts his hands on the barrier, palms flat. His calm expression is in sharp contrast to the twisted grimaces of the other zombies. As I stare at the man, wondering why he looks different, light flickers in his eyes. I realise that the ball of light has wormed its way into the zombie and possessed him. Before I can do anything, the man steps through the barrier and clutches me.

"Do not fight," he gurgles, pushing me towards the window.

"Let go!" I roar, wrestling wildly. I manage to slip loose. I think about darting through the window, but that's where the light wants me to go. Before I can come up with an alternate plan, the zombie grabs me again.

"We do not want to hurt you," he says, nudging me closer to the window of white light. "You must trust us. We only want—"

I knee the man in the stomach. Even though he's dead, he winces with pain or the memory of it.

As I prepare to break free, I spot Bec, Sharmila, Dervish and a man I don't recognise. They're fighting against the tilt of the ship, forcing their way towards me, battling through zombies. Bec spots me locked in combat.

"Kernel!" she shouts. "Hold on. We're almost with you. We—"

"The lights!" I roar back in reply. "The lights are doing this! Don't—"

"Enough," the man snaps. "You are coming. *Now.*"

I reach for his head, to tear it all the way off. Before I can, the man's eyes open wide and the ball of light gushes from them, as well as from his mouth and the gap in his throat. The light is blinding. I squeeze my eyelids shut, but the glare sears through them and I see almost as clearly as if they were open.

As light streams from the man, he explodes, his body ripping apart as if someone had planted a stick of dynamite inside him. The blast sends me flying backwards, through the window, which shatters behind me, stranding the others and cutting me off from the world of all things human.

TRIPPING THE LIGHT FANTASTIC

→The ball of light sails through the window with me. It completely envelops me, crackling over my creamy brown skin, tickling my hairless scalp, buzzing in my ears. I'm warm and comfortable in its embrace. I think this is what it must be like for a baby in its mother's womb.

I try to fight the enveloping light, to break free of its hold, but it just buckles and bulges to match my movements. Finally I settle back and conserve my energy, saving it for when I can focus it more usefully.

I study my surroundings. Though the multicoloured ball of light holds me in its grasp like fingers clutched around a coin, it's translucent. There are other lights beyond, patches and panels, a dazzling variety of colours and sizes. They fill the area around us completely. No stars, sky or planets. A universe of lights.

We're floating through them, sliding from one patch to another, following some sort of hidden path. I hope. Or maybe there's no path and we're lost. Perhaps this is what the lights wanted all along, to strand me in this wilderness. But I don't think so. We seem to be moving meaningfully. Or is that just wishful thinking?

Whatever the truth, I've never experienced anything like this before. Whenever I've stepped through a window, I've emerged instantly on another world. This is like travelling through an immense tunnel.

"Correct," the voice says. The ball of light can evidently read my thoughts, which is bad news — I can't spring any surprises. "We are travelling further than you have ever been, but we are still in your universe. Space is not as easily traversed here as in the Demonata's realm."

"Where are we going?" I ask. Except I don't ask out loud. My mouth won't open. "What's going on?" I cry silently.

"There is no oxygen," the voice explains. "You are cocooned. It is the easiest way to travel. Don't worry — it will not last long and you won't be harmed."

I'm not sure I trust the voice, but there's nothing I can do except lie back and accept it. "So where are we going?" I ask again, trying to sound casual.

"You will find out soon," the voice replies and says nothing more, leaving me to study the spectacular light show in awed, helpless silence.

→After several minutes we zone in on a massive patch of green light. As we pass through, the cocoon around me slips away and I tumble to a cracked stone floor. My mouth opens and I drag in a lungful of acidic but breathable air. Pinching my nose shut to block out the stench, I look around. I'm in a domed chamber. The ball of light hangs in the air several feet away, pulsing steadily. The stones around us are throbbing in unison.

Blanking my thoughts, desperate not to betray myself, I back away. There's an exit behind me. As I reach it, I pause, expecting the ball of light to shoot across and block my way. When nothing happens, I slip out of the chamber and scurry through a short, narrow tunnel.

The tunnel opens out on to a plateau. I race away from the chamber, planning to put plenty of space between myself and the ball of light. But the air here is foul and my body revolts. As a stitch hits me hard, I collapse, gasping for air, lungs straining, head aching.

After a minute of painful gasping, the stitch eases and I stand. Instead of running again, I turn slowly and study my surroundings. I'm on a ruined world. The sky is a dark purple colour, full of poisonous-looking clouds. Forks of lightning split the air every few seconds although I can hear no thunder. When the lightning hits the ground, the dark earth flashes and explodes in short-lived funnels of dirt, mud and pebbles.

Huge, bone-like pillars jut out of the scorched, pockmarked earth. At first I think they're the remains of giant demons. I've seen plenty of sky demons in my time, massive monsters, some the size of a world. But the longer I look, the more convinced I become that these aren't bones, but rather the remains of buildings.

Wandering slowly to the nearest pile of pillars, breathing shallowly, I find that they're made of some sort of metal. That confuses me. Demons aren't builders. Some create houses or palaces, even towns and cities, modelled after those on Earth. But they use bones, flesh, cobwebs, plants and other organic substances to fashion their facsimiles. I've never known a demon to utilise metal or concrete.

The voice told me we were still in the human universe. I thought we slipped out of it when we crossed through the window, but it looks like we didn't. I don't know where I am, but I'm pretty sure it's not a demon world.

As I move through the ash-ridden remains of what was once maybe a skyscraper, something moves in the filth nearby. Jumping backwards, I try to absorb magic from the air, but there's virtually nothing to tap into. Like Earth, this is a zone of little or no magical energy.

The thing wriggles clear of the hard mud and debris it was nestling beneath. It looks like a giant slug, but with six small eyes, a jagged gash for a mouth, and other human-looking bits and pieces — a few fingers, a toe, a strip of flesh that might be an ear. The eyes stare at me for a moment, then the mouth opens and it thrusts itself at my face, making a gruesome, high-pitched noise.

The slug creature strikes my chest and I fall. It's on me in a flash, slithering to my face, leaving a slimy trail. Thin fingers scratch at my chin, then a grey, cold slit clamps over my mouth and nostrils. I feel it tighten on my lips and nose, and the slug squeals with excitement as I struggle for air.

I punch the slug, but my fists make little impact, merely sinking into the gooey, sticky layers of its body. Disgusting slime oozes from the slit, filling my mouth. I collapse, my lungs straining, still pushing and punching the slug, but feebly now. My strength is fading. Soon I'll be slug fodder and the beast will be able to feast on my flesh at its leisure.

As the world starts to darken around me, the slug is abruptly ripped away. I catch a glimpse of it flying through the air, squealing frantically. It lands hard, rolls a few times, then straightens and propels itself at me again.

Somebody steps in front of me and meets the charge of the slug. It looks like a boy, but with pale green skin. He's small but strong — he catches the slug and slams it down in a neatly executed wrestling move. While the slug writhes beneath him, the boy grabs one of the creature's fingers and bites it off with… a small mouth set in the palm of his hand!

The slug stunned me when it attacked, but when I realise who the boy is I'm shocked to the core. I stare with mounting horror and bewilderment as the slug shrieks, then quickly slips away when the boy releases it. He makes sure it isn't going to attack again, then turns to face me.

He has the body of a young child – maybe three years old – but a head that's bigger than an adult's. Mouths in both palms, full of small, sharp teeth. No eyes — instead, balls of fire burn deeply in his empty sockets. And no hair — in its place, small slugs, much like the one he just saved me from, slide slowly around his skull.

"*Artery!*" I moan. I have no idea how Lord Loss's familiar came to be here – he was killed a year ago – but I'm certain he only saved me from the slug in order to kill me himself.

The hellchild cocks his head and frowns. "No," he

growls, and it's the first time I've ever heard him speak. His green flesh ripples and the colour fades. His head shrinks and the slugs burrow into his scalp, then turn into hair. The fire in his empty sockets dies away and eyes sprout to fill them. His large mouth tightens a couple of notches and his sharp teeth soften into a more human-like shape. The mouths in his palms disappear, flesh closing over them.

"No," he says again, and this time his voice is softer. "Not Artery." He glances at his skin – pale, like Mum's – and smiles. Almost no trace of the monster remains. I'm gazing at what looks like an ordinary boy. And he's every bit as familiar as the green-skinned demon.

"I'm *Art*," he says, then steps forward and sticks out a small, delicate hand.

THE MAN FROM ATLANTIS

→"You can't be real," I gasp, backing away from the figure. "You're not my brother. You never really existed. I made you up."

"Yes," the boy nods. "You transformed Artery into this shape and kept him safe, even though he should have perished on your world, by subconsciously utilising the power of the Kah-Gash. We were surprised it cooperated with you. But the Kah-Gash never ceases to surprise us."

"You're not Art!" I shout. "Art didn't speak like this. He never spoke at all."

"True," the boy says. "Artery could communicate with his own kind, but only telepathically. Art would never have been able to speak, even if he'd grown up.

"I'm not the demon you stole or the child you turned it into," the boy continues. "I am the ball of light from the ship. Sensing the difficulty you had accepting my natural form, I adopted the body of someone you would feel more comfortable with. If you prefer, I can switch to the shape of your mother or father, but I think you will find me easier to deal with this way."

My head's spinning. "Are you a shape-shifter?" I ask, getting to my feet and walking around the boy, checking him from every angle.

"No," he says. "I have no physical body. I assembled this from a corpse, remoulding its flesh and bones. It was a creature like the one which attacked you. They are pitiful beasts. Hard to believe they are descended from beings once as industrious as yourself."

"What do you mean?" I frown.

"It's a descendant of the Atlanteans," Art says. "They were bipeds, like you, and their society was similar to yours. Indeed, your distant ancestors were strongly influenced by the beings of Atlantis."

"*Atlantis?*" I croak. "What are you talking about? Atlantis was a mythical city."

"No," Art corrects me. "It was a world of immense, amazing cities, the closest inhabitable planet to Earth. The Atlanteans explored this world to its fullest, then the lifeless planets nearby, finally extending to their neighbouring galaxies. They visited your world. Your ancestors worshipped them, built monuments like theirs, dressed in their honour, wrote things down as they did."

"Are you pulling my leg?" I growl.

"I do not understand," Art responds.

"Are you trying to fool me?"

"No. Atlantis was an advanced planet. The Atlanteans were wise and kind. But they harnessed the raw energy of this universe and that is dangerous. They knew the risks and accepted them. It was the price they paid to explore further afield, beyond the confines of their own sector of the universe.

"They fell within the space of an hour," Art goes on, and although he has a child's face, he looks like an adult as he gazes upon the wrecks of the buildings. "An explosion set off a chain reaction and their society crumbled. The ships they'd sent off into space were linked to the home world, so they were destroyed too. The sky filled with pollutants and ash. Death claimed nineteen billion souls. A few Atlanteans survived and mutated, but I doubt they would have wished for their offspring to end up like this. It would have been better if they'd all perished."

Art falls silent. I stare at the boy who is the image of the child I once thought of as a brother. Now that I'm over my initial shock, I find that he was right — it's a lot easier talking to someone who looks like a boy than with a ball of light.

I study the graveyard of the world around me. Art could be lying, but I don't think so. I'm standing on the remains of Atlantis. The most famous lost city of legend was never a city at all, but a different world. The information is mind-boggling. If Art's telling the truth, the Atlanteans visited mankind in the past. They taught us to read and write, to build. Maybe they even bred with us and—

"No," Art interrupts. "The Atlanteans did not breed with lesser beings."

"This is incredible," I gasp, the word not doing my feelings justice. "But if they travelled to our world by rockets, not windows, is this still the human universe?"

"Of course." Art sounds surprised. "I thought that was clear."

"You said we hadn't crossed but I wasn't sure."

"We have not left your universe and will not during the course of our travels," Art says.

"This isn't the end?"

The boy giggles the way Art used to when he bit someone. "Hardly. This is merely the beginning of an amazing journey."

"Where are we going?" I ask.

"Far away," he answers mysteriously.

"What if I don't want to go with you?" I counter.

"You have no choice," Art says.

"Is that a threat?"

"No," he shrugs. "It's just the way things are."

"Who – or what – the hell are you?" I snap.

"Those who know us give us many names," Art says. "Your people called us the Old Creatures."

"Beranabus told me about them. He…" That reminds me of the ancient mage's death and the danger the others face. "We have to go back!" I cry. "You've got to take me home, so I can—"

"That won't happen," Art says firmly. "Purge yourself of the notion. We have come far from your world. As skilled as you are at manipulating the strings of the universe, you cannot find your way back alone. You must see this journey through to its end."

"What sort of an end?" I hiss. "Where are you taking me? And if you're not specific this time, forget it — I'm not going to wander aimlessly through the universe with you. I'd rather stay here with the slugs."

"Very well," Art says. "We are travelling to the birthplace of all things, where time and space began. We call it the Crux. And it lies at the centre of both this universe and the Demonata's."

"That doesn't make sense," I complain.

"Don't worry," Art smiles smugly. "By the end it will."

UNDER THE SEA

→I try thinking of a way to outwit the Old Creature. While I might not be able to open a window back to Earth, I'm sure I can open one to the demon universe and return home from there. But Art reads my mind and chuckles.

"I will not permit it."

"You can't stop me," I retort.

"Actually I can. I have the power to tear apart any window that you create, and I can do it before the window opens. If necessary, we can stay here for decades and duel with one another, but I would not recommend it. You would lose."

I start work on a window, to test him, but Art's smug expression stops me. He's telling the truth. Cursing, I begin to question him again, but he only turns and walks back to the stone chamber, where a dark grey window is waiting for us.

"What is it to be?" Art asks.

Since I've no real choice, I snarl and step forward with him.

Just before I reach the window, Art's body unravels and he becomes a ball of multicoloured light again. "I have to travel like this," he tells me, his words sounding inside my head. "I need to cocoon you again. But I will resume the shape of Art when we come to our next stop."

"Whatever," I sniff unhappily, bitter at being manipulated.

The light sweeps over and surrounds me. When Art gives the command, I step into the window and we progress.

→Over the next few hours we pass through several chambers similar to the one on Atlantis. Some are made of stone, but others are carved out of wood, metal or other substances. One is simply a chamber of lights, a dome of panels and patches. We don't leave any of these chambers, just stay long enough for Art to open a new window, then move on again.

I'm still amazed by Atlantis, stunned by the proof of other life forms in our universe. I always assumed we weren't alone, that there were intelligent beings on other worlds. But to see an actual alien was an incredible experience. Even if it did just look like a big slug!

Art's a quiet guide. He concentrates on steering us from one chamber to the next. I don't think it's easy.

These patches of lights aren't as easily mastered as the ones I'm accustomed to. It seems to be hard work.

I'm still worried about Dervish and the others, and in shock about the loss of Beranabus. But there's nothing I can do, so I lie back and bide my time. I'm in the grip of something more powerful than myself. I don't understand it and I can't fight or escape. *Yet*.

→We pass through another window and I find myself in a water-logged chamber. I'm not sure what the walls are made of, but it looks like seaweed. As we slip through, parts of the walls glow. It's not magic — I can see small organisms in the crevices of the greenish blocks. They're like underwater glow-worms.

"We will rest a while," Art says, letting the window close behind us. The lights surrounding me shimmer, then slip off, although a layer remains, keeping me dry and providing me with air.

"That's clever," I note as the ball of light transforms into a boy.

"What?" Art frowns.

"The shield."

"It is nothing special."

"Are you tired?" I ask, detecting weariness in his tone.

"Yes." He sighs. "Travel of this nature is draining. We

don't normally cross vast distances so swiftly. But time is against us, so I must push myself."

"How far have we come?"

He pauses, then says, "You do not have words to describe it. Your scientists do, but their terms would mean nothing to you."

Art heads towards a gap in the glowing blocks and I glide after him. We exit the chamber and I'm confronted with an underwater paradise. I'm blown away by what I see and it takes a minute before I can do anything except bob up and down in the water and stare.

We're in the middle of a city. The buildings are all kinds of weird shapes, made of seaweed, shells and huge, twisting roots. Many rise far above and deep below us, two hundred floors high, maybe more. Most sway gently. All sorts of colours, illuminated by enormous swathes of the glowing organisms I saw in the chamber.

There are no roads, just avenues between, through and around the buildings. No glass or doors, only scores of holes in the structures.

I spot some creatures. There are hordes – schools? – of them all around us, floating along the avenues, darting in and out of holes in the buildings. They look like the sea life of my world, only more varied.

As I'm watching, a shark-like beast with several mouths and one giant eye chases an animal that looks like a cross between a seal and a deer. The predator runs down its prey and rips it to shreds. Clouds of scavengers move in quickly and finish off the scraps that the shark leaves behind.

"Are we safe?" I ask nervously. There are more of the sharks around, and other mutations that look even fiercer.

"They won't harm us," Art says. "This is a perfectly balanced world. Nothing would attack anything that it was not, by nature, designed to prey upon."

As he says that, a sea snake the size of a redwood tree passes beneath us. It raises its huge head and studies us. I feel like I'm going to be its lunch. But then it moves on, jaws opening and closing slowly, in search of other food.

"I don't like this," I mutter. "When can we leave?"

"Soon," Art says. "First I must acknowledge the greeting of the natives."

A ring of creatures closes around us. Each looks like a cross between a small whale and an octopus, large but graceful. Their many arms are adorned with shells and sea flowers, and intricate designs which might be tattoos. They swirl over, under and around one another, as if dancing.

"They *are* dancing," Art says. "They worship my kind and wish to perform in our honour. We have not passed through here in a long time. They are excited."

"Why do they think so much of you?" I ask.

"We saved them from a demon attack long ago."

"The Demonata cross to other worlds?" I frown.

"Of course," Art says. "They hate all life forms. You are not the first to suffer at their hands. And you won't be the last. Far from it."

Other creatures gather round us, joining the dance. Their movements become more involved, dozens of different species sweeping around one another, every blink of an eye or swish of a tail carefully choreographed. Through the crush I spot something weird rising from the depths.

"Is that a chess board?" I ask. It's much bigger than any board I've ever seen, but it's the right shape, with the usual arrangement of black and white squares.

"There are Boards like this on almost all the worlds where we have had an influence," Art says. "The Boards are central to the development of intelligence. Some species forget about them as they evolve, but most remember in one way or another."

"I don't get it. What's the big deal about chess?"

"The game means nothing," Art answers. "The *Board* is everything."

Something about the way he stresses the word sparks a memory. I recall a visit I paid to Lord Loss's kingdom several years ago. The demon master loves chess. One of the rooms in his web-based castle was full of sets. He produced a board which he referred to as the Original Board. Each square was a self-contained universe of its own, filled with an array of demons.

"Yes," Art says before I can form a question. "That was the Board we used on your world."

"I still don't understand," I frown. "The Board was just a toy."

"The Boards are not toys," Art says. "Each is a map of the original universe, a link to the past before time."

"You're talking gibberish," I scowl.

"It will become clear soon," Art assures me, then pushes through a gap that the sea creatures have created. "Come. I am fully rested, and the dance has moved into its final arc. It is time for us to depart."

TAKING TO THE SKIES

→We skip from one world to another, chamber to chamber, through the sub-universe of strange lights. I try to figure out how the windows are being opened, hoping to use the information to break free and make my way back home. But I don't know how Art gets the panels to pulse and merge.

"Tell me about yourself," I suggest, partly to break the monotony, partly to learn more about my mysterious guide.

"What do you wish to know?" he replies.

"Where are you from? Beranabus only said that the Old Creatures were beings of ancient, powerful magic, who left our world long ago."

"We leave every planet eventually," Art sighs. "We are nomads, moving from one world to another, never settling."

"But you must have a home," I press. "Everyone comes from somewhere."

"Not us," Art says. "We are of the original universe. We had no beginning."

"That doesn't make sense," I grunt.

"It will—" Art begins.

"—*soon*," I finish sarcastically.

"Sorry," Art says. "I know this is hard. But there is much we have to tell you and it is complicated."

"Let's try something simpler then." I think about the sort of things I'd ask any stranger. "How old are you?"

Art makes a sound like someone clearing their throat.

"Oh, come on!" I shout. "Surely you can tell me that much."

"There is no easy answer," Art says. "We are as old as this universe but we existed before it. In the original universe, there was no such thing as time. We were not born. We did not age. We simply *were*."

"You can't be as old as the universe," I challenge him. "It's billions of years old. Nothing lives for that long."

"We do," Art insists. "We exist as spheres of light, and light is almost ageless."

"*Almost?* You're not immortal?"

"Not any more," Art says.

"This is crazy," I mutter.

"Be patient," Art urges. "By the end of this journey we'll reveal the secrets of the universe, the origins of life and the cause of the Big Bang."

"What's the Big Bang?"

Art is silent for a long time. Then, in a dejected tone, he says, "This is going to be harder than we thought."

→More worlds and chambers. I doze during some of the journey. In the demon universe I can go weeks or months without sleep, but here I grow tired, just as I do on Earth. I start to wonder how long we've been travelling.

"This is the fourth day," Art answers.

"How much longer will it take?"

"I cannot say."

"A week?" I snap. "A month? Years?" I lick my lips and ask quietly, "You *will* take me back, won't you?"

There's a pause. "If you choose to return, we—"

"What do you mean?" I roar. "Of course I'll return! Why shouldn't I? Are you going to try to—"

"Peace," Art hushes me. "The choice will be yours. I don't think you'll want to go back, but we will not prevent you from following your destiny."

"I'll definitely want to go back," I growl.

"You should not make such sweeping statements," Art says. "When you went in search of the demon masquerading as your brother, you were certain you'd return home when you found him, but you didn't. There are no certainties except death. And even that—"

Whatever he was about to say is lost, because we pass through a window into a chamber made of moss-covered stones. And the place is crawling with demons.

They're foul beasts, shaped like horses, but their flesh is rotting away and their bones poke through. Yellow blood drips down their legs from their rib cages. The heads are larger than on any horse I've seen, and each has two sets of mouths, one above the other. There are no teeth — instead, human-looking fingernails jut out of their gums, blood and drool dribbling between the cracks.

The demons had been fighting or playing with each other — hard to tell with these monsters — but they stop when we pop out in the middle of them. Then, with howls of hunger and delight, they hurl themselves at us.

I react automatically and fire a ball of energy at the nearest beast, then leap clear, on to one of the higher stones of the chamber. The roof caved in long ago and I can see out. A quick survey of the land beyond reveals a scorched, ruined world teeming with monsters. A massive demon is rising into the air a few miles away. Hundreds of beasts are clinging to it, or settled on its back in rows. Fleshy strands dangle from its stomach. Large rocks are attached to the lower ends.

A horse-demon jumps, rears its hooves and slashes at my throat. I duck, slam my shoulder into its face and knock it back. "Art!" I scream as others come pounding closer.

"Cover your eyes," Art says. "Use magic as well as your hands."

"What good will that do?" I yell, jumping to another stone.

There's a flash of light and my eyes melt in their sockets. The pain is intense but nothing new. It's just like when my original eyes were stabbed out.

As I howl and fight off waves of pain and madness, Art says, "You should have done what I told you. These demons are called the Sligstata. Light is my only weapon against them. Most can construct new eyes, as you can, but you have done it before, so you should be faster. Set to work immediately, but focus your other senses on the Sligstata. You can avoid them if you concentrate."

"But I can't see!" I howl. "I'm blind!"

"You'll be dead if you don't do what I tell you," Art snarls. There's real fear in his tone. "I can't fight these creatures, even if I turn into Artery — there are too many. I can blind them again, but they'll soon grow wise to that trick. I'm opening a new window but it will take a few minutes. You must defend yourself."

I curse the Old Creature, then set to work on

building a new pair of eyes. It was a long, complicated process before, but this time they grow swiftly, smoothly.

As the eyes form, I listen to the demons and sense their positions. They're stumbling around, lashing out at one another, wild with blind panic. No threat as long as I remain up here. But others are coming. They swarm over the ruins of the chamber, knocking each other aside in their eagerness to tear into me, the echo of their hooves ringing louder as they draw closer.

There's strong magic in the air. I let a ball of power build in my fists and wait until the monsters are several feet away, packed tight, focused on me. Then I let them have it, a blast straight down the middle, scattering them, ripping open stomachs and heads, incinerating eyes, faces and internal organs.

The demons screech with pain and anger, falling beneath the hooves of those behind them. One of the Sligstata hurls itself at me, both sets of mouths gnashing, fingernails twitching. I pirouette away from it like a ballet dancer and end up on the opposite side of the chamber. My eyes have almost completed the healing process, but I still can't see.

"Protect yourself," Art hisses. I was letting another ball of magic build in my hands, but now I divert the power to my eyes and erect a wall of blackness. I see nothing but I know when the light flashes by the screams of the Sligstata.

One of the beasts must have expected the flash and guarded its eyes, because while the others thrash around and topple into the chamber, it makes a beeline for me. No time to dance aside. Planting my feet firmly, I grab the monster by its neck and hold its spitting mouths a few inches from my throat. The stench of its breath would floor a lesser mortal.

As I'm struggling with the demon, my eyes connect with my brain and the world swims back into sight. The Sligstata's mouths are closer than I thought. Gritting my teeth, I push hard and its jaws slide back. But it's tenacious and my fingers are damp with sweat and blood. In a few seconds it will wriggle forward and finish me off.

When I first tried to fight in the Demonata's universe, I was so scared I threw up. I was ashamed at the time, but since then I've learnt the value of a good stream of vomit. I send a magical buzz down my throat and a wave of digested food rises. I spray the demon with hot, thick puke. It gurgles happily, then screeches as I turn the liquid to acid. As the Sligstata burns and writhes, I drop it and look around.

Dozens of fresh demons are racing towards the chamber. Too many to fight. Some of those beneath me have grown new eyes and are knocking aside the blind Sligstata, zoning in on me, hell-bent on making me pay for their torment.

"It's looking bad," I yell at Art, firing a magical bolt at a demon as it tops the chamber wall, driving it back.

"A few more seconds," Art says calmly, pulsing steadily, hovering in the air above my head.

"We don't have that long."

"Just keep them busy a couple more…"

A blue window blinks into life. I don't wait for Art to give the order. With a yell of fear and triumph, I throw myself at it, linking my hands like a person diving into a swimming pool. The Sligstata snap at me with their nightmarish mouths, but miss, and a second later I'm flying through the panel of light. I start to cheer but the sound catches in my throat as fingernails bite into my left leg. I kick but the beast holds firm and drags me back. The patches of light are twinkling seductively but I'm being hauled away from them, back into the chamber of death.

I try summoning magic to fry the Sligstata, but I'm temporarily drained. This looks like the end of Cornelius Fleck. I just hope they kill me quickly. Some demons can keep their victims alive for thousands of—

A crackle of electricity shoots through my leg. It sets my skin tingling but hurts the demon more. It starts to lose its grip. I glance back and see that the Old Creature has once again taken on the shape of Artery. The fire in the green-skinned demon's right eye socket narrows then expands — he's winking at me! Then he grabs hold of me and leaps. We shoot forward and the window snaps shut behind us. Art transforms back into a ball of light and wraps around me. We swoop towards the pulsing lights like a pair of birds, laughing hysterically at our narrow escape.

GOING UNIVERSAL

→It takes a while to settle down. "Thanks," I say when I've stopped chuckling. "You saved my life."

"That's my job," Art says wryly.

"I thought I was done for. There were so many of them…" I frown. "That wasn't the demon universe, was it?"

"No," Art says. "I told you we would not be crossing to their realm."

"Then what were the Sligstata doing there?"

"That world was demon-free a few months ago," Art says. "They must have broken through recently. I wouldn't have come this way if I'd known."

"Even so, how could so many…" I stop as the answer pops into my head. "They opened a tunnel between their universe and that world."

"Yes," Art says.

"The sky demon," I say slowly. "Did you see it?"

"Yes. There were more, a convoy of them in the sky."

"Where were they going?"

"Other worlds." Art sighs. "There were stones of

magic hanging beneath it. You call them lodestones. We set such markers in place on all the worlds we visit. They help us hold the Demonata at bay and give the inhabitants of the planets a chance to evolve.

"The defensive power of the stones fades when we move on. As the safety net crumbles, demons seek to open windows and tunnels. If they succeed, they wipe the world clean. Then, in most cases, they return to their own universe. But sometimes on a world where lodestones are plentiful, they use it as a base to launch more attacks.

"The sky demon and its passengers are heading for neighbouring worlds, using the stolen, corrupted magic of the lodestones to sustain them. It will take millennia, but they are patient. The power will drain from the stones eventually and they'll have to return home, but that might not be for millions of years."

"And as long as the stones hold, they can stay in this universe?" I ask, feeling sick.

"Yes."

"How far is that sky demon from Earth?"

"Billions of miles. It will never trouble your people."

"But if it was setting off from a nearer world, like Atlantis, it could descend on us one day, carrying hordes of demons?"

"Yes," Art says.

"Is our universe full of sky demons, slowly making their way from one world to the next?"

"Hardly *full of*," Art mutters. "But there are many of them."

"Then we can't beat them," I croak. "We thought if we stopped them crossing, we were safe. But if armies are already here, making their way towards us..."

"All worlds will fall eventually," Art says glumly. "All beings will die. That is the nature of the universe. Nothing is forever. Death claims all things in the end."

"Sure," I grunt bitterly. "But I didn't know there were scores of demons cruising the skies, working hard to wipe us out."

"It is not an issue," Art says. "Your world will have fallen long before any sky demon reaches it."

My eyes narrow. "What are you talking about?"

"The lodestones are a temporary form of protection," he says. "Demons always cross. The only hope any beings have is to master the skies. If a species learns to move on to other worlds, they can stay ahead of the Demonata. Your people haven't made that crucial step to the stars. Your planet will fall within the next year. It is inescapable."

My jaw drops, then firmly closes. I breathe in and out through my nostrils, waiting until I'm calm. When I'm in control, I say very clearly, "I want to go home."

"It would be pointless," Art says. "You could do nothing to stop it."

"I have to try. Even if I fail, I want to be there at the end. If Earth's going to fall, I'll fall with it."

"No," Art says. "You have a greater destiny."

"I don't care about–" I begin to snarl.

"Life must continue," Art interrupts. "We realised, billions of years ago, that this universe was doomed. The Demonata are stronger than those who populate our worlds. In time they'll conquer all. We devoted ourselves to denying them that victory. We vowed to find a way to ensure life continued."

"I thought you said all things perish."

"Ultimately," he replies. "This universe is a living thing, and it will die of old age eventually. But we can make sure that the end comes in its own time, not at the hands of the Demonata. *If* you help us."

I'm silent a long time. I can't understand everything Art is talking about, but if he's right... if there's some way to thwart the plans of the Demonata...

"How much further do we have to go?" I ask.

"Not far," Art says. "Another day, perhaps, and we will reach the Crux."

"And you'll tell me everything?" I press. "No more riddles or half-answers?"

"Everything will be revealed," Art promises. "After

that you can stay or go as you please."

"Then I'll come," I sigh, and although my intentions are good, it feels like I've just sold my soul to the devil — or worse.

THE CROX

→More worlds and chambers. Pretty much all of the planets have fallen. They feel old and cold. Art says these were some of the earliest settled worlds, the first planets that the Old Creatures populated.

"You're like gods," I mutter. "You spread life across the universe."

"We nurture life," Art corrects me. "We don't create it. We don't know where the living things of this universe came from, how life was born out of fire and chaos. There are forces at work beyond even our knowledge."

"Then gods – or God – might be real?" I press.

"Perhaps."

"What about an afterlife?" I ask. "Do you know what happens to our souls when we die?"

"No," Art says. "We will talk more about that later, but first…"

We're approaching a small window. We've been moving at a constant speed, but now Art slows.

"We are almost at the Crux," he says and there's a nervous edge to his voice. I feel the ball of light tighten around me.

"What are you doing?" I ask suspiciously.

"The Crux is a place of great danger," he replies. "We cannot stay long, and I must cling tightly to you while we're there, or you will be disintegrated."

"Hold on!" I yelp. "You never said anything about disintegration!"

"I didn't want to frighten you," Art chuckles.

I stare anxiously at the window, wondering if there's anything I can do to stop this.

"Don't be afraid," Art says. "I know what I'm doing."

"Wait!" I cry as we draw close. "Have you ever taken anyone like me into the Crux before?"

Art hesitates, then says sheepishly, "No."

"Then how do you know—"

Before I can finish, we smash through the window and I scream at the top of my voice, as if riding the wildest rollercoaster in the universe.

→As soon as we slip through the window, the temperature skyrockets. We're gliding towards a massive orb of seething fire. This must be what the sun is like close up. The space around us throbs with magical energy. I sense Art tapping into that magic, using it to shield us from the unbelievable heat, glare and radiation. I can't imagine anything non-magical surviving here.

We zip closer to the ball of fire. It shimmers savagely as I stare at it, awestruck and horrified. It doesn't have a constant shape. The edges buckle and warp, bulge out, then twist back in on themselves. Pillars of flame shoot from the surface, spiral around the face of the orb and are absorbed by it again. Sometimes it turns a blinding white shade. Other times it goes black and becomes almost invisible against the expanse of space around it. Most of the time it flickers between the two colours, waves of fire lashing across the surface and bubbling over without pause.

The sun-like ball terrifies me. It's not just the heat. Being here is wrong. I feel like I'm breaking a sacred law by looking at this wild globe of wondrous fire.

"We've broken more laws than you could imagine by bringing you here," Art says. "But we cannot always be prisoners of the laws we live by. Sometimes we have to transcend them."

We press closer to the orb. We're almost upon it. My mouth is dry. My skin feels like it's burning. My eyes seem to be roasting in their sockets. I want to turn and get as far away from here as possible. But before I can beg Art to stop, we hit the outer rim and are swallowed by a billion licks of ravenous flame.

→It takes several minutes to cut through the outer ring. I've fought demons made of fire, so a realm of flames is nothing new. But this fire is hotter than any I've experienced. It roars about us like a living, furious sea. But Art holds firm and guides me through the billowing walls of the furnace.

Finally we break through the flames and enter a realm of bewitching marvels. It's a vast, oval, grey space, illuminated by constant bolts of lightning. There's debris everywhere, asteroids, pebbles and dust swirling around. The lightning regularly splits rocks and splinters them, but the pieces join with other shards to form new, larger rocks, which in turn are split again.

The space is dominated by a series of enormous square panels. Half are black, half white. The panels revolve slowly around the sphere, never meeting. Anything that hits the panels – lightning forks, rocks, flickers of flame – is absorbed, then spat out moments later.

Balls of multicoloured light – Old Creatures – float around the black panels. Hundreds of demons cluster around the white squares. My insides tense when I spot the Demonata but Art speaks quickly to calm me.

"They Will Not Harm Us," he says. "This Place Is Sacred To Both Sides. We Do Not Kill Here."

"You could have warned me earlier," I growl, then frown. "What happened to your voice? It's deeper than before, and echoey."

"We Are All Speaking To You Now," Art says stiffly. "We Do Not Experience Individuality When We Are Together."

I glance around at the various balls of light. They were pulsing in unison as Art spoke. It's too confusing to think of them all speaking at the same time, so I focus on Art and pretend I'm talking to a single entity.

"What's the story?" I ask, shivering as a bolt of lightning strikes the film of light around me and is deflected. "Why are we here? What are the big secrets?"

"The Panels Are The Key," Art says. "You Remember The Chess Board We Saw On The Earlier World?"

"Yes, but what does..." I stop and cast an eye over the panels again, doing a quick count. There are thirty-two black squares and an equal number of white.

"The Original Universe Was Shaped Like A Chess Board," Art explains. "There Were Sixty-Four Zones, Half Black, Half White. Each Zone Was Limitless In Size. Time Did Not Exist. The Universe Had Existed

And Would Exist Forever. It Was The Same For Us And The Demonata."

"I don't understand," I interrupt. "Everything has to begin somewhere."

"Only If Time Exists," Art corrects me.

"How can time *not* exist?" I huff.

"Time As You Know It Began With The Big Bang."

"I told you I don't know what that means."

"Peace," Art calms me. "We Will Come To That. First, Accept That This Was The State Of The Universe. Sixty-Four Zones, Equal In All Respects, Black Separated From White By A Force We Called The Kah-Gash."

I focus intently when he mentions the Kah-Gash, ignoring the things I don't understand. I can try to make sense of the bewildering bits later.

"Demons Existed In The White Zones," Art continues. "Vile, Violent Monsters Who Could Reproduce. We Inhabited The Black Zones And Were Sterile. That Did Not Trouble Us. Since There Was No Time, We Were Immortal. Death Did Exist — We *Could* Be Killed — But It Rarely Bothered Us. We Roamed The Endless Depths Of Our Zones, Peaceful And Content.

"Demons And Old Creatures Were Never Meant To Mix. The Kah-Gash Kept Us Separate."

I spot a disturbance among a group of demons clustered around one of the white panels. Until a few seconds ago, they swarmed around the panel like ants, but now they part, forming two neat ranks. One of the beasts glides between the others, angles for the panel, then brushes against it and is absorbed. I wait for it to emerge, but nothing happens.

"The Demon Is Dead," Art says. "It Was Ancient, One Of Those Who Existed In The Original Universe. No Living Creature Can Touch The Panels And Survive. Most Of The Original Demonata And Old Creatures Choose To Perish Here When It Is Their Time."

"One down, just a few trillion to go," I chuckle humourlessly. Then I pause. "Is that why the other demons are here, to bid farewell to the dead one?"

"Yes."

"I didn't think demons worked that way. Those I've known don't care about any of the others."

"The Original Demons Are Different," Art says. "They Have Known Each Other For So Long That They Have Formed Bonds. We Would Normally Stay Away At A Time Like This, As They Do When We Gather Here For A Funeral. But It Was Important To Protect You."

"I thought you said you don't kill here."

"We Don't," Art says. "But If They See A Human, They Might Attack. We Will Distract Them If They Grow Curious, And Defend You If Necessary."

We watch the end of the ceremony. Nothing much happens. The demons hold their ranks for a while, then break apart and drift towards the ring of fire which encircles the Crux.

"Initially We Were Not Aware Of The Demonata And They Knew Nothing Of Us," Art resumes. "But The Demonata Were Curious. They Tested The Barriers Where White Met Black, And Found A Way To Cross. They Discovered Us."

"And they attacked," I guess. "They set out to kill you all."

Art sighs. "We Knew Nothing Of War. We Fled For The Furthest Reaches Of Our Zones, Hoping The Demonata Would Lose Interest And Let Us Be."

"Some hope!" I snort.

"It Was Brutal," Art says softly. "We Learnt About Pain, Suffering And Loss For The First Time. We Were Innocent, But We Matured Fast. We Had To Or They Would Have Slain Us All.

"We Fought Back. Your People Know Much Of Warfare, But They Have Never Seen It On Such A Scale. Universal, Timeless, A War Of Magic. The Universe Burned. The Kah-Gash Buckled. Ultimately It Could Stand The Strain No Longer."

We've been drifting closer to one of the black squares. It's bigger than I assumed, several miles high. I feel tiny as we pass within its shadow.

"We Knew We Should Stop," Art whispers. "The Laws Were Shattering. The Universe Was Crumbling. The Kah-Gash Could Not Hold. But Still We Fought. We Had Become Slaves To War.

"In The End The Kah-Gash Fractured. In A Blinding, Destructive Flash, All Sixty-Four Zones Shrank To The Size Of A Speck. A Split-Second Later, The Ball Of The Universe Exploded. Everything Was Destroyed And Reborn. Life As You Know It Began."

"And that's when the universe was created?" I ask.

"*Universes*," Art corrects me. "There Are Two. Although There Were Sixty-Four Zones Before The Big Bang, There Was Only One Universe. The Laws Of The White Zones Differed To Those Of The Black, But They Were Held In Place By The Kah-Gash. Now The Two Universes Are Separate."

"I don't understand why they exist at all," I mutter. "Why wasn't everything wiped out in the explosion?"

"The Kah-Gash Protected Us. Its Last Act Was To Create Two Individual Universes, Dividing The Warring Races. It Hoped The New Structures Would Keep Us Apart. As You Have Seen, They Did Not."

"OK," I say slowly. "Our universe and the Demonata's were born out of the ashes of the old one, like a phoenix rising from the flames after it dies. So what's this place?"

"This Is The Crux, The One Point Common To Both

Universes. The Explosion Happened Here. The New Universes Spread Out In All Directions From This Area. The Universes Overlap Each Other. They Share The Same Space But Never Touch. Except Here. The Crux Exists In Both Universes At Once."

"And those black and white panels are the remains of the Kah-Gash?"

"Yes, But Only Of Its Body. All Conscious Beings Have A Body And A Soul. What You See Here Are The Kah-Gash's Physical Remains. The Segments Of Its Soul Flew Off Along With Everything Else."

"Does that mean there are sixty-four pieces?" I ask.

"No. There Are Only Three. You, Bec And…" Art falls silent, then says, "Something Is Happening."

"What do you—" I start to ask.

"Quiet!" Art snaps.

I look around, trying to determine the source of Art's unease. My first thought is that the demons are mounting an attack, but they don't seem to be paying any attention to us. And the panels are revolving the same as before. So why…

Wait. I'm wrong. The panels aren't the same. They're not circling any longer. They're gliding forward now. Towards us. Towards *me*.

"Art?" I mumble. "What are they doing?"

"Gravitating Towards You. Possibly Trying To Reunite."

"Is that bad?" I ask.

Art doesn't answer. Instead he reverses direction and suddenly we're flying towards the ring of fire as fast as we can.

"What's going on?" I shout.

"We Do Not Know," Art says. "We Had Not Expected Such A Reaction."

"What will happen if they join?"

"We Are Not Sure. Maybe Nothing. Maybe The End Of All We Know."

"The end of the universes?" I gasp.

"Perhaps."

I stare with horror at the giant squares. They're coming together slowly, but not slowly enough for my liking.

"Will they stop if we get out of here?" I ask.

"We Think So," Art says. There's a brief pause. "We *Hope* So."

I watch helplessly as we draw away from the panels. It looks like we'll make it out of here before they join. After that we'll just have to pray that –

A blast of magic strikes us and Art makes a high-pitched shrieking noise. We're knocked sideways. I glance to my left, the direction the shot came from. I spot a pack of demons streaking towards us. They unleash more bolts of magic, but the Old Creatures intercept them and blast them aside or absorb the shots themselves.

"Art?" I whisper, fearing the worst.

"I Am Not Dead," he says. "You Will Perish Too If I Die."

We pick up speed again.

"Why are they doing this?" I pant, keeping a close eye on the fighting. The Old Creatures and demons aren't engaging at close quarters – they hover apart and take long-range shots at one another – but it looks ugly. A few of the balls of light are shattered while I watch, and several of the demons are ripped apart.

"The Demonata Wish For The End Of The Universes," Art says. "They Must Have Seen The Panels Move, Spotted You And Guessed You Were The Source Of The Disturbance. Like Us, They Cannot Know What Will Happen If The Panels Join, But They Clearly Wish To Keep You Here And—"

Art is struck again. He doesn't slow this time, but his scream lasts even longer than before. We're almost at the ring of fire, but a demon has broken through the ranks of Old Creatures and is narrowing the gap, moving faster than we are.

We hit the wall of fire and plough through. It feels even hotter than it did the last time. Areas of my skin start to smoulder.

"You Must Use Magic," Art says calmly. "I Cannot Protect You As I Did Before. I Am Wounded And Must Focus On Opening A Window."

"If we make it through the fire, we'll be safe, right?" I yell, doing what I can to counter the burns breaking out across my flesh. "They can't follow us into the human universe, can they?"

"No," Art says. "But We Will Not Make It. The Demon Will Catch Us. We Have To Open The Window From Here."

"Can you do that?" I ask.

"In Theory," he says, doing nothing to calm my frayed nerves.

Art is struck again, but pushes on, concentrating on the small patches of light which I glimpse through the flicker of the flames. I try to create a barrier to help but there isn't a strong supply of magic here, at least not the sort I can tap into. The best I can do is cool my skin and quench the worst of the flames.

The demon looks nothing like those I've fought in the past. It's huge, a mass of bulges, not shaped like any animal I've ever seen. I'm not even sure where its face is. All I know is that it's utterly evil, determined to kill us and closing quickly.

"Art…" I mutter.

"We Know," he replies. "I Have Almost…"

A window of red light forms in the distance, almost impossible to see against the fiery backdrop. I give a shout of triumph, but it's drowned out when another blast of magic hits us. Art screeches. The bolt of energy drives us closer towards the window, but Art's scream cuts out midway and the lights around me shatter.

I realise with horror that Art has been killed, but there's no time to mourn. My flesh erupts, fire exploding from every pore. I scream silently, consumed by flames. In a mad fury I try to slap them out. It's a hopeless task, but before the fire can finish the job, I hit the window and plunge into the sub-universe of multicoloured lights without anyone to protect or guide me.

NEW FACE, OLD STORY

→There's no oxygen, so the flames die away. The pain doesn't, but I've no time to focus on that. It's freezing and there isn't any air. If I can't construct a shell around myself, and swiftly, I'm finished.

I search for magic, but there's nothing I can make use of. This zone of lights contains even less magical energy than there was on Earth. I thrash about like a fish on dry land, lips shut, eyes bulging. I feel my skin tighten from the cold but that doesn't bother me. I'll suffocate long before I freeze to death.

As my lungs strain for air that isn't there, my limbs go still and a calm wave spreads through me. In a way this is fitting. I was always a lonely child. I often felt out of place, not in sync with the people around me. Now I'm going to die in true isolation, more alone than any human has ever been.

A gloomy mist crosses my eyes. I think it's the shades of death drawing over my face, but then I blink and realise it's a dark green window which has opened ahead of me. As I stare at it numbly, a ball of light shoots through and envelops me from head to toe. I've just enough time to marvel at the warmth it brings. Then my eyelids flutter and I fall unconscious.

→I awake on a grey, cold, ashen world. I sit up, groaning. My skin is blistered. Parts feel raw. But I'm alive.

Something moves nearby.

"Art?" I call.

"No." A tall black man steps into view. He's fat, with very dark skin, dressed in an expensive-looking suit.

My eyes widen. "*Raz?*" I gasp.

"Only in appearance," the man says solemnly.

"I don't understand." I start to rise, but pain prevents me. Grimacing, I frown at the fat man. Raz Warlo was a Disciple. I met him when I first joined Beranabus. He was killed during the quest to find my baby brother. "Why change?" I wheeze.

"The one you knew as Art is dead," Raz says. "Although shapes mean nothing to us, we know you need them to make sense of the universe. We felt it would be easier for you if I took a different form." He looks down at himself and frowns. "The suit was a difficult touch."

"What happened back there?" I ask.

"The panels of the Kah-Gash reacted to your presence," Raz says. "The demons attacked. We managed to get you out before they killed you."

"And the panels? Did they stop?"

"The fact that we still exist makes me think so," Raz says drily.

I nod slowly, then clear my throat. "Art sacrificed himself to save me."

"Evidently."

"And you placed your life at risk by coming after me."

"Yes."

"*Why?*" I groan. "Why take me to the Crux and risk your lives for my sake?"

"That will become clear very soon," Raz says and nods at a rock behind me. "That is a lodestone. It is the reason I brought you to this world. I suggest you use its power to heal yourself before we continue."

Now that I focus, I realise there's a strong current of magic flowing around me. I tap into it gratefully and set to work on my wounds, patching up the holes burnt in my flesh.

As I'm sealing the last of the gashes, Raz looks around at the dead land, then says, "Did you ever plan to have children?"

The question throws me and I squint at him. "I

hadn't given it much thought. Probably not. It's hard to bring up a child when you're busy battling demons."

"The Old Creatures can't reproduce," Raz says. "It didn't matter in the original universe, since we were immortal. That changed when the Kah-Gash fractured. Now every creature ages. We are captives of time and the price of our captivity is death."

As Raz speaks, I stand and stretch. My stomach rumbles. I'm ravenous and thirsty, but there's nothing to eat or drink, so I do my best to ignore the cries of my deprived body and focus on the Old Creature's lecture.

"We accepted our mortality," Raz continues, "but the Demonata craved a return to the way things were. They wanted to live forever. So they set about thwarting the hold of death."

"How?" I frown.

"As long as the new universes exist, death will claim us all," Raz says. "But if those universes are eradicated... if the Kah-Gash is reassembled and the old laws are re-established..."

I start to tremble. "Beranabus said the Kah-Gash could destroy a universe. But you're saying it could destroy *both?*"

"Yes. The Kah-Gash could draw everything back through time to the moment of the Big Bang, eliminate all that has happened since and restore the original universe."

"What would happen to us?" I gasp.

"You would have never existed," Raz says. "Time would be reversed. All the creatures and planets of the new universes would be wiped out. Only the Old Creatures and the Demonata would survive."

"Why wouldn't you be killed too?"

"We think we would be protected, as we were when the Kah-Gash exploded. If we are correct, even the new Demonata – the spawn of the original beasts – would be spared, since they carry the genes of their parents."

"Then why not us?" I ask hollowly.

"You are not our offspring," Raz says sadly. "New life was created when this universe was born. We have guided many species and helped souls develop. But you are not ours.

"We must go," Raz says abruptly. "You need to eat, so we will move on." He sets to work on the tiny patches of light in the air around us.

"What world of wonders are we heading for now?" I ask.

"We're not going to a world," Raz says. "We are going to a *spaceship*."

PICKING UP THE PIECES

→I wanted to be an astronaut when I was younger, walk on the moon, fly around in a rocket, zap aliens with a laser gun, teleport across galaxies. I've done a lot more than that in the years since, boldly going to places where no man would ever *want* to go. Still, that love of spacemen and rockets remains, and when Raz tells me we're heading for a spaceship, I fill with excitement. But when we slide through the window, it's into a large room of concrete walls, boxes stacked neatly at the sides, fluorescent lights overhead. There's a small garden in the middle of the room.

"This isn't a spaceship," I grumble. "Spaceships are made of metal, full of stuff like…" I stop, realising how ridiculous that sounds. Spaceships in movies and comics might be like that. But in the real world, built by beings of another planet, why should they be?

"Precisely," Raz says. "This is a massive craft designed to navigate the vastness of space. It is the size of a city, home to two million creatures. They fled their dying planet long ago and have sailed among the stars ever since.

"Now eat."

"Eat what?" I ask, looking around.

"Anything," Raz says. "The crates are packed with nutritious substances. And there are bottles of liquid in those." He points at the boxes to my left.

"Won't anyone mind?" I ask nervously, not wanting to get on the wrong side of short-tempered aliens.

"These are excess supplies. Nobody will notice."

I shuffle over to the crates and lift off the lid of the nearest box. There are large plastic bottles inside. The liquid in them is an unpleasant green colour. The stench, when I snap the top off, is vile.

"Are you sure this is safe?" I ask.

"Yes."

"Why aren't you drinking any?"

"I don't need it."

Sceptical, I raise the bottle and take a sip. It's disgusting! I spit it out and grimace, then reluctantly drain a mouthful and swish it around. The taste doesn't improve, but after half a minute of swishing, I gulp, then lower the bottle and wait to be sick. When nothing happens, I drink some more, then look for something to sink my teeth into. The food is as unappealing as the liquid, but it fills me up. When my stomach can hold no more, I wipe my lips with a hand and glance at Raz.

"Done?" he asks.

"Done," I confirm.

"Are you ready to go on a quick tour?"

"Can I?" I ask eagerly.

"I know you want to. I can disguise us to look like natives."

"Great! Let's do it."

Leaving the storeroom, we walk down a long corridor, then take an elevator to an upper level. It looks remarkably like the elevators on Earth.

"You shouldn't be surprised," Raz says. "We sowed the seeds of intelligence among most of the universe's beings, and the rest were assisted by those we first helped. There are many similarities between species."

The elevator comes to a halt and the doors slide open. I step out into a noisy street that could be in any of Earth's busier cities. Buildings like ours, vehicles that look like cars, streetlamps and power cables. The only difference is that instead of a sky, there's another level overhead. Otherwise it's unnervingly familiar.

The same can't be said for the *people*. They have no human traits. Long tendrils instead of arms and legs. Their faces, which are in the middle of their bodies, have several gloopy eyes set in a semi-circle around a small, toothless mouth. No ears or nose. Each is a mix of colours. They're slimy, dripping freely as they pass. Smaller creatures feast on the mucous, an army of insect-like slime-eaters who gobble it up, keeping the paths clean.

I stare for a long time at the aliens, then glance at Raz and myself and frown. "We don't look any different. I thought you were going to disguise us."

"I haven't altered our bodies," Raz says. "I'm affecting the visual sensors of those around us, so that to their eyes we appear as they do. Yes," he adds with a grin before I can say anything, "that *is* pretty cool."

We wander down the street. I peer in windows as we pass, and even enter a few of the buildings, trying to figure out what the stores are selling, what the creatures are doing, what the buildings are for. Raz whispers in my ear as we wind our way down the street, then turn into another, and another, exploring.

"When the Kah-Gash split, the pieces of its soul shot off ahead of the blast, travelling faster than light or any of the other forces unleashed by the explosion. They darted in and out of the new universes, passing from one to the other as they flew further apart.

"Eventually they slowed and drifted. Sometimes they floated across realms like cosmic butterflies. Other times they disappeared from one part of a universe and popped up on the opposite side in the blink of an eye.

"The patches of light you have seen since birth are physical remnants of the Kah-Gash. There were barriers of energy and magic between the squares of the original universe. When the Kah-Gash exploded, the barriers shattered, but their fragments were used to stitch the fabric of the new universes together. It took us a long time to realise that, since we cannot see them."

"You can't see the lights?" I frown.

"No," Raz says. "They only reveal themselves to the eyes of the Kah-Gash."

"I don't understand."

"There are three parts of the Kah-Gash," Raz says. "The trigger, memory and eyes. The trigger is the commanding force. The memory stores all that happens. The eyes see the hidden strings which bind the universes in place.

"This only became clear to us over the long course of time. In the beginning we didn't know how many pieces there were, what function they played, where they'd gone. We were not even sure that parts of the Kah-Gash still existed.

"The Demonata knew no more than we did, but threw themselves into the search. Their desperate plan was to find the parts of the Kah-Gash, reassemble them and restore the original universe. It's a plan they haven't wavered from.

"For a time we saw no threat. We thought it was a fool's quest. But then the parts began to reappear. They had the ability to turn up anywhere, in a comet, a rock, a tree, an animal, even in one of the new demons. The pieces never merged with any of the Old Creatures or original demons, but all other forms were fair game. They caused no harm, existing in harmony with their hosts, but their re-emergence filled us with panic."

Raz shivers, then continues. "The Demonata pursued the pieces with a mad passion. When they finally found one, they experimented, seeking ways to harness its power. They found they could influence its destination when it moved from one form to another, ensuring it stayed within their grasp.

"The demons searched hard for the other pieces. They couldn't cross from their universe to ours, but they didn't need to. The parts of the Kah-Gash passed freely between universes. The Demonata could wait, even though it might take billions of years."

We come to another elevator and ride it down to a random lower level. I find a park, full of strangely shaped trees and bushes. I dodge between them as Raz speaks.

"We couldn't let them reunite the Kah-Gash," Raz says. "We felt responsible for this universe's new life forms. They were simple creatures, but they had a right to exist. So we counter-plotted. Although the demons couldn't cross universes, we had the power to enter theirs. We launched a raiding party. After a brief battle, we freed the piece of the Kah-Gash and fled. The Demonata couldn't follow. All they could do was keep searching and waiting.

"That's how things continued over millions of years," Raz says, as if talking about the passing of a couple of weeks. "The Demonata imprisoned pieces of the Kah-Gash. We crossed, fought and freed them."

"Are you stronger than the demons?" I ask.

"No," Raz says. "But we only needed to destroy the form in which a piece was stuck. When that happened, it shot free. If the demons had been able to focus, they could have directed it into another form of their choosing, but we distracted them.

"We also searched for pieces in our universe," Raz goes on. "We had no wish to reassemble the Kah-Gash, but we hoped to capture the pieces and hold them from the Demonata forever. We learnt to influence the pieces, but only as the Demonata did. We can keep them in place a while, but eventually they slip free."

"Is that the same when the demons capture them?" I ask.

"Yes."

"Then why worry?" I shrug. "If they can't hold on

to a piece forever, they can't collect them all, can they?"

"Unfortunately, yes," Raz says. "Sometimes all three pieces exist in a universe at the same time, as they do now. When I say we can't hold on to a piece for long, I mean tens of thousands of years. That's more than enough time for the Demonata to unite the parts. All they need is a lucky break.

"So we continued to fight," Raz says wearily. "Every time they captured a piece, we set it free. It could have gone on like that until the end of time, except there were casualties. Some of us always died when we raided. A few here, a few there. When you add them up over millions, then billions of years..." He shudders.

"We're not afraid of death," Raz says. "But we couldn't continue that way indefinitely, because–"

"–you can't have children," I interrupt, beating him to the punch.

"Correct." He smiles sadly. "At some point we would become extinct. Then the demons would be free to track down the pieces of the Kah-Gash and restore the original universe, only this time it would be exclusively theirs.

"We couldn't accept such a fate, so we did something we were never meant to. We played God and interfered with the creatures of the new universe.

We've been paying for that mistake ever since. And the universe has been paying for it too."

Raz turns his face away and says with shame, "We're the reason the Demonata can cross from their universe to ours." He brushes a hand across his cheeks, and though I can't be certain, I think the Old Creature is wiping away guilty tears.

WORLD OF THE DEAD

→We return to the room with the garden and Raz constucts a new window. We travel for a long time through the sub-universe of lights, finally emerging on top of a stone slab. The walls of this chamber are dotted with holes and windows, through which I can see thousands of tombs and monuments, encircling us like silent, frozen sentries.

Raz slips through one of the larger holes and I follow, gazing solemnly at the ranks of graves. Even though the tombs differ in style and size to those on Earth, there's no doubt that this is a graveyard. It has the feel of death.

"This place is massive," I whisper, goosebumps rising.

"It is a cemetery world," Raz says.

"You mean everybody's dead?" I gulp. "Was it a war?"

"There was never life on this planet," Raz says. "But there are populated planets nearby and advanced beings move freely between them. For centuries they have been bringing their dead here, laying them to rest on a world of their own."

A world of the dead. My goosebumps spread. I'm not easily spooked, but this is creeping me out big time.

"By shaping the minds of this universe's creatures, we hoped to cheat destiny," Raz says softly, returning to his lecture. "We knew we would die before the universe ended. We thought if we spread intelligence, the beings we created might carry on the fight.

"There are now millions of races with the power of thought. Many are more advanced than your people. But intelligence was never intended for this universe. The earliest creatures showed no signs of evolving and developing souls."

"What do you mean by that?" I stop him.

"Every intelligent being has a soul," Raz says. "Animals don't. A soul forms when a creature thinks for the first time, when it reasons and makes plans. It is a fascinating process. In some species it happens in every member at the same moment. In most, one of them makes a mental leap, then bears young and they pass it on, intelligence spreading like a disease.

"We cultivated the *disease*. It was much harder than we imagined, but once we made the breakthrough, we quickly mastered the arts of education, then split into small groups and set off for the far reaches of the universe, sowing intelligence everywhere we went.

"We had no right to disturb the natural balance," Raz sighs. "But *you* are a child of our meddling. Would you rather exist as a mindless beast, running wild, no understanding of the past or plans for the future?"

"No," I answer after a short pause.

"Nor do most others. They *have* the choice. We can't force a species to evolve. Some fight it and return to their simpler ways. But most rise to the challenges we set. Life is easier for animals, but so much richer for those with the ability to love and hate, fight and make peace, dream and hope."

Raz falls silent as we walk among the tombs and headstones. After a while I come to a small, unimpressive tomb. I almost walk past, but Raz coughs softly and points towards the upper right corner.

A tiny chess board has been carved into it. As my eyes narrow, Raz points to the left corner, where another board has been carved. Then he nods at a tomb four rows over. A large, intricate board has been painted over the centre of this one, the name of the deceased worked in among the black and white squares.

"The Boards are key to the process," Raz says. "We created them out of material drawn from the Crux.

Modelling them after the Kah-Gash, we created mini-universes of sixty-four zones. Once a species evolves to a certain point, we isolate their souls and take them into a Board, so that they can develop at an accelerated rate. We also teach them about the origins of the universe, the Kah-Gash and the Demonata, the need to reach for the stars, to fight for the future of the universe."

"How come I don't know all that?" I ask.

"You have an undeveloped brain," Raz says, then raises his hands as I bristle. "I mean humans in general. You have not evolved to the point where you can make sense of all that we taught you. Every species is the same. It takes time to work your way through the mysteries of life." Raz grimaces. "Humans will never complete that journey. The Demonata will cut short their growth. Universal understanding is not to be yours."

I blink and look away, stomach tightening. I spot something far overhead. I think it's a falling star, but as I focus, I realise it's a spaceship. Unlike the floating city, this looks more like the rockets I've seen in movies and on the covers of science-fiction books.

"A glorified hearse," Raz says.

We watch in silence until the ship settles out of sight beyond the ranks of tombs. "Can we go and see the burial?" I ask.

"No," Raz says. "I have something else to show you." He leads me through a maze until we come to a black, round stone. Its edges are as smooth as a polished gem's. It's set in a small pit, circled by a number of large tombs. Candles burn around the edges of the pit, but they're not normal candles — the wick doesn't burn down and the flames never flicker in the soft wind.

There's a magical buzz coming from the stone. My fingers curl inwards and my nostrils widen. Magic floods my pores.

"It's another lodestone," I note.

"Yes," Raz says. "Beranabus thought the stones were of our making, but they are actually the remains of planets from the original universe. Most were reduced to dust, but fragments of some survived and drifted through space, sometimes burying themselves in the fabric of freshly forming worlds.

"The stones were charged with the magic of the original universe. We used them to travel swiftly from one planet to another. They acted as universal markers, guiding us, allowing us to cross vast expanses of space swiftly. Unfortunately the lodestones could be used to serve the forces of evil as well." Raz laughs bitterly. "We never guessed that the species we assisted might prove as vicious as the demons we hoped they would fight."

"Mages used lodestones to open windows to the Demonata universe," I groan.

"We assumed this universe's creatures would care primarily for their own," Raz says. "But many craved power. Each world produced individuals with magical talent. Most used their power to do good, but some became tyrants. They crushed their enemies and ruled with a monstrous authority."

"You could have stopped them," I growl.

"And replaced them?" Raz asks wryly. "Established our favourites as rulers? No. We were determined to guide, not rule. We looked on with despair as the rotten few caused misery for millions. But we never intervened. Every species must be free to make their mistakes, enjoy their triumphs, lament their catastrophes. That is our fundamental belief."

Raz sighs again. "The windows were bad enough, but then some used more powerful lodestones to create tunnels and entire civilisations fell. We realised more would follow, that the Demonata would cross in greater numbers and spread. We thought about shutting the project down." He chuckles humourlessly.

"Why didn't you?" I frown.

Raz shakes his head. "You don't realise what that would have entailed. We had visited millions of worlds. There were billions of intelligent beings scattered through the universe. We'd have had to—"

"—kill them all," I finish hoarsely.

Raz nods. "That was not an option, so we dismissed it. Besides, the demons could not ruin *every* world or kill *every* living being. It was physically impossible. The Demonata might destroy much, but not all. Life would continue, even when we were gone.

"That changed sixteen hundred years ago." Raz's features darken. "We had pressed on with the programme. All looked positive. But then, on your world, an insignificant, unremarkable girl altered everything. She turned the laws of life on their head, and introduced a new player to the game, one who could guarantee victory for the Demonata."

I gulp. "You're talking about Bec, aren't you?"

"Yes," Raz says angrily.

"And the new player?" I ask.

He stares at me heavily, then says, "*Death*."

THE REAPER UNLEASHED

→"What are you talking about?" I mutter. "According to Art, death always existed, even in the original universe."

"As a force," Raz says. "Death was like time or gravity. It was simply a thing that happened. Bec changed that. First she stole a piece of the Kah-Gash from Lord Loss. Then—"

"From Lord Loss?" I interrupt, startled. "Art said the pieces never turned up in demons who were alive before the Big Bang."

"They don't," Raz says.

"Then Lord Loss isn't one of the major demons?" I whisper. The demon master is by far the most powerful foe I've ever faced. If there are others even stronger than him...

"There are many greater than he is," Raz says gloomily, "but he has a unique power. The piece of the Kah-Gash nestled within him for thousands of years. That's why he alone of the masters is able to cross freely between universes.

"When Bec unconsciously stole Lord Loss's piece of the Kah-Gash, it was cause for wonder — that had never happened before. But then she did something even more incredible. When Lord Loss killed her, her soul remained.

"Death has always meant the end. When a body dies, the soul moves on, maybe to another realm, maybe to be reincarnated, maybe to nothingness — we can only guess. But no soul ever cheated death."

"Bec was just a ghost," I mutter. "Ghosts are nothing new."

"Ghosts are shadows of the living," Raz says. "They're after-images of people, like the temporary glow a light leaves when it's quenched. Bec was different. She was fully conscious, memories intact, a complete spirit."

I shrug. "She's part of the Kah-Gash. She used her power to stay, just as Lord Loss used it to cross universes. What's the big deal?"

"Death was an absolute," Raz snaps. "The Kah-Gash had no control over it. All beings had to answer death's summons. Until Bec."

The rocket we saw touch down rises with a roar that shakes the tombs around me. I think the structures are going to shatter, but as the rocket parts the clouds and powers away from the planet, they settle down again.

"We don't know how Bec cheated death," Raz says softly. "We're not sure if she chose to remain, or if the Kah-Gash kept her, aware of the side-effects."

"What side-effects?"

Raz is silent a moment. Then he moves away from the lodestone, through the tombs, back to the chamber. As I follow, he speaks.

"Death was a force, but when Bec defied it, that force developed a mind. It became aware of itself, the universes, its role. And unfortunately it reacted with anger."

"This is madness," I grumble. "Death's not a person. It can't *react*."

"It can now," Raz disagrees. "It constructed a body. Prior to Bec, beings died and souls passed on. But the new Death has the power to harness souls. It can deny them passage to whatever lies beyond. It built a huge, shadowy body out of—"

"*The Shadow!*" I cry, coming to a standstill, eyes widening with horror.

I'm trembling. It all makes horrible sense now. Beranabus was right — the Shadow *is* the greatest threat we've ever faced. Only it's far worse than he imagined. You can't cheat death and you can't hide from it.

"Precisely," Raz sighs. "Since death claims all things, Death knows where all things are. The body of Death can only thrive in an area of magic, so it resides in the demon universe. But its reach extends to all worlds. It can guide the Demonata to wherever there is life."

"But why is it working for them?" I moan.

Raz makes a humming noise. "This is speculation, but we believe the Demonata and Death share a common goal — the restoration of the Kah-Gash. If they achieve it, the life forms of this universe will cease to exist. The Demonata will return to their immortal ways. The Old Creatures will drift along sadly. And Death's task will be vastly lessened."

"What task?" I frown.

"The harvesting of souls. Death's job is far harder now than it was before the Big Bang — so many souls to process. It seems to think the job is *too* hard, and is working to – as you humans would aptly put it – lighten its workload."

"We have to stop it," I gasp. "We have to find the Shadow and destroy it. If Death has a body, it can be attacked. If we kill it, maybe its mind will unravel."

"We do not think it is possible to kill Death," Raz murmurs. "It will simply put another body together. There will never be a shortage of souls."

"The Kah-Gash," I snap. "We can use that."

Raz pulls a face. "The Kah-Gash never had power over death. Also, as I said, it might have worked through Bec to grant Death consciousness in the first place. The Kah-Gash has changed. In the past, the pieces cut random paths through the universes. But since Bec defied death, the other parts have worked their way to your planet. They both cropped up there shortly after she died. We could do nothing about Bec's piece – she was beyond our grasp – but we directed the other pair into forms of our choosing and sent them far away.

"They escaped and returned to Earth, in Grubitsch Grady and you."

"You think the Kah-Gash wants to reunite?" I frown.

"It looks that way. Perhaps the Kah-Gash wishes to fight Death, to preserve the universes. Or maybe it too yearns for a return to simpler ways, and is using Death to achieve its goal. We don't know. We can only fear."

"I guess there's only one way to find out," I grunt. "We have to go back. I'll join with Bec and Grubbs, try to control the Kah-Gash, and hope for the best. There's no other way, is there?"

"Actually," Raz coughs, "there is. But you're not going to like it…"

NOAH MK II

→When we cross to the next world, I find myself on a large, circular, metallic platform. It's covered by a domed glass roof. There are banks of sophisticated-looking computers running along the sides.

"Not so sophisticated really," Raz murmurs. "This was designed as a viewing station by one of the lesser species. We could have arranged a more advanced craft, but they like to do things themselves. Look down."

I nudge to the edge, not sure what to expect. As I approach, panels of glass slide back and a telescope revolves into place before me.

A world like Earth lies a few miles below. There are massive buildings, wide roads, parks and ponds. Some of the buildings have glass roofs or are open topped. I can see all sorts of creatures moving around inside them, a bewildering variety of animals, birds, lizards and more, many defying description.

"It looks like a zoo," I remark.

"It is," Raz says. "But all of them have souls and are here of their own choice. They know of the Demonata and the threat this universe faces, and have pledged themselves to our cause."

The air hums with magic. As I cast my gaze around, I spot lodestones dotted everywhere, of all shapes and sizes.

"It's an ark," Raz says. "You know the biblical story of the ark, how Noah took in a pair of every species and spared them from the flood."

"Was that real?" I ask.

"It doesn't matter." He waves the question away. "*Our* ark is real, and we have to deal with far worse than a flood. This is why you're here, why we've shown you all that you've seen and revealed so much."

"I don't get it. You want me to live here?"

Raz laughs. "We'd have brought you here directly if that was the case, telling you only as much as you needed to know, as we did with the others. There are already humans on this ark. Your people are not among the more advanced, but we brought some here anyway, for *you*."

"I'm still lost," I mutter.

"We want you to be the new Noah," Raz says. "We want you to protect these creatures and guide them, evading the Demonata and Death, always remaining one step ahead of those who would destroy them. We want you to save the universe."

It sounds ridiculous. I'm tempted to laugh. Except I know Raz isn't joking.

"How?" I whisper.

"We've planted scores of lodestones across this planet," Raz says. "Enough to last an eternity. This is a world of never-ending magical energy. We designed it to be a haven, a warship, a nursery. Food will always be abundant. Species will never struggle with infertility. Magicians will be born to every generation."

"You're going to make a last stand here?" I frown. "This is a fortress?"

"No fortress could stand against our enemies," Raz says. "If this world was a thousand times more powerful than it is, it still wouldn't hold long against a mass demon attack. The Demonata don't know about the ark yet, but they'll discover it eventually and come. When they arrive, it must not be here."

"Huh?" I gawp.

"We will ensure they never open a tunnel to this world, by guarding each stone zealously. With no direct route of attack, Death will lead them to nearby planets and they'll launch armies from there. When that happens… when the net is closing and the end looks certain… it will be *your* time."

"What am I supposed to do?" I scowl. "Hold up a STOP sign?"

"You will open a window and slip away to another part of the universe," Raz says. "And you'll take the planet with you."

He says it so simply that at first I nod as if it's no big thing. Then it hits me and I turn from the edge of the platform and stare incredulously.

"Take the *planet* with me?" I repeat stupidly.

"When you've opened windows before, others have been able to slip through. This will be similar, only you'll have to open a bigger window."

"You're insane!" I yelp. "I've never opened a window more then seven or eight feet tall."

"That's because you never needed a larger window," Raz says calmly. "You can do far more than you've demanded of yourself. With our guidance you'll learn to open a larger window and curve it, so it surrounds the world. That way, rather than propel the world through the window, it can close around the planet."

I stare at Raz wordlessly. I don't know what to think.

"Think of victory," Raz growls. "Think of life. Think of the demons you'll defy, the doom you'll spare everyone here."

"It's impossible…"

"No," Raz insists. "It *can* work. That's no guarantee that it *will* – there might be obstacles ahead which we can't predict – but we believe in the plan."

My mind's whirling. "But when I die, my piece of the Kah-Gash will link up with the others. You've already said you can't control it."

Raz clears his throat. "That brings us to the part you're not going to like. As you say, we won't be able to harness your piece of the Kah-Gash when you die, so we need to find a way around that. Kernel, what would you think if we asked you to make the ultimate sacrifice for the sake of the universe?"

"You want me to kill myself?" I ask with surprising calmness.

"No." Raz leans forward, eyes sparkling. "We want you to live forever!"

A WARNING

→We spend the night wandering the ark, sharing food and drink with some of the many creatures aboard. They don't know who I am or the special task Raz has asked of me. They think I'm just another face in the crowd.

I'm surprised, as I talk with the sometimes multi-limbed, multi-headed, multicoloured aliens, by how alike we are. Not in looks, clothes or customs. But they have the same concepts of good and evil. Family is important to them. Most are religious. They have dreams and hopes for the future.

"Are all civilisations like this?" I ask Raz as we stroll beneath trees full of bat-like beings. A few are playing a game on a chess board.

"No," Raz says. "We chose from the more compassionate species. They have a fighting spirit – we need warriors – but they can control their tempers. This world has to last an eternity. We cannot tolerate internal conflict."

"It might happen anyway," I note, watching a couple of bats chase each other through the branches, squealing happily. "People change, so I guess this lot do too. You can't know what they'll be like in a million years. Groups might splinter. War could erupt."

"Perhaps." Raz sighs. "We'll use magic to preserve the balance as best we can. Evolution will be curbed, so there'll be no physical changes, but we can't take all possibilities into consideration. We'll plan as far ahead as possible. After that... As you would say, it's in the lap of the gods."

I still haven't reached a decision. I'm weighing up all that the universe stands to gain against all that I will personally lose.

They want me to become a living tunnel between universes. Sometimes a mage becomes part of a tunnel and lives as long as the tunnel remains open. They don't age or die. If I agree to this, I'll live until the end of time. Death won't be able to claim me. I can keep moving the ark around, protecting this small pocket of survivors while all others are tracked down by the Demonata and slaughtered.

It's not foolproof. My piece of the Kah-Gash might desert me when it realises what I'm doing, or Death might find a way to trap the ark. But the Old Creatures think it will work. *If* I play along.

In their position, I'd force the guy with the power

to accept. I wouldn't give him any say in the matter. I'd open a tunnel, make him part of it and leave him with no option but to do what was necessary.

But the Old Creatures believe I have the right to choose. It's the creed they live by. They'll guide their foster children in the right direction, but they won't force us. Ever. Even if the fate of the universe is at stake.

It's not a nice future – I don't want to spend the rest of eternity as a cog in a machine – but if I refuse to cooperate and everything falls to the demon hordes, there won't be any kind of a future at all. The Demonata will either get their hands on all three pieces of the Kah-Gash and destroy everything immediately. Or they'll work their way through the universe, world by world, and gradually grind us into dust. Either way, universal catastrophe.

But if I stay, I'll be surrendering all but a slim fraction of this universe to the demons. I might keep the millions on this world alive, but trillions of others will perish horribly. If I go back and link up with Bec and Grubbs… if we reassemble the Kah-Gash and test it against Death… then the universe has a chance. It might even be possible to save Earth.

Is it better to make a stand, fail and lose all, or sacrifice unimaginable numbers of lives in order to keep a select handful alive? I don't know! This task should have fallen to someone equipped to meet it, like Beranabus. He'd have said yes to the Old Creatures in an instant, without batting an eyelid.

"Perhaps that's why he wasn't chosen," Raz murmurs. "We don't know why the Kah-Gash selects those it inhabits. It might be random, or it might be the work of a higher force. Maybe the universe chose someone who would weigh both sides equally, who wasn't so certain of his path that he'd ignore all others."

"But what if I make the wrong choice?" I groan.

"You can only do what you believe is right," Raz says. "Consider the angles. Heed your instinct. Decide. If you are wrong, at least you will have been true to yourself. Life asks questions of us all. We don't always know the answers. Most times we have to guess."

"But you think I should stay," I press, trying to force Raz to decide for me.

"Yes," Raz says. "But we also believed we were acting in the universe's best interests when we encouraged evolution. We are not always right."

I nod glumly. We've passed from beneath the trees and I can see the sky again. There are several moons, smaller than Earth's, different colours. They look like huge marbles. Thinking of marbles, I remember when Art was stolen by a monster from another world. I darted through a window of light to try and rescue him. I didn't know what lay on the other side. The safe option would have been to wait and consider my actions. But then the window would have closed, Art would have been lost. I'd have regretted my indecision for the rest of my life.

Raz squints at me. "You are going back," he notes with surprise.

"Maybe Death can't be defeated," I sigh. "Maybe the Demonata have won and this ark is all we can hope to protect. But I have to *try* to stop them. If I run now, I'll always wonder if there wasn't something I could have done to save *everyone*.

"If I fight Death and fail, I'll return to do what you wish, assuming I survive. But if I quit now, it'll gnaw away at me... at my soul... forever."

I lower my gaze and wipe tears from my eyes. I don't know when I started crying, but my cheeks are soaked. "Open a window," I croak. "I'm going home."

→The journey back passes unremarkably. A series of lights, windows and worlds. We follow a different route most of the way, but the chambers we pass through are much the same. I don't explore any of the worlds. I'm fully focused on the battle to come, the huge risk I'm taking, what will happen if I fail. I wish I could be positive about my decision, but I'm full of doubts. I think about changing my mind at least ten times an hour.

Eventually we start passing through worlds I remember from the trip out. I get excited as we draw closer to Earth. I might be going to my death, but if that's to be my destiny, at least I'll die on home soil.

Finally, as my stomach's starting to rumble again, we hit Atlantis and come to a stop. Raz looks around to make sure there are no giant slugs, then glances at me. "I'll wait here for you."

I'm surprised. "You're not coming with me?"

"No. I will escort you back, but I won't cross with you. You must face Death by yourself, as everyone must when their time comes. If you wish to return, you can find me here."

"But I can't operate the smaller lights," I remind him.

"You won't need to," Raz says. "You will be able to use the normal lights to search for me. It will take a long time to piece them together – at least several hours – but just think of me and you will find the way."

"How will I breathe while crossing?" I ask.

Raz goes to one of the lodestones and cuts off a sliver of rock with a fingernail, as easily as slicing through paper. "Put this in your pocket," he says, handing it to me. "Draw on its power if you come back. It will sustain you."

"You're sure?" I ask, eyeing the tiny chip of rock suspiciously.

"Yes."

"How long will you wait?" I ask.

"As long as it takes," he says. "I will know when you are... finished."

"You mean when I'm dead," I smile.

"If the hand plays out that way, yes. But I hope it doesn't."

Raz sets to work on the window and it materialises minutes later. I start to tremble and my stomach clenches. I was never the bravest. I hate fighting. But when I have to, I do. Wincing, I step forward.

"One last thing," Raz stops me, then hesitates. "This is a delicate matter. I don't wish to cast doubts without proof, but it's important that you know about the possibility of the threat."

"What threat?" I grunt.

"The girl," Raz says softly. "Her piece of the Kah-Gash was originally part of Lord Loss."

"So?" I ask warily.

"It was in the demon master for a long time. Pieces normally merge with beings who live no more than a few hundred years. They're influenced by those they share a life with. Having been part of Lord Loss for so long, her piece might have been more affected by the demon than by other hosts."

"Are you saying…?" I stop, the thought unfinished, not wanting to continue.

"The Kah-Gash could be manipulating the girl," Raz says. "Perhaps it spared her soul in order to give Death its freedom. Maybe it wants to restore the original universe. Bec is of good heart, but the best of people can be tricked and misused.

"We might be worrying unnecessarily," Raz concludes. "You may have nothing to fear. But watch her, Kernel. Use those sharp eyes of yours. Look for treachery and be prepared for it. *Beware the priestess, Bec.*"

WELCOME HOME

→Raz leads me through the sub-universe of lights for the last time, then bids me a quick farewell and propels me forward. Before I can yell goodbye, I'm thrust through a window and straight into the middle of a nightmarish war. No time to gather my senses. I have to adapt immediately or die.

I'm in the middle of a city. Blood and corpses everywhere. The air's thick with the scent of demons, and also with the buzz of magic, which I swiftly tap into. I try to erect a shield around myself, but something clatters into me before I can complete it. A beast rolls with me to the ground and comes up spitting. It's a wolfish creature, long fangs, claws the size of butchers' knives, hot yellow eyes. It turns, faces me, snarls — then leaps.

I raise my hands to repel the monster, but instead of attacking me, it jumps over my head and tears into something behind, howling with bloodthirsty delight. Whirling, I spot the wolfish beast battling a demon.

The wolf rips at the demon's ribcage, fangs snapping in search of guts.

Wary and confused, I cast my gaze around. There are more wolfen animals on the street and they're all fighting demons. Soldiers are at work too, tackling the demonic invaders, showering them with bullets. They can't kill the Demonata but they can injure, disrupt and stall them.

There's a burst of magic to my right. I spot a small girl rounding on a demon, frying it with magic until its head explodes and its brains splatter the wall behind it. I'm so pleased to see a familiar face, I forget all about Raz's warning and call enthusiastically, "Bec!"

She looks up. Her eyes widen with shock, then her lips spread into a smile. She yells something, but as she does, one of the wolf-like beasts wraps its arms around me and howls into my ear, obscuring all other sounds.

I lash at the creature, trying to wriggle free, gathering my energy to fight back. Before I can, the beast laughs and says, "Surely you recognise me."

I place the voice instantly, but can't believe it. I stare at the creature. He's two or three feet taller than when I last saw him, and his face is warped — dark skin, lots of blood vessels, tufts of wiry ginger hair, a yellow tinge to his eyes, mouth bigger, teeth sharper. His body is lacerated with cuts and bruises. But it's definitely—

"*Grubbs!*" I roar. "What the hell's happened? You look like a werewolf."

"I am," he chuckles. "That's my pack." He waves a hairy hand at the wolves. His fingers are twisted and bulging, the nails more like claws. He could probably pop my head one-handed.

"But... how... what...?"

"I'll deal with this lot first and explain later," he growls, tugging at the waist of his trousers. They only just fit him. He's naked otherwise, chest exposed, rippling with muscles. He's stained with blood — different colours, so I know it's demon blood, not his own. Some of the stains are fresh, dripping from his skin and soaking into his hair. But others are caked in. He's been in the wars since we parted, and he looks like he's been loving every moment.

As Grubbs pounds away to attack a group of vicious demons, I put my questions on hold and focus on how best I can help. It's a dirty, messy battle. Normally demons cross singly or in small groups. But there are dozens running riot here. This is no ordinary crossing. It's the work of a powerful, organised, intelligent foe.

As the battle rages around me, I complete my shield, then focus on the patches of light in the air. A quick check reveals two windows set a few hundred feet from each other. Demons are pouring through both. That suits me perfectly. I might not be a great fighter, but I can turn the tide of this battle single-handed.

Picking a path through the warring forces, I hurry to the nearest window. It's a large pink panel. Ignoring the demons spilling out of it, protected by my shield, I thrust my hands into the centre of the panel and pull at the patches. Within seconds the window pulses, tears apart, then snaps out of existence.

The demons closest to me become alert to the threat I pose. If I can shut down the second window they'll be stranded and demons can't survive long on this world. Screeching for support, they hurl themselves at me. For a split-second I think I'm doomed. But then the road explodes at my feet, scattering the converging demons. As they scream, blinded and injured by the flying debris, sheets of fire drop on them from the air, setting them ablaze, sending them thrashing away madly.

I look for my saviour and find two angels, Bec and Meera Flame, standing side by side, hands raised, energy flowing through them, wreaking havoc. Meera's always been a stunner, but she looks more beautiful than ever now, and Bec is no strain on the eyes either. Having said that, I'd probably think anyone who saved my life was gorgeous — even Grubbs!

"Come with me!" I yell at them and press towards the second window. Meera and Bec back me up, blasting the demons ahead of me, calling for support from the soldiers and werewolves.

The smarter demons realise they're fighting a lost cause. Cursing foully, they dash through the window to the safety of their own universe, driving back those who were trying to cross. More break for the window, but get tangled up with each other or waylaid by our forces. Panic sets it. The street echoes with the hysterical wails of monsters who know they don't have long to live.

A minute later I'm ripping apart the window, and once it dissolves the demons are finished. As magic drains from the air, some of the weaker specimens collapse and rot. The others battle on hatefully, wanting to kill more humans before they die. But it's hopeless. The bullets from the soldiers' guns rip them to shreds, and without the aid of magic they have no way of putting their forms back together. They're torn to pieces. Soon only humans and werewolves are standing. We laugh and cheer, punch the air with fists, then hurry to embrace one another. We might be standing ankle-deep in rancid guts, blood and other vile juices, surrounded by corpses, but we're standing victorious — and that feels *good!*

→Grubbs wants to press on as soon as the danger's been averted. The Demonata and their twisted, human mages have been working flat out, crossing in waves. This is the fifth city Grubbs and Bec have defended in less than three days. And they've already received word of a planned sixth crossing. Grubbs is eager to get there as swiftly as possible, to stop the mage if he can, or prepare for the demons if not.

"Do you know when the window will open?" I ask.

"Within the next thirty-six hours."

"No sooner than a day?"

"No."

"Then what's the rush?"

"It's on the other side of the globe," he growls. "By the time we get to the airport, load everyone up, make the flight, roll off at the other end…"

"You don't have to do that any more," I tut. "I'll open a window and we can be there in a matter of minutes."

"Oh. I forgot." He squints. "But the mage…"

"As soon as we get there, I'll locate the forming window and we'll put a stop to it. Let's rest a while. You lot look beat. We can afford to take a day off now that *I'm* back on the scene."

"Show-off," Grubbs grunts, but he can't hide a grin.

Teams move in to clean up. I was expecting hysteria, crowds of terrified onlookers, confusion and chaos. But it all runs smoothly. Grubbs explains that the world has woken up to the existence of demons. They've attacked five densely populated cities in swift succession. Even though they've been driven off each time, thousands have been killed, cities torn apart, in full view of camera crews.

The Disciples kept the war with the Demonata quiet for a long time, with highly placed allies in most of the major news agencies and governments. But it's no longer possible to cover up. The world knows about demons now, and while panic has swept the globe, most people are behaving sensibly and heeding the advice of the Disciples. They're evacuating targeted cities quickly and calmly, or staying indoors if they can't get out in time. Volunteers have flocked to recruiting centres — Disciples test for mages each time a window opens. Those with no magical ability are working with soldiers, doctors and nurses, street cleaners, electricians, plumbers... rallying to the call, doing all they can to restore order and sweep up after an attack so that life can continue as normal.

While Grubbs gathers his pack of werewolves – there were thirty-seven to start with, but only sixteen remain – and takes them off to their holding pens, I retire to a deserted hotel with Bec, Meera and a guy in a tattered stage-magician's outfit. It's ripped all over, revealing more than it conceals, and is caked with dirt and blood. But he wears it with pride, knotting the strips of cloth around himself. His fingers (two on his left hand are missing) tremble as he ties the knots. He looks like a man who's only just holding himself together.

A frightened manager – but one who stayed when all else fled – shows us up to the hotel's finest suite. He treats us like celebrities, takes our orders, promises to do his best to process them promptly, and leaves us to collapse into chairs (Meera claims the bed) and stare at each other in weary silence.

"This is Kirilli Kovacs," Bec finally says, introducing me to the guy in the magician's costume. "He's a Disciple."

Kirilli waves weakly. Blood is seeping through the bandage around the two missing fingers on his left hand, and also through the many bandages wrapped around his body. Bec sighs, rises and limps across the room. She sets to work on healing the worst of Kirilli's wounds, drawing on the traces of magic that remain in the air. He studies her blankly while she works, like a child being cleaned by its mother.

"Where have you been?" Meera asks, then snaps her fingers at me before I can reply. "No. Let's eat, grab some sleep and wait for Grubbs. We've got loads to tell you and I guess you've got lots to tell us too."

"More than you could ever imagine," I mutter.

"Will it save for a few hours?" she asks and I shrug.

"Great." Then, forgetting about the food, she drops back, shuts her eyes and is snoring softly a minute later.

→Grubbs joins us as the food's being wheeled in. He tucks into Meera's meal — nobody wants to wake her — and asks the manager to deliver more food in nine hours. Then we retreat to different corners of the suite and make ourselves comfortable. I use magic to help me sleep.

We rise nine hours later and feast on the waiting meal. Meera's especially ravenous. I thought Grubbs was a big eater, but she beats him hollow and is still chewing at strips of chicken long after the rest of us have set our plates aside.

We swap tales while we eat, and the stories continue long after we've finished munching. Grubbs and Meera tell me all that happened once he left us at the hospital. With Shark and a squad of soldiers, they went in pursuit of Prae Athim, the head of the Lambs, and tracked her to the appropriately named Wolf Island. A load of Grubbs's cousins had been genetically modified and bred, producing hundreds of savage, wolfen offspring. They were waiting for the trio on the island.

Juni Swan was also waiting. She drove them back and left them at the mercy of the werewolves. The plan was to get her hands on Grubbs's piece of the Kah-Gash and deliver it to her new master. The simplest way was to let the werewolves butcher him, then direct the piece into a form of her choosing when it soared free.

They'd have all perished, but Grubbs unleashed the werewolf within himself and took command of his hairy relatives. He turned the tables on their foes, and although Juni escaped, they killed her conspirators.

Grubbs is sullen when he describes his fight with Juni. He doesn't look anyone in the eye. He's clearly hiding something from us, but I've no idea what.

Twelve of them hit the island. Prae Athim made it thirteen. But only Grubbs, Meera, Shark and someone called Timas Brauss made it off, leaving Prae behind to look after the werewolves, except for the thirty-seven Grubbs brought with him — his own personal army.

"That's pretty much it," he grunts. "Shark's out of action for a while. Timas is busy elsewhere, looking in on Shark whenever he can. Meera and I linked up with Dervish, Bec and Kirilli, and we've been fighting demons ever since."

"Where is Dervish?" I ask, anticipating the worst. "Is he…"

"…dead?" Grubbs snorts. "Hardly. I wanted to send him back to the demon universe – he'd live longer there – but he wants to stay and fight till he drops. He stood by us in the first two battles, but he was wrecked afterwards. Now he's acting as a talent-spotting scout. He's on the edge of this city with thousands of people. When the window opened, he tested them for magical ability. He's come up with some decent mages at the last two stops. I hope he finds more this time. We could use them — I'm running out of werewolves."

Nobody seems bothered by Grubbs's appearance. He looks like something out of a horror movie, twisted and misshapen, picking bits of flesh from between his teeth and under his fingernails. But they're all treating him as if nothing's changed. I guess, in times as deadly as these, you can't worry too much about the looks of those who stand beside you.

But I don't like it. He's not just physically different. Something's changed inside him too. He's rougher than before, more accepting of violence and death. He reminds me of Beranabus, the way he callously wrote off human casualties, like he wasn't truly one of us. Raz told me to watch out for Bec, but I think Grubbs is the one I need to worry about.

I ask how Beranabus died. Bec answers, telling her story swiftly. They found Kirilli on the ship after they left me, then descended to the hold, where Juni was waiting. She used a lodestone to open a strange window, through which the Shadow crossed. As Bec fought it, she absorbed some of its memories and realised it was Death. She informed Beranabus and he sent them packing, staying behind to fight their shadowy foe and buy them time.

"He transformed," she whispers. "He let his demonic half take over. I think he meant to die, whether he won or lost. He wasn't sure he could change back once he set the demon free."

"Nobody can ever change back," Grubbs rumbles, scratching a cut on his chest, then licking flaky blood from his fingers.

Beranabus destroyed the lodestone, sending Death back to the universe of the Demonata. But the shadowy creature struck before it was whipped away, and the ancient magician died in the hold, to be swallowed by the sea.

Bec, Dervish, Kirilli and Sharmila made it back to the deck, fighting their way through an army of zombies. But they were trapped there, imprisoned by a barrier of magical energy as the ship sank.

"Sharmila sacrificed herself to save the rest of us," Bec says miserably. "She lay against the barrier and we exploded her, punching a hole through to safety." She stops, tears welling in her eyes.

"It should have been me," Kirilli says. He hasn't said much so far. Now when he speaks he keeps his head low, embarrassed. "I was the weakest. I ran when the others fought. I've served the Disciples well in a non-combative capacity, but I'm no hero. She should be here now, not me."

"You got that right," someone laughs and when I look round I find Dervish standing behind me, smiling weakly. He looks even older than he did on the ship, frail, trembling, about two steps away from death. The six silver, purple-tipped spikes he grew on his head in the oasis are as impressive as ever, but apart from that he looks like a man on his last legs.

"Good to see you, old-timer," I grin.

"You too," he says. "We thought you were zombie pâté." He winks at Kirilli, who's glowering. "Modesty doesn't become you, Kovacs. I prefer you when you're blowing hot air and claiming credit for every kill in a five-kilometre radius."

"I claim nothing from any man," Kirilli snarls.

Dervish chuckles, then says, "What have I missed?"

"We've been bringing Kernel up to date," Grubbs yawns, as if the stories of their adventures bore him. "Now he's about to return the favour."

Nodding reluctantly, not sure how to begin, I cast my mind back to when the dead first stirred on the ship, take a quick breath and launch myself at it.

RESTLESS SOULS

→I speak clearly and concisely. I don't think I miss anything important, though I have to backtrack a few times when I recall bits that I overlooked. The others listen in silence, their faces lengthening as I reveal the direness of our situation, the belief of the Old Creatures that the universe is doomed.

There's silence when I finish. Everyone's brooding. Even Grubbs looks troubled — his face has altered and become more human.

"I wouldn't have returned," Dervish finally says. "I've faced a lot in my time, stepped up to all sorts of challenges. But in your position, I'd have stayed on the ark. I wouldn't have had the guts to come back with so much at risk. I'd have gone with the safe option."

"Coward," Kirilli laughs.

"I don't like being the practical one," Meera mutters, "but what if he imagined it all? Travelling to the centre of the universe… life starting with a chess board… aliens nudging us up the evolutionary ladder… an ark world. That's pretty far-fetched, even by our standards. What if he's crazy? No offence, Kernel."

"None taken." I sigh. "I wish it *was* my imagination. But I'm sure it wasn't."

"The Kah-Gash told me I was the trigger," Grubbs says slowly, and he has that shifty look in his eyes again. "In the hospital, when the three of us were together, it said I had the power to unite and direct it. So that part of the story's true."

"It's all true," Bec snaps. "Let's not waste time pretending otherwise. Our world is doomed. The universe is damned. Unless we defeat Death."

"No one ever cheats death," Dervish says.

"I did," Bec reminds him.

I said nothing of Raz's suspicions about Bec. We need to work together, not abandon ourselves to paranoia.

"We need a plan," Meera says. "Mr Trigger Man — any ideas?"

Grubbs shrugs. "Track Death down and rip it to pieces. Easy."

"You almost sound like you believe that," Dervish snorts.

"I do," Grubbs insists. "Death made a mistake when it took a body. That puts it on a par with us. From what you told me, Beranabus gave as good as he got when he went up against the Shadow. He sent it screaming back to the foul realm of the Demonata. We're stronger than Beranabus. We can inflict more damage. I say we reassemble the Kah-Gash, hit Death hard and end this."

"I don't know," Bec murmurs. "The Kah-Gash frightens me more than Death or the Demonata. They can only kill us, but the Kah-Gash can wipe out the universe, so we never even existed in the first place. I don't think we should unleash its power unless we absolutely have to."

"Do you have any idea if we can control it?" I ask. "You're the Kah-Gash's memory. Is there anything you can tell us about how it functioned in the past?"

Bec shakes her head. "I've always had a perfect memory, and now I can absorb the memories of others. This explains why. But I can only recall the memories of my own life or the lives of those I touch. Perhaps, if we joined, the Kah-Gash would reveal more to me, but the dangers…"

"What dangers?" Grubbs snorts. "We're wrong to be afraid. This is *our* weapon. We own the pieces — hell, we *are* the pieces. We're the Kah-Gash's masters."

"No," I correct him. "We're its *hosts*. The pieces have been in thousands of other creatures before. We have no more claim over it than any of them did."

"Let's just do it," Grubbs groans. "It wants to be

used. I feel my piece straining to link with yours."

"I feel that too," Bec says, "and it scares me. Why is it so eager to be restored, now, after all this time, with Death on the loose and hordes of demons bearing down on our world? It could be plotting against us."

"It did what we wanted when we linked before," Grubbs protests. "It took us back in time so that we could stop the tunnel being opened."

"What if that was a mistake?" Bec argues. "What if we join again and it takes us further back, to when this universe was born? What if it stops that?"

Grubbs scowls and looks away impatiently.

"I share Bec's concerns," I tell them. "Even the Old Creatures don't know what the Kah-Gash is really like, and they've been studying it for billions of years. We can't know its true intentions."

"Can we afford to wait?" Dervish asks. "If we're as close to the end as the Old Creatures predict... I think we should test it."

I sigh. "If it goes wrong, we'll be condemning all those creatures on the ark."

"This will sound callous," Meera says, "but I don't care. If our world ends, for me *everything* ends. I'm not concerned about other planets, Old Creatures or aliens. You feel that way too, Kernel. You wouldn't have come back if you didn't."

"But there are so many worlds... so many species..."

"Tough," Meera snorts. "They're not our problem. You came back to help save Earth, not the universe. Am I right or am I right?"

I smile weakly. "I can't argue with that. OK, I'll give it a go. But if I start to think we can't beat Death — if it looks like we're fighting a losing battle — I *will* return to the ark. I won't go down with a sinking ship."

Dervish claps my back. "I think you were mad to return, but I like your style! Here's what I suggest. We move on to the city where the next crossing's going to happen and we let the window open. You three link and test yourselves against the demons. If you don't wreck the universe, we'll take that experience forward and confront the Shadow. If you *do* wreck the universe… well, we'll all be dead, so we won't have to worry about it. How does that sound?"

"Good to me," Grubbs grunts.

I shrug.

"I suppose," Bec says hesitantly. "But assuming we pass the test, I'd like to try and learn more about Death before we attack it, find out if it has any weaknesses, if there's a way to defeat it."

"How are we supposed to do that?" Grubbs sneers. "Send it a questionnaire?"

Bec licks her lips nervously. "We might have an inside man who can help us."

"What are you talking about?" Dervish frowns.

"It's something Beranabus said before he died." Bec shudders. She was close to the old magician. His death hit her hard. "In the hold of the ship, after I told him about Death, he said to tell Kernel to find him."

"He wanted me to open a window out of the hold," I mutter, feeling guilty even though I know there's nothing I could have done to help him.

"That's what I thought," Bec nods. "I assumed he planned to escape or knock the lodestone through the window. But the more I think about it, the more I doubt that assumption. He knew he couldn't last long against the Shadow, that it would take us several minutes to climb the stairs. He knew you were part of the Kah-Gash and that the Shadow wanted to get its hands on you. Why would he ask you to risk capture? He was doomed and he accepted his death. His only concern was that we evade the Shadow and live to fight another day.

"I don't think he was asking for help." Bec licks her lips again. "I think he was looking ahead. Once he knew what the Shadow was, he resigned himself to dying. But he didn't give up the fight. Juni and I are proof that death isn't the end. When he found out who his enemy was, I believe Beranabus saw a chance to learn more about it and share that information with us.

"Death uses souls to create its body. Maybe it held on to Beranabus's soul when it killed him. Part of him might be alive inside that monstrous mass of shadows."

Bec looks at me and grins shakily. "You can locate anything in the universes of the living, Kernel. Do you think you could find a ghost in the realm of the dead?"

SHADES OF THE FALLEN

→There's uproar when Bec suggests Beranabus might still be alive in some form. Grubbs accuses her of living in dreamland. Meera gently suggests that she's in denial, that she needs to accept the ancient magician's death. But Bec stubbornly pushes her case, and as she elaborates, our scepticism fades.

We know souls can be separated from bodies — that happened to me in Lord Loss's kingdom years ago, when I entered the Board. In the past, a soul couldn't survive a body's death, but things have changed. Death is claiming souls and using them. We've no way of knowing if a captured soul remains conscious or not. But if they do... if Beranabus has made a study of Death from the inside and uncovered its secrets... maybe he can tell us how to kill it.

It's probably a wild shot in the dark. Grubbs certainly thinks so and says that it's a waste of time, but the rest of us believe it's worth trying.

But before we can set off in pursuit of a dead man,

we have the living to take care of. The new window is almost open. In another few hours, dozens of demons will be streaming across.

While Grubbs fetches his werewolves and Meera rustles up battle-hardened soldiers, I slot patches of light together. Dervish and Kirilli are resting — Dervish looks shattered, Kirilli scared. Bec's watching me. Something about her gaze makes me feel uneasy.

"It must have been amazing," she says. "Your trip to the stars and beyond sounds incredible."

"Yes," I grunt.

"I was wondering…" She coughs. "I'd like to touch you."

"What?" I squeak, startled, thinking she wants to kiss me.

"I can absorb your memories if we touch," she says.

"Oh." I chuckle at my mistake. Then I grow serious. "Why do you want to take my memories?"

"Not take," she says. "Share. I want to see everything you saw. The lights, the worlds, the Crux. If you grant me access, I can see all that you did."

"What does it matter if I show you or not?" I snap.

She looks surprised by my harsh tone. "Well, of course I'm curious," she says, stammering a bit. "But apart from that I have perfect recall. If you share with me, I might spot something that slipped your mind."

"I doubt it," I sniff.

"But it can't do any harm, surely, if I just…" She reaches out, then stops as I glare at her. Letting her hand drop slowly, her expression darkens. "You're hiding something from us. Just like Grubbs."

"You saw that too?" I hiss.

"Everyone sees it. Something happened between him and Juni that he doesn't want us to know."

"What do you think it might be?" I ask.

"I've no idea. But I think I know what *you're* holding back. You look hostile. I've done nothing to make you dislike me, so you must be… afraid."

"I'm not afraid of you," I sneer.

"Maybe not. But you're nervous… more than that… *suspicious?*"

I fidget uncomfortably.

"The Old Creatures said the pieces of the Kah-Gash have been influenced by the hosts they've inhabited," Bec says thoughtfully. "If my piece of the Kah-Gash was in Lord Loss for thousands of years…" Her expression clears. "You don't trust me. You think I might betray you, or that my piece of the Kah-Gash might trick us."

"Can you say for sure that it won't?" I ask quietly.

Bec starts to respond hotly, then pauses. "Actually no," she admits. Then she looks at me piercingly. "But can *you* make any guarantees? Can Grubbs? You don't know where your pieces were before, or why they ended up in you. Maybe we'll all be played for fools."

"Maybe." I nod slowly.

Bec smiles thinly. "Go on watching me, Kernel. I don't mind. But I'll be watching you too. And Grubbs. I don't think any of us can be trusted."

"You're right," I say glumly, then return her smile. "And *we're* the ones who are supposed to save the world? I don't fancy our chances!"

"Me neither," she laughs, and we grin at each other, united by our uncertainties, paranoia and fear.

→We could stop the mage before he opens the window, but then we wouldn't have a chance to test ourselves. I don't like the course we're taking — people will probably die — but there's no other way. If we want to learn about the Kah-Gash before we go looking for the Shadow, we have to fight. We could cross to the demon universe and test it there, but that would mean unleashing the Kah-Gash in an area of total magic. If the weapon's on the side of the Demonata, that would hand it the perfect opportunity to break free of any confines we might seek to impose.

"Stick close to me," Grubbs growls. I'm on his left, Bec on his right. Meera, Kirilli, the werewolves and soldiers are behind us. Dervish is a bit further back, observing. I sense the window forming. Just minutes to go. The mage is working inside a nearby building.

"We're not going for a full union," Grubbs says. "Just a partial link."

"Are you sure we can do that?" I ask.

"Yes," Grubbs says. "I'm the trigger. I can control it. Follow my lead, don't react when you feel my magic mingling with yours, and everything will be coolio."

I share a troubled glance with Bec – she doesn't like this either – but before I can say anything the window opens and demons scurry out of the building. There are dozens of scaly, bloody, multi-headed monsters, oozing pus and slime, slithering down the steps, smashing through windows, hunting for victims. A river of nightmares.

But nothing new. I faced worse with Beranabus. I'm more concerned about the werewolf between me and Bec than I am by the demons bearing down on us.

Grubbs stares at the Demonata, eyes narrow and glinting yellow. His fangs grow an inch, his lips stretching with them. He grabs hold of my hand and Bec's. Energy spirals up my arm. I tense against it but then the voice of the Kah-Gash murmurs to me. *It's all right. Don't fight. No harm will come of this.*

I don't entirely trust that inner voice, but even if I wanted to reject the union, I couldn't. The magic within me warms to Grubbs's and I feel power well up from nowhere. The shock of it makes me gasp. My skin crackles and my fingers dig into Grubbs's huge paw. My legs go weak, then steady.

We're drawing power from all around, from the earth, people, demons, the sky. Everything's linked. There are connecting lines everywhere, between humans, objects, the Demonata, the stars. The Kah-Gash was here before any of us, holding the sixty-four zones of the original universe together. And it still binds us in place — it just doesn't define the universes as tightly as it used to.

But it could. With the power coursing through me now, I could quench the sun by snapping my fingers, and open a tunnel between universes. Make myself ruler of all worlds, people and demons. Limits exist only in the mind. As the Kah-Gash, I'd set those limits, not be bound by them. I could–

"Let's just kill these demons and leave it at that," Grubbs says, shattering my dreams of universal dominance.

I blink, coming out of the spell I was under, amazed by how swiftly I gave in to temptation. Grubbs and Bec might not be the jokers in the pack. Maybe *I'm* the weak link, the one the Kah-Gash can exploit.

But there's no time for self-doubt. The demons are almost upon us. Our werewolves are howling and the soldiers are readying their rifles. Another second or two and all will be chaos.

Grubbs roars and I feel the magic of the Kah-Gash

draining from me — from Bec too. Grubbs is the focal point through which the power is channelled. No way of fighting it now. The energy that we've sucked in explodes through Grubbs, mixed in with his roar.

A stream of raw power envelops the demons and stops them cold. Their eyes bulge as they choke in a net of magic. We hold them in place a moment, as easily as we'd trap a colony of ants by lowering a jar over them. Then Grubbs blows on them the way he'd blow on a feather.

The demons shoot backwards, through the walls of the building, then through the window between universes. The startled mage is blasted through as well, torn to shreds with most of the demons. When the area is clear, the stream of energy fans out and crackles across the face of the window. It glows brightly, then crumples, and the patches of light which were used to create it flood back to us along with the magic. The stream swirls around us, breaking up into vortex-like tendrils. Then Grubbs lets go of my hand and Bec's.

The power dwindles in seconds and the lights drift away. It's like nothing ever happened — apart from the huge hole in the front of the building.

"Wow," Grubbs says, flexing his fingers and staring at them. "That was great." He looks up at us and grins. "Let's find more demons and do it again!"

→A couple of hours later, in a hotel suite even grander than the last we stayed in, Grubbs is still itching to pick another fight, but Bec insists we should focus on Beranabus. The pair are arguing heatedly. I've kept quiet. Dervish, Meera and Kirilli say nothing either. We chipped in during the early stages of the argument, but for the last hour it's been pretty much Grubbs and Bec yelling at each other.

"Forget about crossing!" Grubbs shouts, towering over the small, slender girl. "I say we wait for them to come. With the power of the Kah-Gash, we'll drive them back every time. They'll soon realise they can't win and head off for softer pickings on other worlds."

"You think that's acceptable?" Bec retorts, not intimidated by the grotesque, wolfen teenager. "We pass them along and let others suffer?"

"Like Meera said, we only care about this world," Grubbs huffs.

"Leave me out of this," Meera snaps, but both ignore her.

"What about Death?" Bec jeers. "Will you repel the Shadow when it attacks?"

"Why not? Death might be more powerful than the Demonata, but the Kah-Gash can trump it."

"No," Bec says. "Death is the ultimate power. If we don't strike now, it will grow stronger and come to find us."

Grubbs shrugs. "Do I look worried?"

Bec smothers a curse. "You were all for attacking earlier. You wanted to go for Death like a dog after a rat."

"That was before you brought Beranabus into the equation. I'd still go if you only wanted to have a crack at the Shadow. But you want to free a dead man. That's what this is really about. Your beloved *Bran* turned coward at the end."

"What are you talking about?" Bec screeches and appeals to the rest of us. "Has he gone mad? Do any of you know what—"

"Beranabus was afraid," Grubbs interrupts. "That's why he told you to send Kernel after him. It wasn't so he could study Death from the inside and learn its secrets. He realised his soul might be trapped and he didn't want to spend eternity in the grasp of the Shadow. He hoped Kernel could get him out. You know that's true. You knew it from the moment you suggested the idea of rescuing him. Tell me I'm wrong."

Bec says nothing. Her face was red with anger moments before, but now the flush fades. Her lower jaw trembles. She looks ashamed.

"This is personal," Grubbs growls, facing us like a lawyer addressing a jury. "She's not thinking about beating Death. She only wants to set Beranabus free."

"What's wrong with that?" Meera asks quietly. "He was her friend. You'd do the same for Dervish in that position. So would I."

"I wouldn't," Kirilli pipes up.

"No surprise there," Dervish mutters.

"It's too dangerous," Grubbs yells. "I liked Beranabus but I'm not going to risk everything to save his soul. Hell, he might not even be there. Maybe Death didn't claim him."

"It did," I say softly. "I've been studying the lights while you were arguing, concentrating on Beranabus. A few started flashing as soon as I focused on him, and more have joined them. It's not like when I search for someone living, but if his soul hadn't been absorbed by the Shadow, no lights would flash at all."

"OK, it took his soul. So what?" Grubbs shrugs. "How many of you want to risk a rescue? Who cared about the mad old buzzard that much?"

He looks around the room. Kirilli instantly shakes his head. Meera nods firmly to show she's on Bec's side. Dervish looks uncertain. "We owe him," he says.

"We owe a lot of people," Grubbs grunts, "but we can't always repay our debts. You taught me that. A Disciple doesn't risk his life to save a few people, not when the fate of billions is at stake.

"If I think we have a real chance of hurting the

Shadow, I'll jump at it. But if we're just going over there to free Beranabus's soul... That's not right. Beranabus wouldn't have thought so either — not until he crumbled at the end."

"What if he didn't?" I ask angrily. "I spent more time with him than any of you. I never saw him ask for favours. He was the most selfless person I knew. What if he really did hope to learn something that might help us?"

"I'm not willing to take that chance," Grubbs says.

"You're a fool!" Bec shouts.

"Maybe," Grubbs sniffs. "But it looks like we have a tie, three votes for each. You, Meera and Kernel want to ride to the rescue. Kirilli and I have more sense. And Dervish..." He looks to his uncle for a final answer.

Dervish sighs. "I agree with Grubbs. We can't let personal feelings cloud our judgement."

"What if it was personal for *you?*" I softly challenge him.

"It's not," Dervish says wearily. "If Grubbs was in that position, I'd do all I could to free him. But he isn't, so there's no point–"

"*Bill-E,*" Bec stops him. Dervish turns slowly, left eyelid ticking, but she isn't looking at him. She's staring at me. "Is it Bill-E?"

I nod slowly.

"Liar!" Grubbs howls, raising a huge, shaggy fist.

"How dare you—"

"I searched for him after I looked for Beranabus," I say quickly. "I was running tests, searching for others I knew who'd died, like Mrs Egin, Logan Rile, Sharmila. I came up blank on all of them. Then I thought of Bill-E and a few lights flashed, the way they flashed for Beranabus."

"If you're lying…" Grubbs growls, fingers clenched tight.

I step forward. I'm shaking like a rattlesnake's tail but I speak clearly. "If you think I'd say this to trick you, you don't know me at all."

Grubbs stares into my eyes. He wants to find deception, but he can't because I'm telling the truth. His shoulders slump and he backs away. He shares a scared look with Dervish, who's been hit just as hard by the news.

Bec could crow, but she doesn't. She merely waits.

"I killed him to free him," Grubbs finally croaks. "It was the hardest thing I've done. I murdered my own brother. I wouldn't have done that to save the world, the universe or anything else. But I couldn't bear to let him live in torment at the hands of the Demonata. I killed him to spare his suffering, to set him free. Now you're telling me I didn't, that the Shadow has him?"

"I'm sorry," I whisper.

Tears of blood trickle from Grubbs's eyes. Raising a hand, he wipes them away, then covers his face with his hand and moans softly.

"We have to free them," Bec says. She crouches by his side and reaches out to embrace him.

"Don't touch me!" he barks, pulling away from her.

"Don't be silly," she smiles. "I absorbed your secret when we linked outside. I know what Juni predicted. But I don't believe her. She's insane. You would never do what she claimed."

Grubbs cries out and wraps his arms around the little girl, hugging her like a doll, weeping while we stare at the pair of them, bewildered. When he finally stops crying, he releases Bec and grins shakily at her, then casts his gaze over the rest of us, his features firm.

"Show of hands. Who's going to help me and Bec kick some Shadow ass?"

Five arms rise immediately. Kirilli is the only dissenter. "You're all mad," he grumbles.

"Overruled," Dervish laughs, then twists his spikes into place and drawls like a gangster. "I always wanted to be part of a jailbreak!"

THE CARRIAGE HELD...

→I try opening a window to Beranabus, then Bill-E, but enjoy no luck. It's too difficult on this world. The lights are few and scattered. I need more power to piece them together. I need the magic of the demon universe.

We cross to a realm we know is safe, where we've based ourselves in the past. Grubbs brings his pack of werewolves along ("For fun," he grins bleakly) but we leave the soldiers behind. I choose a place where time operates like it does on Earth. That way we should be back to face the next assault. Assuming we survive our brush with Death. Which is a pretty big assumption.

As the others prepare for battle, I use the lights to pinpoint the position of our enemies. I still can't get a fix on Death, even though I now know its identity. But I find Lord Loss and Juni Swan easily enough. They're on a world I've never been to, surrounded by thousands... no, *millions* of demons. The thought of entering the midst of such an army is terrifying.

I think of telling the others, but what's the point? We have to do this. Bec, Dervish and Grubbs for personal reasons, me because I believe – *hope* – Beranabus can reveal something about Death which will give us the power to defeat it. If all goes well, we won't have to face the demons, just their shadowy master. If it goes poorly...

Best not to dwell on that.

I turn my thoughts away from demons. Breathing calmly, I focus on Beranabus. Lights begin to pulse, but there aren't many of them and I have a tough time piecing them together. Normally lights flock to me when I summon them, but these patches resist. I have to focus harder than I've ever had to, and even then they only drift towards me sluggishly, reluctantly.

Gritting my teeth, I bully the patches into place, slotting them together as if they were pieces of a crudely carved jigsaw puzzle. I'm aware of time ticking, the others growing impatient, especially the werewolves, who howl and hammer the ground with their fists, eager for action.

I push the distractions from my mind and focus on the lights. Normally I can multi-task, chat with others while I'm working on a window. Not now. This will take everything I have. I'm doing something no one has ever done before, breaching the barriers of life itself.

Eventually, after hours of fierce concentration,

when I'm starting to think it's impossible, a small window opens. It's an unimpressive, jagged panel of brown light, and it flickers alarmingly at the edges. But I don't care. It shouldn't by rights be open at all, so I'm more proud of it than any window I've ever created.

"Come on!" I shout, reacting quickly to push the outermost lights back in place before they can buckle. "This will only hold for a few seconds."

"Where does it—" Grubbs starts to ask.

"No time!" I yell. "We have to go *now* or not at all."

"Then let's go," Grubbs grunts and dives blindly through the window.

The werewolves rush after him. When the last of the sixteen has vanished, a nervous Meera crosses, followed by Bec. Kirilli steps forward, but hesitates.

"I really don't want to do this," he mutters.

"Too bad!" Dervish laughs and pushes the startled stage magician through.

"Hurry," I gasp, feeling the window start to disintegrate.

Dervish ducks past my whirring arms. As soon as he's out of sight, I throw myself after him. I sense the window collapse as I sail through. Whatever happens next, whatever dire mess we wind up in, there's no quick way out. We're in this to the end whether we like it or not

→I find myself in a realm of shadows, dark and swirling. The shadows whip at me and then flit away as if blown by a strong wind. But there's no wind here, just the ever-circling shades of the dead.

I was expecting cries and moans of torment, but it's silent. That surprises me. At the least I should be able to hear the howls of the werewolves. But when I open my mouth to call for the others – I can't see any of them – I realise why it's so quiet. Sounds don't carry. Though I shout at the top of my voice, nothing emerges.

I hunker down, fighting the dark wisps which threaten to bowl me over and sweep me away. There's no floor, just banks of shadows all around. I'm not floating. It's more like being stuck in a pool of mud.

I try to create a ball of light, but nothing happens. There's magic here, waves of energy washing between the shadowy souls and binding them, but it's a different type of magic and I'm unable to channel it.

As I try again, something solid strikes my left shoulder. Cringing away from my assailant, I peer through the streams of shadows masking my eyes. I spy a bulky shape bearing down on me. Impossible to tell if it's friend or foe. I back up, desperately scouring the space around me for a trace of magic I can use. Then a pair of huge hands grasps my arms and tugs me to a halt. A face thrusts up next to mine. It's a fearsome, demonic face and my first instinct is to lash out. But as a veil of shadows whisks away from over the creature's eyes, I realise it's Grubbs.

He says something. I shake my head and mouth back the words, "I can't hear."

Grubbs narrows his eyes. Nothing happens for a few seconds. Then I hear his voice inside my head. "—me now? Can you hear me now? Can you—"

"Yes," I stop him, replying silently, thinking the words instead of voicing them.

"Are you able to channel the magic?" he asks.

"No."

He tuts, then grins. "I couldn't either. Nobody could. But Bec adapted swiftly and showed the rest of us. Come on."

He leads me through the shadows, half-staggering, half-swimming. The others aren't far away, grouped together, Bec at the centre, the rest huddled round her, lit dimly by flickering balls of light which she has generated. They all look scared, especially Kirilli. Even the werewolves are subdued, whining silently and glancing around uneasily.

Once I'm in physical contact with the group, Bec speaks. "We haven't much time. Death isn't aware of us yet but it will discover us soon. You have to find Beranabus and Bill-E as quickly as possible."

I realise she's talking to me. "How can I find them?" I protest. "I opened the window and brought us here. What more can I do?"

"You're the eyes of the Kah-Gash," she snaps. "You see more than any of us. To me there's no difference in the shadows. They all look the same. But I'm sure you can see more."

"Well, I can't," I snarl, hating the way she's heaping the pressure on to me.

A wave of energy floods through me, opening doors within my brain, clearing passageways. Suddenly I find myself absorbing and converting the magic of Death. I fill with power and breathe out easily, smiling at the buzz of it.

"How did you do that?" I ask, relaxed and cool.

"I used my gift," Bec says. "Now use yours and *look*."

Still smiling, I cast my gaze around and see that Bec was right. Now that I've tapped into the magic, the shadows have taken on a new consistency. There are thousands of individual shards and shapes whirling around us, no two alike. I can't believe I didn't see them before. Each has its own shade, form and way of moving. They're all a grey-black colour, but there are more variants of grey and black than I would have dreamt possible.

My first thought is, "So this is what souls look like." But that's not right. This is only what they look like *here*. Death has taken these unfortunates and moulded them into what it wanted them to be.

As I study the souls, I extend my thoughts, focusing on individuals, trying to communicate. Nothing happens for a while. Then, all of a sudden, I'm struck by a burst of voices, screams and yowls, tormented cries for help and release. Wincing, I shut out the noises. After a brief pause, I open myself to the voices again, but put filters in place, blocking out the worst of the background noise.

"Who are you?" I ask a nearby shadow as it floats past.

"Free me!" it screams.

"Who are you?" I shout again, but it only repeats its plea. Others that I focus on are the same, impossible to question, wailing for freedom.

I turn to tell the others, but I don't need to. Bec has been in touch with me the whole time and has broadcast the short snippets to the rest. They look distraught. The suffering of these souls is awful. In life, no matter how bad things get, at least you have the release of death to look forward to, the belief that no matter what lies beyond, nothing can be as bad as *this*.

But these people have shuffled off their mortal coils, only to find themselves ensnared by the force they were relying on to set them free. Every soul here knows it wasn't meant for this hellish realm. Having escaped the confines of natural life, they've found themselves caught in an unnatural web and it's driven them mad.

"We have to get out of here!" Kirilli shrieks. "We can't help them!"

"Bran won't have given in to madness," Bec insists. "Find him, Kernel. He won't have surrendered. Not Bran."

I don't have her faith in the ancient magician, but I search anyway. Using the magic of Death, I send a radar-like cry out in all directions, calling for Beranabus, trying to locate his position. Once I've sent the signal, I wait for it to echo back. If he's still conscious, he'll respond. But if he's like the others... if he's lost his senses and forgotten his name... become just a swirling shadow with no idea of self...

"Bill-E," Grubbs snarls as we wait. "Look for Bill-E too."

"I will," I tell him, "but give me time. Beranabus first. If we—"

I stop, jaw dropping. Because an answering burst of energy has echoed back to me from a point far away.

"Was that Bran?" Bec hisses.

"I think so," I say hesitantly. "But it was very weak. I guess there's only one way to find out." I look around to make sure everyone's ready, then start forward, wading through the sluggish swirls of shadows, repeating the signal, zoning in on the area where the soul of Beranabus seems to be signalling back.

→We reach the place where the response came from. I don't see anything different at first. It looks like any other part of this wretched no-man's-land. The souls cluster and swirl around us. I call Beranabus's name, but there's no reply. I study the river of souls, but it's impossible to say who they might have belonged to in life. Maybe the reply was a fluke, or I only heard –

"That was always your problem," a voice snaps inside my head. "You take too many things into consideration."

"Bran!" Bec cries, head whipping from side to side, searching the gloom for her childhood friend.

"I'm here," Beranabus says, and I trace the voice to a shadow circling overhead, no more remarkable than any other.

"Where is he?" Bec shouts. "I can't see him."

"Relax, Little One," Beranabus hushes her. "Kernel's the only one who can see me. You'll have to be content with my voice. Not that it's a bad voice. I've roared down demon masters in my time."

I burst out laughing. This is the most incredible thing ever. I never thought I'd be in direct contact with my old mentor again. But before I can tell him how sorry I am that he was killed, Grubbs shouts at the dead magician.

"Is Bill-E here?" he cries.

"Aye," Beranabus rumbles.

"Where? Let me talk with him. Bill-E!" Grubbs swivels wildly, shouting his dead brother's name.

"Were you always this stupid or is it a result of your recent metamorphosis?" Beranabus snaps. "I was thousands of years old when I died, more powerful than any human in history. Yet it took everything I had to hold my thoughts together and not become one of the wailing cretins this place is stuffed with. Do you really think your young brother fought off the madness that all the others succumbed to?"

Grubbs draws to a stop and turns to face me, his eyes cold with hatred. "Show me where that vile old buzzard is. I'll kill him again."

Beranabus laughs cruelly. "Control yourself. I never put things politely when I was alive, so I'm hardly going to start now that I'm dead! Your brother's here, he's lost his mind and is suffering, and unless you free us all, he'll remain trapped indefinitely."

"Then we *can* free you?" Bec shouts hopefully.

"I think so," Beranabus mutters. "That's not why I told you to ask Kernel to find me, but it will certainly be a bonus. I can't hold my mind together much longer. The effort…" In those few words I get the sense of how close Beranabus is to snapping. Despite his brave front, he's terrified.

"Before we try that," Beranabus says more brightly, "I want to know everything that's happened since I died. Bec — open your thoughts to me."

The shadow of Beranabus's soul darts closer to Bec and hovers over the girl's head. A tendril gently touches her forehead. She closes her eyes and smiles. I get the impression of memories being transferred, like data being uploaded from one computer to another. Then Beranabus sighs.

"I'd gathered some of that already – you can learn a lot here if you keep your eyes and ears open, metaphorically speaking – but there's much more to consider now. I don't think…"

He falls silent. Bec's eyes half open, then close again. She nods softly and I realise he's speaking privately to her.

Grubbs steps up beside me. "Can you find Bill-E?" he asks.

"Even if I could, would you want to speak to him like this?" I answer quietly. "Wouldn't it be better to just free him?"

"But I never said a proper goodbye. There are so many things–"

"Kernel's right," Dervish says, laying a trembling hand on Grubbs's shoulder. "Better to remember Bill-E as he was. If we can set his soul loose, that will be enough."

Grubbs nods reluctantly, then squints at Bec. "What's going on between those two? Why the secrecy?"

"I was wondering the same thing," I whisper.

"Such suspicious minds," Beranabus barks. "You'll need to trust each other if you're to defeat Death and save the universe. Haven't you heard of teamwork?"

"You think we *can* beat it?" I ask eagerly.

"Not a hope in hell," Beranabus chuckles. "But you have to try, don't you?"

Bec's eyes are open. She looks troubled. I don't know what Beranabus shared with her, but I'm reminded of Raz's warning. I have a bad feeling. Suddenly I wish I hadn't insisted on this mission, that I'd left Beranabus alone. I thought he could teach us how to vanquish our foes, but all he's done is predict doom and tell Bec something that's set her mind awhirl. But awhirl with what? *Deceit?*

Before I can press the issue, a cluster of shadows to my left bunch together, throb, then rise high above us like a cobra's head.

"Ah," Beranabus sighs. "The behemoth awakes."

"It's alive!" Kirilli shrieks as the shadowy growth studies us ominously.

"This would be a good time to split," Meera mutters.

The pillar of shadows smashes down on us before

anyone can volunteer a plan. We're thrown apart, yelling with panic. The werewolves howl and lurch at the massed head of shadows, but it bats them aside with ease and rises above us again. As it does, more shadows converge around us. Death might have taken a while to note our presence, but it's moving swiftly to turn its imprisoned souls against us.

"Bec!" I roar, dodging another of the Shadow's blows. "How do we get out?"

Beranabus answers mockingly. "Can't you open a window, Kernel? That was always your speciality."

"No time!" I yell. "Bec?"

"The Kah-Gash," she says shakily, reaching towards me. A twisting fist of shadows slams into her right arm, snapping it at the elbow. She screams as her hand goes limp, then grits her teeth and unleashes a burst of energy at the fist. The shadows shatter beneath the force of the blow. Bec clutches me with her left hand. "Grubbs!" she yells.

He's already making his way towards us, lips moving silently as he speaks to his piece of the Kah-Gash. A sword of shadows slices across his back, drawing blood, but he just grunts and pushes on.

Kirilli's bouncing about like a Mexican jumping bean, dodging the spines and hammers that are forming and striking at us, yelping with each narrow escape, the rags of his tattered suit flapping up and down to comical effect.

"That's the way," Beranabus laughs at the petrified stage magician. "Dance, fool, dance!" He cackles madly. I think he's closer to insanity than he realises.

Grubbs reaches us and lays a powerful paw on my neck, the other on Bec's. I immediately feel the Kah-Gash flare into life. There's not as much power as before because we're surrounded by Death, unable to draw energy from the stars. But I still feel about ten times more powerful than normal.

As a hammer of shadows crashes upon us, Grubbs roars and it disintegrates. He releases Bec and me but the link remains. With his hands, he claws at the shadows around us, ripping dark holes through the fog of souls. Bec and I follow his lead, using magic to split shadows and blast through thicker banks of them. The others join in – except Kirilli, who's still leaping about – and we attack the formations that Death has sent against us.

"This way," Beranabus calls, shooting ahead. I don't know how anyone could find their bearings here, but I have to trust him. It's not like we have much choice.

We struggle after the fleeing shadow. I'm following Beranabus, the others are trailing me. Kirilli is the only one who doesn't come. He hasn't looked around. I call his name a few times, but he doesn't respond. In the end I curse and leave him. I feel bad, abandoning the Disciple, but you can't save everyone. Some of the werewolves have already been killed. The power of the Kah-Gash is fading, having no outside source to draw from. If I went back for Kirilli, I'd waste energy and time, and that would prove the death of us all.

A noise grows as we push on. It's a hissing sound, the spitting of a million furious snakes. Death is venting its rage. I've heard all sorts of shrieks and cries during my years in the demon universe. Nothing sent a shiver down my spine as much as this.

A spear of shadows strikes Grubbs just above his heart and shoots out the other side. With a roar of pain he falls to his knees, but is up again instantly. His fangs lengthen and as another spear arcs towards him, he snatches it between his oversized teeth and grinds it to pieces, then spits them out.

A shadowy scythe splits the flesh of Meera's lower back. She staggers, finds her feet, then is struck by a thick club. She falls unconscious, but Dervish is there to grab her and haul her forwards. His face is flushed, his limbs are trembling, his heart must be pounding fit to burst, but he carries on. I don't know if it's for Meera's sake or his own, but he doesn't quit, even though it would be easier for him to lie down and die.

I've been hammered all over and I'm bleeding from a variety of cuts, like the others, but Bec's hardly been touched. She's the strongest of us in this place of death. Grubbs might be the trigger, but Bec is pulling the strings at the moment, directing the energy of the Kah-Gash, using it to keep the lights going, protect herself from the blows of the Shadow, and help the rest of us as best she can. For such a small girl, she packs one hell of a lot of power.

"Here!" Beranabus calls. He's come to a halt by a thick bank of souls. "This is a wall. Focus on this spot. Quickly — you're almost out of time."

Bec unleashes a ball of energy at the wall. I do the same. Grubbs starts to, then snarls and hurls himself at it instead. He hits the bank of shadows and rips into it, roaring as he scoops dark handfuls out of his way. The surviving werewolves crowd around him and tear at the shadows too.

"Nearly there!" Beranabus roars cheerfully as Dervish and Meera are knocked aside, and I narrowly avoid being speared through the centre of my head.

A hole appears in the side of the Shadow. Light shines through, blinding after the gloominess of this unnatural realm. The werewolves howl gleefully and double their efforts. The hole widens and I hit it with another blast of energy. Bec focuses on the area around it. Grubbs rips at the shadows like a madman. More holes and tears appear. Some of the souls drift free and disappear as they hit the air outside. Others follow, streaming after the first few. The holes widen, then the fabric around them crumbles away. The hissing reaches its peak, only now it's a scream of pain. Souls dart from their prison, sensing escape, surging towards the exit from all parts of Death's makeshift body.

Beranabus yodels enthusiastically, fighting the flow, holding his position. "Not bad," he chuckles approvingly.

"Is that it?" I cry, hardly daring to believe it could be this simple. "Have we killed Death?"

"Don't be ridiculous," Beranabus snorts. "Death can't die."

"But conscious Death... the Shadow... have we destroyed it?" I yell.

"No," Beranabus says sadly, sounding more like his old self. "You've delayed matters, that's all. It will have to find new souls and create another body. That will take weeks, maybe a month or two. Then it will be back, stronger than ever. Having learnt from this setback, it will be more vigilant. You won't pierce its defences so easily again."

"Then how will we beat it?" I shriek. "How will we win?"

"You won't," Beranabus whispers. Then he's gone, whipped free of his prison, cheering wildly, to depart the universe of the living once and for all, bound for whatever lies beyond. Bec yells a frantic farewell, but I don't think he hears. He doesn't care about life now or those who inhabit it. He's done.

As I stare at the souls flying past, shocked by Beranabus's parting prophecy, Death's brittle shell dissolves and I fall through the layers of shadow on to hard, dry land — and drop into the middle of an army of millions of demons.

SWAN SONG

→Ranks of monsters surround us, stretching far into the distance. This must be the world from which the Demonata are plotting their invasion of Earth, the base from which they send troops when they open windows to our world. We knew an army was massing, but we never dared confront it. Beranabus was a reckless fighter, but he wasn't crazy. He knew we couldn't hope to face this many demons and walk away alive.

The demons have backed off from the disintegrating mammoth of the Shadow. They're watching it with alarm, chittering and bellowing, not sure what's going on. It's their leader. Death drew them together, promising them control of the universe and eternal life. Now it's falling to pieces like a punctured Zeppelin. They don't know what to do.

"*There!*" shrieks an all too recognisable voice. Pushing myself to my feet, I spy her near the fore of the demons to my left — Nadia Moore, aka Juni

Swan. She's by the side of her eight-armed master, Lord Loss. Both are staring at us with a mix of hatred and uncertainty.

I look around slowly, showing no signs of panic in case I incite the Demonata. Grubbs and Bec are nearby. Grubbs has also seen Juni and Lord Loss. He's taking deep breaths, preparing for battle. Bec is fixing her arm and doesn't seem to be aware of the trouble we're in. Dervish is using magic to revive Meera, glancing around anxiously as he fans her back to life. The ten surviving werewolves have gathered in a circle behind Grubbs, growling softly as they eyeball the demons. And a little further over, hopping around, unaware that we've escaped the stomach of the Shadow, is Kirilli Kovacs.

"Grubbs," I hiss. "Any ideas?"

"Can you open a window?" he mutters, cracking his knuckles.

"I've already started," I whisper, nudging patches of light into place with deft flicks of my fingers, not wanting to alert our enemies to the fact that I'm at work. "It'll take a few minutes. Can you cover me?"

"I'll give it a good shot," he growls, then bellows at Lord Loss. "Where's your mighty leader now? Death offered you the universe and immortality. Hah!"

Bec finishes setting her arm and calmly walks over to Grubbs. She stands behind him, back to back.

Dervish and a woozy Meera shuffle up beside them. When Kirilli hears Grubbs, he stops dancing and stares around. The werewolves haven't moved, awaiting Grubbs's command.

"Very commendable, Grubitsch," Lord Loss says. His voice silences the mutterings and snarls of the other demons. He drifts to the front of the army, Juni by his side. When he's in the open, he looks at each of us in turn and smiles. "But Death cannot be destroyed. You have merely inconvenienced it. A valiant victory, but you have only won a battle, not the war. You know that. We *all* know that." He addresses the last cry to the army of demons, raising his voice, and they roar back encouragingly.

"This feels like a reunion," Lord Loss says, smiling sadly, the snakes writhing in the hole where his heart should be, blood oozing from the many cracks in his pale red flesh. "So many familiar faces. Grubitsch, Dervish, Cornelius, even little Bec, back from the dead and as tenacious as ever."

"Master," Juni murmurs, nodding sharply at me.

"I am aware of Cornelius's efforts," Lord Loss chuckles. "Don't worry, sweet Swan, he will not have time to open a window. I let him get this far in order to fan the flames of hope in their hearts. Now that those flames are flickering nicely—" His red eyes flash dangerously. "—it is time to quench them." He shouts at the millions of demons, "*Attack!*"

With a volley of deafening screams and howls, the army surges forward and smashes to the ground around us, a living wave of chaos, barbarism and death.

→We'd perish in seconds without the power of the Kah-Gash. But as soon as Lord Loss roars, Grubbs grabs Bec, leaps to my side and wraps an arm around me. Unifying our magic, he draws from the power in the air and erects a hasty but sturdy barrier around us. Instead of driving us to the floor and ripping us to shreds, the demons deflect off the shield.

I work on the window as the demons lash and claw at the barrier. It covers all of us except Kirilli, who was too far away and has been cut off, swamped by the army of demonic warriors. It's a powerful shield, impervious to physical assault. If the demons continue to hurl themselves at it, they won't inflict any damage and we'll be out of here in another couple of—

"Stand aside!" Lord Loss yells, blasting his way through a pack of gibbering beasts. He studies the barrier and sneers, then howls a phrase of magic. Energy crackles in all eight of his hands. He lets it build, then directs it at the barrier, a stream of sizzling, purple power. Lord Loss is a demon master, far superior to any human in the ways of magic.

Nothing should be able to stand against him. But we're the Kah-Gash and I sense within seconds that we're stronger than our foe. I laugh confidently. We're going to walk out of this without even a scratch. I can't wait to see the look on his face when…

Juni lays a hand on Lord Loss's lumpy flesh. She's changed a lot since I last saw her, become a mutated, flesh-dripping, impossibly ugly beast. Her eyes flare with shocking madness and naked hate. I remember when, as Nadia Moore, she saved my life. She'd committed herself to Lord Loss by that stage, but there was still room in her heart for human feelings.

Not any more. She's become that which she once fought, every bit as heartless as a true child of the Demonata. She screeches vilely and unleashes a burst of magic at the barrier. At her cry, demons huddle around the pair and link with them, adding their energy to hers and Lord Loss's, focusing their combined forces on the shield.

"Grubbs!" Bec pants, feeling the barrier give. "We need more power."

"I can't," he gasps, sweating as we all are, buckling under the strain. "This is as far… as I dare unleash it. If I give it more freedom… I won't be able to control it. Anything could… happen."

I don't understand what he's saying. He must be mad. The barrier will break and they'll be on us in seconds. We have to throw everything we have at them or else we're doomed.

Then I remember when we last gave the Kah-Gash absolute freedom. It drove the universes back in time. If we could count on it working in our favour again, there'd be no need to worry. But we don't know what it will do if we set it loose a second time. Maybe it would give us the strength to defeat the demons — or maybe it would wipe out our universe and hand victory to the Demonata. We dare not play that card unless all else is lost. Our situation is desperate, but not hopeless, and until that changes, Grubbs is right to hold back.

"We have to fight," he roars. "Are you ready?" I nod weakly. "Bec?"

"Go for it," she growls.

With a battle-hungry cry, Grubbs explodes the barrier. A wall of energy spreads like a ripple from a nuclear explosion, flattening the demons closest to us. For a few seconds we're standing at the centre of a clear circle, confusion reigning all around. Then the demons further back recover, bellow brutally and push forward, clambering over the bodies of the fallen, to surround and enclose us.

The real fight begins.

→It's wilder than any battle I've ever been involved in. I've laughed in the face of overwhelming odds before, but nobody's laughing now. There are too many of them, demons of every rank, from familiars up to masters like Lord Loss. All they share is a total hatred of us and a determination to strip our flesh from our bones.

We strike without pause, bolts and fireballs of magic. Hundreds perish within seconds, but still they press on, thousands of fresh monsters to replace each that falls.

I try to stay in touch with Bec and Grubbs, but we're forced apart. Grubbs is dragged away by several demons at least five times his size. A winged beast snatches Bec from the ground and shoots into the air with her.

I go down under the feet of dozens of hard-shelled demons. Claws slash, fangs and pincers snap. I feel rips open down my legs and arms, across my stomach and chest. I ignore the pain, use magic to numb the worst of it, and with a great effort thrust off the demons. Yelling, I stagger to my feet, then collapse again beneath a dinosaur-shaped beast.

Fangs lock around my throat and tighten. I turn the flesh of my neck to steel but the fangs continue to grind together. This is the end. There's nothing I can do. Some wounds are fatal, no matter how magical you are. Once my throat's been crushed, I'm as dead as—

A silver, purple-tipped spike pokes sharply through the centre of the dinosaur's head. It squeals, then falls aside. A panting Dervish pulls me to my feet. The spikes on his head have tripled in length and writhe like snakes, independently of each other, jabbing at the demons around us, driving them back.

"How much longer will it take you to open that bloody window?" he roars.

I look for the patches of light. They're twenty feet away, drifting apart. With a curse, I summon them, pat the stray patches into place and start adding new lights to the pack.

"How long?" Dervish screams again, blood flowing from a chunk that's been bitten out of the left side of his chest — I see snapped white bones poking through the streams of red.

"Maybe a minute," I gasp, hands blurring.

I glance around as I'm putting the window together. Grubbs is back on his feet, supported by his retinue of werewolves, who've torn into the demons around him, attacking rabidly, tearing strips out of their foes. Bec is still fighting with the winged demon and has forced it towards the ground. Meera's close by, doggedly working her way back to us. Her left arm's been severed at the shoulder. Half her face is a clawed-up, blood-soaked mess — her beauty's been spoiled forever. But more worrying than that are the guts dangling from a hole in her stomach, and the small demon wrapped around her waist, tugging at the intestines, reeling them out like a cat unravelling a ball of string.

"Meera!" I scream, desperate to help, but needing to stay focused on the window. It's our only hope of escape. If I abandon it, we're all doomed.

Dervish has spotted Meera too. He begins to dart to her rescue, then swears and drives back a multi-eyed monster that was about to snap off my hands. He has to stand guard. I can't protect myself while I'm working on the window. He's tied to his post, as I am. He weeps with frustration as he fights off the hordes clustered around us, muttering Meera's name over and over.

The demon working on Meera's guts sticks its head into the hole in her stomach. It's giggling sickeningly, like a child tucking into a box of treats. But then its head explodes and it topples to the ground. A figure breaks through the demons around Meera and hauls her forward, towards us. I think my eyes are playing tricks, but when I blink and see the same thing, I realise I'm not dreaming.

Kirilli Kovacs is ploughing through the ranks of demons. One of his hands has turned into a steel scythe and he's mowing down all who come too close. He's the one who rescued Meera.

"Kovacs, you lunatic!" Dervish yells with delight. "You're supposed to be a coward!"

"I am!" Kirilli screeches.

"Then what the hell are you doing?"

"I don't know! I think I'm saving the day! It feels—"

A demon sweeps Kirilli's legs from under him. He flies into the air with a yelp, then is knocked sideways by a bellowing, half-human beast intent on getting her hands on us before any of the others finish us off. Juni Swan is back in the thick of the action.

She angles for Dervish, dripping flesh as she charges, swiping demons out of her way, teeth bared, eyes rolling madly. With a welcoming grunt, Dervish sets his feet firmly and snarls, losing interest in all the other monsters, forgetting his duty to protect me. As Juni rushes him, he grabs hold of her arms and swings her around like an adult whirling a baby. Juni spits acid into his face. He neutralises it swiftly but not before a wide swathe of his flesh bubbles away. The pair fall to the ground, wrestling savagely, stabbing, biting, punching and spitting, each hell-bent on murdering the other.

The window's almost fully formed, but there's no one to watch my back now. Several hound-like demons press tight around me, snapping at my face, digging channels in my flesh with their jagged claws. "Grubbs! Bec!" I scream, turning from the window to drive back the demons. "I need help!"

Grubbs roars at his werewolves. Slipping free of the giants, they struggle towards me, blasting and chewing a path through the packed ranks of monsters.

In the air, Bec's seen off the challenge of the winged demon, but Lord Loss has hit the scene. The pair tumble and roll around overhead. Half his arms are holding her rigidly against his rancid flesh. The other half are lashing her, pulling her hair, trying to gouge out her eyes, digging into her soft flesh.

Meera's in bad shape, but she shoves fistfuls of guts back into the hole in her stomach and dives to Dervish's rescue, pulls Juni Swan off him and scratches at the traitor's eyes. Juni screeches and tries to knock her away, but Meera's stronger than she looks, and she loves Dervish as much as Juni hates him. Grabbing hold of Juni's bloated, rotten head, she jerks her hard and they spin away. Dervish tries to follow, but gets tangled up with another demon.

Grubbs and the few surviving werewolves make it to my side. They're all badly wounded, but they fight as viciously as ever. As they form a half-wall around me, Grubbs yells at me to finish the window and I hurry to obey. The fingers of my left hand have been crushed, but I can still manipulate the patches. Sobbing with pain and fear, I slot one after another into place, praying for the lights to gel and the window to open before it's too late.

Juni's laughing. She's got both hands inside the hole in Meera's stomach and is forcing them up through the layers of guts that still remain, seeking to crush lungs, the heart... whatever she can find.

"Meera!" Dervish howls, trying to force his way through to her but failing.

Meera smiles painfully. She's got her arms wrapped around Juni, holding tight. As Juni tears at Meera's insides, the Disciple catches our gaze and winks wearily. "No... Shadow," she wheezes.

"What's that?" Juni roars.

"No... Shadow," Meera repeats. "When I die... I'm finished... and so... are you."

Juni's face freezes. She catches on to Meera's plan a second too late. Her eyes widen with alarm as she tries to detach herself and dart to safety. But before she can, Meera explodes. She must have been working on the ball of energy since she realised she was beyond help. It bursts from her in a blazing flash of light, shatters her bones, incinerates her flesh — and rips through the mutated, twisted form that Juni built for herself when Death restored her soul to life.

Juni's final howl is lost in the noise of the explosion. She's torn to shreds along with Meera and both women fall to the ground in ragged, bloody, lifeless chunks, their souls freed or lost, however you choose to look at it. Meera has gone to the great beyond, which is a sickening blow. But I experience a burst of joy as well as sorrow, because Juni Swan has perished too and this time no power in the universe can bring the vindictive harpy back. We're rid of her at last!

CASUALTIES OF WAR

→It sounds like the entire universe is screaming. Dervish and Grubbs wail for Meera. In the air, Lord Loss bellows Juni's name and reaches out to her with a couple of his arms, offering Bec a brief respite. The demon hordes screech with delight, the scent of human death like a red rag to a bull. They press even tighter around us, each wanting to be next to claim a soul.

I drown out the screams and focus on the window. It's all that matters now. We have seconds to get the hell out of here, or we'll wind up like Meera. No time for misery or joy. Just focus, work fast and pray.

A werewolf is slaughtered and collides with me as it thrashes in its death throes, opening a new, deep cut down the side of my head, just behind my left ear. I shrug it off and concentrate.

Kirilli leaps high into the air, raining handfuls of bone down upon the demons. He must have picked them up from the floor of the battlefield. They strike like shrapnel, blinding, wounding, killing. He roars with delight — then shrieks as a demon's jaws flash and his right foot is bitten off at the ankle. Kirilli collapses. His foot drops on top of me and I head it away like a football, never pausing, right hand moving mechanically, fending off demons with my damaged left hand.

Grubbs headbutts a demon and smashes its skull to pieces. His forehead comes out drenched in brains and foul-smelling fluid. Extending his tongue, he licks his eyes clean and fights on, laughing through his tears.

Lord Loss and Bec crash to earth, then rise again. They're still struggling with each other, but he doesn't seem to be inflicting as much damage. His hands move lazily, more like they're caressing Bec than savaging her. And she doesn't react as violently as before. She wriggles less frantically in his embrace, almost as if...

Before I can complete the thought, a window of pale blue light blinks into existence. I stare at it stupidly. Then exhilaration sweeps through me and I yell at the top of my voice. *"The window is open!"*

The Demonata scream hatefully and lash at us frantically. The smarter beasts try to crowd around the window, to block our path, but they're hampered by the mass of demons. There are too many of the monsters. They get in each other's way.

Kirilli hops to the window, grabs Dervish's right

arm — he's still staring at the spot where Meera fell — and topples through, dragging Dervish after him.

A bloodied, panting Grubbs draws up beside me. He casually repels a handful of demons with one swipe of a massive arm. We're both looking to the sky overhead where Bec is locked in the embrace of Lord Loss.

"Go!" she yells. "Leave me!"

"We can't," Grubbs croaks.

"We must," I mutter as more demons bear down on us, snarling, spitting, claws and fangs at full stretch.

"But—" Grubbs begins.

"We're demon fodder if we stay," I snap, then throw myself through the window and out of the demonic universe of death.

→I hit a hard floor and I'm on my feet a split-second later. This is the cave where Beranabus and I were based before our quest to find the Shadow began. It was the first place that popped into my mind when I started putting a window together.

I rip at the fabric of the window, dismantling it, not waiting for Grubbs. If he crosses within the next few seconds, fine. If not, he's a fool and he'll deserve all he gets.

As my hands move within the panel of light, tearing at the individual patches, a werewolf stumbles through, wrapped in the arms of a giant insect-shaped demon. They crash past me and continue their fight on the floor. As Kirilli yelps and slips out of their way, Grubbs backs through the window, bolts of magic flying from his fists, roaring a challenge at those he's leaving behind.

Two more werewolves follow their leader into the cave. The head and shoulders of a third appear, but something clutches its legs and hauls it back. It howls and kicks at whatever has hold. Grubbs grabs the creature and pulls. But then the window comes undone. The patches of light pulse and snap free of each other. The panel vanishes and the werewolf's cut neatly in half, its lower body stranded in the universe of the Demonata, its head and upper arms dropping to the floor here. Its death roar catches in its throat.

It's over.

Well… almost. The insect demon gibbers and breaks free. It darts at the place where the window was, pauses when it realises it's trapped, then turns on me. Before it can strike, all three werewolves pounce. They rip it to pieces and feast on the brittle remains, instantly forgetting about the trauma of the battle, fully focused on their meal, ignoring the rest of us as we sink to the floor and stare silently at each other with shock, bewilderment and dismay.

→Grubbs is the first to move. Rising slowly, groaning

painfully, he hobbles over to check on Dervish. His uncle's in bad shape, the worst of any of us. Blood is pumping from the hole in his chest and I don't think any amount of magic will stop it. Grubbs starts arguing with him. He wants to open a window back to the demon universe, where Dervish will stand a chance of recovery, but the battered Disciple is having none of it. He told Grubbs a while ago that he wanted to die on Earth when his time came. It looks like he'll soon be granted his wish.

"How's the foot?" I ask Kirilli, who's sitting nearby, staring at the place where his right foot used to be. He's crying softly.

"It's gone," Kirilli moans, then looks up. "I don't feel any pain."

"You will soon," I tell him. "But I can work some magic here. I'll bandage it up and help numb the pain. Then I'll open a window and drop you off at a hospital before I leave."

Kirilli doesn't ask where I'm going. Instead he grins weakly. "I did good, didn't I?" he asks hopefully.

"You did great," I smile.

"I never thought I'd be a hero," he whispers. "I dreamt of it many times but I never believed…" He falls silent, reliving the highlights, conveniently ignoring the part where he danced like a fool in the stomach of the Shadow. I don't remind him of that, but fetch bandages from behind the spot where I used to sleep. He's earned the right to be proud. It's not stumbling along the way that matters, but how you finish.

Grubbs limps over as I'm bandaging Kirilli's ankle and healing it with magic, closing off the veins and arteries. He watches silently until I'm done, then nods at me. Leaving Kirilli, we squat near the place where we once kept a fire burning. Grubbs's face has altered. He looks more human than he did when he was fighting. He also looks like he's in a lot of pain, but he says nothing of it.

"Meera's dead," he mumbles.

"I know."

"She took Juni with her. I'd have rather killed that traitor myself, but as long as she's gone…" He sighs, then says quietly, "Dervish is dying. He asked me to take him up top, so he can die outside. I need you to open the trapdoor."

We're deep beneath the ground. A rope ladder leads to the surface, but a stone slab blocks the way out. It's operated by magic. Focusing, I mutter the correct phrase and set it sliding free. "Done."

"Thanks," Grubbs says and starts to rise.

"I could take him to hospital with Kirilli," I suggest.

Grubbs shakes his head. "No point. They couldn't do anything for him. What a moron, letting the demons bite a chunk out of his chest. He should have kept his guard up. The old fool deserves…" He shudders, fighting hard to hold back tears.

"I'll wait for you to return," I tell him.

"That's OK. Take care of Kirilli. You can come back for me."

"I'm not coming back."

Grubbs had made it to his feet, but now he pauses, stares at me and squats again. "What are you talking about?" he asks gruffly.

"It's over. I'm going to the ark."

"You can't. We need you. This isn't finished."

"Of course it is." I wipe blood and sweat from my forehead. I feel so weary. It will be a relief to leave this world and the fighting behind. "We gave it our best shot. We tore the Shadow to pieces. But you heard Beranabus. Death will return, and it'll be even stronger next time. We can't defeat it."

"We have to try," Grubbs growls. "We got the better of it once — we can beat it again. I'll unleash more of the power of the Kah-Gash next time."

"How?" I snort. "We don't have Bec. It's just you and me now."

"We'll rescue her," Grubbs says as if it's the simplest thing in the world. "Lord Loss won't kill her. He'll want to torment her first. I'm guessing he'll return to his kingdom to wait for the Shadow, and he'll take her with him."

"What if he does?" I sigh. "We can't fight him there. We'd stand no chance of defeating a demon master on his home turf."

"Maybe not," Grubbs agrees curtly, "but we have to *try*. Everyone's depending on us. Meera died for this. Dervish will be dead soon too. Beranabus and Bill-E. All the others who've given their lives. They can't have died for nothing. We fight on until the demons kill us all. Only then do we stop."

I shake my head. "If I stay here and perish, the demons will conquer the universe completely. I shouldn't have come back at all, but I did, for one last stab at success. We tried and failed. The ark is all that's left."

I reach out and squeeze Grubbs's arm. "Come with me. They'll welcome you. You can help us keep the ark safe from demons, ensure it never falls to Lord Loss and his stinking kind. It's the best we can do. Staying here is pointless. The fight has moved on. We have to move with it."

"Abandon our world?" Grubbs sneers. "Leave Bec in the clutches of Lord Loss? Run while the demons are weak? Never! They've lost their master. The army will split. They'll fight with each other and return to their own realms. We can harry them, hit hard, drive the fear of the Kah-Gash into them. This isn't the end — it's the beginning. We have the advantage. Now's the time to press it home and make sure that even if Death does return, it has no army to support it."

"That won't work," I say impatiently. "Death's stronger than us, and it's eternal. No matter what we do, it will rise again, recruit new followers and lead them to victory. It's over."

I stand and roll my neck. I want to sleep so badly. But I'll wait until I find Raz, then sleep as we travel to the ark. Forcing off the waves of pain and weariness, I focus on the lights in the air around me and think about Raz in the chamber on Atlantis. As patches blink, I start the long, laborious job of piecing them together.

"That's it?" Grubbs grunts. "You're just going to leave us?"

"It will take several hours to open the window. I'll be here when you get back. You can decide then if you want to come with me or—"

"What about Kirilli?"

I wince. "Damn. I forgot." The stage magician is resting, eyes closed, breathing heavily. I let thoughts of Raz slip from my head and think about a hospital instead. It only takes a few minutes to open this window. When it's ready, I ask Grubbs if he'll help me carry Kirilli through.

"Leave it to me," he says, then picks up the wounded Disciple, slings him over his shoulder like a slab of meat and steps through before the groggy Kirilli has a chance to say goodbye.

While Grubbs is gone, I think about what I'm going to say when he returns. I have to warn him about Bec, tell him what the Old Creature cautioned. I recall the way Lord Loss eased up on her and I realise why I felt so troubled. It looked like they were going to stop fighting, as if she'd said something to make peace with him. Could she have betrayed us like Nadia did? I need to alert Grubbs to the threat before he races after her. Maybe she doesn't want to be rescued. Maybe she's on *their* side now.

As I'm trying to decide where Bec's loyalties lie, Grubbs steps back through the window. I prepare myself to argue with him again, but he smiles and waves my protests away before I can voice them.

"You're right," he chuckles. "You have to go. I wasn't thinking straight."

I sigh with relief. "Will you come with me?" I'm hoping he says yes. Accepting my role on the ark will be hard. It would be a lot easier if I didn't have to face it alone.

"My place is here," he says. "Dervish, Bec, Shark... those are the people I care about. I don't give a stuff about other worlds. I'll fight and I'll die, and if that's not enough, at least I'll have done all that I could. That's what matters most, isn't it, doing all you can, regardless of the consequences?"

"Yes." I smile and extend a hand. "No hard feelings?"

"None," Grubbs says, taking my hand in one of his huge, hairy paws. His smile fades. "But *you* might have some."

I frown curiously. Grubbs is gripping my hand tightly. "What do you–"

Before I can complete the question, Grubbs slashes at my face with his other hand. The sharp, bloody, jagged nails that he was gutting demons with just minutes earlier carve my left eye open. As it pops and I howl with shock and agony, he sweeps his hand back in the opposite direction and rips my right eye out. Then he lets me go.

I fall to the floor screaming, and blindly try to scoop the contents of my ruined eyes back into their sockets.

"I didn't enjoy that," Grubbs says, his words only barely penetrating my veil of screams. "But you agreed — *regardless of the consequences*. I need you, Kernel. I can't fight on without you. So you're staying. End of story."

"My eyes!" I bellow, lashing out furiously, hoping to strike him dead. "Give me back my eyes, you son of a–"

"Can't," Grubbs says calmly. "But what I will do,

once I'm done with Dervish and we've had time to patch up our wounds, get our breath back and link up with support troops, is open a window back to the universe of the Demonata. You'll be able to build another pair of eyes there. And then you'll use them to find Bec and help me rescue her."

"You're mad!" I holler, swinging for him again. "Come here so I can kill you!"

"There'll be plenty of time for killing," Grubbs says, backing away. "Forget your crazy ark. I'm your keeper now. All other bets are off."

"Come back!" I yell, stumbling after him and falling. "You don't know what you're doing. You're handing victory to them. We can't trust Bec. She'll betray us. Lord Loss will be waiting. Death will…"

I stop. I've been shouting to myself. I can hear Grubbs scrabbling up the rope ladder with Dervish, ignorant of my cries. Apart from the werewolves, which are still snacking on the insect demon's remains, I'm alone.

Abandoned and blind, I strike the floor pitifully, then moan softly and lower my face into the blood and dust, wishing the roof would cave in and finish me off. If I still had eyes, I'd weep, not for myself, but for the multitudes of creatures who'll have nowhere to hide when their worlds burn.

"What the hell have we done?" I sob.

All that you could, I imagine the voice of Beranabus whispering. And then, after a short, bitter pause, he adds with a sarcastic chuckle, *But it wasn't enough. This universe is finished. Goodnight, Vienna!*

HELL'S HEROES

For:

Liam, Biddy and Bas — the Father, the Mother
and the Holy Bust!!!

OBEs (Order of the Bloody Entrails) to:
Geir, Wiedar, Jon and all the other nocturnal
Norwegian Shan crew

Road Managers:
Geraldine Stroud — the ripper skipper!
Mary Byrne — the tipsy first mate!

Editor-in-chief:
Stella Paskins — 10 rounds, not out!!

Apocalyptic agents:
the Christopher Little chorus line

And an extra special thank you to all of my demonically
delightful Shansters, especially those of you who have kept
me company on the web through the run of the series.
But take heed — if you desert me at this point,
heads will roll!!!

"What happens when you lose everything?
You just start again.
You start all over again."
'Apply Some Pressure' by Maxïmo Park

THE LAST LAUGH

→"I miss Cal," Dervish says. "We fought a lot when we were young, like all brothers, but we were always there for one another."

We're lying in the mouth of a cave, admiring the desolate desert view, sheltered from the fierce afternoon sun.

"It's strange," Dervish chuckles. "I thought I'd be the first to go. The life I chose, the risks I took... I was sure I'd die young and nastily. I pictured Cal living to be eighty or ninety. Funny how things work out, isn't it?"

I stare at the hole in the left side of Dervish's chest. Blood is seeping from it and I can see bone inside. "Yeah," I grunt. "Hilarious."

Dervish shifts and grimaces. He's in a lot of pain, but he won't have to suffer much longer. My uncle was in bad shape before we took on an army of demons. Now, having come through hell, he doesn't have a prayer. He's finished. We both know it. That's why we came up here from the underground cave, so he could die in the open, breathing fresh air.

"I remember one time," Dervish continues, "not long after Cal married your mum. We had a huge row. He wanted me to quit being a Disciple, marry and have kids, lead a normal life. He thought I was crazy to do what I did."

"He wasn't wrong," I snort.

"You love it really," Dervish grins. Blood trickles down his chin.

"Save your breath," I tell him, trying not to shudder.

"What for? I won't need it where I'm going." He raises an eyebrow. "You don't think I can survive, do you?"

"Of course not. I'm just sick of listening to you whine."

Dervish laughs softly. The laugh turns into a blood-drenched cough. I hold him as he shakes and moans, spewing up blood and phlegm. When the fit passes, he asks me to move him out of the cave. "I don't think I need worry about sunburn," he murmurs.

I pick up my dying uncle and carry him outside. He doesn't weigh much. Thin and drawn, overstretched by the world. He rests his head on my chest, like a baby cuddling up to its mother. I prop him against a large rock, then settle beside him. His eyes stay closed. He's dozed off. I study him sadly, memorising every line of his creased face, brushing the wilting spikes of hair back from his forehead, remembering all the nights he comforted me when I'd had a nightmare.

With a jolt he wakes and looks around, alarmed. When he sees me, and the hole in his chest, he relaxes. "Oh, it was only a dream. I thought we were in trouble."

"Nothing can trouble us here."

Dervish smiles at me lopsidedly. "I loved having you live with me. You were like my son. Billy was too, but I never got to spend the sort of time with him that I did with you."

"If you were my real dad, I'd have asked to be fostered."

Dervish's smile widens. "That's what I like to hear. You're a true Grady. We don't do sympathetic."

His eyes wander and he sighs. "I hope I see Cal again. Billy and Meera. Even Beranabus. So many who've gone before me. Do you think there's an afterlife, Grubbs? Will I be reborn? Or is there just… nothing?"

"There has to be *something*," I mutter. "Why would the universe give us souls if not? It'd be pointless."

Dervish nods slowly, then frowns at something behind me. "What's that?" he wheezes.

My head shoots round and I scan the surrounding area for danger. But I can't see anything except dry earth and rocks. "There's nothing—" I begin, then stop. Dervish's eyes have glazed over. He's not breathing. His face is calm.

I tremble and reach out to close his eyelids, blinking back tears. My fingers are just a few centimetres from his eyes when... *snap!* Dervish's teeth clamp together and he bites the tip of my index finger.

"Hellfire!" I roar, toppling backwards, heart racing.

"Your face," Dervish snickers — always the bloody joker!

"Try it again," I snarl. "Next time I'll dig a hole and bury you alive."

"Don't be so sensitive," Dervish coos, still giggling. He runs an eye over my unnatural muscles, the tufts of ginger hair sprouting from my skin, my wolfish features, yellow eyes, jagged claws and blood-spattered fangs. "You're a real mess."

"With a role model like you, I never had a hope," I sniff.

"Poor Grubbs." Dervish makes goo-goo eyes at me. "All you ever wanted was for someone to show you some love."

"Get stuffed."

We both laugh.

"I'm going to miss you," Dervish sighs.

"Yeah," I mutter. "I'll... y'know... you too."

"Part of me wishes I could hang on and see how it all turns out. But then I think about the odds..." He shakes his head.

"Don't worry," I say grandly. "I'll take care of the

Demonata. The Shadow too. I've seen enough movies to know how these things end. We'll all be high-fiving each other and celebrating a famous victory by this time next month. But you won't see any of it. Because you'll be dead."

Dervish scowls. "You really know how to comfort a dying man."

We're silent a while. The flow of blood has slowed, but I don't kid myself — it's only because he doesn't have much left. There's no getting better, not this time. Dervish has cheated death for the last few months, but he played his last card when we faced the demon hordes.

"What's going to become of you, Grubbs?" he asks. "This new look... the way you kill so freely..."

"I'll be fine." I poke the ground with my bare, hairy toes.

"No," he says. "You've changed, and not just on the outside." He lays a weak, bloodstained hand on mine. "Don't become a monster. Remember who you are, the people who love you, why you fight. Beranabus acted inhumanly, but he was never fully human to begin with. You were. You *are*. Don't lose track of that."

"Is this really how you want to go?" I squint. "Lecturing me like some second-rate TV psychiatrist?"

"I'm serious," he growls.

"Don't be stupid," I smile. "It's far too late for that."

Dervish rolls his eyes, then shrugs. "Don't say I didn't warn you."

"I won't."

Dervish shivers and glares at the sun. "It's so cold. Why's there no warmth in that thing?"

"Eclipse." It's the first thing that pops into my head. Dervish cocks an eyebrow, but otherwise ignores the inanity.

"I wish we could have had more leisure time," he says. "Apart from the trip to Slawter, I never took you on any holidays."

"If Slawter was your idea of a holiday, that was probably a good thing."

"Orlando," Dervish nods. "That's where we should have gone. Roller coasters. You, Billy and me. We'd have had so much fun."

"We were never meant for a life like that," I mumble. "I used to think I could choose it, just turn my back on magic and demons. But I've been locked into this course since birth, just like you. Bec, Beranabus – all of us – we never really had a choice. I hate the unfairness of fate, but…"

I pause. Dervish's head has slumped. I tilt his head back, keeping my fingers clear of his mouth, expecting him to bite again. But this time it isn't a joke. His eyes are closed. The last breath has slipped from his semi-parted lips. His heart has stopped beating.

"Guess the last laugh's on you, old-timer," I croak, letting his head rest on my shoulder and patting him clumsily.

Rising, I gently lay him back against the rock, then pad away and choose a spot in the shade. As I bend, I get the feeling that Dervish is sneaking up on me. I turn quickly, lips lifting into a smile, but he hasn't moved. He never will again.

Sighing emptily, I clench my fingers tightly, then drive them into the dry, hard-packed soil, scooping out the first fistful of my dead uncle's grave.

CLOCKING OFF

→Creeping through a factory, in pursuit of a snake demon seven or eight metres long. I wouldn't have thought a beast that size could hide easily, but I've been searching for several minutes without success. I should be out on the streets, battling the masses, but this demon killed a Disciple. She was an elderly, frail lady, but she could swing a spike-headed mace more effectively than anyone I've ever met. I never asked her name, but I liked her. I'm going to make her killer pay.

I slide around a corner, checking the pipes overhead. I feel edgy, which is odd. I haven't felt anything but cold, detached hatred recently. I guess the tension of the moment has got to me. I'm sure the demon won't prove to be a serious threat — I'm more than a match for any of the familiars who cross through windows — but it's fun to pretend I'm in danger. I'd almost forgotten what fear was like.

A scraping noise behind me. I whirl, a ball of magical energy crackling at my fingertips. But it's only Moe. He followed me into the building, even though I told him to stay outside. Moe's one of three werewolves who've been with me since Wolf Island. Werewolves don't need names, but after a few weeks with the trio, I felt like I should call them something. So I christened them Curly, Larry and Moe, after the Three Stooges. I never had much time for the Stooges, but Dervish loved them, so I named the werewolves in his memory.

I growl at Moe to let him know I'm displeased. He makes a soft whining noise, but he can tell I'm not that bothered. Moe takes his bodyguard duties seriously. He never likes to be too far from me. I think he feels a bit lost when I'm not there for him to protect.

Letting Moe fall into place behind me, I push further into the factory, past a long conveyor belt. Workers were sitting in the chairs alongside it just an hour ago. It's been nearly a month since Dervish died in the desert. There have been dozens of crossings since then. Hundreds of thousands of humans have been killed. People are terrified and desperate, but life goes on. A few of us know the cause is hopeless, but we haven't shared the bad news. As far as the general population is concerned, we can beat these demonic invaders.

So, as the body count mounts, folk carry on normally, manning their posts even in the face of an impending crossing, slipping away to safety at the last moment, returning as soon as the window closes.

Moe growls and darts to a nearby locker. I start to follow, assuming it's the demon, but when he rips the locker door off and tears open a lunchbox, I realise he's found a sandwich.

"Idiot," I grunt, turning back to the conveyor belt.

Fangs sink into my thigh. Yelling, I fall and the snake drags me into the gloom beneath the belt, where it's been lying in wait. I strike at its eyes, but it doesn't have any. Gripping me tightly, it drives its fangs further into my flesh, crushing the bones in my leg.

I once read a survival pamphlet that said if a giant snake ever got hold of you, you should lie still, so it thinks you are dead. Then, as it swallows your legs, you free your knife (too bad if you don't have one) and hold it by your side. As the snake devours your thighs and sets to work on your stomach, you drive the tip of the knife up through the roof of its mouth and deep into its brain. That always grossed out girls when I told them!

I'm sure it's sound advice, but I don't have time to test it. Unlike most large snakes, this demon's poisonous and I can feel its venom coursing through my veins. I don't have the luxury of playing possum. Besides, that's not my style.

Grunting against the pain, I grab the demon's fangs and snap them off. The beast chokes and releases me, spewing poisonous pink blood. I drive one of the broken fangs into the side of its head. It squeals like a baby and thrashes across the floor. I hang on, riding it bronco-style, stabbing at it again and again. More blood froths from the wounds, soaking my face and chest.

As the snake slams against the conveyor belt, knocking it over, I thrust my head in its mouth and roar down its throat. A ball of magic bursts from my lips and rips through the demon's body. It explodes into tattered, slimy shreds. I pick some of the foul scraps from between my teeth, then focus magic into my leg and repair the damage. Getting to my feet, I look for Moe. He's still munching the sandwich.

"Great help you were," I snarl, using more magic to clear my veins of poison.

Moe looks at me guiltily, then holds out the last piece of sandwich. I turn my nose up at it and hobble for the doorway, eager to squeeze in more killing before the window between universes shuts and robs me of my demonic punchbags.

→The streets are awash with demons, the usual assortment of vile concoctions, many cobbled together from bodies resembling those of animals, fish and birds. Demons are an unimaginative lot. Most can use magic to mould their forms, but rather than give themselves original, amazing bodies, they copy ours.

Dozens of werewolves are fighting the demons. I had them imported from Wolf Island, to replace those of my original pack. Most of the new specimens aren't as sturdy, fast or smart as those I first chose, but they get the job done. Curly's in the middle of them, acting as pack leader in my absence. She's a fierce creature, taller than me, though not as broad. Sharp too. She can always spot if one of the werewolves disobeys orders and attacks a human instead of a demon. She pounces on the offending party in an instant and slits the beast's throat without blinking. No second chances with Curly.

Soldiers and freshly blooded mages support the werewolves. The soldiers don't do much damage — you can only kill a demon with magic — but the mages are doing a pretty good job. They're learning quickly. Not up to the level of the Disciples, but getting there fast.

I move among the apprentices, taking the place of the mace-wielding old lady. There aren't many Disciples left, so they're spread thinly across the world, one or two per group of mages. I see the men and women around me flinch as I pass. They know who I am. They've seen me kill more demons than anybody else. They know they're safe when I'm around. But I'm a fearsome sight and most find it hard to suppress a shudder when they find themselves beside me.

I could change back if I wished, resume my human form. But I prefer it this way. It's easier to lead people to their death if you're not truly one of them.

A girl, no more than twelve or thirteen, is playing

with a wooden yo-yo. As a demon comes within range, she snaps the yo-yo at it. The wood splinters and the shards puncture the demon's eyes. She replaces it with another yo-yo, this time a plastic one.

"Nice work," I grunt.

She looks up at me and fakes a yawn. "Whatever."

Magic isn't a natural part of our universe. But some humans – mages – are born with the ability to tap into it. When a demon opens a window from its universe to ours, magical energy spills through. If you're a mage, you're in business.

In the past, very few mages got to unleash their power. Windows weren't opened often. It was hard for the Disciples to find new recruits. Now that demons have gone into overdrive, and two or three windows open every day, it's simple. When a window is forming, we arrange for crowds of people to wait close by, then test them for magical prowess. Those who show promise are thrown into the fray after a quick burst of training, to perish or triumph.

I see a window in the near distance. A child, even younger than the girl with the yo-yo, stands to one side. A man and woman are behind her. I guess they're using the girl. She probably had no choice in this. But, innocent or not, the Demonata are working through her, so she has to die.

As I push through the battling demons, werewolves

and humans, I marvel at the greed of mankind. I should be accustomed to it, but I'm still astonished every time it happens. Most mages use their powers for good, especially now that people can clearly see the full, destructive evil of the Demonata.

But there are others who side with the demons. They seek power, wealth, a longer life. They scent an opportunity to get ahead and sell off their souls to the highest bidder without a second thought. It never seems to occur to them that there will be no place in a demon-run world for *any* humans, even the most evil. Demons don't do coalitions.

The woman behind the girl spots me. She taps the girl's shoulder and mutters in her ear. The three of them edge closer to the window. Uh-uh! Can't have them slipping away early. That wouldn't be fair. I bark a phrase of magic and erect an invisible barrier between the trio and the window. Panic shoots across the faces of the adults. The girl simply looks confused.

The man hurls himself at the barrier, trying to smash it with his shoulder. The woman curses and draws a gun. As she trains it on me, I turn it into a posy of flowers. She stares at the petals, sadness filling her eyes as she realises this will serve as her death wreath. Then Moe barrels on to the scene and knocks her to the ground. Her screams excite the wolf in me and I fall on the man, snarling. He just has time to beg for mercy. Then my teeth are around his throat and the sweet taste of human flesh fills my mouth.

I gulp the man's blood, then toss his carcass aside and loom over the girl. She gazes up at me, that confused look still crinkling her features. She's even younger than I thought, maybe seven or eight. She's clutching a small teddy bear in one hand.

"Are you the bogey man?" she whispers, eyes round.

"Yes," I croak, then take hold of her head with my huge, scarred, blood-soaked hands and crush.

Thoughts of Juni Swan flicker through my mind as the girl shakes and drops the teddy bear. Juni was Lord Loss's assistant. She could catch glimpses of the future. We fought on Wolf Island. She had me beaten, but then let me go. Because, in a vision, she saw me destroying the world.

I've tried to dismiss Juni's prophecy, but I'm sure it's true. I often think that I should throw myself off a cliff or let the demons kill me. The world would be a safer place without me. But I can't do it. Life's too sweet. So I lie to myself and cling to false hope that she was wrong, even though I know it's selfish madness.

As the girl goes still, I set her down and wonder if I'll crush the world as easily as her head.

The window flashes out of existence, stranding the demons. With screams of despair, they battle furiously, eager to kill as many humans as they can before this universe rids itself of their ugly stain. But they're already weakening, robbed of the magic they need to survive.

I feel my strength fading too. I'm a magician, so I can operate in the absence of a window. But I'm nowhere near as powerful as I am when the air's thick with the delirious energy of the Demonata.

It doesn't matter. I'm not essential in this final stage. Nor are the mages. This is where the werewolves and soldiers come into their own. They rip apart the weakened demons with fangs, claws, bullets and machetes. The demons don't die, but they no longer have the power to put themselves back together, so they can only lie there in pieces and wait to dissolve as magic drains from the air.

Moe cocks a deformed eyebrow at me and grunts questioningly.

"Go on," I sigh, wincing at the pain in my leg. That's the downside of using magic to heal a wound. It's fine while there's magical energy in the air, but once that passes, pain kicks in with a vengeance.

As Moe joins the bloodletting, a pale, thin, icy-looking woman approaches me. It's Prae Athim, head of the Lambs, a group which once acted as executioners of Grady children who'd turned into werewolves. Now they supply me with fresh recruits from Wolf Island.

"That looks nasty," Prae says, nodding at my leg. It's

purple, and pus seeps from the cuts which have reopened.

"I'll be fine," I mutter. "I got rid of all the poison before the window closed."

"Does it hurt?" she asks.

"Yes. But it won't kill me."

"Still, you should have it looked at."

I grin. Prae loves to mother her wolfen wards, even a semi-werewolf like me. She's cold with humans, but has a soft spot for those who've turned into savage, mindless killing machines.

"Will you look after the others?" I ask.

"Of course," she snaps. "Don't I always?"

Prae can't directly control the werewolves – only I can do that – but she's had years of experience and commands a team of specialists. When I'm tired or don't have the time to round up the pack and settle them down, she moves in with her troops. They use electric prods, nets and shackles where necessary, though having feasted on so many demons, most of the werewolves are happy to do as ordered.

"Will I see you later?" I ask. Prae often spends the night after a battle with me, looking ahead to the next assault, discussing tactics.

"No," she says. "We're accepting a new shipment from the island. I want to make sure the transfer goes smoothly and get them quartered close to the others."

"Do you want my help?"

She shakes her head. "I'll make them comfortable first. You can give them your pep talk in the morning. I'm sure they'll be impressed."

Prae leaves and I chuckle softly. I've grown fond of her in recent weeks. She reminds me of Dervish. He could be a distant customer too, when he needed to be.

Thinking of my dead uncle wipes the smile from my lips. I spend a few minutes remembering some of his finer moments — when he came to see me in the asylum after my family was killed, fighting Vein and Artery in the cellar at Carcery Vale, battling Lord Loss in the town of Slawter, dying with dignity in the desert.

Then I recall his love for Juni, when we thought she was on our side, and that reminds me of her dire prophecy. Sighing miserably, I shuffle off to hospital, wishing I could avoid quiet, human moments like these. Life's a lot easier when chaos is erupting all around and the beastly wolf within me rises to the fore.

MR GRUMPY-PUSS

→I'm not going to the hospital to have myself tended to. Prae's concern was touching, but unwarranted. I'll be in a lot of pain until the next attack, but as soon as a window opens and magic floods the air, I'll revive spectacularly. No, I'm going to look in on a patient. A guy not much older than me, whose eyes I clawed out a month ago.

As I enter the ward where I left Kernel before the battle started, I fill with guilt, as I do every time I face him. My stomach still gives a turn when I recall the callous way I blinded my friend, ripping his eyes from their sockets the way a bully might swipe a bag of sweets from a child.

The doctors and nurses are rushed off their feet trying to deal with a flood of casualties. Abandoning the more seriously wounded to chance, they focus on those most likely to respond to treatment.

Nobody pays much attention to me as I pad through the corridors. I've made myself a bit smaller, but I still cut a sinister sight. I'm taller and broader than any human, naked except for a pair of torn, tattered trousers, hairy, bloody and foul-smelling. I'd inspire terror if these were normal times. But we've passed way beyond the bounds of normality. These days, in the cities and towns where the war takes me, I draw nothing more than curious glances.

I stop at the door of Kernel's room and study the bald, brown-skinned teenager through the glass. He's sitting on a chair in the corner. I left him lying on a bed, but he's given that up to one of the recently wounded. Kirilli Kovacs is by his side, chatting animatedly, making sweeping gestures with his hands. I smile at the ridiculous Kirilli. He still wears a stage magician's costume, though he replaced his ruined original suit with a new one a few weeks back. It didn't have gold and silver stars down the sides, but he found some and has been stitching them on in quieter moments.

Two fingers on Kirilli's left hand are missing, he's scarred and bruised all over and his right foot was bitten off at the ankle — he wears a prosthetic. Kirilli is proud of his injuries. He whined to begin with, but when he saw the impression they made on people – especially pretty nurses – he adopted a stoic stance. He loves telling exaggerated tales about how he lost his various body parts.

Kirilli's a natural coward, but he came good when we

last fought the demons in their own universe. He was a hero that day, surprising even himself. He hasn't been called into action too often since, but has handled himself capably when required. I think he's over the worst of his cowardice, though he'll never be an out-and-out warrior.

I push the door open. Kernel is smiling at whatever tall tale Kirilli's spinning. The pair have become good friends. Kirilli helps Kernel forget about his missing eyes. I should really set the Disciple more demanding tasks – he's too important to waste on babysitting duties – but guilt over what I did to Kernel stays my hand.

There's a growl to my left. It's Larry, crouched in the corner. I leave one of my most-trusted werewolves with Kernel whenever I'm not around. Officially they're here to protect him. But the truth – as Kernel knows – is that I don't trust my blind companion. I'm afraid he'll create a pair of eyes when a window is open and slip away. Larry's instructions – hammered into him with difficulty – are to watch over Kernel and disable him if the teenager ever starts fiddling with his sockets.

Kernel and Kirilli glance up when Larry growls. Kernel's expression instantly changes, even though he can't see me. I guess the smell gives me away.

"Here comes our triumphant general," Kernel sneers. "Kill many demons today, Grubbs? *Blind* any of them?"

"How is he?" I ask Kirilli, ignoring the taunts.

"Blind!" Kernel snaps before the Disciple can answer. "In agony. A doctor had a look at me earlier, before the window opened. Infection has set in. I used magic to clean it – carefully, so as not to arouse my *guard's* suspicions – but the rot will return. I'll probably drop dead of some disease of the brain any day now. Give me back my eyes, you son of a wolfen hound!"

"Does he ever change the track?" I sigh.

"He only gets like this when you're around," Kirilli murmurs. "And, as I'm sure you acknowledge, he has genuine cause for complaint."

I grunt sourly and step aside as a patient is bundled past by a couple of nurses. "We've had this conversation too many times. I won't restore your eyes until we rescue Bec. If you promised not to take off, I'd let you fix them now."

"I promise to kick your ass every day for all eternity in hell," Kernel snarls. "How about that?"

I scowl at the blind magician, hating myself more than him. Kernel's part of a demonic weapon known as the Kah-Gash. I am too. It can be used to settle this war, handing ultimate victory to us or the Demonata. The third part is in a girl called Bec, currently a prisoner of the demon master, Lord Loss.

The original plan was for the three of us to unite, unleash the power of the Kah-Gash, destroy the

Demonata and ride off into the sunset, champions of the universe, the greatest heroes ever. Easy.

Then Death came along and complicated matters. Death used to be a force, the same as gravity or light, without thought or form. Now it has a mind and it created a body from the souls of the dead that it reaped. We christened it the Shadow before we found out its true identity.

Death doesn't like us. Life's too abundant in this universe. It wants to go back to the way things were, when only demons and the Old Creatures were around. It's thrown its support behind the Demonata. Under Death's guidance, the demons have banded together and launched an assault on Earth. Their reward if they triumph will be the obliteration of mankind, control of our universe and immortality. Not a bad little package!

One of the ancient Old Creatures took Kernel on a trip to the centre of the universe, explaining the origins of life along the way. Apparently there was one universe to begin with, divided into sixty-four zones, half white and half black, like a chess board. The Kah-Gash held it all together, keeping the demons and Old Creatures apart. Then law and order broke down, the Big Bang shattered everything and life as we know it began.

The Old Creatures protected us from the Demonata as long as they could, but they've been fighting a losing battle. Unlike the demons, they can't reproduce, so when the last one dies, we'll be left to the devices of the inhuman armies. That spells curtains for this world and all the others in our universe.

To deny the demons their triumph, the Old Creatures created an ark. Like Noah's, only this is an entire world, staffed by a variety of the universe's more magical creatures. They want Kernel to captain the ark. As the *eyes* of the Kah-Gash, he can find shortcuts between any two points in the universes. By keeping him alive forever, the Old Creatures hope that he can steer the ark one step ahead of the pursuing Demonata, ensuring that a small section of our universe survives until the end of time.

It would have been easy for Kernel to accept their offer. But he came back and pitched in with us for one last assault. The Old Creatures said we couldn't beat Death, that it's invulnerable, but Kernel refused to write off our chances. He joined with Bec and me, and we confronted the Shadow.

We managed to destroy Death's body, but it's only a matter of time before it returns, bigger and badder than before, to lead its followers to victory. Seeing this, Kernel chose to return to the ark. I asked him to stay and fight. Bec had been captured by Lord Loss and I wanted us to free her, then unleash the full force of the Kah-Gash on Death when it returned.

Kernel refused. He thought Bec had switched

allegiances and sided with Lord Loss. Even if she hadn't, he couldn't see any way of defeating Death. He got ready to open a window and take off for pastures unimaginably distant.

That's when I lost my cool and tore out his eyes. I needed Kernel to find Bec for us to stand any sort of chance against Death. If I had to blind and imprison him to force his hand, so be it. The human Grubbs Grady could never have acted so viciously, but the new, wolfen me… Well, I don't sleep with an easy conscience, but I can live with it.

"How does he look?" Kernel asks Kirilli. "Ashamed? He should. What he did to me, I wouldn't have done to a dog. Or a demon. Not even a werewolf."

"He looks tired," Kirilli says, offering me a slight smile.

"Poor Grubbs," Kernel sneers. "Are you overworked? You should take a week off, treat yourself to a holiday."

"That's right," I sigh. "Go on hating me. It's not like you've got anything else to hate, is it?"

"The Demonata?" Kernel shakes his head. "I *don't* hate them. They're doing what they were born to. Nature spat them out as foul, heartless killers. That's the way they are. You, on the other hand, chose vileness over humanity. We were friends. I trusted you. But then you did this to me and keep me here against my will, even though you know it's wrong. I despise you more than I ever thought possible."

I sniff away his insults. "Whatever," I deadpan, echoing the girl with the yo-yo. "We're staying here the rest of the night, then moving out at ten in the morning. If you want anything, ask a nurse."

"I want new eyes," Kernel snarls. "Can a nurse fetch me those?"

I start for the door.

"Grubbs," Kernel stops me. I glance back wearily, preparing myself for more insults. "Why are we still here?"

I frown. "I told you, we're staying overnight, then–"

"I mean on Earth," he interrupts. "When you blinded me, you said you needed me to find Bec, that we'd wait for our wounds to heal, then rescue her. But it's been a month and we haven't gone after her. Why not?"

I'm surprised Kernel hasn't mentioned this before. I kept waiting for him to ask and had all sorts of responses lined up. But now my tongue freezes. I flash on the dreams I've been having, think about sharing them with him, then shake my head.

"We're not ready. We'll go for Bec when the time is right. We can do more good here at the moment."

"*We?*" Kernel replies archly. "All I do is wait around in hospitals for you to return from the killing fields. If you're not going to use me, set me free."

"I will use you," I mutter. "When it's time, I'll take you back to the demon universe and let you build new eyes."

"And then?" Kernel prompts.

"We'll find Bec."

"*Find* her?" He pounces like a cat. "Not *rescue* her?"

I gulp, then nod at Kirilli. "I'll see you in the morning."

"Not if I see you first," Kernel calls after me, then raises his voice as I exit, to make sure I hear his parting shot. "Not that *that's* very likely!"

→I find an unoccupied room on an upper floor of the hospital and make a bed out of some balled-up surgical gowns. I'd rather not sleep, but rest is vital, even for a creature like me. I have to be at my sharpest to keep on fighting demons.

I think about my conversation with Kernel, and about Dervish, Juni, Lord Loss, Bec. I recall the prophecy again, the way Juni cackled, her delight as she described seeing the world explode, the universe burning beneath my twisted hands.

It's too much. Guilt, fear and loneliness overwhelm me. I'm not in close touch with my human emotions these days. I've become a detached, brutal excuse for a person. But tonight, for a few brief minutes, my defences crumble. I become an awkward teenager again. I feel the weight of the expectations that ride upon me… the awful price the world will pay if I fail… those who've been lost… the lives I've taken, like the confused little girl tonight… the fear of what might be waiting for me when I cross to Lord Loss's realm… Juni's prophecy.

As my face contorts and becomes more human, my chest heaves and I weep. Hot, thick, salty tears run down my cheeks as I sob and beg for help from the dead — Dervish and Beranabus, Mum and Dad, Meera and Bill-E. I've blinded a friend. Hidden terrible truths from those who've placed their trust in me. Killed and lied. And, if Juni's to be believed, there's worse to come.

I wail and mumble madly, biting into the gowns to stifle my cries, pounding my chest and face with my fists. I curse the universe, God if he exists, the Old Creatures, the Disciples, Lord Loss and all the demons. But most of all I curse myself, poor, pitiful, apocalyptic Grubbs Grady.

Then, as the tears dry… as the werewolf regains control and my features harden and transform… as I bury my humanity deep again… as the Kah-Gash whispers and tells me I'm not alone and to stop behaving like a child… I gradually calm down.

I turn and readjust the gowns. Make myself comfortable. Breathe more slowly. Mutter a short spell. And fall into what should be a pure and dreamless sleep — but isn't.

IN DREAMS I WALK WITH YOU

→The spell I use when I want to sleep is meant to stop me dreaming. It's designed to provide me with a good night's sleep, free of nightmares, so I can wake fresh and bright in the morning. But it hasn't been working since Bec was abducted. I've tried different spells, having asked a number of Disciples for advice, but nothing keeps the dream at bay. The same disturbing scenes unfold every time and they're the real reason why I haven't tried to rescue Bec.

As the dream kicks in again, I flow along with it as usual. I've tried fighting, struggled to change the sequence or details, but without success. Tonight I accept my lack of control with as much grace as a savage beast like me can muster.

I'm in a room made of cobwebs, staring down at a sleeping girl — Bec. She lies on a bed of thick webs, covered by a blanket of much finer strands. She looks pale and exhausted, but bears no wounds and breathes easily, calmly.

Her left hand moves upward and brushes her cheek, as I knew it would. Her nose twitches and again I'm not surprised. I've seen it all a dozen times. When you experience the same dream over and over, you start paying attention to the details, to stop yourself going mad. I try to find something new tonight, a little movement or quiver that I missed before, but everything is exactly the same as before.

Bec's eyelids flutter open. A moment of panic — "Where am I?" — then her look of alarm fades and she rises. She's dressed in a beautiful nightgown, the sort I've only seen in old movies. It's not made of webs. I guess Lord Loss took it from one of his victims — I can't imagine him going shopping for it.

Bec walks to a small, round window and gazes out over a landscape of cobwebs. This is Lord Loss's realm, a world of countless sticky strands, a massive network of despair and sorrow. The air is thick with misery and suffering. I can sense that thousands of people have died here, crying out for their loved ones, alone and separated from all they'd ever known.

Bec turns to a table and chair, both carved out of webs. There's a mirror set in the wall over the table. The girl sits and studies her reflection. She looks tense, but not scared. She reaches out to touch the face in the mirror, as if she's not sure it's really hers, then pauses and lowers her hand.

Standing, she walks to a wardrobe on the other side of the room. The doors open as she approaches and a clothes rack slides out. Long, frilly dresses hang from it, the sort a princess or movie star would wear. I don't think they'd suit a plain girl like Bec. She must think the same thing because she smiles at the dresses and shakes her head.

"You do yourself a disservice, Little One," says a voice. Bec stiffens, then turns slowly and regards Lord Loss. He's hovering in the doorway, blood seeping from the many cracks in his pale red skin. His dark red eyes are as kindly as I've ever seen them. Even the snakes in the hole where his heart should be look harmless, hissing playfully, seeming to smile at the young girl by the wardrobe.

"Of course you deserve such finery," Lord Loss continues, floating into the room and running a couple of his eight arms over the dresses. "You are a priestess of high standing. You should expect only the best from your world and its people. They exist to serve your pleasure and revere your beauty."

"You flatter me," Bec says shyly.

"No," Lord Loss says. "Power is beauty, and as you are the most powerful of all humans, you must be the most beautiful. Wear these dresses and think of them as rags. We shall find finer robes for you later."

He picks out a green dress and smiles. "This matches

your eyes. Will you try it on, to please me?"

"Very well." Bec sighs and slips out of her nightdress, not embarrassed to be naked in front of the demon master. Bec's nudity made me uncomfortable at first, but I'm used to it now. What I find more unsettling is the fact that she seems to want to please Lord Loss. Why should she care about his wishes, or dress to impress him? This is our enemy, a vile, twisted monster. Yet she's letting him treat her like a doll.

When Bec has dressed, Lord Loss leads her to the table and applies make-up as she sits patiently. It's obscene, watching his mangled hands brushing across her face. I want to knock him away and slap Bec back to her senses. It wouldn't be so bad if he was controlling her thoughts, brainwashing her to do his bidding. But I don't get any hint of that. Bec looks nervous, but her mind appears to be her own.

When Lord Loss is finished, he drifts back a few metres and studies her. He nods with satisfaction, as he does every time, and murmurs, "What a vision."

Bec blushes, unable to hide a timid smile. I've grown to loathe that smile. It's wrong. This should be a place of tears and heartache, not shy smirks.

"Come," Lord Loss says, offering Bec an arm. "Let me show you more of my palace."

Bec gulps, then takes his arm and lets the demon master lead her out of the bedroom. They descend a staircase of webs. Some of Lord Loss's familiars scurry past as the pair walk gracefully down the steps. The lesser demons scowl at Bec, but steer clear of her, afraid of angering their master. Bec knows they hate her, but she doesn't care. She's safe as long as she stays by her protector.

They stroll through the castle, Lord Loss polite as a prince, the perfect host, pointing out features of special interest. Bec admires the chandeliers and statues, and coos when Lord Loss modestly admits to designing them himself.

"You're so creative," she says.

"That is kind of you, but untrue," he replies. "They're modelled after objects I have seen on Earth. I have a certain workmanlike skill, but no real artistic streak. Unoriginality is the curse of my kind."

They descend further, to a cellar deep beneath the ground. In my sleep I tense. I know what's coming and I hate it. This is one of the worst parts of the dream. If I could skip it, I would, but it draws me on as it always does, an unwilling viewer, unable to pull back or look aside.

We enter a chamber of torture. Savage implements of torment are strapped to the webby walls. Brands glow red in burning fires. The air is pierced by the screams of the dying. Bec flinches and her fingers tighten on Lord Loss's arm. He pats her small hand, comforting her. She gulps, then takes a trembling step forward. Lord Loss nods approvingly and leads her on.

I've never been able to count all the people in the cellar, since many are hidden behind walls or cabinets. There are at least thirty, probably a lot more to judge by the volume of shrieks and moans.

"Do you feel sorry for them?" Lord Loss asks as Bec shudders.

"Yes," she whimpers.

"Good," he says. "Pity is a virtue. I feel sorry for them too. It's true," he insists as she shoots him a dubious glance. "I take pleasure from their torment, but I feel pity too. That is how I differ from my fellow demons. I don't hate humanity. I crave their torment and sorrow, but I also adore them. I torture with love, Little One. Can you understand that?"

"No," she frowns.

He sighs. "At least you are honest. I'm glad you can reveal your true feelings to me. I don't want there to be any deception between us. Always tell me the truth, even if you think I won't like it. Lies belittle us all."

Bec observes silently as Lord Loss sets to work on a few of the humans hanging from the walls or lying across hard tables. He acts like a nurse as he tortures them, every movement deceptively gentle and loving. He purrs softly, telling them how sorry he is, how he wishes he could free them, how it won't be much longer now.

Bec doesn't look as if she shares the demon master's enjoyment, but she doesn't object either. I've tried to read her mind every time we get to this point, but I can't. I'd give anything to know what's in her thoughts. I hope she's putting on a detached face to fool Lord Loss, to stay on his good side and trick him into thinking she doesn't hate him. I hope this is a masterful act, that she's plotting to betray him, waiting and praying for Kernel and me to burst in and rescue her.

But her eyes are calm and emotionless, and when she licks her lips, it looks as if she's fighting a desire to try what Lord Loss is doing.

As the demon master continues to extract fresh pain from his victims, Bec casts her gaze around and my virtual head swivels too. This is the part I hate the most. I try to look away or shut my eyes, but I'm locked in. I have to see what she sees, even though it sends a chill through my bones that will still be there when I wake.

The people chained to the walls and torture devices are a varied mix. Men and women, boys and girls, of different races. No babies — Lord Loss likes to be able to hold discussions with his victims. With a single exception, I don't recognise any of them, though I know by his magical aura that one – a thin, blond-haired man – is a Disciple.

Bec studies the Disciple – he's in the worse shape of anyone, kept alive only by magic – then moves on, her gaze sweeping over a girl my age. I didn't notice her the first few times. To Bec she's of no more interest than any of the others. It's a blink-and-you-miss-it moment. It was only after the fourth or fifth time, when I was concentrating on details to keep boredom at bay, that I focused on the girl's face and got a shock that echoes even now, twenty or so viewings later.

The girl is pretty, but her face is covered with blood and scrunched up with terror. Her clothes hang from her in filthy rags, but I'm sure they originally came from the finest designer boutiques. And although her hair is a tangled mess and her nails are long and cracked, once they were as carefully tended as a model's.

Apart from the blood, the girl doesn't seem to have been tortured, but many of Lord Loss's victims look unmarked. He patches them up and lets them recover a little when he's done, to make it all the more painful next time. Inside, I'm sure she's been twisted and torn in more ways than most humans could imagine.

As Bec's eyes dart about, I snatch the same quick glimpse of the girl that I've been horrified by ever since I realised who she was. Back on Earth, in a quiet hospital room, my lips move as I mutter in my sleep. "*Bo Kooniart…*"

EXECUTIVE BOARD

→Bec and Lord Loss move on eventually, up another set of stairs, to a different part of the demon master's palace. Blood drips from his doughy flesh as he floats along, but it's not his own. Bec is silent, head bowed, brooding.

I'm thinking about Bo Kooniart. It seems like a lifetime since I last saw her, racing back into a demon-infested town in search of her horrible father and pain of a brother. Bo was one of the actresses in *Slawter*, a movie about demons made by a crazed director who decided to use real-life monsters in the name of art.

I despised Bo. Her father, Tump Kooniart, was a powerful agent, which was the only reason she and her brother were cast in the film. He was working in league with the director and Lord Loss. He thought the Demonata would spare him and his children. He thought wrong.

Bo was a spoilt, snobbish, sneering little brat. But when the demons ran riot and our lives hung in the balance, she acted selflessly, heroically. We might not have escaped without her help. Then, rather than follow us to freedom, she went back to try and rescue her father and brother.

I assumed Bo had been killed along with the hundreds of others who died, but Lord Loss must have spared her and taken her to his own universe, where he could torture her at his leisure.

When I realised Bo was still alive, trapped in that chamber of nightmares, I felt that I was directly to blame. Lord Loss authorised the attack on the film set in order to wreak revenge on Dervish and me. All those people died because of us. Bo is in torment because of *me*. I feel compelled to cross and break her out. But I don't dare, not until I've decided what to do about Bec. I might get away with one sneak attack on Lord Loss's kingdom, but never two.

The tour continues. Bec is quiet for the most part and looks gloomy, but I'm sure I'd look a lot worse in her position. How can she walk alongside that beast so calmly? Unless she's considering joining him…

I wish they'd have a conversation about it. In movies, the villain always gives his plan away by talking too much and revealing his secrets. But Lord Loss never discusses Bec's state of mind. There's no mention of the war between the Demonata and mankind, or what role he wants Bec to play in it.

The pair enter a room filled with chess boards and the demon master's face lights up. After our showdown in Slawter, he said I'd spoilt chess for him, but that's not true. He's still a fanatic, as evidenced by the care he takes of the boards and the way he describes them to Bec, telling her where he got them, the games he's played, the opponents he's faced.

"Did you carve any of these yourself?" Bec asks.

"No," he says morosely. "I started to, several times, but chess is like a religion for me. Whenever I sat down to make a set of my own, it felt like sacrilege."

Bec looks around at the array. She seems to be searching for one in particular. "What about the original Board?" she asks eventually.

"Why do you seek that?" Lord Loss's eyes narrow.

"I don't *seek* it," Bec smiles. "I'd just like to see it again. I know you took it from the cave after Drust died."

"You mean after you killed him," Lord Loss murmurs.

Bec stiffens, then tilts her head. "Aye."

Lord Loss clicks several fingers. A demon with five legs and a neck like a giraffe scurries away and returns with a crystal board, the first that was ever made on this world. According to Kernel, it was a tool of the Old Creatures. They used it to help mankind evolve.

Lord Loss holds the Board reverentially, then passes it to Bec. She treats it the same careful way he did, examining it closely. "It's amazing," she whispers. "I can feel the power, so different to ours."

"The magic of the Old Creatures," Lord Loss sniffs. "It's nothing special."

Bec hides a smirk behind the Board. I don't see what all the fuss is about. It's just another chess board as far as I'm concerned. I know it has magical properties, but I've seen a hundred more fascinating objects in my travels.

Bec hands the Board back to Lord Loss. The dream's almost over. I'm anticipating the end. But before the conclusion, there will be one last conversation.

"I'd like to enter it," Bec says.

"Why?" Lord Loss snaps suspiciously.

"I know of its splendours. Kernel went there once, many years ago. I want to experience them for myself."

Lord Loss is frowning. "You cannot escape me in there," he growls. "If you think you can tap into the magic of the Old Creatures and use it against me, you are gravely mistaken."

"That's not my intention," Bec says calmly. "You said earlier that you didn't want me to lie. So I'll tell you truthfully, I *do* have a secret reason for wanting to enter the Board. But it has nothing to do with escape."

Bec's eyes flicker. It's the furtive look of someone who suspects they're being watched, who wants to go somewhere private to discuss dark deeds. I think, as I've thought every time I see her eyes move, *Does she know I'm here?*

This is no normal dream. I'm certain these events are real, that they happened, are happening or will happen in the future. I suspect my ability to follow Bec through the castle is the work of the Kah-Gash. If I'm correct, maybe it's working through her too and she can sense me watching.

Maybe Lord Loss senses Bec's nervousness too, because after a brief pause, he accepts her request. "Very well. I will grant your wish, as I grant the wishes of all who are honest with me."

The pair go rigid and their eyes frost over. Their souls have entered the Board. If I knew for sure that this was happening in the present, I'd cross immediately and strike while the demon master's soul was absent. I'd kill him where he stood, and that would be the end of lowly Lord Loss.

But time works differently in the demon universe. This might be something that took place in the past, or that hasn't happened yet. I'd be a fool if I rushed in without knowing for certain that the demon master was distracted and defenceless.

I wait for the scene to fade and the dream to pass. It always does at this point. I'll slip into unconsciousness and won't stir until morning. A few more seconds and...

Nothing happens. For several minutes I watch the motionless pair, Lord Loss cradling the Board, Bec leaning close to him, both with their eyes half closed. I wonder if the scene has frozen, like when a DVD sticks, but then a demon slinks by and I realise time *is* passing.

For the first time ever, the dream is different. I don't know if that's a good or a bad sign. I try looking away from the Board, but my gaze is fixed. I start to fidget, wondering if this is a trap, if my mind will remain stuck here while my body shrivels up and dies. Have I been lured in and ensnared? If so, I can't see any way out. I'm helpless in this dream zone.

Time drags on. Hard to tell how long. I wish I had a watch. I become more certain that I've walked into a trap, that I'm going to perish slowly and stupidly. Then, as I'm cursing myself for being so gullible…

Bec blinks and Lord Loss clutches the Board to his chest. The pair breathe out and smile shakily at each other. "Interesting," Lord Loss mutters.

"Isn't it?" Bec grins.

"I will need time to ponder and reflect."

"Of course."

"If you're wrong… if it doesn't go the way you think…" His face darkens.

"It's a risk no matter which way you play it." Bec shrugs, then turns. "I can find my own way back."

She walks out of the room and I automatically trail

her, thinking to myself, *What the hell?* Lord Loss stays where he is, fondling the Board, staring after Bec with an unreadable expression.

→I stay with Bec as she weaves through rooms and corridors of webs, eventually ending up back in the bedroom where she started. She looks exhausted. I think more time passed for them inside the Board than it did for me as an onlooker. But what did they do in there? What did they talk about? It sounded like Bec made some sort of an offer to Lord Loss. But *what?*

She undresses and wipes the make-up from her face. Steps into her nightgown, then returns to the seat by the table and stares into the mirror. She looks doubtful, like she's gambled everything and doesn't know which way the dice will roll. For a moment I believe she's tried to persuade Lord Loss to throw in his lot with us. Perhaps she's been playing him all along, waiting until the time was right to sign him up for our side. I have crazy thoughts of the demon master doing a Darth Vader and joining our side to stop the evil Emperor of Death.

But this isn't *Star Wars*, and almost as soon as the childish hope forms, reality knocks a thousand holes in it.

"I reached my conclusion sooner than I anticipated."

Bec turns. Lord Loss has entered the bedroom. He's

smiling. She stands and walks over to him, trembling. "You've decided?"

"Yes." He leans down and kisses her. For a second I think he means to draw the life from her lips, but this is a kiss of passion, not destruction.

"I admire your daring and cunning," he murmurs. "We will proceed as you suggested. If you can find the lodestones, I'll help open the tunnels."

Bec throws her arms around Lord Loss and hugs him. As she does, I'm torn from my dream. Snapping awake, I hurl myself from my makeshift bed in the hospital, smash a fist into the wall, then howl at the ceiling like a madman.

HOME SWEET HOME

→I cancel my plans to travel to the city where the next crossing is due. Instead I send the werewolves, under the guidance of Prae Athim and her Lambs. They'll have to handle this one without me.

I catch a separate plane, with Kernel, Kirilli, Moe and Curly. I leave Larry with the other werewolves to keep them in line. I'm twitching with nerves, unable to forget the dream for an instant, wondering about the pact Bec made with Lord Loss, recalling the way she embraced him. The memory chews me up inside. I wish I'd gone after her as soon as she was kidnapped and killed that damn priestess from the past.

On the plane, I tell Kernel and Kirilli about the dream. It's essential they know about the threat, in case anything happens to me.

Kernel hits the roof. "Why didn't you tell us before?" he roars. I claim innocence – until last night, there was no hint that Bec might betray us – but he doesn't buy that. "You should have told us anyway. You know better than to hide something this important."

There's nothing I can say to defend myself, because he's right.

Moe and Curly hate planes. They cower in their seats, as far from the windows as they can squirm, whining at the noise of the engines and every bump caused by turbulence. All of the werewolves hate flying. They only suffer it because they know there will be rich pickings at the other end.

At least we don't have to bother with connecting flights. The governments and armies of the world work hand-in-hand with the Disciples now. A jet is put at my disposal as soon as I ask for one. It makes getting around a hell of a lot easier.

Kernel is still griping as we hit the runway, saying he warned me about Bec, that this wouldn't be happening if I'd listened and that I should return him to the demon universe and set him free. He insists we're wasting our time trying to thwart the plans of Bec and Lord Loss. Although many of the world's lodestones – reservoirs of ancient, magical power – were destroyed or drained long ago, an unknown number still exist.

"The locations of most are a mystery to us," Kernel says, "but Beranabus knew about a few stones that he either wasn't able to destroy or wanted to keep intact. He never told us where they were, but Bec absorbs the memories of everyone she touches, and she spent a lot of time with Beranabus. She'll lead Lord Loss to the lodestones and we can't stop her. We're done for."

Again, I can't argue. The more potent lodestones can be used to open a tunnel between the demon universe and ours. The Demonata can cross without limits through such tunnels and stay here as long as they remain open, which could be years or even longer — some can stay open until the end of time itself. If Bec and Lord Loss get hold of those stones, this war is finished.

But we have to *try* to stop them. I despise Kernel's defeatist attitude. And we're not entirely helpless — if Kernel's eyes are restored, he can target Bec and we can maybe kill her before they get going. But I don't say that to him because it would set him off on another rant.

A helicopter is waiting for us when we disembark. Again, a perk of the job. I've never ridden in a helicopter for fun. I'm always zipping off to one fight or another. I'd like to take a scenic flight one day, but the way things are stacking up against us, I doubt that will ever happen.

Once we're all strapped in, we take off. Curly and Moe howl happily and stick their heads out of the windows. As much as they hate planes, they love helicopters. Werewolves — go figure!

It's a short flight, and although Kernel carries on with his tirade, I tune him out, thinking about the past, my history, all that I've lost and left behind. I haven't been back here since the night Bill-E died — the night I killed him. Scores of dark memories bob to the surface, mixed in with happier recollections.

We hit the outskirts of Carcery Vale and skim over the houses, shops and schools. They look unfamiliar from up high. It's evening and the streets are quiet, with only a few people strolling or driving around. We might be facing the end of the world, but life carries on as normal for the most part.

The plan was to head straight to the cave, but on an impulse I lean forward, tap the pilot's shoulder and point him in a different direction.

"What are you doing?" Kernel asks, feeling the helicopter bank around.

"I want to visit the mansion first."

"What's the point? If we're going to do this, let's crack on and do it. We don't have time for trips down memory lane."

I ignore him and watch intently as we home in on the massive house a few kilometres outside the town. This is where I lived with Dervish after my parents were slaughtered. It's the last place I was able to call home. Probably the last place I'll *ever* be able to call home.

We touch down in the large courtyard and the pilot kills the engines. Curly and Moe are first out, sniffing the ground, marking their territory, making sure it's safe for their leader. I slide out next, leaving Kirilli to help

Kernel down. The pilot stays with the helicopter.

I stare up at the gigantic house, recalling a variety of memories, a mix of good and bad. The glass in the windows has been shattered by gunfire, but otherwise the building looks much the way it did when I cast my final look back on that sad night.

The spare key isn't under the pot to the left of the front doors and I prepare to break in. But when I try the doors, they're not locked. Entering, I call "Hello?" but nobody answers. There are no noises apart from the creakings of the house.

As the others follow me in, I spot scores of bullet holes in the walls and ornate old staircase that is the spine of the house, and much of the furniture has been torn to pieces. On Dervish and Bec's last night here, they were attacked by soldiers in the employ of Antoine Horwitzer, a rogue Lamb.

"It smells stale," Kirilli says, limping along behind me.

"It's been deserted for ages," I tell him.

"Not that long," Kernel mutters.

"Perhaps it's mourning the death of its owner," Kirilli says. "Houses have feelings too. They don't live and feel like we do, but they absorb part of the spirit of those who inhabit them."

"Weirdo," Kernel grunts and I laugh with him. Kirilli shrugs and shuffles off to explore.

"Do you want to come with me?" I ask Kernel,

feeling faint traces of the bond that once existed between us.

"No," he sighs, moving to a window and standing by it as if he can see out. "I'll stay here and admire the moonlight. You go cheer up the house. Grubbs?" he adds softly as I turn to pad up the stairs. "I know how much this place means to you. Take your time."

"Thanks," I smile.

I head for Dervish's office first. This is the room he spent most of his time in, where he worked, plotted and relaxed. It's been shot up badly, but it still reeks of my uncle. His books lie scattered across the floor. His computers have been blown to smithereens, but I can picture him hunched over the screens, frowning as he read about some old spell or other. And maybe it's just my imagination, but I'm sure I can smell the musty stench of his feet — he loved to kick his shoes off in here, but he wasn't great at changing his socks regularly.

I want to say something to mark the occasion and pay homage to the memory of my dead uncle. But everything I think of seems trite and clichéd. I was never the best with words. They've failed me often in the past, and they fail me again now. In the end I just pat the back of the chair where Dervish used to sit.

I visit the hall of portraits and run my gaze over the faces of the dead, all our family members who have perished over the centuries, most as a result of lycanthropy. I'd like to add photos of Dervish and Bill-E to the rows of frames, but I don't have any on me. I could fetch a couple from the study, but I don't want to go back there.

I settle for writing their names in the dusty glass of a couple of the larger pictures, along with their dates of birth and death. Pausing, I smile and add a line under Dervish's name. "Died fighting the good fight." A longer pause, then, with no smile, I write under Bill-E's name, "Killed by his half-brother."

Let future visitors make of those epitaphs what they will.

→My old bedroom. I lie on the bed and sigh happily. Wouldn't it be great if I woke up now and everything had been a bad dream? I could have a good chuckle with Dervish and Bill-E, tell them how they'd been killed off, play up the grisly circumstances of their deaths, stick some hair around my face to make me look like a werewolf.

But it's not a dream and I can't pretend that it is. Too much about me is different, not least the fact that my legs stick way out over the end of the bed, far past the point where my feet used to stop.

I look through my old clothes and CDs, remembering a time when such things were important. I go to the toilet and think about Reni Gossel, Loch's sister, as I'm washing my hands. We would have become an item if the world hadn't spun off its rails. Maybe I should look her up, kiss her farewell, tell her something corny like I'll always hold her dear to my heart.

Then I catch sight of my twisted face in the mirror, the fangs, the bloodshot eyes, the tufts of coarse hair, the way one ear sticks out about six centimetres higher than the other. Some boyfriend I'd make in this state! Best to give Reni a wide berth. I'd terrify her if she saw me like this and I didn't come back to freak out my ex-girlfriend.

Why did *you come?* the Kah-Gash asks. The voice of the ancient weapon usually only speaks to me when the situation is dire. But its curiosity has been aroused.

"To say goodbye," I tell it. "I want to see the old place one last time. Kirilli was right — houses are like people. I want to let the mansion know how much it meant to me."

Very peculiar, the Kah-Gash says drily. *I thought you had put such quaint human ways behind you forever.*

"I thought so too," I mutter, then wink at myself in the mirror. "But I'm glad that I haven't."

I head for the ground floor. The others are drinking in the kitchen, Kernel and Kirilli from glasses, Curly and Moe from bowls. I tell them I'll be a few more minutes, then steel myself and open the door to the cellar.

Dervish's wine collection — his pride and joy — is a

mess. Lots of the racks have been knocked over and hundreds of bottles lie smashed on the ground, their contents spilt. I was never bothered about wine, but I feel sad viewing the destruction, knowing how rare some of the bottles were and how much they meant to my uncle.

Stepping carefully through the wreckage, I open the secret panel that nestles behind a false wine rack. I trudge down a long tunnel to the house's second, secret cellar. This was where Dervish cast his more dangerous spells and communed with Lord Loss.

There's magic in this room. I never asked Dervish where it came from. Maybe it has something to do with the lodestone buried in the cave not far from here.

I use my power to light the candles dotting the walls. The room flickers into view and my eyes are drawn to the remains of a steel cage. We kept Bill-E in it when he was turning. I was a prisoner there too for a while. Hard to believe such puny bars could ever have held the likes of me. But I wasn't a monster in those days.

I wander round the cellar, looking at the books, the scraps of burnt paper, the chess pieces left over from when we challenged Lord Loss. I never liked this room, but it doesn't scare me as it once did. Nothing really scares me now. Except the thought of Bec collaborating with the demons, or me destroying the universe. Heh!

A book among the debris catches my attention.

There's a picture of Lord Loss on the cover. I pick it up and study the demon master. My lips curl. Of all the monsters, this is the one I hate most. I'd give anything to look in his eyes and laugh as I throttled the life out of him. I'd maybe even accept defeat in the war if I could settle the score with this lowly one first.

As I'm thinking about Lord Loss, the picture moves. His eyes come into focus and he leers. "Grubitsch..." he whispers. "Come to me... Grubitsch..."

"In my own good time," I growl.

The face presses out of the page like a 3D image. "Give yourself... to me. Let me end... it all now. No more pain. No more sorrow. No more—"

"—of your bull," I snort, then roar at the book. Lord Loss's face wrinkles, then flattens. Seconds later it's just a picture and his voice is gone. I toss the book aside. "That's enough nostalgic crap," I huff and head back to the house, all my goodbyes completed, ready for business.

ROCK ON

→We walk to the cave, leaving the pilot and the helicopter at the house. I know this forest so well, even having been away so long, that I could go through it with my eyes closed and never stumble. I savour the familiar sights and smells, taking it all in. I sense things kicking into high gear. This could be my last quiet night for a long time, maybe ever.

When we reach the place the cave is, there's no sign of an entrance.

"What's happening?" Kernel asks, sniffing the air uneasily.

"The hole's been filled," I tell him.

"Then we've nothing to worry about," he says. "They can't do anything with the lodestone unless they can access the cave from this side."

"I'm not taking any chances." I grab Kernel's hand and squeeze hard. As he yelps, I use the power of the Kah-Gash to unite with him. Our potential skyrockets and I draw energy from everything around us, and from the reservoir of magic beneath our feet.

With my free hand, I point at the spot where the hole used to be and bark a command. Rocks and dirt – along with lots of insects and a few startled rabbits – fly into the air in a funnel and arc over our heads.

Kernel trembles when I release him. "How did you do that?" he croaks. "You took power from me without my permission."

"I'm the trigger," I remind him. "The guy who fires the Kah-Gash into life. I don't need permission."

"So you can steal from me whenever you like," Kernel snarls, relations between us deteriorating as swiftly as they'd started to improve.

"Don't have a heart attack," I mutter, then scramble down the hole into the gloom of the subterranean world.

Kirilli helps Kernel as we climb down a steep wall. Moe and Curly flank them, growling softly, wary of this underground den. I'd be happy to descend in the dark, but Kirilli creates a ball of light. "There," he beams. "That's much better."

As he says that, his prosthetic foot slips and he drops. A yell escapes his lips and his eyes widen with alarm. But before he can plummet to his death, Moe grabs his left arm. The werewolf braces himself and clings to the wall as Kirilli jolts about. Once the startled magician has regained his wits – along with his grip – Moe lets go.

"He saved my life," Kirilli gasps, looking like he's

about to be sick. "These beasts are becoming more human every day."

"Don't bet on it," I grunt. "He only kept you alive in case he gets hungry later."

Kirilli chuckles weakly. "You're joking, right, Grubbs?" I carry on climbing down. "*Grubbs?*"

→The cave hasn't changed since the night Bill-E died. I can still appreciate its spectacular beauty, the amazing array of stalagmites and stalactites, the unusual formations, the waterfall cascading from one of the walls. That surprises me. After everything that happened, and all the wonders I've seen in the demon universe, I thought I'd be immune to the charms of the cave. But it thrills me almost as much now as when I first discovered it with Bill-E and Loch.

"Impressive," Kirilli murmurs, strolling through the fields of stalagmites. "I did a bit of potholing in my younger days. This is a splendid fissure. I'm sure it's the start of a chain of caves. If I had the proper equipment, I'd love to explore fully."

"We're not here to map cave systems," I growl, marching over to the waterfall. I squint at the wall around it. There's a thin crack which was once much larger. That was where the tunnel would have opened if the demons had been successful.

"Kernel," I call. He approaches warily, guided by

Kirilli. I gouged out his eyes in a cave. I'm sure he's thinking about that now, wondering if I plan to slice off any more body parts. "I want to link up with you again. Do I have your *permission?*"

"You'd do it even if I refused," Kernel sneers, but sticks out a hand.

Using the Kah-Gash, I power up, then roar at the cave wall, the same way that I roared at the picture of Lord Loss in the cellar. The rock quivers, like it would in an earthquake. The crack splits further, widening until it's a two-metre high chasm. I let the roar die away and the wall stops shaking, but the gap remains.

"Do you think this might be part of Bec's plan?" Kernel asks as I step forward. I freeze and glance back. He's smiling angelically. This isn't something he just thought of. He's been saving it to hit me with at the most distracting moment.

"What are you talking about?" I snap.

"Maybe she orchestrated the dream," he says sweetly. "For all we know, the other lodestones might not be suitable. Maybe they can only manipulate this one and she needed you to clear the way."

I stare hatefully at the bald teenager. Right now, I'm glad I popped his eyes. I just wish I'd ripped his tongue out too.

"I guarantee one thing," I say stiffly. "If they attack,

and I think all is lost, I'll toss you to my werewolves before I die."

Kernel laughs, then sticks out his hand again. "Lead on, sweet prince."

"Get stuffed," I spit, leaving him for Kirilli. Tensing, I crouch, then jump and grab hold of the bottom of the crack. Dragging myself up, I peer into the darkness. I can't see or hear anything, but Kernel's warning has unsettled me and I stand guard as the others climb, not wanting to venture further without back-up.

When we're all gathered in the mouth of the tunnel, we advance. It's hotter than the cave, and even though it's wide enough for a couple to walk side by side, I keep imagining the walls grinding shut, pulping us to mincemeat. Kirilli and Kernel are nervous too, while Moe and Curly whine unhappily as they trudge along reluctantly.

Eventually the tunnel opens out into another cave. There's a lake of calm, clear water covering most of the floor. In the centre stands an island of bones, on top of which rests a large, jagged chunk of rock — the lodestone.

"I'm not a good swimmer," Kirilli says uncertainly.

"I doubt if it's deep," I say, striding into the water. Even with my hairy legs, it feels cold.

"Should we undress?" Kirilli asks.

"Don't bother."

"But if we have to walk around all night in wet clothes…"

"You're a mage," I remind him. "You can dry them off once we get out."

"Oh," he says brightly. "I forget sometimes." Chuckling, he leads Kernel into the lake. His chuckles turn to yelps when he feels the icy bite of the water, but he presses on. Curly and Moe start to follow. Then Moe splashes Curly. She yelps and splashes him back. Within moments they're involved in a water fight, rolling around, wrestling and dunking each other, barking like a pair of puppies.

I reach the island and climb on to the mound of bones. A brittle skull cracks beneath my feet. I almost apologise, but there's no point. The person this belonged to passed far beyond the need for apologies centuries before I was born.

Kernel and Kirilli climb out of the lake as I study the rock in the middle of the bones. It's rectangular, rough around the edges. A skeleton is propped against it, kneeling, its skull resting on the top. I guess these are the remains of someone whose throat was slit over the rock — lodestones need blood to thrive.

"What's it like?" Kernel asks.

"Nothing special. I've seen better in the local quarry." I push the skeleton out of the way and rub my hands together. "Down to business. Beranabus simply broke the lodestone on the ship, right? No spells or magic required, just brute force?"

"This might be different," Kernel says. "I think it's a more powerful stone."

"Only one way to find out." I grab hold of the rock. I'm expecting a shock of energy to shoot through me, but although I can feel the buzz of Old magic in the stone, it doesn't affect me. I let my fingers wander and find cracks and holds. Then I take a firm grip and strain, trying to snap the rock in two.

Nothing happens. I release the stone and scowl. "Think you're tough?" I growl. "You won't get the better of Grubbs Grady." I get hold of it again and strain once more.

"He's talking to rocks now," Kernel says.

"A definite lunatic," Kirilli purrs.

I ignore them and brace my muscles. The stone continues to resist. Losing patience, I pick it up, look around, then plough into the water, holding the rock over one shoulder. My legs buckle and I use magic to steady them. Moe and Curly gawp at me as I stagger past. The lodestone weighs me down, even though I'm using magic to support it. A few more seconds and it will drive me under the water. That wouldn't be the best way to go — pinned beneath a stone to drown.

With a savage curse, I swing the lodestone around, raise it over my head, then hurl it at the wall of the cave.

The rock slams into the wall and shatters. Shards litter the floor, and chunks bounce off and rain down on the underground lake. The werewolves howl at the echoing retorts and the cave fills with waves of noise. I crawl out of the lake, pick up the larger fragments of the lodestone and hammer them into the wall or off each other, reducing the rock to dust. This is one stone Bec and Lord Loss won't be able to use. No tunnel will ever be opened in Carcery Vale again.

When I'm done, I lean against the wall and look around, panting. Kernel and Kirilli are wading through the lake. Moe and Curly have climbed out and are drip-drying. The island of bones looks far less menacing now. I think about dismantling it and scattering the bones. I don't have time to bury them all, but I could hide them in the lake, grant the dead at least that small measure of privacy.

As I'm deciding whether or not to set to work on the island, I hear footsteps in the tunnel. I spring away from the wall and land in the lake close to where Kernel and Kirilli were about to step out. "Wait!" I hiss, holding up a hand for silence. I listen closely, hoping I was wrong about the footsteps. But a few seconds later I hear them again. Two sets, edging closer slowly, cautiously.

"Company?" Kernel whispers.

"Trouble most likely." I bark softly at Moe and Curly. Obeying my command, they move to the mouth of the tunnel and take up position, one on either side.

"Shall I douse the light?" Kirilli asks. He's trembling. It might be from the chill of the water, though I suspect fear plays more of a part.

"No," I tell him. "When I give the order, intensify it and direct the rays at whatever comes through. If they have eyes, maybe we can blind them."

"You're good at that," Kernel mutters sarcastically.

We fall silent. The footsteps draw closer. Then I see shadows. Two separate figures, one tall and skinny, the other shorter but broad. The tall, skinny one might be the shadow of Lord Loss, but the other can't be Bec. Not unless she's chosen a new form, like Nadia Moore did when she joined the demon master.

Their feet come into view. I see boots and the hems of trousers. They both look human. Soldiers perhaps, sent to assassinate us? Mages? Potholers like the young Kirilli Kovacs? Some chance of that!

The pair pause, perhaps sensing trouble. Then the broader one shrugs and steps forward quickly, the taller one taking a hasty stride to keep up. Curly and Moe howl and leap, claws extended.

"No!" I roar and they wheel away instantly.

The two humans were raising guns in self-defence, but now they lower them and stare at us.

"Who is it?" Kernel hisses, fingers twitching. "What's going on?"

"It's me," the broad one says.

"And me," the lankier one adds.

"Shark?" Kernel gasps.

"Yeah," the soldier grunts.

"And Timas Brauss," the computer whizz says.

Shark looks at the werewolves, the island of bones, the shattered lodestone and the three of us shivering in the water. Then he grins. "So," he drawls, "have you missed me?"

SHARK ATTACK

→The last time I saw Shark was just after we escaped from Wolf Island. He'd been mauled by werewolves. Any normal person would have died from his wounds, but Shark is as stubborn as they come. He refused to roll over and die.

He's still in bad shape. His left ear was bitten off and a raw-looking stump remains. He can see out of his right eye, but only just — the flesh around it is scarred and pink. All four fingers on his left hand were severed, leaving the thumb looking lonely and strange. The thumb and index finger on his right hand are gone too. And he's wearing a brace from his waist to just beneath his chest.

"You look like hell," I roar happily, picking him up and swinging him round.

"Mind the ribs," he wheezes and I immediately put him down. He scowls at me. "You don't look any great shakes yourself. Haven't you heard of razors?"

"No time for shaving. I've been too busy killing demons."

"That's no excuse," he says, then winks with his good eye.

"Hi," Kernel says, shuffling forward and extending a hand.

"How you doing, kid?" Shark asks with unusual kindness, ignoring the hand and giving Kernel a hug.

"Surviving," Kernel sighs.

"I'm Kirilli Kovacs," the stage magician introduces himself, straightening like a soldier presenting himself to an officer. "I'm a Disciple."

"That so?" Shark grunts, running a bemused eye over Kirilli's costume.

"Nobody has to bother with me," Timas says cheerily. "I don't matter."

"Of course you do," I chuckle, moving forward to shake the hand of the tall, thin, red-haired computer genius.

"I was eagerly looking forward to seeing you again," Timas says. "Primarily, I must admit, because of the chance to renew my relationship with the delicious Meera Flame. But I understand she has been taken from us."

"About a month ago," I nod, my smile fading as I recall her grisly death. "She took Juni Swan with her. Blew her into a thousand lumpy pieces."

"Some small comfort," Timas says. "I have been seeking solace in the world of computers, but since Meera, I find it hard to summon up the same enthusiasm as before. I think I might be in mourning. Or perhaps it's just that I changed my diet recently."

Kirilli raises an eyebrow. I smile and whirl my finger around beside my head.

"What have you two been up to?" I ask. "It feels like years since Wolf Island."

"I've been recovering," Shark says gruffly, hating to admit to his wounds.

"And I've been playing nursemaid," says Timas.

"I wanted to join up with you earlier, but my doctor wouldn't let me," Shark complains. "She kept me sedated. I'd be there still if she hadn't been eaten by a demon. Her replacement was less concerned about me."

"Are you sure you're OK?" I frown. "I don't want you dropping dead on us."

"Some hope! I've been in a couple of fights already. I wanted to limber up before I tracked you down, make sure everything was in working order. As dozens of dead demons would tell you if they could talk — it is."

"How do you fight with so few fingers?" Kirilli asks.

Shark bends his thumb. "I gouge." Kirilli laughs, but stops when he realises Shark is serious. The ex-soldier glares at Kirilli, then turns his gaze to me. "What about you? Anything new I need to know?"

"Yeah. But let's go back to the other cave. The skulls and bones are giving me the creeps."

"You're getting soft," Shark snorts, but follows me up the tunnel to the cave of natural wonders.

As we settle down close to the waterfall, we fill Shark in on all that's been going on. Kirilli tells him what happened on the ship of zombies. Kernel gives him a quick rundown of his trip across the universe with the Old Creatures. Then I describe our battle with Death and the demons. When I get to the bit about Kernel's eyes, Shark interrupts forcefully.

"What the hell do you mean?" he shouts, staring from me to Kernel. "I assumed some demon blinded him. Are you seriously telling me *you* did it?"

"I had to," I mutter. "He was going to leave."

"So what?" Shark roars. "He's one of us. You never turn on your own."

"See?" Kernel smiles tightly. "That's what I've been saying for a month."

"You don't understand." I hate the way Shark looks at me. "We're up against *Death*. We can't beat it by normal means. Our only hope is the Kah-Gash. If Kernel leaves, we're finished. I need him to help me find Bec and unleash the full power of the weapon."

"I keep telling you there's no hope," Kernel snaps. "I won't waste my time fighting a losing battle. Even if you could convince me to stay, we'd still need

Bec, but now that she's turned against us..."

"What are you talking about?" Shark frowns.

I tell him about my dream, how I saw Bec ally herself with Lord Loss. "She vowed to lead him to the lodestones. With the help of those, he can create tunnels between universes."

"What makes you think it wasn't just a nightmare?" Shark asks.

"This was no ordinary dream. It's real, trust me."

"Let me get this straight," Shark says grimly. "You three are the Kah-Gash, the most powerful weapon ever. One of you has turned into a savage werewolf, the second wants to quit and head for the far side of the universe and the third appears to be a traitor. You guys are supposed to be our best hope? Sounds to me like we'd be better off without the whole damn lot of you!"

"We're doomed without the Kah-Gash," I retort. "The demons will wash over us. Earth won't see out the year."

"At least we won't be torn to shreds by our *friends*," Shark fires back at me. "I'd rather be gutted by a demon than stabbed in the back by you."

My temper flares and I lean forward menacingly, growling. Moe and Curly lean in beside me — any foe of mine is an enemy of theirs.

"Easy, doggies," Shark murmurs, making soothing gestures with his mangled hands.

"Don't bait me," I snarl. "I'm not in the mood to be insulted."

"I don't care about your mood," Shark says. "You're putting yourself forward as our champion, but I think the wires in your head have got crossed. Hell, even Timas seems normal compared to you."

"I object to that slur on my good character," Timas says, but Shark ignores him.

"I'm serious, Grubbs. It takes a lot to scare me, but listening to you and seeing that crazy look in your eyes... I'm not sure you're in control any more."

"I'm in full control," I say through clenched teeth. "I didn't enjoy blinding Kernel, but it needed to be done. You've done things you didn't like in the past, so don't get high and mighty with me. I couldn't have faced this as a human — I was weak. Now I'm strong and heartless, like the demons. I can do whatever it takes to save the world."

"You reckon?"

"Yes."

"You're afraid of nothing, ready to face anything the Demonata can throw at you?"

"Damn straight."

Shark smiles icily. "Then why haven't you gone after Bec?"

I blink. "I had to come here first, to destroy the lodestone."

Shark shakes his head. "There are other stones. Bec might be revealing their location to Lord Loss even as we speak. You should have targeted *her*."

"I thought she'd come here," I mumble. "This was one of the most powerful stones. They've used it before, so I figured—"

"Bull!" Shark stops me. "You came here to stall for time because you're afraid. I see it in your eyes, inhuman as they are. You can't mask the traces of fear, not from those who know what to look for."

"What the hell do you know about fear?" I challenge him hotly.

"More than I ever wished to," Shark says softly. "I've lived with real terror, as have most of us who fight these demonic beasts. I've seen horror in my eyes when I've woken in the middle of the night and looked in a mirror. Hell, I've seen it in daylight too. I don't let fear distract me, but it's always there. It's in you too. And I think it's misleading you."

I start to roar a denial... then stop.

He's right. As soon as he says it, I know. Shark isn't the most vocal of people, but he has the knack of hitting the nail clean on the head when he does speak up. I *am* afraid. Not of the Demonata or Bec, but of myself and Juni's prophecy that I'd destroy the world.

I should have gone after Bec once I'd recovered from my wounds. I could have let Kernel leave, just asked him to locate Bec and open a window before he went. I don't truly believe we can defeat Death, even with all three pieces of the Kah-Gash. People wiser than me have said it's impossible and I'm sure they're correct.

I kept Kernel because I was afraid. I didn't want to go after Bec. I preferred to carry on fighting, doing what I was good at — what I was *safe* at. If I'd let Kernel go, it would have meant returning to the demon universe and running the risk of becoming a world-destroying monster. By staying here, I childishly hoped to avoid my destiny. It was a delaying measure, nothing more.

I thought I was Grubbs Grady — superhero. But I've been trying to hide from the universe – from myself – ever since our escape from Lord Loss and his army. Now that Shark's opened my eyes to the truth, I know it's time to stop.

"Kernel, I'm sorry," I mutter. His features crease with surprise. "I was wrong. I was cowardly. I was vicious."

"Keep going," he says.

"I won't hold you any longer," I tell him. "I'll take us back to the Demonata universe and set you free. All I ask is that you locate Bec and open a window for us before you leave. I hope you'll come with us, to rescue her if we can, kill her if we must, but I won't force you. It's your choice."

"If I thought we could make a difference…" he says miserably.

"You don't have to explain." Cracking my fingers, I shoot Shark a wry glance. "You should have been a psychologist."

"And put up with whining brats like you every day? No thanks."

"Excuse me for pointing out the obvious," Kirilli says, "but isn't Kernel the only one of us who can open windows?"

"No," I say. "I can too, just nowhere near as easily as him, and only to a single place in the demon universe. It'll take a few hours, but we're in an area of magic, so I'll be able to tap into that energy."

"There would have been much more magic to tap into if you hadn't destroyed the lodestone," Kirilli murmurs.

I lean in close. "See those werewolves?" I hold my thumb and index finger half a centimetre apart. "I'm this close to serving you to them for lunch."

As Kirilli blanches, I close my eyes and draw all the power that I can from the air. It's fading now that the lodestone's been smashed, but I don't give the stage magician the satisfaction of telling him he was right. Taking a deep breath, I recall the first line of the spells that Beranabus taught me, and begin.

WHO'S THAT GIRL?

→It takes longer than I thought it would to open the window, and it's bloody uncomfortable. Kernel makes it look easy — he just moves his hands around and *voilà*! Even Beranabus was able to open one with relative ease. But I operate more like Dervish did when he once summoned Lord Loss in the cellar at Carcery Vale. Lots of huffing and puffing, incantations, smoke steaming out of my pores.

Finally, after hours of intense effort, a weak-looking window of yellow light forms. "Quick," I groan at the others. "I don't know how long it will last."

Shark is first through. He moves stiffly, hindered by his brace, and looks quite pitiful, but I wouldn't like to be the demon who mistakes Shark for an easy target. Timas hurries after him. I don't think he'll be much use over there — he has all the magical talent of a slug — but he won't abandon Shark.

Kirilli hesitates. "Maybe one of us should stay here to…" He stops, unable to think of a valid excuse.

"Cower?" I suggest.

Kirilli shoots me a dark look, then steps through. I bark at Moe and Curly and they cross. Then I take Kernel's hand and lead him to the window. He pauses in front of it.

"I can still sense the lights," he whispers, moving his head as if he had eyes.

"I bet my window doesn't compare with any of yours."

"No." He smiles. "But you did good for a novice."

He steps into the window, sighing happily, and disappears.

Are you sure this is wise? the Kah-Gash asks as I lift my leg to cross.

I frown. "You don't want me to go?"

My wants are yours, the voice of the ancient weapon says. *I have always served, hiding myself when you wished, fighting your wolfen half when you were afraid of it, helping you take the world back through time when the Demonata crossed. You don't trust me, but I have always respected your desires.*

"Then tell me if this is the right thing to do."

I cannot judge. I merely question your actions because I sense your uncertainty.

"Will I destroy the world if I go after Bec?" I press. "Should I flee with Kernel to the other side of the universe? Throw myself off a cliff?"

I don't know, the Kah-Gash says. *I have no insight into the future. I only know that you mistrust this course, so I ask as your friend — is this wise?*

"You want me to find her, so we can unite and set you free," I challenge it.

I have always been free, the Kah-Gash retorts. *I choose my hosts and stay of my own free will.*

"But you want to be made whole again?"

There's silence for a few seconds. Then a sigh. *The window is about to close. Cross or stay, the choice is yours. But choose now.*

I want to question it further, but there isn't time. Cursing, knowing this might be the worst move I ever make, I throw myself through the window just before it blinks out, severing the link between universes.

→We're in the middle of an oasis. At least that's what it looks like, but on closer examination you can see that the trees are made of bones and scraps of human skin, and the pool at the centre is alive and carnivorous. This was one of Beranabus's favourite spots in this foul universe. He often rested here.

"What kept you?" Shark asks.

At the same time Kernel says, "We shouldn't be here."

"I was tying my shoelaces," I tell Shark, then turn to answer Kernel.

"You're not wearing any shoes," Shark notes.

"You're *so* observant," I respond drily.

"Bec knows about this place," Kernel says, raising his voice. "We stayed here after the attack at the hospital. She might be keeping tabs on it."

"I already thought of that," I scowl, "but this is the only place Beranabus showed me how to get to. I couldn't guide us anywhere else."

"That's stupid," Kernel barks. "The location is irrelevant. You could have—"

"You can stand there and lecture me," I snap, "or you can build a fresh pair of eyes and lead us all to safety."

Kernel grumbles, but turns, sits and focuses on his empty sockets. As he directs magic at the place where his eyes once were, Moe growls and advances on him, followed by Curly.

"Easy," I soothe them. "Change of plan. Let him work on the eyes."

The werewolves stare at me. Sighing, I thicken the cords in my throat and growl their new instructions. Once the message has penetrated, they explore the trees around us, chasing each other through them, munching strips of flesh and breaking off bones to gnaw.

"Is the water safe to drink?" Kirilli asks, stepping towards the dark pool.

"It's not water," I tell him. "If you get close, it will pull you in and eat you."

"Nice," Shark grunts. "You know how to pick the perfect spot for a date."

"Are there any computers here?" Timas asks, studying the trees.

"This is the universe of the Demonata," I remind him. "The home of magic and monsters, nightmares and madness. Of course there are no bloody computers!"

"Why not?" he asks. "Maybe demons like to surf the web too."

I roll my eyes, but inside I'm smiling. They're a weird, wounded lot, but I can rely on every one of them to stand by me in a fight. Well, maybe not Kirilli if his yellow streak kicks in… or Timas if he gets bored… or Kernel once he takes off for his rendezvous with the Old Creatures… or Shark if the brace holding his guts in place cracks open…

"What are you grinning at?" Shark asks.

"You wouldn't like it if I told you," I chuckle. To hell with the odds — at least they're my friends. If things go bad, I'd rather die in the company of this bunch of misfits than with anyone else.

→Kernel's still working on his eyes. They're starting to come together. At the moment they look like a runny egg that's been poured back into the two halves of its shell. The rest of us are sitting nearby. Moe and Curly lie by my feet, panting after their playful chase.

I'm in the middle of telling Shark and Timas about Beranabus's soul, how we found it inside the Shadow and freed it, what he told us before he departed. I'm interrupted by choking noises. Glancing over, I spot Curly shaking her head and retching. I grin, figuring she swallowed a bone the wrong way, but then Moe growls and edges away from her. I sense something's wrong.

"Move back," I tell the others. They shuffle away, Kernel too, knowing better than to question me. Moe is snarling, his teeth bared, eyeing Curly darkly.

The female werewolf rolls around, whining and gasping. I howl a question but she either doesn't hear or can't respond. She's clawing at her face. I howl again, trying to calm her, but she staggers to her feet and whirls away, making horrible sounds. She crashes into a tree, rebounds and picks up speed. She's unconsciously heading for the pool. I see the liquid draw towards the edge closest to us. It senses a victim and is getting ready to pounce.

I race after the distressed werewolf and tackle her. She lashes out at me, but feebly, no power in the punch. I get a glimpse of her face and shudder. Her flesh is bubbling as if she's been dunked in a bucket of acid. Her eyes bulge and her tongue swishes madly from one side of her mouth to the other.

"What's wrong with her?" Kirilli yells.

"Damned if I know," I mutter, nudging her away from

the pool, ready to defend myself if she attacks.

Curly lurches to her knees, then throws herself down and buries her face in the soil. She thrashes wildly, sending clouds of dust shooting into the air. She slams her face harder into the ground, as if she wants to destroy it.

Curly screams, squeezes her head, then slumps. Her hands fall away. Her legs shiver, then go still. She lies face down, breathing shallowly, silent. I edge closer, wary, expecting her to leap up and attack. But she's not playing possum. She doesn't move as I poke her with my right foot, or when I kneel beside her and pull her head up by her hair.

There are gasps from the others when they see her face. I frown at them, then rotate her head. As her face swings into view, I see what disturbed them. Her features have altered. There's another face poking out of the flesh and bones. It's still forming, the skin around the cheeks bulging and warping. But I recognise it in spite of all the blood and goo.

"Bec!"

Her eyes snap open and focus on me. I almost drop her and stamp her head into the ground. But that wouldn't achieve anything. This isn't the real Bec, merely a projection. I might as well hear her out. If I do any damage, I'll only hurt Curly.

Bec's lips move and she spits out clumps of Curly's

hairy flesh. She tries to speak. Blood gurgles in her throat and she chokes. Spits it out, then retches. Curly's hand twitches and rises towards her mouth. It's probably just to wipe blood away, but I'm taking no chances. I pin her with a wrestling move and clamp her hands behind her back. There are now only centimetres between my face and Bec's. I draw back slightly, in case she bites.

"You don't look worried," Bec says, her voice rougher than usual, a bit of Curly's growly tone mixed in with it.

"I've seen a lot weirder than this," I shrug.

"Is that really Bec?" Shark barks.

"Quiet," I tell him.

"We should kill her if—"

"Shut up!" I roar.

Bec smiles crookedly. "You've been spying on me. I thought I sensed you, but I wasn't certain until now. You'd be more concerned if my appearance had come as a complete surprise. Will you try to kill me, Grubbs, or do you still hold out hope of reassembling the Kah-Gash?"

"What have you done?" I growl. "Have you pledged yourself to that foul hunk of rotting demon meat?"

"We can't beat them," she sighs. "Everybody realises that except you."

"So we join them instead?" I sneer. "Never. I'd rather die than fight beside the likes of Lord Loss."

"I tried death," Bec says. "It wasn't much fun."

"Are you having more *fun* now?" I want to pound her face to bits, but it wouldn't change anything.

"Enjoyment isn't an issue any longer," Bec says. "I won't become a shrieking harpy like Juni Swan. I take no pleasure from this. But I want to survive. There's no point sacrificing ourselves when the fight has already been lost."

"Of course there is," I protest. "Dying for the people you care about has always been the ultimate point."

"But who do *you* care about?" Bec asks softly. "Your parents and Dervish are dead. Your sister, Bill-E, Meera, Sharmila. Who's left? Who are you fighting for? I think you're only resisting because it's expected. You've never looked around and said, 'I don't have to do this.' Try it, Grubbs. Ask who you fight for. Then tell me I'm wrong for choosing life over a pointless death."

I shake my head. The scary thing is, it's tempting. I could easily accept everything she's said, choose the same way she has, abandon the post of protector that Beranabus saddled me with, ride off into a gleeful, savage sunset with Bec and Lord Loss. I never wanted to be a hero. Why die miserably when I could live triumphantly? All it takes is a slight adjustment in the way I think, and...

"No," I whisper, putting temptation behind me.

Bec smiles. "I almost had you for a moment, didn't I?"

"Almost," I admit, chuckling wolfishly.

"Grubbs," Kernel says.

"Not now," I snap, staying focused on Bec. "What else do you have to say? I doubt you went to all this trouble just to tempt me."

"I wanted to warn you," Bec says. "I feel I owe you that much."

"Warn me of what?" I frown.

"Grubbs!" Kernel yells. "A window is opening. I can feel it."

"*That*," Bec says sadly. Then her face freezes, turns a paler shade and starts to disintegrate.

I drop Curly's head, lurch to my feet and scan the surrounding area. I can't see anything, but I don't doubt Kernel. "Your eyes!" I shout.

"Not finished," he says.

"Do I have time to open a window back to Earth?"

He shakes his head.

"Then get ready to fight."

As soon as I've said it, a dark, grey window snaps into existence and hordes of Lord Loss's familiars spill through. They overrun the oasis in seconds, screaming and spitting, bearing down on us in a blast of frothing, demonic hellfire.

UNSTILL WATERS

→I'm driven to the ground by gibbering demons, but back on my feet moments later, scattering the beasts with a burst of magic. I look over their heads, searching for Lord Loss. The familiars don't bother me – I'm far stronger than them – but their master is a different matter. If he crosses, we're in real trouble.

But there's no sign of the eight-armed sentinel of sorrow. Demons are spilling through the window, but only underlings. Maybe he's saving his grand appearance for the end, to make more of an impression. Or maybe he's wary of Kernel and me, and wants to see how we fare against his familiars first.

Several small, furry demons attack the blind teenager. They have long snouts with sucker-like mouths at the end. I think their orders were to focus on his eyes if he'd reconstructed them.

"Kernel!" I roar.

He bats most of them away and smashes the snouts of

another pair with a karate kick that Bruce Lee would have been proud of.

An octopus-like demon launches itself at me and wraps its tentacles around my throat. I bite through a couple – sushi… yum! – then grab one and yank the demon in hard. I head-butt it and send a thousand volts of magical electricity crackling through its brain. The octopus drops, its remaining tentacles withering. Stepping on to its carcass, I bound into the air and rain a sheet of fire down on the demons closest to me. Their screams are music to my ears.

Kirilli is warding off monsters, firing weak bolts of energy at them, yelping and staggering around anxiously. He'd be a good fighter if he could forget about his fear and focus. Even in this agitated state, he's powerful enough to drive back the demons who attack him. His biggest worry will be tripping over his own feet and leaving himself open to assault.

Timas and Shark are fighting side by side, with their bare hands and feet. Shark prefers the old-fashioned ways, punching, kicking, throttling. He likes to get his hands – well, thumb! – dirty. Timas isn't able to do anything magical, but he's fast and sharp, and although he can't kill the demons, he repels them artfully and calmly. He wouldn't last long by himself, but with Shark by his side he holds his own.

Moe is slaughtering the stampeding creatures with

delight. It's Christmas come early as far as he's concerned. He rips throats open, tears off limbs, disembowels viciously. His only regret is that he can't stop to feast on the spoils.

Curly staggers to her feet, her face a broken mess. She lasts about three miserable seconds, mewing painfully and trying to push the pieces of her cheeks back into place. Then demons drag her down and finish her off. A sad end for a fine warrior.

Five large, burly beasts slide through the window. They're giants, four metres tall. I get the sense that they're tough as rocks, but not much on the magical front. If these are the fiercest foes we have to deal with, it will be a breeze. It'll take a while, but we can wipe out this crowd without having to go into second gear.

I don't get it. There must be more to come, or maybe there's a hidden threat among the smaller, yapping demons. Lord Loss wouldn't waste his familiars on us. He'd happily sacrifice them if he thought they could wear us down and leave us ripe for the picking, but these guys wouldn't even test a run-of-the-mill mage.

As I'm trying to figure out the method behind his apparent madness, the giants grab the smaller demons and lob them through the air into the pool of living liquid. It bubbles and seethes, swiftly stripping the skin and burning through the bones of the familiars, dissolving the shells of the more heavily protected.

"What's going on?" Shark yells, throwing a poodle-like demon with four heads at one of the giants, who grabs it like a frisbee and spins it off into the pool, where it only has time to bark twice before its tongue is fricasséed by the foaming liquid. "They're doing our work for us."

"Maybe they're on our side," Kirilli squeals happily. "They think we're going to win the war, so they've betrayed their master and are trying to prove themselves worthy of our mercy."

"I doubt it," I mutter, head-butting another octopus demon, watching warily as more demons are thrown into the pool. The liquid's glowing with different hues of demon blood. I've a bad feeling about this.

As another demon is tossed into the ravenous pool, the liquid throbs. The giants kneel in front of the pool and bow their heads. Some of the demons attack them spitefully, but the giants ignore their blows and wait patiently, like monks praying at an altar.

The liquid throbs again, then rises up in a circular sheet of dripping darkness. It looms over the kneeling giants and lesser demons. For a mad moment I think it's going to form legs and stride towards us. But instead it crashes down over the giants and those around them, breaks like a wave, then re-forms and rises again, even larger than before.

The sheet of lethal liquid sloshes forward several

metres, by means I can't work out, then collapses over another pack of demons, smothering and dissolving them, expanding again as it pulls itself up to its full, majestic height.

The pool is getting closer to us. Most of the demons have realised they're in trouble. Some try to attack the moving pool, only to be scorched and torn apart. The smarter beasts flee for their lives.

Shark, Timas, Kirilli and Moe have clustered around me. They're all staring with disbelief at the aqueous, mobile tower. I call Kernel to our ranks, then prepare a ball of energy, taking power from Kernel and the others. I unleash it at the sheet of liquid. The ball punches a hole through the sheet and sizzles angrily as it shoots out the other side. But then the liquid oozes shut over the rip and the pool sways on, undaunted.

"Bloody Beranabus!" I howl. "He told us the master of this realm had left or been killed. He was wrong. The pool *is* the master. It's been dormant, lacking the power to move, but now that it's been fed enough demons…"

I try a freezing spell, but although part of the pool half-frosts over for a couple of seconds, it doesn't take hold and the killer sheet presses on, destroying more of the demons which I now realise were sent here for the sole purpose of empowering the slumbering behemoth.

"We can't defeat it," I huff, backpedalling.

"Perhaps an evaporation spell?" Kernel suggests.

"Nothing will work. It's a demon master and this is its realm."

"Surely we can outrun it," Kirilli says.

I laugh. "You can always rely on Kovacs to opt for a hasty retreat. But this time he's right. Let's make like sprinters and…"

I draw to a halt. The trees around the perimeter of the oasis are snapping together, bones and flesh linking, forming an unbroken ring. Demons screech and hurl themselves at the bony, fleshy fence, or try to scale it, but are swiftly speared by some of the longer, sharper bones.

"So much for scarpering," Shark sniffs. "What now, oh wise and noble leader?"

"We could offer Kirilli as a sacrifice and hope it leaves the rest of us alone," I murmur, drawing a satisfactory yelp from the terrified stage magician. "Kernel — any luck with those eyes?"

"It'll be a while," he says.

"What's taking you so long?" I growl.

"Bite me," he retorts.

The pool breaks over another group of demons. This time when it rises, it splits into two sheets which glide apart — double trouble.

"A multiplying demon," Timas says. "Fascinating. Based on those it had to devour in order to divide once, and on those who remain… assuming it can split again…" He does a quick head count of the remaining demons. "We might have to face as many as eight clones within the next six minutes."

"We could do with a plan," Shark barks.

"I'm working on it." I look around, weighing up my options. Trying to punch a hole through the wall of bones and flesh is probably our best option. Maybe we could explode a demon against it. But I'm not convinced that will work. Demon masters make many of the rules in their own realms.

If we link, Kernel and I *might* get the better of it in a fight to the death, but again I'm dubious. Even Beranabus avoided direct confrontation with the stronger Demonata on their home turf. We'll be taking an awful risk if we pit ourselves against it.

There's one other option. The words *frying pan* and *fire* leap to mind as soon as I consider it. But if it's a choice between facing a firing squad and jumping off a cliff, I'll always opt for the jump because you might get lucky on the way down.

"Follow me!" I shout, grabbing Kernel's hand and darting forward. I narrowly dodge the pillars of liquid, racing past them as they crash to the ground less than a metre to my left. I head for the spot where the pool used to rest, and where the window that the demons crossed through is still hanging in the air.

"You've got to be joking!" Shark roars. "That leads to Lord Loss's realm!"

"That's where we were heading anyway, wasn't it?" I yell back.

"But the plan was to take him by surprise. If we jump through a window that he made…"

"Hell," I chuckle, "if I was in his shoes, and some nutcase jumped through my window and straight into my arms, it'd sure take *me* by surprise!"

Before Shark can argue, I hit the window of light and throw myself at it, bursting through, bellowing wildly, relishing the insane buzz of my suicidal lunge.

KNIGHTS IN SLIMY ARMOUR

→Nothing but cobwebs. I whirl wildly as the others crash through after me, sure Lord Loss and his minions are hiding in the shadows. But we're alone in a large, bare room. No time to wonder at that. I don't know if the mobile pool can cross after us, but taking no chances, I cast a spell over the window, establishing a shield to block anything else from following.

"Where is he?" Shark growls, casting an uneasy eye around the room.

"I don't know." I try sensing the demon master's presence, but I've never been good at that type of magic.

"Let's get out of here," Kirilli moans.

"Don't be stupid," I snap. "This is where we wanted to get to."

"But it's different now," Kernel says, taking Kirilli's side. "Lord Loss herded us here. It's obviously part of a plan. We'd be crazy to go on."

"That's the way it always is," I shrug. "Lord Loss sets a trap — I blunder into it and hope for the best. So far I've got the better of him. My luck's bound to run out eventually, but there's nothing else I can do. I don't have the brains to outwit him, just the brawn and guts to fight back."

"So you want to walk into his den and take things from there?" Kernel asks.

"Yeah," I grin.

"That's madness."

"Maybe. But in my experience, the cleverer you are, the more ways you find to shoot yourself in the foot. Juni, Davida Haym and Antoine Horwitzer were way smarter than me and each set me up for an elaborate fall. But I'm here and they're dead. Sometimes it pays to be simple."

Kernel frowns. "In a strange way, that almost makes sense."

"Stop talking!" Kirilli shrieks. "Get us out of here!"

"We're not leaving," I growl. "Kernel, how are those eyes coming along?"

"I reckon another ten minutes if we aren't distracted."

"Coolio." I crack my knuckles. "We could wait here, but I think we're better off taking the fight to them."

"Knowing you as well as they do, that's probably what Lord Loss and Bec are counting on," Kernel warns me.

"Good. I'd hate to disappoint them. But there's a personal matter I want to settle first."

"What are you talking about?" Shark scowls.

"You'll see," I mutter, then head out of the room and set off through the castle that I've explored a few dozen times in my dreams.

→Timas is intrigued by the webby mechanisms of the castle. If he had his way, we wouldn't move on until he'd made a full study of each room. But I ignore his pleas to slow down and instead plough on until I find a corridor that I remember from my nightmarish meanderings with Bec and Lord Loss.

Once I've got my bearings, I pick up speed, leading the others through a series of corridors and rooms, down into the dungeon. We encounter none of Lord Loss's familiars. That's weird – this place should be packed with nasty little demons – but I've no time to worry about it. If I don't do anything else right, there's at least one wrong I'm determined to fix. It's a minor matter in the grand scheme of things, but it's important to me.

I'm nearing the door when Kernel stops and says, "Peekaboo!"

I face the bald teenager with the caramel-coloured skin. His bright blue eyes are back in place, little flickers of light dancing across his pupils. He stares at the air around me, smiling widely.

"You can still see the lights?" I ask.

"Oh yes," he breathes, extending a hand to caress an invisible patch. He parts his fingers and stares at me through the cracks. "This is where I say goodbye." He says it warily, expecting me to argue.

I nod shortly, then jerk my head at the corridor ahead of us. "Around that bend is the door to a dungeon. Lots of humans are imprisoned there. Lord Loss tortures them in his spare time. I'm going to free them. Want to help?"

"You told me I could leave," Kernel says guardedly.

"You can. But if you do and we fail, you'll condemn these captives to suffer at the hands of Lord Loss, maybe for thousands of years."

Kernel licks his lips and frowns. I almost have him.

"One of the prisoners is a girl called Bo Kooniart. She helped Dervish and me break out of Slawter. She could have left with us, but she went back to find her father. And her brother." I smile crookedly at Kernel. "She risked all to save her brother. You and I know what that's like, don't we?"

Kernel nods unhappily.

"You can tell where Lord Loss and Bec are," Shark says. "Search for them. Check if they're waiting in the dungeon for us."

Kernel studies the invisible lights for a few seconds. "They're on one of the higher levels, at the centre of the castle."

"Then what are you scared of?" Shark grins.

Kernel glares at me. "One last favour, then I'm out of here. Agreed?"

"Do whatever the hell you want, baldy," I sniff and press on, hiding my smile behind a bloodstained, hairy hand.

→The door, like everything else, is made of cobwebs. It's the only door we've encountered in the castle. Timas bends to study the hinges as it swings open. The rest of us move forward, me first, followed by Shark, Kernel, Kirilli and Moe. We hear the victims before we spot them, low moans, pained weepings, soft cries for mercy and death.

We fan out and Kirilli edges ahead of the rest of us, eyes widening as he studies the humans strapped to the walls and tables, the implements of torture lying like toys across the floor and webby shelves.

"This is despicable!" he splutters.

A man with half a face lifts his head at the sound of Kirilli's voice and stares at him through one eye. "Have you come to kill us?" he wheezes.

"We've come to save you," Kirilli says, hurrying to his side.

The man sneers wearily. "Don't make fun of me. Lord Loss sent you to give us false hope."

"No, honestly," Kirilli insists, "we're here to –"

"Watch out overhead!" Timas shouts behind us.

I look up and spot a huge spider-shaped demon descending on a strand of web, fast as an eagle swooping on a rat. I lunge forward to protect Kirilli. Shark and Kernel react a split-second later. But the furious stage magician doesn't need our help. Neatly sidestepping us, he points a finger at the spider and screams a phrase of magic, unleashing twin lightning bolts from his eyes.

The bolts strike the spider and it explodes, showering us with goo and slime. As I spit out the mess and wipe it from my eyes, I stare at Kirilli. He's standing rigidly, finger still outstretched, features contorted with contempt.

"Nice work, Kovacs," I murmur. "But next time, try not to splatter us. If you'd waited till it was lower, you could have killed it *and* spared us the splashback."

Kirilli blinks and stares at me, then realises I'm joking and smiles tightly. "The way you smell, it wouldn't make much difference," he says.

"I'm liking you more and more," I laugh, slapping his back. "Now, shall we free these poor devils and send them home?"

"Hell, yes." Kirilli sets to work on the bonds imprisoning the sceptical half-faced man.

As the others dart about the dungeon, freeing the tormented humans, I hurry to the spot where Bo Kooniart has always been. My stomach lurches when I don't find her — the shackles which held her in place lie open on the floor. I turn to the captured, blond-haired Disciple who I saw every time I trailed Bec and Lord Loss here. His expression is torn between hope and disbelief.

"Bo – the girl who was here – where is she?"

He doesn't respond, only stares, still not sure I'm real.

"The girl," I growl, pushing my face up to his.

"You're not… a demon," he croaks. "But you're not… human either. What… are you?"

"That doesn't matter. I'm here to rescue you. But where's the girl? Did Lord Loss…?" I don't finish, not daring to voice my worst fears.

"Back… there," the Disciple wheezes, nodding at a barred door behind me.

Hurrying to the bars, I spot Bo and two others chained to the floor. It's a small room filled with insects made of fire. They slither slowly across the helpless captives, leaving small, flame-filled channels in their flesh. Bo is gagged – they all are – so she can't scream, but I can see the pain and terror in her eyes.

Cursing, I rip the door off its hinges and toss it aside. Bursting into the room, I stamp on as many of the fiery insects as I can, then pull Bo and the others free and toss them out into the dungeon. Taking a deep breath, I blow on them, quenching the flames and killing the insects still burrowing across their chests, faces and limbs. With a quick swipe of a claw, I cut the gags from their mouths. As they whimper and sob, I find clothes nearby and toss them to the naked prisoners. While they pull them on, I do what I can to heal their wounds. Then I turn to free more of the inmates.

"Wait," Bo croaks. "I've seen you before, but I don't know where." Her voice is surprisingly strong for one who's been through hell. Then again, remembering how she went back into the bedlam of Slawter to search for her father and brother, maybe I shouldn't be so surprised.

"Grubbs Grady," I grunt, letting my face change back to the way it was when she knew me.

Her eyes widen. "*Grubbs?* What happened to you? You look like…"

"…something from the cast of *Slawter*," I grin.

"Is it a curse?" she asks. "Did the monsters do this to you?"

"Yeah," I mutter. "Something like that."

I help her to her feet. "Are you OK?"

"I don't know," she sighs. "It's been so long… years… yet I don't look old, do I?" She stares at her hands. Although they're rough and scarred, and stained with blood, they're the hands of a girl, not an old crone.

"You look fine," I tell her. "You'll look even better once you've had a hot bath."

Bo frowns. "A hot bath? Here?"

"No," I say softly. "You're going home."

She starts to tremble. "Don't say it, not if it isn't true."

"It's true," I promise, then shout, "Kernel, where's that window?"

"Working on it," he calls back.

"Another minute or two," I tell her. "Then it will all be over."

Except for the impending apocalypse, the voice of the Kah-Gash adds inside my head, but I ignore it.

"Abe?" Bo asks quietly. "My dad?"

"You haven't seen them here?" She shakes her head. "Then they didn't make it out of Slawter."

Tears well in her eyes. "You're sure? There's nowhere else they might be?"

"No."

She nods sorrowfully and I marvel at the strength of humans. Despite all that she's suffered, her first thoughts are of her dead relatives. I thought I grew stronger when I became a wolfen beast, but in some ways maybe I lost more than I gained.

"It's open," Kernel calls and ushers the first of the prisoners through a window of yellow light.

"Come with me," I tell Bo and the others, leading them towards the window. "There'll be people on the other side. They'll help."

"Aren't you coming with us?" Bo asks.

"No."

"He'll find you if you stay," she whispers. I don't need to ask who she means.

"He won't have to. We're going after him."

"You think you can fight him?" She stares at me as if I'm mad.

"We'll give it a good shot."

She shakes her head wordlessly. Then we're at the window. Before she can think of anything to say, I gently push her through. I don't need thanks. It's enough to see her to safety. A small, unimportant triumph — but to me, it matters a lot.

The prisoners continue filing through, but some are beyond help. A grim-faced Shark takes care of those, breaking their necks, freeing their souls swiftly and painlessly. Sometimes that's the most you can do for a person.

The blond-haired Disciple pauses at the window and looks at us. "I should stay with you and fight," he mutters. "It's my job."

"You wouldn't be much good to us the state you're in," I say as kindly as I can.

"But I know how to do things."

"You've done enough," I smile. "Go home. Rest up. Recover. Take a long holiday. God knows, you've earned it."

"Before I leave," he says. "The war… who won?"

"Which war?" I frown.

"The World War."

"One or Two?"

His face blanches. "There was a *second*?"

"Go home," I tell him, insistent this time, feeling sorry for this confused man who's going to have to learn to adapt to what's left of life in the twenty-first century.

Soon they're all gone or beyond the reaches of pain, and it's just us in the dungeon. I look from Shark to Timas to Kirilli. "If you want to leave, I'll understand. This is probably the end for anyone who pushes on with me."

"Do we look like cowards?" Shark snorts.

"Well…" I was about to say Kirilli did, but one glance at his determined face and I button my lip. The time for mocking Kirilli Kovacs has passed. He's truly one of us now. "Sorry. I guess I've seen too many movies. Let's go."

I start for the door.

"Aren't you even going to say goodbye?" Kernel asks.

"Why?" I grunt. "You're not going anywhere."

"You said I could leave," he snarls.

"You can," I chuckle, "but you won't. Walk out on a showdown with Lord Loss? Abandon us when there's still hope we can beat this thing? Leave Bec to ruin the world, knowing you could maybe have stopped her if you tried? Nuh-uh. You're going nowhere."

Kernel grumbles darkly and I feel his scowl burning a hole in the back of my neck. But I know, as I step through the doorway, that he'll follow. They all will. Hell, we're heroes — this is what we do.

SOULFUL

→ We creep through the corridors of the high-ceilinged castle, our footsteps muffled by the thick strands of web which serve as floorboards. We still haven't seen any demons. Maybe Lord Loss's familiars are with the demon army we fought the last time we were in this universe. But it's strange that he should choose to face us by himself. As a master, in his own realm, he can be confident of success, but it would be easier if he had hundreds of his henchthings to throw against us. Lord Loss doesn't usually take chances. Why do so now?

Kernel's busy juggling patches of light as we walk, putting the framework for a window together, so he can complete it quickly and make a swift getaway if he has to. I'm stunned that he came with us. I was bluffing when I said I was sure he'd stay. I totally expected him to leave. He's spent the last month going on about how he needs to return to the ark. Why the sudden change?

Guilty, the Kah-Gash murmurs inside my head.

"You did this?" I growl.

I'm able to nudge when the wish already exists, the Kah-Gash says. *I can't make any of you do something you don't want to, but I can tip the balance if you're in two minds. Kernel knew he should leave, but he wanted to stay. I played on his wishes and turned him from the path of reason.*

"I bet this isn't the first time you've manipulated us," I accuse it.

It's not manipulation, the Kah-Gash protests. *I merely give you the confidence, from time to time, to do that which you truly desire.*

"But it's what you desire too, isn't it? You want us to join. You're using us."

Such a suspicious mind, the Kah-Gash sighs, then falls silent.

I think about telling Kernel what the Kah-Gash said, offering him the chance to leave. That would be the decent thing. But I'm a slime-covered, hairy, mutated, wolfen beast. What the hell do *I* know about decency?

We push on until we come to a huge room, the largest in the castle. The floor is littered with toys, dolls, clothes and other bits and pieces from Earth. In the centre a huge chandelier hangs above a massive spider-shaped throne, both carved from webs. There's a painting of Lord Loss done in the style of Van Gogh pinned to the wall to the rear of the throne.

Lord Loss squats at the base of the throne, not quite touching the floor, head bent over a chess board. Bec is his opponent. She sits cross-legged with her back to us. She's making a move as we enter, engrossed in the game.

"A moment, good people," Lord Loss mutters without looking up. He purses his blood-red lips, studies the chess pieces, then moves one of them. He smiles at Bec and says, "To be resumed." Then he straightens and Bec turns to face us.

"Hello, Grubbs," Bec says quietly. "Kernel. Shark. Kirilli." She nods at the tall, red-headed man and the werewolf. Timas beams at her, but Moe just snarls. "Are these all you brought? I thought you'd come with an army."

"These will do," I tell her, moving closer, scanning the room for hidden threats. But it seems to be deserted except for this pair.

"Welcome back, Cornelius," Lord Loss says. "It seems like an age since your last visit. What a shame young Artery isn't here to greet you."

Kernel says nothing but he looks like he's about to be sick. This is hard for him. Maybe the persuasive power of the Kah-Gash has faded and he's wondering what the hell he's doing here.

"No greeting for me?" Shark asks.

"You require none," Lord Loss says calmly. "You were always a bit player. One does not waste pleasantries on pawns."

"You're hurting my feelings," Shark sniffs. His gaze

falls on Bec and he draws his thumb across his throat, trying to freak her. But if she's worried, she doesn't show it. Her expression hasn't changed in the slightest.

"This place is amazing," Timas says, squinting up at the chandelier, then at the painting behind the throne. "That's woven out of coloured cobwebs, isn't it?"

"Yes," Lord Loss says, smiling with genuine warmth. "You're the first visitor to notice. It looks like oil on canvas from a distance, but in fact..." He draws to a halt and coughs into a fist. "We could be friends, Timas Brauss, if circumstances were different. You strike me as a man after my own heart." He runs a hand over the snake-filled hole in his chest. "So to speak."

"We freed your prisoners," Kirilli growls, brushing slime from the sleeves of his jacket.

"How daring of you," Lord Loss murmurs. "I am devastated. What shall I play with now in my idle moments?" His eyes twinkle viciously. "Perhaps I'll focus my attention on *you*, Master Kovacs."

Kirilli produces a playing card out of thin air, then rips it in two. "That's what I think of your *attention*."

Lord Loss frowns. "I was told you were of a cowardly nature. It seems I have been misinformed."

"No," Kirilli says. "The reports were accurate. But I've changed."

Moe growls at me questioningly.

"Yeah," I reply. "You're right."

"About what?" Lord Loss frowns.

"Moe thinks there's been too much talking and not enough killing." I slam my hands together and send a wave of magic shooting at the pair in front of the throne. I race after it, fangs and claws extended, readying myself for battle.

The wave of energy ruffles Bec's hair and sends a few drops of blood spraying from Lord Loss. But that's all. The demon master tuts and waves a hand at me. I crash to my knees, my mouth sealing as if glued shut, the hairs in my nostrils knitting together. I can't breathe. I slash at my lips with my claws, ripping them open, then dig a couple of fingers up my nose, breaking through the web of hairs.

As I draw a welcome breath, Moe, Shark, Timas and Kirilli bound past. The werewolf's howling, Shark's roaring and Kirilli's shrieking. Timas just whistles softly, as if heading out to work.

Lord Loss could repel them easily, but he lets the quartet close on him, then grapples with them, slapping them back, playing, letting them think they have a chance of defeating him. I know better. I felt his power as he stitched my lips and nose shut. I was wrong to think we had even a sliver of hope. This is his kingdom. He's unbeatable here.

I glance at Kernel. He's still working on a window, but he pauses when I catch his eye and raises an eyebrow, asking if I want him to fight. I shake my head, letting him know that he's fine as he is. Then I face Bec, who still hasn't moved. She's observing the fight with calm disinterest.

"Why?" I snarl, moving in on her, sure Lord Loss will intervene, tensing myself against whatever he throws at me.

"What option did I have?" Bec asks quietly. "The demons have won. There's no profit in dying heroically but uselessly."

I'm drawing closer. Lord Loss hasn't made any move to stop me. My mouth is wet with saliva and blood. I spit to clear it, then growl at her. "You fought in the past when it seemed hopeless."

"I was younger then," Bec sighs. "I believed in miracles. Now I know we can't win. Bran knew that too at the end. You can't defeat Death."

"But he didn't give up," I remind her. "He tackled the Shadow and bought us time. He sacrificed his life to save you. And now you've pledged yourself to the beast he hated most of all."

"If I could save humanity by sacrificing myself, I would," Bec says quietly. "But nothing would be gained." She stands, picks up the chess board and holds it out to me. "This is the Board. It's what the universe was like in the beginning, and what it will soon be like again. Sixty-four zones, half for the Old Creatures, half for the

Demonata. No room for humans. I don't think that's a good or a bad thing — it's just the way things are."

"No," I snap. "That will only happen if we let it. And we won't. *I* won't."

I'm within striking distance. Making a fist, I lash at her. I expect her to duck, but instead she swings up the Board and deflects my blow, then slams it into my chin, knocking my head back. That stuns me — I hadn't anticipated the small girl standing up to me in a fair fight. Before I can recover, she touches my stomach and sends a shockwave of magic crackling through my flesh.

I collapse in a ball, howling with pain. Bec cracks the Board over my head. I raise a hand to swat it away, but it smashes down hard on my knuckles, breaks the bones in my wrist and hammers my face into the ground.

If the floor was concrete, my skull would be crushed and my brains pulped. But the webs give beneath me, so although I come up with one side of my face feeling like it's been caved in, my eye shut, blood pumping from any number of wounds, I *do* come up. I should be dead, but I'm not. And that's bad news for Bec.

Springing to my feet, I snap my teeth around her wrist. She didn't expect this rapid response. She thought she'd have time to attack me again. As Bec prepares a spell to repel me, I bite down hard and chew her hand off. She gasps and falls away, using the magic which was on her lips to cauterise the wound and numb the pain.

Before she can reattach the hand, I drive for her throat, meaning to bite her head off as smoothly as her hand.

My jaws freeze and an electric shock courses through my veins. I fall away, spasming. As I thrash on the floor, I spot Lord Loss waving a stubby finger from side to side. "No, Grubitsch," he admonishes me. "I lost one assistant when Juni Swan was killed. I shall not lose another."

Shark roars and jams a hand into the hole in Lord Loss's chest. The snakes bite him, but he keeps his hand in, grabs a couple of the serpents and squeezes them to death. He tosses the corpses into Lord Loss's face. Blood spatters the demon master's eyes, momentarily blinding him.

As Lord Loss wipes the blood away, Shark, Moe and Kirilli jump him. Timas starts to follow, then hesitates and turns instead to Bec. "Are you good at chess?" he asks.

Bec frowns. "I—"

He strikes before she gets any further, lashing out with his right foot. He looks like a gangly, awkward man, but he can move swiftly when he wishes. His foot connects with the side of Bec's head, knocking her sideways. She cries out with surprise.

As my jaws unlock, I scrabble after Bec, desperate to finish her off. Timas steps aside. I claw closer. Bec hears me before she sees me. She focuses on my hate-filled eyes and hisses like a cat. A phrase of magic bursts from her tongue. A split-second later, her severed hand shoots across the floor, flicks on to her wrist and dances feverishly as tendons, bones and blood vessels fuse at a furious pace.

I throw myself at her, roaring wildly, but Bec flies out of reach, sliding across the floor to the nearest webby wall. When she hits it, she shimmies several metres up the wall, then glares at me from a safe height.

Lord Loss has cleared the mess from around his eyes and is back in business. He looks annoyed. Shark reaches into the demon master's chest cavity to kill a few more snakes. This time one of them darts from the gap and wriggles up his arm. He tries to slap it away, but it slides over his elbow, bites a hole in his biceps, then sinks its head into his flesh. Its body follows and it starts to disappear beneath his skin. Shark yelps and grabs the snake's tail. He falls away, tugging on the snake, screaming with pain and horror.

Moe howls louder than ever and digs his fangs into the doughy flesh of Lord Loss's stomach. He chews a chunk loose, then rips a thirty-centimetre strip of skin away. Lord Loss groans and half-turns. Another two snakes dart from the hole in his chest and shoot at Moe's eyes. Their fangs hit before the werewolf can whirl aside, puncturing the globes. Moe shrieks and hits the floor, blind and in agony.

Kirilli backs up, isolated and trembling, looking from Moe to Shark.

"What now, little man?" Lord Loss whispers, rising in the air before the stage magician, all eight arms extending to their fullest length.

Kirilli gulps, takes a few more steps back, then stops. "I guess this is where I pull off my masterstroke," he grins and whips out a couple of knives. He tosses them at the demon master and they strike either side of the beast's right breast. As soon as they hit, they turn into weeds. Lord Loss laughs, then chokes as the weeds spread and burrow into his flesh. Within seconds his entire chest is a bed of suffocating greenery. The weeds wrap around his throat and climb his neck to his face, which is turning a beautiful purple colour.

"Master?" Bec calls from her perch, looking troubled. I should go after her, but I'm transfixed by the sight of Lord Loss. It's incredible that he's struggling like this, especially at the hands of a Disciple as insignificant as Kirilli Kovacs. But maybe Kirilli is the ace up our sleeve. Nobody expected him to be a threat. Lord Loss probably didn't bother to shield himself as fully as he would have against the rest of us. If Kirilli can take advantage of that…

But even as I'm thinking the impossible, Lord Loss shudders, then smiles. The weeds die and peel away in dry clumps. Moments later only a thin rash remains.

"Impressive," Lord Loss acknowledges, "but hardly enough to bring down one such as I. Was that your best shot, Master Kovacs?"

"Pretty much," Kirilli sighs.

"So again I ask, what now, little man?"

Kirilli manages a shaky smile. "You kill me?"

Lord Loss nods and points a couple of arms at the mage.

"No!" I bellow and hit the demon master with a burst of magic.

Lord Loss is knocked aside. Steadying himself, he glares at me. "Are you still alive? I thought you would have dealt with him by now, Little One."

"It's hard," Bec says softly. "They were my friends."

"I understand," Lord Loss purrs. "But you must kill at least one of them for me. To prove you are truly on my side."

My heart gives a hopeful leap. It seems Bec might still be torn between her original loyalties and the new vows she made. If she's wavering, there's a chance to save her. She hasn't crossed the final line yet. Maybe I can draw her back.

"Help us," I plead, locking gazes with the troubled-looking girl, letting my face soften and become more human. "If the three of us unite, we can kill him."

"I came back!" Kernel shouts. "I didn't need to. But I returned. For *you*."

"To kill me," Bec says sullenly.

"To rescue you," I disagree. "You haven't passed the point of no return. You can be one of us again. It makes sense to stick with your own. No matter what you do, you'll never be a demon."

"No," Bec says. "But I'm not really human either. I'm an agent of Death. I've passed beyond the ways of the living. This is all that's left for me."

"No!" I cry. "You can—"

"My people are dead," she interrupts. "Those I owed loyalty to died many centuries ago. Bran was the last. You're not part of my world. I'm tired of trying to do the right thing. When my soul didn't pass on, I unleashed Death. In a weird kind of way, I'm its mother. Now I need to fully pledge myself to it."

Bec stretches out a hand towards the Board. It flies into her fingers and glows. Lord Loss sighs happily and rises above Shark and the others. As he floats, he waves at the walls around us and they dissolve, the strands of webs unravelling and dropping, revealing the areas previously walled off.

There are humans in the rooms around us. Thousands of people, standing frozen in place, eyes blank, arms by their sides. For a few seconds I think they're dead, but then I see their chests rising and falling as they breathe in unison.

"This looks ominous," Timas remarks.

"The Board!" Kernel yells. "Their souls are in the Board."

"Neatly tucked away," Lord Loss says, moving closer to Bec, a perverse smile lifting the corners of his mouth.

"Wait," I gasp, seeing the dark intent in Bec's eyes. "Don't do this. You're still one of us. Beranabus would hate you if he saw you now. Those are real people. There are children…"

"You're all children in my eyes," Bec says quietly. "I've lived for more than fifteen hundred years. Even your eldest are babes to me." Her face hardens. "And it's time to put the babies to bed."

"No!" I scream, feeling the bonds between us snap forever, seeing the last trace of humanity blink out of her eyes. I try to stop her, to jump and knock the Board from her hands. But Lord Loss waves and subdues me.

As Kernel lurches forward and Shark struggles with the snake… as Kirilli stares at Bec and a frown creases Timas's forehead… as Moe writhes blindly on the ground and Lord Loss floats next to his protégé and nods encouragingly…

Bec places her right hand on the Board and sends waves of fire burning through the layer of crystal. I sense the flames billowing through all sixty-four zones. It's almost infinite inside, each zone the size of a galaxy, but the fire scorches through faster than the speed of light, destroying all in its path, demons, worlds, skies... and the souls of the people around us.

They fall in lines, bodies slumping and twitching, butchered by the sad-faced girl from the past. Thousands of innocent, defenceless humans — all murdered without mercy by pale, warped Bec.

AN UNHOLY QUARTET

→I roar wordlessly, filled with horror and hate. Bec's face is lit by the glow of thousands of burning souls. She looks awestruck and damned.

"My beloved," Lord Loss gurgles, running a sticky hand down the side of Bec's face. She doesn't respond. She's staring into the flickering glow of the Board, transfixed. She does nothing to stop the massacre, even as the bodies topple and writhe around us. I've never seen someone consciously turn to the path of evil. If it wasn't so sickening, I'd be fascinated.

"What the hell's going on?" Shark yells. He's torn off the snake's tail and sucked out its entrails. It's dead, but most of its body remains stuck in his arm.

"She killed them!" I scream, trying to climb up the wall after Bec. It's the only stretch of wall left, standing like a pillar in a huge, corpse-strewn room.

Shark looks at the falling humans. "No," he moans, struck hard by the appalling tragedy of it, even though he's seen so much in his time.

"We have to stop her," Kirilli says, stepping forward and flexing his fingers.

"I think it's passed beyond that,"Timas says, squinting up at the Board. "A most remarkable device. I'd love to know how it works."

"I'm going to kill you," I vow, pointing a trembling finger at Bec. "You can't stay up there forever. As soon as you come down, you're dead."

Lord Loss laughs. "You're such a brute, Grubitsch. You think mindless violence is the answer to all the universe's troubles."

Bec blinks, then stares into the Board again. I don't know if she's heard anything we've said, if she's even aware of us. She watches the souls burn, but takes no pleasure from the slaughter. This is destroying her. Her human emotions are burning away with the spirits of the dying.

"Why?" Kernel mutters. "It doesn't make sense."

"She wants to prove herself to her new master," I snarl.

"But Lord Loss didn't ask her to kill them," Kernel presses. "He asked her to kill one of *us*. There must be another reason why she targeted them instead of you or me."

"You were always smarter than your burly companion," Lord Loss says. "Not as clever as sly young Bec, but definitely several rungs higher up the IQ ladder than the somewhat dense Master Grady."

The last of the humans hits the ground, but the Board is still glowing. It's a dark glow and it pulses steadily, a gloomy, grey, *shadowy* throb.

"It's Death!" I shout, realisation coming too late to be of any use.

Wispy tendrils rise from the Board and snake into the air around Bec. From a distance you might mistake them for smoke, but this close I can see that there's nothing natural about the sinewy strands. They have the same consistency Death had when we faced it before. It looks like our shadowy foe has found its way back. The humans were slaughtered so that Death could stitch together a new body from the fabric of their souls.

With a scream of failure, I unleash all of my power in a ball of magic. It roars towards Bec like a missile. Nothing should be able to halt or divert it. Bec should be smashed to pieces.

But Lord Loss intervenes, slides between Bec and me, and absorbs the blast. It slams him into Bec, who falls to the floor. But it doesn't destroy him. This is his realm. He can take all that I throw at him here and still bounce back.

Shark and Kirilli hurl themselves at Bec as she falls, murder in their eyes. But she's on her feet before they strike. With a lazy gesture, she sends them flying. She's still clutching the Board. More shadowy tendrils rise from the sixty-four squares and wrap themselves around her, caressing her, sliding up her throat, brushing across her lips. Her mouth opens and she inhales. The shadows slip down her throat and her eyes take on a darker, more menacing colour.

"Grubbs," she says, and the word rolls flatly from her mouth. "Come to me."

There's something commanding and seductive in her tone. I know she plans to kill me, but that doesn't seem like such a bad thing. If I give myself to her, it will all be over in an instant. No more pain, guilt or suffering. One hug from the girl encased in shadows and I can join with her, become part of that gloomy subworld, seek refuge in oblivion.

"Grubbs!" Kernel shrieks. I frown at him and start to tell him not to disturb me. But then I spot a window of red light. He's opened a way out.

"I don't think so," Lord Loss snarls. He tries to intercede, but although I didn't seriously injure him when I unleashed the ball of energy, I stung him. He's slower than normal. Shark and Kirilli flee ahead of the demon master and stumble through the window. Timas takes his time, watching the Board and the way the shadows stream from it and dance across Bec's flesh. A cloud of shadows is forming around and behind her. Timas looks like he'd be happy to dive into the heart of that cloud and lose himself in it.

"Come on!" Kernel roars. "I won't wait any longer. Come now or stay and die."

Timas sighs, his shoulders slumping. He shoots Kernel a scowl, then slips through the window instead of into the cloud of shadows, choosing life over death. It's a choice I haven't made yet.

"Come to me, Grubbs," Bec whispers and staggers forward, raising a dark hand. She tries to smile, but it's as if she's forgotten how.

"Don't kill him," Lord Loss pleads, real longing in his voice. "You said you'd let *me* murder this one. You gave your word. It was all I asked for."

"Grubbs!" Kernel yells warningly.

We can keep him, the voice of the Kah-Gash says. *We can block his retreat and hold him here. Take him into the cloud with us. All three pieces reunited by Death, a union of the most powerful forces in the universes, a quartet instead of a trinity. It would mean power beyond all measure. You're the trigger. You can make it happen.*

"Power…" I murmur, eyes wide, torn in ways I don't fully understand.

"To hell with you," Kernel sobs, then steps up to the window of red light.

I extend a hand to hold him back… then pause and let him go.

"No," I croak, my mind clearing. "I don't want this."

Bec hisses, her semi-smile crumbling. "Come to me,"

she growls. Not a plea this time. An order.

"Get stuffed!" I snort, then throw myself at the window. The cheated howls of Bec and Lord Loss echo after me as shadowy tendrils shoot towards me, trying to haul me back. But Death is too slow for this fleet-footed wolfen boy. I'm gone before it can grab me, and the darkness — for the time being — is left behind.

LIGHTS OUT

→Kernel is already dismantling the window as I crash through and roll across the ground. "I thought we'd seen the last of you," he says as the window blinks out of existence, securing our safety.

"You wish." I grimace as I stand. I took a hammering in Lord Loss's realm, not least to my face. That was fine when I had the magical energy of the demon universe to tap into. I could numb the pain. But back on Earth I feel like I've been run through a meat processor.

Shark groans as he prises the remains of the snake from his flesh. Blood gushes from the hole it leaves. Timas makes a tourniquet out of his belt and tightens it around the ex-soldier's arm.

"I never liked snakes," Shark wheezes. "Now I bloody hate them! I'll have nightmares about that."

"You don't have enough imagination for nightmares," Kernel laughs, slumping beside his friend. He runs an eye over me and frowns. "Are you going to be OK?"

"Yeah," I mumble, coughing up blood.

"The left side of your head looks like it's been caved in with an iron."

"Thanks for pointing that out."

"I could take you to a hospital, but I doubt they'd be able to do much for you."

I wave away his concerns. "I'll be fine. A short rest, then we'll go somewhere magical and I'll patch myself up."

"She was a vindictive little wench, wasn't she?" Timas says cheerfully, as if discussing a cat who'd shown her claws.

"I'd have drowned her if I'd known what she was going to turn into," Kirilli snarls. "She saved me on the ship when we first met. I thought she was kind. But she murdered those people as if they were ants."

"We've lost her," I sigh. "She belongs to Lord Loss and Death now. We'll have to kill her the next time we meet."

"You think you can?" Kernel asks quietly.

"Over there, no. But here, where they're weaker? We stand a chance."

Silence falls as everyone thinks about Lord Loss, Bec, Death. We know we're done for. I can see it in their eyes. We can talk the good talk all we want, but the demons are stronger than us, even on our own turf. Winning is a dream, not a real possibility.

Kirilli lets out a deep breath and chuckles wryly. "We

left Moe behind. I'll miss that dumb hairball. He might have thought of me as lunch, but I had a soft spot for him all the same."

"There's only one of the original werewolves left now," I nod. "Assuming Larry hasn't been killed." I glance at Kernel. "How long have we been gone?"

He shakes his head. "I'm not sure. But it's too long, no matter what." He backs away from me, his expression changing. "You know what I'm going to say."

"You want to leave?"

"It was madness, staying when I did. I have to go."

"You're our secret weapon," I tell him, knowing it's a waste of breath but feeling like I should go through the motions. "With your help we can make sneak attacks, dart in, strike, nip out again. If you abandon us, they'll grind us down."

"They'll grind you down regardless," Kernel sighs. "And you're forgetting, my eyes are no good here. They're already starting to sting. A day or two and they'll be gooey blobs again."

As I'm trying to think of some fresh way to argue with him, Kirilli clears his throat. "Why don't we ask for help from the Old Creatures? If they told you the truth, they have the power to hold the demons back. If we put a strong enough case to them…"

Kernel shakes his head. "They're looking at the bigger picture. Earth is just another world, one of untold billions. They don't care about us. They only want my part of the Kah-Gash."

"We could barter," Kirilli says. "What if you promised to help them, but only if they reinforced Earth's defences? They used lodestones to deter demons in the past. Surely they could recharge or replace them and erect a ring of magic around the planet through which the Demonata couldn't cross."

Kernel looks uncertain. "I think Death has changed things. I don't know if the old ways work any more."

"But we could ask," Kirilli presses. "If they say no, we haven't lost anything. There's no harm putting in a request, is there?"

I seize on Kernel's hesitation. "Why not try? Even if they turn you down, they won't punish you for asking, will they?"

"Probably not," Kernel says. "But…"

"What?" I snort. "Afraid of upsetting them? Will you condemn the rest of us just to make a good impression on your new friends?"

Kernel's face stiffens. "That's a cheap shot."

"Maybe. But it's not an unreasonable request. Take us to the Old Creature who came back with you. Let us discuss it with him. If he turns us down, at least we'll have tried. You can go, the rest of us will stay. Where's the harm in that?"

Kernel shrugs. "I'm sure he'll reject you, but I guess

we might as well try. Let me open a window to the demon universe, then I'll—"

"Why do we have to go there?" I snap suspiciously.

"It will take several hours to open a window to Atlantis," Kernel says. "My eyes might not last that long here. Plus it's easier for me over there."

"OK," I growl, but edge to within striking distance in case he's trying to con us.

→Kernel takes us to a few different worlds, trying to find a spot where our enemies can't track us. Eventually, on an asteroid in the depths of space, he sets to work on building a window to Atlantis, the world where the Old Creature is waiting. Far from being a mythical country which sank beneath the waves, Atlantis is the nearest inhabitable world to Earth. It was once populated by advanced beings. They mastered space travel and visited our planet, influencing mankind's early progress. Then there was some kind of meltdown, like a nuclear war but worse. The Atlanteans perished.

I'm not looking forward to meeting the creature from the original universe, older than time itself. They're obviously a superior species and Kernel thinks they're much wiser than us, that we'd be crazy not to follow their plans. But by their own admission they've messed up before. I don't have the same faith in them that Kernel has.

Even if the ark they've built is the only hope for survival in the future, how can they turn away from the needs of the present? The Old Creatures told Kernel they believe every species has to follow its own path. They protect us in our formative years, hold back the Demonata so that we can develop. But then they withdraw, leaving us to fend for ourselves or perish at the claws of the demons.

What the hell kind of thinking is that! If I had their power, I'd never abandon a world. The Old Creatures won't live forever. They say they can *only* hold back the demons for a few billion years. Like that's nothing! A billion years is an eternity for most civilisations. If they spared us the agonies of the Demonata that long, by the time their power waned, Earth would be a shell of a planet anyway. They could save us all this suffering.

I know they have other worlds to think about. The universe is teeming with intelligent beings and Earth's just one small rock among billions. But if we were worth helping in the first place, they should have seen the job through. To me it's the same as if a parent teaches its child to walk, then drops it into a pit of snakes and says, "You must prove yourself worthy of survival. Good luck!"

I've all sorts of bones to pick with the Old Creatures. But I'll have to hide my feelings, smile big and play it humble. Because these guys are our only hope. If we can convince them to help, maybe the Demonata can be driven back. I might even avoid the future that Juni prophesied and not destroy the universe. It will stick in my throat, but I have to play up to these cold, ancient life-givers. If I don't, we're on our own, and that will truly be the end.

Temper, Grubbs, temper!

→It's taking Kernel ages to open the window to Atlantis. He works hard, sweating with the effort, but apparently there's no quick way because of the distance involved. When I asked him how far away it was, all he said was *far*. We can't get closer to it in this universe either — space doesn't work the same way here. Kernel has to construct a window that links back to Earth, then on to Atlantis. I'm glad I'm not the eyes of the Kah-Gash. Having to deal with technical issues like this would drive me mad. I'm much happier gutting demons.

The rest of us patch up our wounds while we're waiting. Shark and I are the worst, battered all over. The brace around his stomach has cracked in several places. He glues it together with magic, but I get a glimpse of the flesh beneath. It's ugly — purple flesh speckled with a mouldy green fungus. There's blood soaking into his trousers and bits of his guts are poking out of ragged holes.

"How much longer do you think you can keep going?" I ask.

Shark shrugs. "I should have been dead weeks ago, as my doctors kept telling me. Having cheated death this long, who knows?"

"Has the infection been there long?"

"Who made you a nurse?" he scowls.

"*Infection?*" Timas barks. "You were supposed to tell me if you got infected."

"It slipped my mind," Shark says drily.

"Let me see," Timas says, reaching for the brace.

"Leave it," Shark grunts. "I used magic to heal myself. I'll be fine." He sighs. "You know what I miss? The ladies. No matter how bad things got, when Meera or Sharmila was with us, I always felt more at ease. Crazy, huh?"

"If they were here now, they'd march you to hospital and have that infection looked at," Timas huffs.

"Why don't you go find a machine to tinker with?" Shark snaps.

"Over here?" Timas replies archly.

"I thought *I* was supposed to be the highly strung one," Kirilli murmurs, and we all laugh.

"Seriously," Timas says, smiling, "that infection will kill you if we don't have it treated."

"Seriously," Shark responds, grinning tightly, "I know it will, but I don't think it's the sort of infection any doctor can treat. Just let me battle on and drop when it's my time. I don't have much longer whether I push on or go back. I'd rather die fighting than tucked up in a hospital bed."

Timas considers that, then nods. "As you wish."

Kirilli chuckles. "That's the one plus point about not having any women around — we can discuss these things logically. No woman would let Shark get away with reasoning like that."

"Our kind of women would," Shark disagrees. "Sharmila and Meera knew the score. They wouldn't have objected. Or wept. They were tough."

"Yeah," I sigh, thinking of Meera on her motorbike, red hair streaming behind her, laughing as she tore past speed signs.

Silence settles over us again as we brood about the friends we've lost, the wounds we've endured. It's a relief when Kernel finally opens a window of white light and staggers away from it, exhausted.

"About time," I grunt. "Let's go."

"Wait a minute," Kernel stops me. "This is a window to a distant place in our universe, not a passageway between realms. It doesn't work like a normal window. It'll take several minutes to cross and there isn't any oxygen. The Old Creature gave me a piece of a lodestone to use."

Kernel digs out a sliver of rock and studies it. "I'll use its power to erect a shield, but I'm not sure it will hold us all. If the shield starts to crumble while we're crossing, I'll have to cut the rest of you loose."

I stare at Kernel suspiciously. "If this is some kind of trick…"

"No trick," he insists. "I wasn't supposed to bring others back with me. I don't know if I can swing it."

"Can't we erect shields of our own?" Shark asks.

"It's a different type of magic. You won't be able to tap into it."

We gaze uneasily at one another. Shark, Timas and Kirilli wait for me to make a decision.

"Will there be any fighting?" I ask.

"On Atlantis?" Kernel shakes his head. "No. A few of the slug creatures might attack, but we can easily repel them."

"Then I'll come by myself. The others can stay here. We'll pick them up on our way back — or *I'll* pick them up if I return alone," I say quickly, before Kernel launches into another of his I-won't-be-coming-back spiels.

"You're sure you'll be safe without us?" Shark asks.

"Yeah." I grab Kernel and settle my fangs close to his throat. "If Window Boy gives me any trouble, I'll chew through his carotid artery before he can blink."

"Charming," Kernel sneers, then creates a tight, invisible barrier around us and we shuffle into the window of light.

→Crossing has always been instantaneous, like stepping from one room to another through a doorway. Not this time. I find myself floating through a weird zone of lights, all sorts of shapes and colours. I cling to Kernel like a child to his father, ogling the lights, feeling completely out of my depth. I try to ask a question but no sound comes from my lips.

"We could speak normally," Kernel's voice says inside my head, "but it would mean more work on the shield. It's easier this way."

"Bloody telepathy," I grumble silently, then nod at the lights. "Is this what you see all the time?"

"These are different to the normal lights," he says. "But they're similar."

"How do you concentrate on normal stuff?"

Kernel laughs. "For me this *is* normal. The only time I was unable to see lights was when I entered the Board in Lord Loss's palace."

"How are we moving?" I ask. "What's propelling us?"

"I'm not sure. I think the lights draw us on. As long as I bear Atlantis in mind, they steer us towards it."

"What if you black out or go crazy?"

Kernel sniffs. "There's no telling where we might end up."

I've never felt so helpless. At least in the realm of demons, no matter how bad things got, I was always able to fight. Here I'm relying on Kernel for everything. I feel useless. On Earth I'm a magician, a leader of werewolves. Here I'm nothing. If Kernel cast me adrift, I couldn't do anything about it.

I get tenser the further we glide. I want to go back and take my chances without Kernel. I don't mind dying on Earth or in the demon universe. But not here, in this unnatural zone of lights. It was a mistake asking him to bring me. I should have stayed where I belonged.

I fight my hysteria as long as I can, but eventually it threatens to overwhelm me. I'm about to demand that Kernel take me back, but before I can he says, "That patch of green light is the entrance to Atlantis."

I fix on the green panel and smile eagerly as we draw closer. The other panels seem to slide away from around us until the whole universe looks like one giant patch of green. Then we slip through and land on a hard floor.

We're in a chamber made of stones. The air is foul, acidic, painful to a nose as sensitive as mine. Squinting against the discomfort, I look around and spot a fat, black man sitting close by. It's the Old Creature in human form, disguised as Raz Warlo, a Disciple who fought with Dervish many years ago.

"Hello, Kernel," Raz says stiffly, eyeing me beadily. "I did not expect you to bring another piece of the Kah-Gash."

"This is Grubbs," Kernel says. "He has something to

ask you."

"Yes," Raz says. "I can read it in his thoughts. The answer is no."

"Hold on a minute," I growl. "You don't know what—"

"You want my help," Raz interrupts. "You want me to return to Earth, recharge the lodestones and provide you with the means to repel the Demonata."

"Well, OK, maybe you *do* know what I want," I smile, trying to make a joke of it. "But you can't refuse before I have a chance to—"

"I can see all of your arguments already," Raz says. "None will persuade me to return with you. The threat of withholding Kernel won't work either, since he is determined to travel to the ark with me. He has a greater calling he must respect. Your world is unimportant in the grand scheme of things."

"It might not matter to you," I snarl, "but it means everything to us."

"No," Kernel says sadly. "It doesn't. I'd save it if I could, but if it's a choice between dying meaninglessly or helping others survive… I've got to go, Grubbs."

"Nobody has to go anywhere," I hiss, trying to rein in my temper. "Come with us. Give us the power to defend ourselves. You made the lodestones work once — why not again? Time means nothing to you guys. Give us a million years. That won't kill you, will it?"

"It would go against all that we believe in," Raz says.

"We protect developing worlds in their infancy, but your people have outgrown the need for us. You had the power to evolve and move ahead of the demons. You failed to nurture that talent. That is your problem, not ours. If we interceded in this case, we would have to intercede in all of the others."

"What's so wrong with that?" I explode. "You have the power to save lives, to save *worlds*. Why don't you bloody use it?"

"We cannot save everyone," Raz says patiently. "The universes do not work that way. Losses are unavoidable."

"Listen to me, you ignorant son of a—"

I freeze. I'd been taking a step towards Raz, but suddenly I can't move. My hand's outstretched, one foot raised, mouth open. I must look idiotic, but there's nothing I can do about it.

"Grubbs?" Kernel squeaks, then turns on Raz. "What have you done to him?"

"Merely halted him," Raz says. "He is not harmed. When we move on, he will be freed. Come, Kernel, it is time to return to the ark."

"But he won't be able to go home," Kernel says.

"We will send him back with a piece of a lodestone to protect him," Raz promises. "He will be safe, at least until he faces the demons and is destroyed along with the rest of his kind."

"You're sure?" Kernel asks.

"I give you my word."

I want to tell Raz what I think of his *word*, but my lips are frozen along with the rest of me. I have as much control over myself as a concrete block has.

Raz gouges a bit of rock out of a lodestone, presses it into my right palm and closes my fingers around it. Then he turns into a ball of light and starts to pulse. The stones of the chamber throb around us. Kernel casts me a shameful look and shrugs. Right now, I almost hate him more than Lord Loss or Bec. How can he turn his back on us? I might be a werewolf, but I still remember what it means to be human and I fight for the things that mattered to me before I changed.

As I struggle to break free of the spell holding me captive, Kernel half turns and sniffs the air. His eyes narrow. He focuses on a spot a few metres away, then says, "Raz..."

"Please do not interrupt. This is very—"

"A window's forming."

The ball of light stops pulsing. "Are you certain?"

Kernel nods. "Over there." He points. "It's not one of yours?"

"No." There's a sighing sound. "How much time do we have?"

"Not—"

A window of grey light opens and Bec steps through. "—much," Kernel finishes glumly.

Bec looks taller than before, but that's a trick of the shadows billowing around her. They encase her from head to toe, rise above her in clouds and trail behind her like robes. Her eyes are pools of shadowy flickers. Vapours dance across her lips. The shadows move constantly, sometimes covering her completely, then parting to reveal a glimpse of her pale face. There's something of Juni Swan about her, but she looks more of a menace than Juni ever did.

"I can't let you leave, Kernel," she says, and there's the same flat tone to her voice that I noted before. She doesn't sound evil, merely determined. There's even a hint of sadness mixed in somewhere, as if she's sorry she has to do this.

"How did you find us?" Kernel mutters, backing away from her.

"I'm the memory of the Kah-Gash," she says. "I remember everything I see or absorb. When we were in contact, I shared your recent memories. I can't see the lights but I can mimic your actions and go where you've gone, and also where the Old Creatures took you. I can go *everywhere* you've been. I can even find the ark."

"No!" Raz gasps, sounding more human than he did before.

"Yes, my ancient friend." Bec smiles thinly. "You hid it masterfully, but your hiding place has been exposed. I will lead the demons to the ark and set them loose on the creatures you have gathered. Without Kernel, they're doomed."

With a shriek, the ball of light shoots at Bec. She laughs and swats it aside as if it was a fly. As Raz smashes into the wall of the chamber, his spell over me shatters and I regain control. I launch myself at Bec and land on her back. I bare my fangs and snap at her neck, but the tendrils of shadow thicken around her and send a wave of electricity shooting through me. With a choking noise, I'm flung against the wall like Raz.

"You cannot fight me," Bec says calmly. "I am two now. Death has joined with me. I am its vessel and mouthpiece. When you attack me, you attack Death — and that is a foe no one can defeat."

Raz recovers and throws himself at Bec again. This time the ball of light engages with the shadows surrounding the small girl. The air fills with high-pitched crackling noises, so shrill that blood trickles from my ears and nose. There are blinding flashes and disorienting blackouts. Bec stands immobile at the centre of the warring forces, fingers twitching but otherwise motionless as the spitting shadows swirl around the pulsating ball of light.

I try to wade in but the air close to Bec is hotter than I can stand. I get to within a couple of metres of her, then the hairs on my arms catch fire and I have to retreat and roll in the dust to quench the flames.

Kernel's staring at the battling pair, jaw slack, eyes wide. "We have to help!" I roar, staggering to my feet, wiping sweat and blood from my face.

"We can't," Kernel whispers. Blood is seeping from his ears and nose too.

"There must be something we can do," I snarl, shaking him roughly.

"Like what?"

"Unite our magic. Hit Bec hard. Unleash the Kah-Gash."

"Are you mad?" he scoffs. "Bec's part of the Kah-Gash, but now she's also part of Death. If we join, we'll link up with the Shadow. Do you want to put the power of the Kah-Gash in Death's hands?"

I stare at Kernel, then at the waves of shadows writhing around Bec. Maybe this is when I make the move that damns the world. Perhaps this is how it ends, with me handing Death the force it needs to reduce everything to ash. If it gains control of the Kah-Gash, it can use me as a puppet, pull my strings as it's jerking Bec's, send me to Earth to wreak havoc.

"We have to get out of here," Kernel pants, dragging me towards the window of green light, which is still open.

"What about Raz?" I growl, breaking free.

"He's lost," Kernel says. "It's over. Bec knows where

the ark is. She can find it. The plans of the Old Creatures are ruined. Raz can't help us now. Nobody can."

"Then let's die here," I say softly and Kernel pauses. I search his bright blue eyes for acceptance. "If this is the finish, let's go out with a bang. You and me, alone against Death. What do you say?"

Kernel licks his lips. His features soften and I think he's going to agree. I ready myself for the final battle, looking forward to the relief of oblivion which failure and death will bring. But then Kernel shakes his head.

"I don't want to die so far from home. If we can't make a difference, let's at least perish on our own world, not on a dead planet."

I sigh heavily, accepting the fact that relief isn't to be mine just yet. Nodding, I edge to the window of green light with Kernel, but stop there and study the warring giants. I don't want to quit until the fight's been decided. If Raz can surprise his foe and chalk up an unlikely victory, there's still hope.

But it soon becomes clear that victory isn't to be ours. The snakes of shadows rip into the heart of the ball of light, tearing chunks out of it. The dislodged scraps drift through the air like bits of plastic, then crinkle away to nothing. There can be no doubt that Raz is going down for the three count.

"Go, Kernel," the ball of light whispers. "You can do no good here."

"I'm sorry," Kernel moans.

"I regret it too," Raz says. "We tried so hard to prevent this but it seems our efforts were in vain. Please forgive us. If we could…"

Whatever he was about to say is lost in a terrible screeching sound, like two huge metal plates being scraped together. There's a flash of light so intense that for a few seconds I think I've been blinded, and fire breaks out all over my body. As my sight returns and I thrash at the flames covering me, I see dozens of shards of light floating through the air. They're all that remain of the Old Creature.

The shadows settle around Bec and her head moves, eyes following one scrap of light to another, watching with grim satisfaction as they blink out. She blows on one that drifts close to her mouth, laughing softly as it catapults through the air.

Kernel grabs my arm and makes a wheezing noise. The flames didn't take hold on him – one of the advantages of having no hair – but there are ugly scorch marks across his face, and a hole in one of his cheeks where the heat burnt through his flesh. He tries to drag me away but I pull against him and lock eyes with Bec.

"I'll kill you before this is over," I vow.

Bec shakes her head. "No."

"I'll rip your head from—" I begin, but she cuts me off.

"The fight with the Old Creature drained Death, but it's recovering swiftly. If you don't leave now, it will destroy you, seize all three pieces of the Kah-Gash and claim victory early."

"Like you care what it—"

"Get the hell out of here, fool!" she screams and the fear in her eyes hits me harder than any threat. With a heavy heart, I wrap an arm round Kernel and dive through the window of green light, roaring with rage and frustration, knowing all is truly lost.

TUNNELLING THROUGH

→Shark, Timas and Kirilli are waiting for us on the asteroid, sitting close to the window, talking in low voices. They don't spot us immediately. It's only when Kernel groans and staggers away from me that their heads shoot up and they leap to their feet.

"Well?" Shark barks hopefully, figuring Kernel's return must be a positive sign.

"We're sunk," I tell him and the hope flickers out in an instant.

"The Old Creature wouldn't help?" Kirilli asks.

"No. But even if he had, it wouldn't have mattered. Bec followed us. She's in league with Death. They crossed shortly after we did and killed the Old Creature."

"What are you talking about?" Shark frowns. "Kernel's the only one who can build a window that quickly."

"Not any more," I chuckle mirthlessly.

"You mean she could come here at any moment?" Kirilli gasps, eyes flicking from one stubby outcrop to the next, searching for unnatural shadows.

"No," Kernel says. "She can't see the lights. She said she could only mimic what I do, and go to the places I'd been to when she touched me and absorbed my memories. She can't track me."

"Thank heavens for that," Kirilli smiles.

"She can find the ark," Kernel tells him. "She'll lead the demons there."

Nobody looks unduly upset. It's hard for us to care about the ark. Earth's in trouble. People we know and love are going to die. So what if some spaceship trillions of kilometres away faces the same threat? Our world is what matters most. To hell with the rest of the universe. We can't think that big.

"What happens now?" Timas asks as Kernel and I sit and stare at the dead landscape of the asteroid. "Are you going to return to the ark?"

"I wouldn't be able to find it," Kernel sighs. "Bec has a perfect memory, but I don't. The Old Creatures guided me there and back. I don't know how to locate it by myself."

"Well, it's an ill wind that doesn't blow anyone a bit of luck," Shark beams. "I guess that means you have to come back with us now."

"For all the good I'll do," Kernel grumbles. "Maybe I'll just stay here and wait for the universe to end. It'd be a lot simpler."

"But nowhere near as exciting." I stand and shake

blood from my face, using magic to heal the damage to my ears and nose. I don't feel depressed. I have a sense of destiny clicking into place, of things playing out the way they were always meant to. We've tried every angle we could think of and they've all failed. We've passed the point where we can save the day with a cunning plan. We're puppets of fate now. There's no use worrying about events we can't control.

"Where next?" I ask cheerfully.

Nobody meets my gaze. They don't have any ideas. We had targets to aim for up to this — Juni Swan, the Shadow, Lord Loss, the Old Creature. Now all we can do is return home, put up a good fight and accept annihilation with a rueful grin.

"We could…" Timas says, then falls silent.

"If Bec is part of Death, and we kill her…" Shark begins.

"There are other Old Creatures…" Kirilli murmurs.

"Kernel?" I cock an eyebrow.

The surly teenager shrugs. "It doesn't make any difference."

"Then take us to Prae Athim," I decide. "If I'm going down fighting, I want to go with my faithful pack behind me."

→We find Prae, a few units of soldiers and my enhanced werewolves battling demons and a bunch of zombies outside a small town. We fall in beside them, surprising and delighting Prae. No time to exchange pleasantries. I howl at the werewolves, letting them know their leader's back. They happily return the howl and fight with renewed vigour, keen to impress.

Larry breaks away from the carnage and loops around me, snapping with excitement, sniffing me all over to ensure I'm the real deal, not some demonic doppelgänger. I bark a few commands to the last survivor of my original pack, telling him to stop sniffing and get back to fighting. As he bounds away, calling others to his side, I focus on strays around the edges and pick them off as they try to sneak away. I don't care whether they're demons or zombies. Some of the others have a hard time slaughtering those who were once living people, but they're all the same in my wolfen eyes.

It doesn't take long to bring the demons and zombies to their knees. The pack had control of the situation before I arrived. My presence merely speeds things up. Within minutes we're relaxing on a mound of mutilated corpses, cheering because it's what you do to celebrate a victory, even though it's just one small triumph in a doomed war.

"Didn't expect to see you again," Prae grins. "It's been hell here. I thought you'd fallen on some far-off demon world."

"Not a hope," I smile wryly, running an eye over my

pack, noting the new arrivals, yapping at some of those I recognise from before.

"What's been happening?" Shark asks and Prae quickly brings us up to date. Earth's in a lot worse shape than when we left. Six weeks have passed. Windows are opening at a rate of four or five a day. Demons are having their wicked way in most countries. The Disciples, mages, werewolves and soldiers have been fighting doggedly, but I see desolation in Prae's eyes. When we left for Lord Loss's realm, people still had hope. Not any longer. From what Prae tells us, realisation has set in across the globe. Even those who've avoided contact with the demons know they're living on borrowed time. They go through the motions, but without any real expectation of victory.

The zombies came from nearby. Prae says hundreds of them – and even more demons – are massed outside a city a few kilometres away. A lodestone must be buried somewhere close. Once Bec located it, the demons set to work, assisted by one of their treacherous mages, and opened a tunnel. Hordes of demons pushed through with vicious glee, and the dead have been coming back to life to help them.

There's a strange magical energy in the air, which Kirilli recognises from when he fought the Shadow on the ship. Death used that energy to reanimate the corpses and it's pulled the same trick here. The blank-eyed zombies are driven by a force they have no control over, killing recklessly, slaves to their ever-hungry master.

The first clusters of walking dead clawed their way out of crypts and graves, but many of the people killed by the demons have also been brought back to life. A lot of victims are ripped to shreds by over-eager demons, but those who are left largely intact are revived by the magic of Death.

"We haven't been able to get close to the mouth of the tunnel," Prae sighs. "So we've been trying to pen them in, to stop splinter groups like this one from spreading. The demons aren't particularly strong, and the zombies are no more powerful than ordinary humans. If this tunnel is a one-off and we can hold them here, it won't prove too much of a problem."

"It's just the first of many," I tell her. "More will open and in time stronger demons will cross."

Prae nods slowly. "I guessed as much, but I still... you know... hoped."

"Forget about hope. We don't have time for such fantasies." I cast an eye over the dead around us, then peer at the city in the distance. Planes circle overhead, dropping bombs. Teams of soldiers and mages are dotted around.

"Call off the planes," I growl at Prae, starting towards the city.

"You're going in?" she asks.

"Yes. I'll find the lodestone, destroy it, and that'll be that."

"But there are a *lot* of them. More crossing all the time. They're not especially strong, but there are so many…"

"All the more for me to kill," I chuckle, then break into a jog, howling for my werewolves, leaving the humans to retreat or follow as they please.

→Carnage. Bloodshed. Mayhem. We cut our way through the ranks of demons and zombies, dismembering, disembowelling. Kernel guides us, tracing patches of light to the location of the tunnel. I've assigned five of the toughest werewolves – including Larry – to serve as his bodyguards, although I don't think he really needs them. Kernel was never the ablest fighter, but he lays into these opponents with determination, using magic to liquefy them or make their heads explode. I've never seen him so bloodthirsty. I guess a lot of people will be acting this way now that we're close to the end. Desperation tends to make humans act unnaturally. But if they all fight like Kernel, that will be a good thing.

Our opponents fall like bowling pins, overwhelmed by the raw force we strike them with. They kill a few soldiers and werewolves, even one or two mages. But their successes pale in comparison to ours, and it's clear within minutes that we outpower them.

They make their final stand on the outskirts of the city, where the lodestone rests in an excavated ditch. Some of the smarter demons retreat through the tunnel, back to the safety of their own universe, but most crowd around it and defend it to the death. I don't think they do so out of loyalty — they're simply too dumb to know when they're beaten.

I gut a boar-shaped demon, spit out entrails and shoulder my way forward. Then I'm on the stone. It's an unremarkable piece of rock, set in the mouth of a small tunnel. I peer over the top of the lodestone and see a woman behind it, joined to the stone by her chin, parts of her body scattered all around, still functioning.

The woman snarls at me and says something in a foreign language. I could use a spell to translate it, but why bother? I'm sure it's more of the same old crap.

I ball my right fingers into a fist and crush the woman's head. Apart from her agonised squeal, this has no effect. Several demons throw themselves on me, but I flex my muscles and swat them aside. Then I lash at the rock with my fists, one punch after another. It cracks on the fourth blow, splits on the fifth, then crumbles after a few more.

As the lodestone breaks, a wind rips out of the tunnel. It quickly picks up speed and sweeps across the land, gathering all the demons and zombies, knocking over some of the humans and werewolves too. Using magic, I root myself and watch as the wind is sucked back up the tunnel, returning its catch to the realm of the Demonata. A few human and wolfen innocents are taken too. I can't say I'm too bothered. This is a tough world and it's getting tougher. Only the strong are worth caring about.

As the wind drops, the tunnel closes and rocks and earth grind together. I glance around at those who remain. Many were knocked over and are picking themselves up, weeping and groaning. Prae has been clinging to a werewolf. She lets go and staggers away, then hurries to check on the rest of the pack, showing that odd maternal concern that she reserves for these hairy misfits.

"That wasn't so hard," I grin at Kernel. His eyes are wild, darting this way and that, looking for something else to kill. "Easy, big guy," I calm him, laying a firm hand on his shoulder. "It's over for now. We can rest a while."

"Rest?" he sneers. "Don't be a child. There's another tunnel. I can smell it."

"Where?" I growl.

"The other side of the world. We can be there in minutes. You game?"

"What's it like compared to the one we just shut?"

"Bigger. It's only been open a few hours, but already

more demons have come through there than here. Stronger ones too. A lot nastier than these familiars."

"Are there Disciples on the scene? Mages? Soldiers?"

"Who cares?" Kernel hoots. "I'll take them on by myself if you're chicken."

"You want to be careful who you taunt," I snarl.

"Don't be ridiculous," Kernel smirks. "You won't harm me. You need me. I'm your quick way in and out of the madness."

I eye Kernel warily as he works on opening a new window. I don't like this new, wilder version of Cornelius Fleck. Something switched off inside him when the Old Creature was killed. He thought he had a greater purpose, that he was going to save the universe. Now he's been reduced to the same level as the rest of us, scrapping to salvage an unremarkable planet on its last legs. The demotion hit him hard. I'm not sure how many brain cells he's operating on. In this state he could do anything.

But there's no time to try and help the borderline crazy Kernel. Because even as I'm worrying about him, the window opens and he darts through. I have no option but to call my pack of werewolves to my side and push on after him, before I lose him to an army of demons and the walking dead.

BIGGER, BETTER, BADDER

→I know straightaway that we're in trouble. When you fight as often as I do, you develop a knack of swiftly judging the course of a battle. To any normal person, this would look no different to the war zone we came from, a group of humans and werewolves up against demons and reanimated corpses.

But looks are deceptive. The magical energy in the air is much thicker than it was outside the city. That's good for us, but even better for the demons. It means stronger monsters can cross, beasts who can channel the energy and wreak more havoc than the creatures we crushed a few minutes ago.

There are already some mages and soldiers on the scene. We wade in beside them, werewolves running wild, Disciples unleashing bolts of magic, soldiers firing concentrated bursts, shredding the bodies of weaker demons and zombies.

A group of the undead are clustered around hundreds of screaming people. I scatter them with a wave of magic that rips most to pieces. "Fight or get the hell out of here!" I bellow at the humans, then grapple with a massive demon that has several heads and more arms than I can count. It tugs and snaps at me, piercing my flesh in dozens of places, focusing its largest mouth on my face.

I roll across the ground with the demon, punching savagely, biting at anything that comes within range of my fangs. I drive a fist into its stomach and feel around for guts to yank out. Before I can finish off the beast, a foul stench fills the air. Looking up, I spot Kernel vomiting over the demon. As the last drops drip from his lower lip, he touches the vomit and it flashes, becoming acidic. The lethal puke sizzles through the demon's shell and it falls away, squealing with agony.

"You love that old vomit trick," I grunt, getting to my feet, wiping slime, blood and some of the remains of Kernel's last supper from my flesh.

"It works," he says, looking for his next victim.

"I could have dealt with the demon myself," I tell him.

"I know. But I didn't like its face."

He whirls away, scanning the masses for another face that doesn't take his fancy. He certainly has plenty to choose from. I fry a few more demons, then push after Kernel. I'm worried he might do something stupid in his wired-up state.

We fight desperately, more demons crossing all the time, each wave stronger than the last. I haven't sensed any demon masters hitting the scene, but these are certainly A+ students. They slaughter soldiers for fun, and don't have too much hassle despatching werewolves or mages either. We've already suffered severe casualties and the battle is only minutes old.

I force my way through a pack of zombies and grab Kernel. "The lodestone!" I yell in his ear. "We have to destroy it. We can't take much more of this."

"It's over there," he shouts, pointing to his left.

I stand on my toes. All I can see are demons and zombies, a few hapless humans trapped among them. "How far?" I ask Kernel.

"A mile, maybe more."

"How are you at flying?"

"Never tried it on this world," he says. "But I'm game."

Linking hands, we jump high. I've flown once before, with Beranabus, when he dragged me out of a plane. I've tried to repeat the trick a few times since, but there was never enough magic for me to tap into. Now there is and we soar forward, shooting over the heads of the warring forces like a couple of blow-ins from *Peter Pan*.

Some of the more powerful beasts fire at us as we flit by. We easily deflect the balls of energy and rocks. But as we get within a hundred metres of the tunnel, a squadron of winged demons flaps into the air. We draw to a halt and eye them warily.

The demons, thirty or forty of them, hang in the air above the lodestone. They're deliberately positioned, an aerial guard to protect the tunnel.

"There are others on the ground," Kernel says sullenly. "More powerful than any we've faced so far."

"Can we take them?" I ask.

"Maybe." He casts an eye over the demons behind us. "But we'd have more fun if we tackled that lot."

"This isn't about fun," I growl.

"Of course it is," he laughs. "You taught me that. We've lost. All that remains is to take as many demons down with us as we can, and have a blast killing them."

I scowl, but I can't refute his statement. If Kernel has become a suicidal, kill-crazy goon, it's because of what I've done to him.

"Let's try for the lodestone," I mutter. "If we slip past the guards and destroy it, this will be a victory to savour."

Kernel considers that, then nods. He swoops ahead of me, issuing a challenging cry to the winged demons. With a curse, I tuck my chin down and fly after him.

The dogfight is short and vicious. The demons aren't just airworthy — they're powerful too. We try to zip through the gaps between them, but they're faster than us and more naturally suited to mid-air manoeuvres. We hit them with balls of energy and acidic, projectile puke, but although we cause damage and kill a few of them, most shrug off our blows and respond with ear-splitting shrieks, two-metre long talons and beaks that can rip a head clean off a neck.

Within a minute we know it's a hopeless task. I catch Kernel's eye, shake my head and peel away. He follows, deciding he'd rather not be pecked to death by a pack of demonic harpies. They don't chase us, but settle on the ground, ready to launch another defence of the lodestone if threatened.

"I told you we shouldn't have bothered," Kernel says sulkily.

"How long can they keep that tunnel open?" I ask.

"Do I look like I'm an expert?" he huffs.

"I know you are — you've boasted about it often enough. How long?"

Kernel chuckles, then focuses on the area around the lodestone, studying the patches of light which are invisible to the rest of us. He sighs. "It won't crash any time soon. I reckon it can be kept going for a few years."

I feel sick. I take a couple of deep breaths, clear my thoughts, then turn and stomp away.

"Where are we going?" Kernel asks, tucking in behind me.

"To signal a retreat."

"We're going to run?"

"Can you think of another course?"

"Not really, no."

"Then shut up and help me pull back as many survivors as we can."

→We summon soldiers, mages, werewolves and civilians, then help them fight their way clear. We lead them to a convoy of trucks and buses which are waiting a few kilometres away, set in place by a forward-thinking general in case the battle went poorly. The demons chase heatedly, eager to chalk up more kills before we slip through the net. Some of the faster monsters target the convoy and clamber over the roofs of the vehicles, breaking in, causing high-speed crashes. A few perish in the flames like the humans they targeted, but most walk away, laughing, lugging severed heads, maybe to settle down over a few mugs of blood later and compare kills with their comrades.

Kernel, Shark, Kirilli and I do what we can to minimise the damage. The others look to us for guidance, since we're the most powerful and experienced. We guide the trucks and buses to safety, repel the demons and zombies, spread ourselves as widely as possible. But ultimately we're just four guys. We can't save everyone. The losses are horrendous, in the high thousands. And they'll get worse once the demons stabilise and branch out.

When we've led the troops to safety, we head for a makeshift camp where scores of medics are tending to the wounded or setting aside the dead. I howl a few times, calling the remaining werewolves to my side. When sixteen – all that appear to be left – are gathered around me, I march to a large, vacant tent. Timas joins us along the way, responding to my howls as the werewolves did. He looks drained, and he's covered in blood splatters, but he doesn't seem to have been injured. Some soldiers try to waylay us to ask for instructions, but I wave them aside, telling them I'll confer with them shortly.

We sink into chairs in the tent and I look around wearily. Larry isn't one of the sixteen werewolves and there's no sign of Prae Athim either.

"If you're looking for Prae, she's dead," Timas says before I ask. "She perished trying to protect a wounded werewolf. I cut her head off and incinerated it, so she won't be coming back as a zombie."

I process the news, then ask, "What about Larry?"

Nobody answers. I doubt if anyone cares. To be honest, I find it hard to work up much sympathy either, not when so many thousands have been killed. Sorry, Larry. I hope you died well, but tough luck if you didn't.

"What now?" Kirilli asks. I've never seen him look so miserable, but it's not the type of self-pitying misery he once wallowed in. He's sad because of what he's seen.

"We try to pen them in," I sigh. "Hit them with all the missiles we can. Drench the land around the tunnel with a circle of petrol. Light it when they try to push out — fire will kill a lot of them if we add magic to the flames. Establish a perimeter of mages. Fly in volunteers, test them for magic, set new mages to work with the others. Make another assault on the lodestone when we have support."

"How far can they travel if they break through?" Kirilli asks. "On the ship, they were confined by a bubble of magic. Is there a similar bubble here?"

"No," Kernel says. "The energy from this tunnel streams out freely. There's a limit to its reach, but that might be a few hundred kilometres in all directions."

"Then we need to evacuate everyone within a two-hundred-kilometre radius," Shark says. "I'll talk with whoever's in charge, set soldiers on the job, turn this into a no-man's land."

"You don't understand," Kernel says. "We can't control this."

"You just said there were limits," Shark growls.

"To *this* tunnel, yes," Kernel snaps. "But there are more powerful lodestones. I'm sure they'll open a new tunnel soon, one of unlimited energy. The demons who cross will be able to go anywhere. And masters will be free to cross too, hundreds of demons as strong as Lord Loss, if not stronger."

"Can't we stop it before it opens?" I ask.

Kernel tuts. "I don't have a magic wand. I can sense a tunnel as it's opening, usually in advance. We can be on the scene within minutes, but what if they open two at the same time? Three? More? Demon masters *will* establish a toehold. If we weren't able to break through the defences of this mediocre lot, what sort of hope do we stand when we're up against the real deal?"

There's a long silence. Slowly, each of them turns to look at me, placing the burden on my shoulders, leaving me to make the fatal call. I don't blame them. I'd pass the buck too, if I could. But if the buck has to stop here, so be it.

"Get your soldiers to move out the survivors," I tell Shark, "then come back. We'll rest up. Kernel will watch for tunnels. When another like this one is due to open, we'll contact those close to it and give the order to retreat. There's no point fighting the stronger demons. We'll tell everyone to run. The fast will survive. The slow…" I shake my head.

"We're not going to try and help them?" Kirilli whispers.

"We'll save ourselves."

"For…?" Shark asks.

"The big guys." I crack my knuckles. "That's my plan. We ignore the smaller, weaker tunnels. We summon the most powerful Disciples and mages, then wait. When a permanent tunnel opens, through which demon masters can cross, we hit with everything we have. If we close it, we relax and wait for the next one, then go through it all again. If we fail, there's no Plan B. We triumph or perish."

"Our last stand,"Timas murmurs.

"It's come to that?" Shark asks quietly.

"Yes."

"Good!" he booms, thrusting himself out of his chair. "I hate pussyfooting around. I'll pass on the word, then grab some shut-eye. Make sure you call me in time for the big show — I don't want to miss this one."

Then he strides out of the tent, leaving the rest of us to smile ruefully, wait nervously and prepare as best we can for the end of the world.

À LA MOSES

→Four days of waiting. We're all restless and itching to go into battle. It would be easier to join one of the many wars raging around the globe than sit here and twiddle our thumbs. But as bloody as the battles are — we see and hear all about them on the constant news reports — they fall short of the apocalyptic mark. Six tunnels have been opened, but all are limited, and though millions of people have fallen to the demon invaders, the world struggles on.

I spend most of the time with my werewolves. I prefer their company to that of humans. I don't have to think when I'm with my wolfen pack, merely growl every so often to keep them in line. I lead them on occasional forays into demon-controlled territory, so they can pull out a few zombies to snack on. But apart from those welcome diversions, we mostly rest from the sun in a tent, relax beneath the moon at night, and pant and scratch a lot.

I don't have much contact with the others. I've seen

Shark and Timas going from one meeting to another with a variety of politicians and army officers. They're putting some sort of emergency campaign together, acting like we have a plan, trying to keep panic to a minimum.

Kernel and Kirilli have gathered an army of mages and Disciples. They've two hundred or so lined up and ready for action. Many refused to answer their call, preferring to fight the demons who've already crossed, defending areas and people close to their hearts. Kernel and the ex-stage magician run the volunteers ragged, testing them in every way possible, toughening and sharpening them for the mother of all battles. I don't think it will make any real difference, but if it keeps them occupied, I guess it serves a purpose.

Finally, when I'm about to go stir crazy, Kernel sticks his head inside my tent. "It's time."

I snap to attention immediately. "A new tunnel's opening?"

"Yes. Not too far from where you used to live. On the coast."

"It's the big one?"

He nods soberly. "Massive. It hasn't opened yet, but already the lights are going crazy, even from this distance."

"Tell the others," I mutter, the many hairs on the back

of my neck rising. "And Kernel?" He stops and looks back. "It's been nice knowing you."

He smiles bitterly. "No it hasn't," he says and goes to summon the troops, leaving me to ready the werewolves for what will probably be our final fight.

→Kernel creates a window of orange light and we step through on to a grassy cliff. The tunnel is being opened in a cave beneath, but we wanted to get all of our troops assembled on this side before facing our foes. I stride to the edge of the cliff as the rest of the mages, Disciples and werewolves cross in orderly file. We didn't bother bringing soldiers — they couldn't do anything against the more powerful Demonata.

It's a wild stretch of coastline, the water dashing against the rocks far below, a sharp drop to a quick, messy death. Rain falls steadily and winds rip in off the ocean, which stretches as far as I can see. The land is barren all around. I doubt if anyone ever lived in this beautiful but desolate spot.

I feel magic building in the air. It's almost the same as being in the demon universe. I let animal-shaped streams of steam trickle from my fingertips and watch as they dissolve in the rain. There are thudding vibrations from deep underfoot, as if goblins or trolls were hammering drums in the bowels of the earth, in preparation for battle.

Shark and Timas have been holding a hushed conversation. Now they move away from the cliff and Timas takes up position, partially sheltered behind a jutting rock. He's brought a stack of laptops with him and quickly sets them up. Shark stabs a few umbrellas into the earth and opens them over the technical genius to provide him with cover. Curious, I amble across to see what they're up to.

"This isn't the time for video games."

Timas looks at me gravely. "No game."

"We had an interesting debate," Shark grunts.

"What sort of a debate?" I frown.

"About the future of the planet and what happens if we lose today."

"And?" I cast a troubled eye over the laptops.

"My way of reckoning," Shark says thickly, "is if we get creamed, the people of Earth are better off dead than left to the vicious devices of the Demonata. We got clearance from most of the relevant authorities, but it wouldn't have mattered if they'd objected. Timas could have cracked the security codes."

"*Maybe*," Timas mutters. "Not definitely. It would have been an intriguing challenge, but one that it is better not to have to face."

"What are you talking about?" I snap.

Shark taps a small camera set in the shoulder of his uniform. "Several of us are wearing cameras like this.

Timas will be watching. If the demons get the better of us, he has orders to press the button."

"What button?"

"The nuclear button," Timas says softly.

I gawp at him, then at the grim-faced Shark. "Are you trying to wind me up?"

"Don't be a child," Shark snarls. "You said it yourself — this is our last stand. If we fall, the planet falls. I'd rather it fell to us than them. Quicker, cleaner, more humane. And we might take some of them with us."

"But…" My head spins. Maybe this is what Juni foresaw. Perhaps Timas won't be able to push the button and the task will fall to me, and that's how I'll destroy the world.

"What's the alternative?" Shark asks. "Let the demons run free, torture and kill at their leisure, make slaves of those they choose to spare? We saw what happens to prisoners in Lord Loss's castle. Do you want your friend Bo Kooniart to have to suffer that again?"

"We don't have the right to make this call," I whisper.

"Of course we do," Shark says. "But even so, we ran it by the watchmen of the nuclear community. There were a lot of dissenters, but a few gave us the green light, enough to make our job a formality. Timas is hooked up to bases across the world. If we run foul of the demon army, he'll bring this planet crashing down around us. There won't be a cinder ball left by the time he's finished. Let's see the Demonata get a kick out of that!"

I stare from Shark to Timas, then nod slowly. "But only if we definitely fail," I tell Timas. "Don't press any buttons just because you *think* we're going to lose. As long as one of us stands, keep your finger clear. Understand?"

"Affirmative," Timas says, then sticks out an arm. As we shake hands, he says, "Give them hell, Grubbs."

"And all the toppings," I promise, then turn my back on the Pied Piper of nuclear destruction and pray he isn't called upon to play the world to its doom.

Kernel's waiting for me. "It's open," he says simply.

"How do we get down?" I ask.

"There's a tunnel beneath the waterline. We jump and swim."

"Don't be ridiculous," I sneer. "You march bravely into a lion's den — you don't *swim* to it."

"You have a better suggestion?" he responds icily.

I stroll to the edge of the cliff. It's a straight drop to where the waves roll in and crash against the base. The easiest way, as Kernel suggested, would be to drop and use magic to protect ourselves. Under normal circumstances, that would be our only option. But there's so much energy in the air, we can be creative, like in the demon universe.

The memory of an old story comes to mind and I grin. Raising a hand, I gesture to the water below. It begins to bubble and spit. Then, as curious Disciples and mages gather around me, the waves part and an avenue opens, a stretch of dry land at the foot of the cliff, surrounded by towering walls of water.

"Hark at the modern-day Moses," Kirilli says jealously. "If I could have done that in my act, I'd have been bigger than David Copperfield."

"You ain't seen nothing yet," I drawl, then point my other hand at the cliff. With a low, rumbling sound, a thick chunk of rock fifty metres to my right grinds out of the wall, forming a step ten metres long, five metres wide, half a metre high. I cock a finger and another chunk of rock slides out of the wall just beneath it, another beneath that, and so on. A staircase swiftly forms, reaching all the way down to the ocean floor.

"Will they hold?" Kirilli asks, eyeing the steps nervously.

"Only one way to find out," I grin, then jump off the cliff and land on a step several metres below. It doesn't even shudder. "Hurry up," I call to the others. "Last one down's a rotten egg."

They laugh, then trail down the staircase after me to the cave where the monsters are lying in wait.

THE MISSING LINK

→We creep down the stairs. Nerves fray the further we descend. I sense a few of the mages lose their resolve and retreat. I don't pause to berate them. This isn't a place for the weak. We're better off without cowards.

That's harsh, the voice of the Kah-Gash murmurs. *It's not so long ago that you would have run too.*

"Here for the big party?" I grunt cynically. "You must be loving this."

What makes you think that? It sounds genuinely surprised.

"This is what you want, isn't it, an excuse to unleash your full power and destroy the human universe?"

If I wanted that, the Kah-Gash says witheringly, *I would have made it happen a long time ago. I wouldn't need to wait for an excuse.*

"You mean you want to destroy the demon universe?" I frown.

The Kah-Gash sighs. *You still don't understand. I don't want anything. When there was only one universe, I had a natural urge to keep it as it was. Since it splintered, I have simply enjoyed the experience of being. I have no vested interest in the result of the battle about to take place. I'm merely a curious observer.*

"But Kernel said you manoeuvred us into place. According to the Old Creatures, you kept Bec's soul intact when her body died. You chose to inhabit three humans at the same time. You set this up."

Guilty, the Kah-Gash chuckles. *But it was the fascination of watching what happens that motivated me. I have no yearning for one outcome over another.*

"So will you help or hinder us?" I press.

Neither, the Kah-Gash says.

"In that case, shut up," I snarl.

As you wish, the Kah-Gash whispers and falls silent.

"Slow up, big guy," Shark says, tapping my shoulder. I glance back at him. He points to a spot behind us — the mouth of a tunnel. "That's the way to the cave. You missed it. I guess your thoughts were elsewhere."

I smile ruefully. "You could say that."

Kernel and Kirilli are waiting on the step by the opening in the cliff face. The Disciples who have come with us are on the steps above, flanked by my pack of werewolves. The mages are scattered across the steps behind. Most are trembling. A few are physically sick. But all hold. There'll be no more deserters today. Those who remain are in this until the awful, apocalyptic end.

"A few words perhaps?" Kernel mutters.

I shrug, then face my troops and roar, "Let's kill some demons!"

With a relieved cheer – I don't think anyone was in the mood for a long speech – the mages, werewolves and Disciples sweep after me into the tunnel. Bidding farewell to sunlight and the world of humanity, we enter the demon-riddled den.

→The tunnel is narrow, but a couple of metres high. The floor is damp and littered with fish and other creatures of the sea, a few of which still flop or slither about. It's hot, the heat coming from the cave ahead of us. It's a dry, unnatural warmth that I've felt many times before, always in the presence of demons.

Kernel is beside me. He's created a ball of light, which trails us like a faithful hound. His sharp blue eyes have lost their crazed sheen. He looks nervous now.

"Stick close to me," I tell him. "We stand a chance if we fight together. Don't hold anything back. We can't worry about the Kah-Gash betraying us. We have to throw everything we can at this lot."

"What about Bec?" Kernel asks. "Do we kill her or try to link up?"

"Kill."

"There's no way we can subdue her, make her power work for us?"

I grimace. "We can try, but I'm not holding out much hope."

"I wish Beranabus was here," Kernel sighs.

"He couldn't make much difference if he was. It's you and me now. The others are for show, to make us feel like we're not alone. But we are. It all boils down to how much damage we can wreak with two-thirds of the power of the Kah-Gash."

"Do you think it will be enough?" Kernel asks.

"We're about to find out," I mutter, and with a few long strides I step into the cave of the Demonata.

It's massive, far bigger than I imagined. There are large stone pillars set in a ring around it, a few dozen or more. One of the larger stones serves as the mouth of the tunnel to the demon universe. A human – I can't tell if it's a man or a woman – has joined with it and I see body parts mixed in with the rock. The tunnel stretches far behind, a mix of stone, flesh and guts, veins running along the sides like railway lines on a map. Enormous demons lurk within, poised to cross. I catch glimpses of tendrils and fangs. They're crawling through the tunnel, which is still widening. It isn't ready to grant them access to this world yet, but in a short while it will stabilise and they'll pop out like mutant babies from a monstrous womb.

On this side of the divide, Lord Loss awaits us. Because he once hosted Bec's part of the Kah-Gash, he can cross freely between universes. He bobs up and down in the air close to the rock, extended arms waving gently, snakes hissing softly in the hole where his heart should be. His dark red eyes are dilated and his lips turn down in a sad frown.

Beside him, shrouded in shadows, stands Bec. She's wearing a shawl of webs which falls to just beneath her knees. The small girl looks even more of a threat than Lord Loss, a result of the strands of shadows revolving around her and the dark, inhuman swirls in her eyes.

"So we come to this," Lord Loss murmurs as the rest of our troops spill into the cave and fan out.

"One chance, Bec," I growl, ignoring the demon master. "Come back to us and we'll forgive you. Stand against us and you'll die along with the rest of the scum."

"You know nothing of the ways of Death," Bec says quietly. "I cannot die. Even if you destroyed my body, my soul would thrive. Death will claim you today and all who come with you. And I will serve as the vessel through which it operates."

"It's not too late to change your mind," Kernel says, his voice cracking.

"Of course it is," Bec says with a thin smile.

"Then let's finish this." I howl at my werewolves and they lunge at Bec. I focus on Lord Loss. As I race towards him, roaring madly, the mages and Disciples crowd after me, each making their own choice whether to target the girl or the demon.

As I close in on Lord Loss, I leap into the air and grab hold of the cold, clammy skin around his throat. I dig my fingers in, snarling into his face, closer to him than I've ever been. He laughs as my thumbs search for his vocal cords and find only doughy flesh. His arms whip around me, the snakes in his chest bite for my heart and we whirl through the air as if dancing.

"You cannot know how I have longed for this moment," Lord Loss purrs, his mouth no more than a centimetre from my left ear. "I hate you as I have hated no other human. Your death will afford me more pleasure than—"

I send a ball of energy shooting through the demon's chin and into his brain. Fire flares behind his eyes and his flesh turns an ugly purple colour. With a gasp, he half-releases me and shakes his head. Loosening a hand, I aim for his eyes, but he catches me by the wrist and bends it back, tutting mockingly. His eyes and flesh regain their normal colour and he smiles as I fail to unleash another bolt.

"Naughty Grubitsch," he teases. "You should play fair. But you always had a problem doing that, didn't you? On the chess boards... in Slawter... in the cave where your brother died. You never had the courage to face me honestly."

I bellow in answer, becoming more of a werewolf, searching for the strength to break free of his hold. All of a sudden he releases me and I drop to the ground. As I lunge back to my feet, I spot Bec repelling my wolfen pack with ease, slitting their throats, setting them afire, swatting them aside like flies. Shadowy tendrils snake from her in all directions and attack the humans behind the werewolves. The shadows only have to brush softly against the cheeks or chests of most of the mages. At a single touch they topple, eyes freezing, skin turning a grey shade, dead before they hit the ground. With each murder, Bec grows stronger as Death absorbs the souls of the slain.

"Kernel!" I bellow, looking for him in the middle of the madness.

"Here," he calls, stepping forward. As I run to him, Lord Loss waves a hand at the roof of the cave. Stalactites drop from overhead. They pierce the skulls of several mages around me. I could protect myself with a shield, but instead I swipe the deadly pins aside in a display of contempt.

Moments later I'm standing beside Kernel. Our eyes meet and we nod briefly. I clutch him to me with a thick arm and level the other at Lord Loss. As magic explodes within Kernel and joins with mine, I let it channel through my fingers and streaks of black energy hiss through the air and strike Lord Loss with the force of a volcano, slamming him back against the wall of the cave.

Lord Loss screeches as we pulp him with the power of the Kah-Gash. We draw energy from all around, even from the tunnel of the Demonata. Hope blooms for the first time in ages. Lord Loss is writhing beneath our touch. If we can do this to one so strong, we can do it to others. Maybe this isn't our last stand. It might be only the first step forward to a new, demon-free future.

"The tunnel," Kernel says through chattering teeth — like me, he's struggling to hold himself together. The Kah-Gash wants to break free of our bodies and become a sheer force of energy. "We have to close it. Forget about Lord Loss."

"Never," I growl, then smile savagely. "But he can wait a while." Closing my fingers into a fist, I sever the lines of energy streaming from them. The demon master slumps to the ground, landing in a sorry-looking heap, no longer able to float with the dreadful majesty that's proved so impressive in the past.

I face the tunnel to the demon universe. The monsters within are almost at the opening. Their faces are twisted with rage and loathing. They've seen what we've done to Lord Loss. They feel our power. They know we're going to thwart their plans.

I laugh and point at the rock. Drawing power from the tunnel, I direct it back, willing the walls to grind shut, the rock to crumble, the tunnel to disintegrate.

The fleshy walls inside the mouth vibrate. The veins throb wildly. Some explode. The demons gibber wildly as blood rains down on them. To come this close to victory, only to be denied at the last moment… excruciating!

Their demented fury delights me. Taking a step closer, I draw yet more power from the universe on the other side of the tunnel. As delicious as this moment is, I can't make it last. It's time to end this battle and move on to the next. We need never be afraid of these creeps again, not as long as Kernel and I are…

Power drains from my fingers as swiftly as it filled them. With a confused cry, my head whips round. Bec is behind me, smirking. Her right hand rests on Kernel's shoulder and she's drawing power from him, and from me through Kernel.

"Stop!" I roar, throwing a punch at her.

She halts my giant paw with a glance, her smile widening, waves of shadows crackling across her pale cheeks. "We're part of the same weapon, Grubbs," she says. "You can't unleash the Kah-Gash without my permission."

"I'm the trigger," I yell. "I can do whatever the hell I like."

I try sapping power from her, as she has from us. But I can't. The flow is one way. I can draw more energy from the air – and I do – but a third of it flows into Bec as soon as I absorb it. And while I'm fighting the shadow-wrapped leech of a girl, I can't focus on anything else.

"Kill her!" Kernel screams, kicking out at Bec. He manages to knock her hand away, but the draining flow continues.

I turn on Bec and bare my fangs. Shadows leap from around her and dart at my eyes, momentarily blinding me. Several strands snake down my throat and I gag. Whirling away from the priestess, I spit out shadows and swipe them from my face. Kernel's shaken from my grip and goes skidding across the floor.

Bec steps in front of the tunnel and spreads her arms. "Come to me!" she cries. I think she's calling Lord Loss and my eyes fix on the demon master. He's dragged himself back to his knees, but he doesn't look ready to rejoin the fighting.

Then I realise it's not Lord Loss she's hailing. It's the others, separated from us by the thinnest of magical veils. Before I can react, a gush of even hotter air washes through the cave. As my heart sinks, the tunnel opens and a score of demons even more powerful than Lord Loss slither from their realm into ours.

THE WINK

→The demon masters are no larger or fiercer in appearance than most of the lesser monsters I've fought and killed. But their power sets the air in the cave throbbing, and the scale of it stuns me. They're way stronger than Lord Loss. I realise, as they rise and look upon us with malevolent glee, that the heartless, chess-obsessed beast is only a minor master. I thought he was a king among demons, the pinnacle of all we'd ever have to face. But in comparison with this lot, he's a novice.

As more slide into view, eager to be in on the killing, the Demonata set to work on the mages, Disciples and werewolves. They butcher arrogantly, at their leisure, picking off individuals and crushing them like balls of paper, relishing their agony. These masters could wipe out everyone with the flick of a wrist, but they want to play with us first.

I hurl myself at Kernel and link with him. He's trembling with shock, and in his eyes I see the reflection of a similarly fearful look on my own face. But I ignore the terror and focus. Drawing power from the air again, I unleash a bolt of energy at one of the masters, a green, bulbous, putrid thing, like a leech gone horribly wrong. I hit it with more power than I struck Lord Loss with. But it isn't even nudged sideways by the blast. It glances at me with a small, pink eye and sneers.

"Oh hell," Kernel moans.

"More power," I snarl. "We're the Kah-Gash. We can take this lot. We just need more—"

"No," Kernel says, looking around. "We need Bec."

She's by Lord Loss's side, helping him. He's hovering again. He looks furious, but shameful too. He glares enviously at the other masters. Earth has always been his private playground. He was the strongest demon who could cross, a true terror for us to tremble before. Now he's been overshadowed by these new, stronger creatures. He knew this would happen — it's what he worked to bring about — but that doesn't make his loss of status any easier to bear.

A frantic Kirilli goes up against one of the masters. He shoots playing cards at it. They pierce the demon's flesh and explode beneath its skin. Kirilli's screaming hatefully, fearfully, but with excitement too. He thinks he can beat this thing.

"Kovacs, you nutter!" I roar. "Get away from there. You can't—"

"I've got it!" he screeches, unleashing a flurry of

cards, face bright red from the heat and adrenalin. "This baby's going down. It should have known better than to mess with—"

The cards halt, quiver a moment, then join and form a blade. Before Kirilli spots the danger, the blade slices across him, severing his head from his body. His head flies high into the air and a startled expression creases his features. As he watches, still conscious, the blade splits into a scissor-like mechanism and chops his head up into halves, then quarters, then eighths. Kirilli's arms twitch for a second or two. Then his body collapses and bits of his head and brains rain down upon it.

"Tah-dah!" I croak miserably, eyes surprisingly welling with tears.

"That's the way to go," Shark yells, leaping over the mess that was once Kirilli Kovacs. He lands by our side, wipes blood from his face and grins ghoulishly. "What's the plan, boys? How do we cream these sons of hellspawn and daughters of demon dung?"

"We don't," Kernel says sullenly, wincing at the screams of the dying.

"They're too powerful," I whisper, staring horror-struck at the carnage.

Shark frowns, then slaps us with the three fingers of his right hand. "Enough of that crap. If they defeat us, fine, but we won't give up. Figure out a way to beat this lot or die fighting. But don't stand here like fools, waiting to be fried."

With a challenging cry he bounds away and lands on the head of a scabby demon with dozens of crab-like pincers. Shark rips off a few of the pincers and jabs at the monster's eyes. He punctures a couple, but the demon has several more. With a snort, it turns its head and blows a sheet of mucous over him. Shark pulls a disgusted face, tries to wipe the snot away, then screams as the snot burns through his flesh and bones.

I try to save the ex-soldier, extending my magic to him, working to nullify the acidic snot. But the demon blocks my attempt and chortles sadistically as Shark splatters into hundreds of pieces, all of which dissolve away to a gooey mess within seconds.

I stare at Shark's remains, dazed that this can be happening so swiftly, so effortlessly. I thought if we failed, we'd go down valiantly after a brutal, gallant fight. But we're being squashed like ants. This is ridiculous. When did the rules change and why did nobody warn us?

"Bec," Kernel growls, gripping my hand tightly. "We have to grab her."

"What for?" I wheeze, face ashen, watching the demons rip the Disciples and mages to pieces. I see the last of the werewolves die in howling torment. One of the demons picks up its carcass and wiggles it around like a finger puppet.

"We can still destroy the tunnel," Kernel hisses.

I stare at him. I'm supposed to be the one with the never-say-die attitude. When I became a wolfen half-human, I put caution aside and became a one-dimensional beast who didn't know the meaning of surrender. I should be the guy coming out with crazy, suicidal plans. But I'm frozen in place, more vulnerable and helpless than I ever was before.

"If we push Bec into the mouth of the tunnel, we can explode her and use the force of the explosion to shatter the rock," Kernel continues, impossibly composed under the circumstances. "We might die too, but at least we'll buy the world some time. And maybe we can protect ourselves from the blast, live to fight another day." He shrugs. "Either way, it's our only hope."

I nod slowly, then with more determination, regaining control. "Aye," I grunt, mimicking the dead Beranabus. "And maybe there aren't any lodestones as strong as this one. If we drive this lot back, they might never be able to cross again."

We share a look that says, "*Riiiiiiight!*"

Kernel grins. "To the death, Master Grady?"

"To the death, Master Fleck," I grin back.

Then we both say together, "But not ours!"

Laughing, we dart across the cave, dodging the

warring humans and demons. Kernel's feet slip in the blood and slime which covers the floor, but my claws and hairy soles are suited to gripping. I steady him and we push on at a good pace.

Bec spots us closing in on her and smiles, spreading her arms as if welcoming us home after a lengthy absence. Lord Loss straightens beside her and snarls. "You should not dare—" he begins, but we're on them before he gets any further.

I leap, using all the power in my legs, and smash into Lord Loss, sending him hurtling against the wall of the cave again. Bec tuts and turns to deal with me. She considers me the prime threat and studies me warily, forgetting about the other third of the Kah-Gash.

Kernel takes advantage of Bec's momentary lapse. He sneaks up behind her and sends volts of magic frying through her brain. She cries out and jerks away from him, arms, legs and head spasming madly. Lord Loss gasps with concern and reaches for her. I drive a hairy elbow into his ugly face, then fall on Bec and pound her as if she was a human drum. I could pop her head like a grape if I tried, but I don't want her dead. Not yet.

The shadows around Bec respond sluggishly, feebly whipping at Kernel and me, nowhere near as effective as they were before. It seems Death limited itself by uniting with Bec. As part of the girl, it suffers if she does.

It can't defend itself as ably as it could when it had a body of its own.

Lord Loss hisses savagely and throws himself at us, arms lashing out, snakes darting from his chest, spitting venom as they fly at our faces. One catches my left eye and sinks its fangs in. My eye bursts and liquid soaks my cheek. I roar loud enough to shake a house. I never thought losing an eye could be so traumatic. No wonder Kernel hated me so much after I put him through twin doses of this.

Kernel tries his old vomiting trick, hitting Lord Loss with a spray of puke that turns to acid, like the snot that finished off Shark. But the demon master has seen Kernel in action before and he's prepared. He freezes the vomit and it falls away in a thin, brittle sheet, to shatter on the floor.

But the vomit distracts the heartless monster and buys us a couple of seconds. Steeling myself against the pain, fighting the disorientation, I grab Bec and lob her at the mouth of the tunnel. As she lands at the base of the lodestone, I leap after her. Kernel scurries along behind me, unleashing bursts of energy at Lord Loss to slow him down.

The walls of the tunnel are vibrating again. It's still widening. In a few minutes, more demons will be free to cross. I hear their excited cries echoing from the universe at the far end. I recall the army we faced when we went in search of Beranabus's soul and flash on a picture of thousands of demons pouring into this cave, obscuring us all, forcing Timas to press his button on the cliff above. Whether nuclear bombs or the crossing demons destroy the planet, it's definitely doomed. Unless…

I pick up Bec and stagger into the pulsing mouth of the tunnel. She stirs in my arms, then squeals and strikes me with blasts of fire. The flames rip up my arms and lick my face, burning my hairs to the roots, then eating deeply into my flesh.

I ignore the pain and focus on Bec. I feel Kernel draw up next to me, then his magic links with mine and we pour it into the struggling girl. I want her to explode in geysers of flesh, bone, blood and magic. For a moment, as her flesh ripples, I think we're going to succeed. But then she smiles and stops struggling. Our magic flows into her, but instead of bursting through her, it circles within the girl, then returns to us, stronger than before, but having caused no harm.

I try again, but although I pump more power into her than I did the first time, it doesn't hurt Bec, just comes back at me with interest. Lord Loss settles beside me and lays a couple of arms across my shoulders. I glare at him, but he doesn't strike, merely smiles wickedly.

"What's happening?" Kernel yells as more and more energy builds between and around us.

"Time to unleash the full power of the Kah-Gash," Bec gurgles, her teeth red with blood from the pounding she took.

"She's using us," Kernel screams, trying to pull away but held in place by the magic which continues to build. "Kill her, Grubbs, kill her!"

I try, but I can't focus. At least not on Bec. I sense the power fanning out, the Kah-Gash taking over as it did in Carcery Vale when it sent us back into the past and gave us the opportunity to defeat the Demonata. But things are different now. Bec's working for the enemy. There's no telling what will happen this time.

I have to stop this. The Kah-Gash is the ultimate weapon. Our world will fall, no matter what, but if Bec gets her hands on the Kah-Gash she can annihilate the rest of the universe too. If the best we can do is deny them that victory, we'll have to settle for that.

I start to cut off the power flooding through me, to thwart Bec's plan. But just as I'm about to take my finger off the trigger, Bec catches my eye and... *winks*.

The wink unnerves me. It didn't look like a mad, victorious, mocking gesture. Bec looked like her old self for a split-second. It was a playful wink, the sort you tip to a friend when you have a secret, mischievous plan. The type that says, "Trust me and play along. This'll be fun!"

It's crazy. I should stop this as I intended. Too much is

at stake to gamble recklessly. But the promise in that quick wink… the spark of humanity I thought I saw lurking behind the shadowy veils of Death…

With a desperate, confused, horrified howl, I make what's probably the worst decision of my entire life, or anyone else's. Instead of freeing myself from the clutches of Bec and Lord Loss, I draw even more power from the air, giving the Kah-Gash all the kick it needs to flare into life and wreak universal havoc.

With a sudden, sickening lurch, a ball of raw, all-consuming energy bursts from every pore of my body. Similar balls explode from Kernel and Bec. The three parts of the Kah-Gash join, sizzle in the air, then strike hard at the heart of the tunnel to hell.

Everything hits the fan.

WITH A BANG

→We needed words when we previously unleashed the full power of the Kah-Gash, spells to direct it. Not this time. We've moved beyond that. Grown, matured, fused completely with the weapon. There's no pulsing sky, clouds bursting into flames, melting rocks. Instead we skip straight to the exploding-into-colours stage.

My body shreds and I know instinctively that I'll never have a use for it again. Grubbs Grady is dead and gone. So are Kernel Fleck and Bec. We're the Kah-Gash now, a bodiless force, purer than light, free of all constraints. We didn't go this far the first time. We didn't understand what was happening. We tried to fight the loss of control, the madness. Now we just swing with it, leaving our humanity behind, bursting forward at a speed I can't begin to describe.

We smash through the tunnel, the world shattering behind us, the Disciples and mages dead in an instant, Timas on top of the cliff a moment later, everyone on Earth a second after that. The planet rips apart as Juni predicted, and I'm to blame. But I don't care. I'm caught up in the moment, crazy with power, oblivious to everything except the rush of the *now*, the *here*, the *us*.

We're in a subuniverse of billions of flashing patches of light. We careened from one to another when we entered this realm before, but now the transition is fluid. Patches join and form windows. We shoot through without pause, picking up speed, the windows becoming a blur, sucking the remains of the world after us… other planets… stars… the universe… all matter… even time itself. And not just the human universe — we take from the Demonata's realm too. Everything is sucked along in our wake.

A voice whispers, "The Crux." It takes me a few seconds to realise it was Bec who spoke. It seems our individual selves still exist on some kind of level. We're not entirely the single entity I thought we'd become.

"The Crux," Bec says again, insistently.

"Why?" Kernel asks.

"I'll explain later. Just direct us there."

"But if we go to the Crux and take everything with us…"

"Trust me," Bec says. "This is the only way. Bran hatched a plan."

"Grubbs?" Kernel asks, still uncertain.

I've no idea what's going on, what the *plan* might be, if Bec's really on our side or playing us for mugs. But what choice do we have? "Make it so," I mutter in my best Captain Picard voice.

Kernel sighs. I get the sense that we've adjusted our position. Our speed increases, the windows becoming a buzz of white light, noise building around us, drowning everything out, making it impossible for us to talk to one another.

I have a bad feeling about this, but it's too late to stop, so I continue supplying power to the Kah-Gash. I take it from the lights and everything behind us, draining the universes dry, using energy, magic, time and all the rest to propel us forward faster. Kernel's guiding us. Bec… I'm not sure what the spirit of the Celtic girl is up to, but I get the impression that she's busy too. Her mind seems to be focused on the flotsam behind us. She's absorbing *something* from the spiralling remains of the universes. Not energy or magic. But what else could it be?

Before I can pursue the query, a fiery ball materialises in the distance. From Kernel's description, I recognise it as the Crux, the centre of all things, the place where the Big Bang happened. There was only one universe originally, sixty-four zones, half black, half white, demons in the white zones, Old Creatures in the black. No other life forms. No time either. During a war between the demons and Old Creatures, it exploded, creating life and the universes as we know them.

We shoot through the rim of the Crux. Kernel said it was the hottest place he'd ever been, but there's nothing hotter than us right now.

There are sixty-four giant square panels floating around the lightning-pierced heart of the Crux. Clustered around them are balls of light – the Old Creatures – and enormous demons even more powerful than the masters in the cave. These are the original Demonata, those who existed before the new universes were born.

The Old Creatures and demons react with shock as we tear into the Crux. Panic-stricken, they try to mount a defence of the giant panels. But we swat them aside and they're torn to pieces by the trailing vortex, sucked in and ripped apart like all the others, perishing with a chorus of confused howls.

I expect us to slow to a halt, but instead we carry on at full speed, then split as we hit the centre of the Crux. There's a blinding flash. We separate into sixty-four fragments and strike the black and white squares. They flare and ripples run across their surface. Sparks shoot out of them.

Then everything clicks together. The sixty-four squares join in less than the blink of an eye. We become one again, only now we're enmeshed with the squares. We explode outwards, the squares expanding with us. We're the barriers between zones, but we also fill the infinite space inside them, everywhere at once.

The expansion lasts millions of years, but it's also instantaneous. That doesn't make sense, but it's the only way I can explain it. Time has shattered. The laws we lived by – that all creatures lived by since the Big Bang – exist no longer. In the absence of time, everything happens immediately yet gradually.

As I'm trying to get my head around the new laws, there's a sudden click and the expansion stops. Everything settles. The last traces of the universes I was familiar with disappear completely. The worlds, stars, people, creatures… gone. Erased from history. The souls of the dead are gone too. In this universe, their bodies never existed, so their souls never developed. All is undone.

Before I can go insane with guilt, I notice beings blinking back into existence. The Old Creatures and Demonata who were alive when Bec, Kernel and I became the Kah-Gash are revived and returned to their proper places in the universe. The dismayed Old Creatures pop up in the black squares and wail at all that has been lost. The delighted Demonata – both the original demons and those they sired – materialise in the white squares and go wild with joy.

Time has been eradicated. Humanity and their kind are no more and never were. The original order has been restored. Death can function as an unconscious force, the way it was meant to. Demons will live forever, breed and kill without limits. The Old Creatures will drift along meaninglessly in their otherwise lifeless zones, or be tracked down and slaughtered by demons. The Shadow and the Demonata have won.

The end.

AH YES, I REMEMBER IT WELL

→ "No, you idiot, it's the beginning."

Bec laughs and light bubbles around me. I blink and shield my eyes with a hand. Then frown. Hang on — I'm a bodiless force. I don't *have* eyes or hands.

"You do now," Bec giggles.

Lowering my hand, I stare with astonishment at the little girl sitting on a couch I know only too well. It's from my old home, the mansion in Carcery Vale. I'm in the enormous living room, in my regular spot opposite the oversized TV. Bec's sitting across from me, smirking. A confused-looking Kernel is in a seat nearby.

"What the hell..." I stop, something about my hand unnerving me. I turn it over, wondering what's wrong. Then I realise — there are no hairs. The skin is smooth and pale. The fingers are large but not inhuman, and instead of claws I have ordinary fingernails. I'm not a werewolf.

"Of course you aren't," Bec snorts. "Not unless you choose to be. You can make yourself muscular and hairy if you want, but I'd rather you didn't. You looked so silly prancing about as a man-wolf."

She gets to her feet and walks to the window. She's dressed in simple clothes, just a cloak or something like that wrapped around her. I'm in my favourite jeans and T-shirt. Kernel's wearing something similar.

I follow Bec to the window. As I cross the room, I spot objects snapping into place around me — vases, books, pictures. The room is still forming.

Bec is staring out of the window at nothing. And I mean *real* nothing. It's black out there, the pure blackness of empty space. As I watch, some of the garden from home sprouts into view and spreads, looking strange against the dark backdrop. I see Bec's reflected smile in the glass. She turns and beams at me.

"What's going on?" I mumble.

"I'm making a temporary base for us," she says. "I figured it might help us adjust more smoothly."

"And these?" I ask, nodding at our bodies. "Are they real?"

"As real as we want them to be," she says enigmatically, returning to the couch.

"What does that mean?" Kernel snaps. "Is this a dream? Reality? How are you…" He stops, head twisting from one side to the other. "I can't see the lights," he whispers.

"Of course not," Bec says. "We *are* the lights now.

They were part of the Kah-Gash. Now that we've become it, you don't need to see them. We've moved beyond that stage. We're not physical beings. We don't really have eyes or ears, or even brains. You have to start thinking bigger than that."

"How about you just explain it to us nice and simply before we lose patience," I growl, flexing my fingers.

Bec laughs. "You can't threaten me, Grubbs. This body's for show. You could grind it to dust and it wouldn't make the least difference." She clicks her fingers and her head explodes. Blood pumps from her neck. Kernel and I yelp with shock. Then a new head grows out of the stump. Her eyes open and she winks. She waves a hand over the blood on the couch and it fades.

"I don't get it," I mutter. "Is this fantasy? Are we dead?"

"No, you moron," Bec says. "We're the Kah-Gash. The universe is us and we're the universe. We're the glue holding everything together, the power that drives it, the force..." She sees incomprehension in my eyes and sighs. "Are you getting any of this?" she asks Kernel.

"I think so," he says slowly. "But..." His face drops. "We destroyed the world! The people we knew — are they all...?"

"Dead," Bec says cheerfully. "Torn to atoms, then broken down even further. None of that universe exists any longer. Time and all its creations are lost forever. In this universe they only ever existed—" She taps her head. "—up here."

"I'm glad you're taking it so well," I snarl, advancing on her, trying to figure out a way to kill her, to make her pay for the awful massacre she tricked us into engineering.

"Don't be a child," Bec tuts. "I didn't trick you into anything. I tricked *them* — the Demonata and Death. It was the only way. Bran figured it out. He couldn't be certain it would work, but in the absence of any alternatives, we had to risk it."

"If you don't start making sense quickly…"

Bec shakes her head. "With such a small brain, I don't know how you made it this far." She points a finger at me as I open my mouth to protest. "The trigger." She points to Kernel. "The eyes." She taps her chest. "The memory. You gave us the power to undo time and all its trappings. Kernel guided us. And I absorbed."

She waves a hand at the ceiling and it turns transparent. The sky above is black. Impossible to see anything. But as we watch, an object comes into focus. I'm not sure where the light that strikes it comes from, but it's fully lit and even more recognisable than the room we're sitting in. It's the moon, full-sized and round, a pockmarked pearl in a sea of darkness.

"I remembered everything about the original

universe," Bec says, smiling up at the lunar giant. "I couldn't access those memories, but they had to be there. If that universe was ever to be reassembled, the Kah-Gash would need the blueprints to restore everything accurately.

"Bran knew that too. It's what gave him the idea. He figured if the memory of the Kah-Gash could store everything from the original universe, it should be able to memorise all of the new universes too.

"I was busy while you two were incinerating galaxies," Bec continues. "To rip the universes to shreds, we had to touch every planet, person, animal, atom. As we touched and tore, I committed everything to memory. The whole of history, from the moment of the Big Bang to the end... it's all up here." She taps her head.

"I know the names of every intelligent being, the spots on the wings of every butterfly that broke out of a cocoon, the genetic codes of the simplest and most complex of creatures. I know how suns functioned, how worlds formed, how life evolved. All of the secrets of the old universes are mine. They can be yours too, if you want me to share, though I suspect you aren't bothered."

"So you remember," I grunt. "So what? It's still gone, isn't it?"

"Gone but not forgotten," Kernel murmurs, his forehead crinkling thoughtfully. "Look at these bodies — they're real. Perfect replicas, down to the smallest detail. That's right, isn't it, Bec?" She nods. "And the moon is real too?"

"Exactly the way it was before we blew it to pieces," Bec grins.

"We can bring it all back!" Kernel shouts. "The Kah-Gash has the power to tear a universe apart, but it also has the power to rebuild it!"

"That's what Bran counted on," Bec chuckles.

I stare at the pair of them, still confused. "What's the point of building a fake universe?"

"It won't be fake," Bec corrects me. "It will be as real as the old universe was. We can do anything. We can make all the solar systems, worlds and creatures the same as they were before. We'll let history unfold the way it did first time round, begin with the initial sparks of life and build from there. Advanced species like humans will live and develop souls again. Everything will happen the way it did from the dawn of time up to the moment of universal destruction. We'll direct proceedings that far, then give the inhabitants of all the worlds their freedom. The future will be in their hands after that."

"What's the point?" I frown. "The Demonata will wreck it all. They exist too. They'll cross and destroy, just like—"

"You weren't listening," Kernel interrupts. "Bec said we could do *anything*."

"You mean we'll protect them from the demons?" I shake my head. "They found ways to twist the laws before. That's why the Kah-Gash shattered. We can't be sure that we can stop them doing it again."

Bec crosses the room and takes my hands. Her fingers are trembling. "We won't have to protect our people if the demons aren't there," she says softly.

"But they are. I can sense them."

"I can too," Kernel says. "I know where all of them are, along with the Old Creatures. If I close my eyes, I can visualise all sixty-four zones and track the whereabouts of every living being."

"The Kah-Gash holds everything together," Bec says. "We *are* the universe. We bind every molecule to those around it. Nothing can hide from us. And nothing can defy us."

The mansion fades and we're floating in space, illuminated by the light of the recreated moon. The freezing cold and lack of oxygen doesn't affect me. Why should it? As the Kah-Gash, we *create* temperature, air, all the rest. I begin to see why Bec and Kernel are so psyched.

"The Kah-Gash never sought to control the universe," Bec says. "It had no will of its own. It simply held things in place. It didn't know why it kept the demons and Old Creatures apart — it just did. It wasn't capable of making choices."

"But *we* are," Kernel says, a twinkle in his eyes.

"Ideally we should respect the order of the original universe," Bec says. "Never interfere. Let things develop in their own way. Stay neutral."

"But to hell with that," Kernel grins. "I think this is why the Kah-Gash began to explore after it split, why it took up residence in a host of different creatures. It was learning, growing mentally, choosing."

Bec nods. "Choice was everything. When the piece in Lord Loss chose to leap into me — that's when the Kah-Gash gave us the means to self-govern, assuming we could work out the kinks."

"Are you getting it yet?" Kernel smirks.

"I think so," I sigh. "We can build it all again, the worlds and people of our own universe?"

"Yes," Bec says.

"We can recreate time?"

"Or the semblance of it," Kernel says.

"But before any of that…" I close my eyes and focus. Like the other two, I can sense the position of the demons, every one of them, spread across thirty-two zones, still celebrating their triumph and return to eternal life. As the Kah-Gash, we're the force holding their bodies together, the blood gushing through their veins and arteries, the cells of their grey, lumpy brains. We bind them. But if we choose, we could just as easily…

"...*un*bind them." I open my eyes and smile. "We can wipe them out. Kill them all. Eliminate each and every one of the beasts."

"Yes," Bec says, then her features crease. "But we mustn't."

"What do you mean?" I frown.

"It would be genocide," Bec says.

"Don't be crazy," I laugh. "They're demons, not humans. It can't be genocide if you only kill monsters."

"They're living beings," Bec insists. "They're cruel and merciless, certainly, but that's just their nature. They have a right to exist."

"No they don't," I protest. "They tried to wipe us out. Hell, they did! They never cared about our right to life. Why should we care about theirs?"

"Because we're better than them," Kernel answers softly, taking Bec's side. "If we kill them, we'll be as bad as they are."

I shrug. "I can live with that."

Bec's eyes flash and she gets ready for an argument. Then Kernel snaps his fingers and says, "Wait. I remember something. Give me a minute..."

While we stare at him, Kernel turns his back on us and hunches down. Moments later a landscape swims into place around us. We're in a valley and everything's a light blue colour. There are jagged pillars all around us. It looks familiar but I don't know why.

"This was the first place in the demon universe you came to when you crossed with Beranabus and me," Kernel reminds me. He waves a hand at one of the shorter pillars and an angular demon steps out. As I gaze at it, Beranabus forms in front of the creature. It's not the real Beranabus, or even a reconstruction, merely a recorded image of him. Bec starts to cry when she sees the magician, but they're tears of happiness.

"No," the recording of Beranabus says to the demon. "We're not going to leave you alone. You know who we are and what we want. Now…"

"I remember," I sigh. "I was surprised. I thought all demons were as powerful and dangerous as Lord Loss."

"Yes," Kernel says. "Before you left, you wanted to know why we didn't kill the blue demon."

As I nod slowly, Beranabus answers the question, as he did that first time. "Not worth killing. There are untold billions of demons. They're all evil, but most can't hurt us or cross to our world. That cretin doesn't even dare leave this valley. It waits, hiding and surviving, doing precious little else."

"*Hiding and surviving*," Bec echoes. "Are we going to slaughter the weak and innocent, Grubbs? Is that what we've sunk to? If it is, I don't think we should stop with the Demonata. We should destroy ourselves too. If we can't grant mercy to those who've done us no harm, we have no more right to this universe than those we've fought so hard against."

"OK," I snap. "There's no need to rub it in. I see where you're coming from. We'll leave the weak ones alone, those who can't cross, those who don't pose a threat. But the masters have to be taken out — I won't budge on that. Any beast that even looks like it has the potential to cross, to defy us, to pick at and weaken the structure of the Kah-Gash... we wipe them out now."

"We could isolate them," Bec murmurs. "Imprison them in a place where they can't–"

"No!" I bark. "They're too much of a risk. We kill every master going. I won't bend on this one. They have this coming to them and I'm going to see that they get it."

"We have to do it," Kernel says, trying to win Bec round. "They found a way to destroy the Kah-Gash before. They could do it again. To guarantee order, we have to remove them. It's the only way to be sure."

Bec sighs, then nods reluctantly.

"I knew you'd see sense," I chuckle, then grin viciously, the old wolfen Grubbs Grady re-emerging momentarily. "Let's give them hell!"

And the massacre begins.

DEVILMENT

→The demon masters perish in their millions. They don't see us coming and are helpless in the face of our wrath. We sweep through the white zones like a cosmic wind, obliterating all who pose a threat. We don't torment those we kill. Unlike these vile monsters, we're not evil-hearted and don't wish to cause pain. I'd be lying if I said part of me doesn't enjoy the cull, but I don't revel in it.

Because time doesn't work like it did before, the culling is both swift and drawn out, lasting the drawing of a breath and the birth and death of a dozen suns. It happens across all thirty-two zones at the same time. We don't have to localise. We can be everywhere at once, moving across the face of a million worlds in the same instant.

We blow through the demonic zones with godlike barbarism, felling all who need to be eliminated. We don't bother with bodies or battles. We move as spirits, a force of nature, and the demon masters are crushed, never knowing what struck them, most dying without a chance to even howl in retaliation.

It's clinical and cruel, precise to a devilish degree. We rip through the white zones, staining them red, killing every demon master in existence… except one. Him we save for the end. The rest are vipers to be crushed. We go about our work dispassionately. But with the last one, it's personal. It's payback time, and I know that when I look into his dark red eyes and see the final flame of life flicker out, I'll be so ecstatic I could burst.

→When all the other masters have been taken care of, and only one remains, deliberately isolated and spared, we create bodies for ourselves and fade into existence outside his castle of webs. The demon is waiting for us at the edge of the moat running around the fortress, sitting on the throne which used to rest inside. He looks more alone than ever, bereft of all his peers. But not scared. He's aware of everything that's happened – I made sure he could hear and see it all, so he'd know we were coming for him – but to my surprise he doesn't look afraid.

"Welcome again, my young friends," Lord Loss says, clapping cynically. "You have grown in stature since your last visit. Your incineration of the demon masters was impressive, if overzealous. Beranabus would have approved, but I wonder if Dervish would have, or Meera Flame?"

"We did what had to be done," Kernel growls.

"I would say you did far more than that," Lord Loss counters. "The powerful masters from the original universe I can understand. They posed a threat and always would have. But what of the lesser masters, those with powers similar to mine? You could have easily prevented them from crossing or attacking you. They posed no threat. You could have left them to patrol the depths of their realms and harm none except their own. Yet you chose to kill them too. You rained hellfire down on all."

"Because you were all as bad as each other," I snarl.

"In whose eyes?" Lord Loss asks. "Yours?"

"Yes."

He smiles mockingly. "Who gave you the right to pass judgement on an entire species, Grubitsch Grady?"

"No one. I took it."

"How *demonic* of you," Lord Loss purrs.

"If you're trying to make me feel guilty, you'll need to do better than that," I sneer.

"I doubt if I am required to sow the seeds of guilt," he murmurs. "Eternity stretches ahead of you. Given time, I believe your conscience will torment you of its own accord."

"He's boring me," I yawn, glancing at the others. "You ready to kill him?"

"Yes," Kernel says eagerly, taking a step forward.

"Wait," Bec mutters. Her cheeks are flushed and she's staring at her feet.

"You don't feel sorry for him, do you?" I ask incredulously.

"No," Bec says.

"You can't feel any loyalty," Kernel half-laughs. "I know you played the part of his servant, but it was only an act." He pauses. "*Right?*"

Bec looks up and takes a deep breath. "We struck a deal," she says and I groan.

"What sort of deal?" Kernel frowns.

"Never mind," I snap before Bec answers. "We're killing him. That's final. I don't care what was agreed between the two of you. Dervish, Bill-E, my mum and dad, Gret… all dead because of *him*. He perishes like the rest of his foul kind. No argument."

"We can't kill him," Bec says miserably. "I hate him too. He killed people close to me or caused their deaths. But you saw us enter the Board together. We made a deal. If I don't honour it…"

"What was the deal?" Kernel asks again.

"No!" I roar. "I don't want to know. He's a demon. We don't owe him anything. I'm going to kill him, and if you try to stop me, I'll–"

"Kill her too?" Lord Loss pipes up, relishing the conflict.

"Enjoy the show while you can," I snarl, raising a hand to obliterate him.

The universe tightens around my fist and it falls limply by my side. I whirl on Bec, fire in my eyes.

"The Kah-Gash can be split again," she says. "If we fight with each other, we risk everything. Our sacrifices and endeavours will have been for nothing if we bicker and lose control. All that we knew and loved will be truly lost then."

I count to ten, reining in my anger. Then, through gritted teeth, I say, "Tell me about the damn deal."

"He helped us," Bec says. "I told him of Bran's plan to let the Demonata build a tunnel and break through, then use the Kah-Gash to tap into the power of the tunnel and take time back to its very beginning."

"Lord Loss knew we'd kill all the demon masters?" Kernel gasps.

"Yes," Bec says. "He thought we'd kill the familiars too. He didn't believe I could persuade you and Grubbs to spare them."

"And you let us go ahead?" I spit at the demon master.

"Why not?" he murmurs. "They meant nothing to me. A vile, beastly lot. The universe is better off without them."

As Kernel and I gawp at Lord Loss, Bec explains. "My

betrayal was a charade. I slaughtered the souls in the Board, but I knew we'd have to kill a lot more than that if we were to triumph. We can bring them back to life later, the same as all the others.

"We tricked Death and the Demonata. Convinced them I was on their side, that I wanted to live forever as one of them. We needed Death to work through me, so I could control and subdue it when the Kah-Gash was reunited."

"But if Death was part of you, didn't it know what you were planning?" Kernel asks.

Bec shakes her head. "It didn't have access to my inner thoughts, only those I chose to share with it. Death was new to consciousness. It had a lot to learn about the mind." She smirks. "I guess now it never will."

"I protected her from my savage brethren," Lord Loss says. "I helped bring the three of you together and did what I could to ensure you were not killed before you had the chance to join. It was a risk, of course, but a calculated one, and in the end it proved to be enough."

"But why?" I croak. "You're a demon. You hate us."

"Not at all," he retorts. "I adore mankind. I'd have happily strung *your* guts out for cats to play with, Grubitsch, had things worked out differently. But humans… the games you invent… the sorrows you suffer…" He smiles at the memories.

"What do you get in return?" Kernel asks. "What did Bec promise?"

"My life," Lord Loss replies. "And a promotion." He looks at the stars twinkling far above us. "I was never as powerful as you believed. You realise that now, having seen and exterminated much stronger masters than me. I was a young, humble demon. That's why I focused on Earth. I knew I could impress there, that if I made it my personal playpen, I could dominate the human realm of fear."

"You chose to be a big fish in a small pond," I snort.

Lord Loss tilts his head. "Stronger masters terrorised galaxies, inspiring horror across a multitude of worlds. I lacked that power, so I concentrated on a single planet. I tested several before I chose Earth. Your people appealed to me, for reasons I cannot put any of my fingers on. Perhaps I was guided by the Kah-Gash. Maybe even then it had selected your world to serve as its dramatic stage."

"You're pathetic," I sneer, seeing my old foe in his true colours, astonished that I lived so long in fear of him, considering him the worst of any imaginable enemy.

"I was," Lord Loss says calmly. "No longer. I am the last demon master, the final sentinel of sorrow. All of this universe's demonic familiars must bow to my power now. I'll also cast a dark shadow across the hearts and minds of the creatures in your universe, weaving my web of misery across more worlds than any master ever came close to before. I'll be the source of every nightmare, the face behind each malicious mask of myth. I'll sow fear everywhere my eye alights, and reap the rich rewards for all eternity."

"What makes you think we'll let you?" I challenge him.

"Bec promised," he smiles.

I cock an eyebrow at the girl.

"We need him," she says quietly. "Every developed world had its bogey men, evil spirits, devils. The universe requires a force of evil for the wicked to gravitate towards, a malevolent being which the dark-hearted can worship. If they can't turn to Lord Loss, we'll have to play that hideous role. I don't want to be a monster to the twisted and the vicious of our own worlds. Do you?" she asks me. "Or you?" she throws the question at Kernel.

Kernel and I look at each other uneasily.

"Why him?" I grumble. "We can bring back one of the others that we killed, or use a familiar. It doesn't have to be Lord Loss. I want to destroy him. After all he did to us…"

"They do say, 'Better the devil you know'," Lord Loss murmurs slyly.

"I gave him my word that we'd let him rule the white

zones," Bec says. "Plus, he vowed never to overstep the mark, to leave the Old Creatures alone, to cross only when authorised and always return to his own realm when his work is done. He won't establish toeholds in the human universe, or allow his familiars to settle there either."

"But the familiars won't be able to cross universes this time," Kernel frowns. "We'll stop them."

"We can't," Bec says. "History demands their presence. If we're to let time unravel as it did before, every demon crossing will have to be recreated. I'll work in tandem with Lord Loss, letting him know when and where his familiars should cross. When we reach the present – the time when we ended the universe – we'll set him free to operate by himself as long as he respects the rules, and at that point we can put a stop to the crossings of lesser demons. Our people can be free of the monsters after that, but not before."

"How can we trust him?" I growl.

"I gave my word," Lord Loss says stiffly. "I have always honoured a promise."

I shake my head. "We're better off without him. We can control and direct the familiars by ourselves. Lord Loss would be a threat. We'd have to watch him like a hawk."

"No," the demon master says. "That's merely an

excuse, Grubitsch. You wish to kill me to exact revenge. You cannot justify my execution any other way."

"Then I won't," I shrug. "I'll kill you and take your place. I'd rather that than let you carry on. You're the reason I'm here, the cause of everything bad that ever happened to me. If it wasn't for you, my parents would be alive, Dervish and Bill-E, all the others. I won't spare you, not after the hell you've put me through. I'd rather burn."

I raise a hand to wipe out the demon master. I'd meant to torment him before I finished him off, but now I'll settle for a quick kill.

"Your words hold the key to my reprieve," Lord Loss says calmly as I point a finger at him. His self-satisfied smirk infuriates me, but for some reason I can't bring myself to strike. "If not for my interference, you wouldn't have joined with Kernel and Bec. The Kah-Gash could never have been utilised as it was. All has been shattered to be rebuilt, but if not for *my* actions, it would have simply been destroyed.

"I put you through hell, yes, but it was a hell you *needed* to experience. The pain, suffering, death… all were necessary. I served the purpose of the universe, just as you did. If not for my dark presence, you would never have found the path you were required to travel.

"People need devils and dark gods, if only to give them a foe to rally against, an obstacle to overcome. Your people understood that there can be no light without darkness, no good without evil, no triumph without setbacks. You can't kill me because I'm part of all that you are, all you've done and plan to do. You don't have to like me. You can even loathe me. But you must accept me."

I tremble with frustration. Part of me wants to whip him down, wipe that smirk from his face, kill him no matter what. But everything he says rings true. I owe it all to him, the good as well as the bad. As despicable as he is, he set this in motion. It wasn't intentional, and he acted selfishly at every turn, but if Beranabus was right and some godly force in our universe chose heroes and moulded them, maybe Lord Loss was part of the *über* plan, as vital a player as Bec, Kernel or me.

"I'll be watching you," I snarl. "If you take just one wrong step…"

"Why should I?" he smiles. "I never yearned to conquer your world, Grubitsch, merely to revel in the torment of its many desperate souls. Now I will become the pit of darkness at the centre of the entire universe, a web into which all the weak, helpess and vindictive must fall. What more could I wish for?"

"I hope you choke on it," I sneer, then let my body unravel and return to my ethereal state. The last thing I see through my human eyes is Lord Loss rubbing his eight stumpy hands together, leering eagerly, awaiting the dawn of time and the birth of the first of the billions whose misery he'll wallow in like the ugly, heartless, flaccid but essential leech that he is.

ONCE MORE, WITH FEELING

Lord Loss sows all the sorrows of the world
Lord Loss seeds the grief-starched trees

In the centre of the web, lowly Lord Loss bows his head

Mangled hands, naked eyes
Fanged snakes his soul line
Curled inside like textured sin
Bloody, curdled sheets for skin

In the centre of the web, vile Lord Loss torments the dead

Over strands of red, Lord Loss crawls
Dispensing pain, despising all
Shuns friends, nurtures foes
Ravages hope, breeds woe
Drinks moons, devours suns
Twirls his thumbs till the reaper comes

In the centre of the web, lush Lord Loss is all that's left

START ME UP

→We pick a black square at random and set about putting together the building blocks of life. The three of us work as one, without having to discuss what we're doing. Bec provides the memories, and thus the blueprints of what we need to start life again. Kernel manipulates the hidden strings of the universe to bring into being anything Bec desires. And I supply the power, channelling the energy of the Kah-Gash through them.

It's a long, complicated process, yet at the same time swift and simple. This is what the Kah-Gash does. It's like a person breathing, walking, talking, clicking their fingers. As humans we performed countless natural functions every second of the day. This is the same, only on a cosmic level.

The Old Creatures are aware of what we're up to and we can sense their seal of approval, even though we never communicate. They're happy to drift along in their own zones. All they ever wanted was to be left alone, safe from the threat of the Demonata, to roam as they pleased. We can guarantee that now, so they have no further interest in us.

I wish we had it so easy. There are hard times ahead. Having to focus for billions of years... put worlds, ecosystems and civilisations back the way they were... ensure every seed finds the egg it was meant to... guide every animal from a single-celled organism upwards, on every planet, in every galaxy... determine the deaths of all creatures, down to the fraction of a second of the date when they were meant to die...

It's no walk in the park!

One problem we don't have to worry about is the harvesting of souls. As strong as we are, there's a higher force than the Kah-Gash. We can sense it, but we can't define it, something greater than power, knowledge, life or death. We could give it a name, but that's not our job or our right. Let the beings of the universe name and worship the force in whatever ways they wish. We're not here to provide answers, just to give others the opportunity to marvel at the secrets of the heavens and perhaps one day unravel the mysteries for themselves.

I'm not looking forward to letting bad things happen. I'm sure I'll be tempted to intervene a million times a day, spare innocents, undermine tyrants, build a better, safer, cleaner universe. But it's a temptation I must ignore. If we start to interfere, we'll rob individuals of the right of self-determination. Nothing good can come of celestial dominance, no matter how noble our intentions. We're architects of this universe, nothing more, and we must never let ourselves forget that.

Having said that, we'll have to direct traffic up to a certain point, to the moment when we tore the universes asunder. We could start fresh if we wanted and let things develop randomly, but there's no telling what would happen then. Life might never evolve at all. We think it's better to start the ball rolling, guide the creatures of this universe along the path they followed first time round, then withdraw and leave them to themselves.

Well… maybe we'll stop a *bit* earlier. We don't have to let time stretch to the very last second. There's no harm tying up some loose ends a day or two before the universe ended. We have to implement change at that stage anyway, fiddle with the order of events to ensure this new universe isn't annihilated. It wouldn't make any real difference if we rounded things off a week or two earlier… maybe even a few months or years…

"That's dangerous thinking," Bec notes, her voice coming from every part of the universe and yet from nowhere in particular. "We agreed we wouldn't interfere."

"But we have to at the end," I argue. "If we let events play out as before, the recreations of ourselves will tear the universe to shreds. We have to make changes. There can be no wandering pieces of the Kah-Gash. Death must remain a force and never be unleashed as the Shadow. No war between the demons and humanity. We have to juggle events, remove a few individuals from the mix, strip some of power, give others more to do. It'll be like a game of chess. We can let the game unfold as it did before, but if we want to avoid checkmate, we'll have to readjust the pieces a few moves shy of the finish."

"That makes sense," Kernel agrees.

"So where do we draw the line?" Bec asks. "Grubbs was the last to be born. Do we set the universe free just before that? Or do we go back to before *I* entered the world and release our grip then?"

"That would be the simplest thing," Kernel says, but there's an uncertain edge to his voice.

"The trouble with stopping there," I mutter, "is that the people we knew might never be born. My parents, Gret, Dervish…"

"Shark and Sharmila," Kernel says.

"Bill-E and Kirilli," Bec sighs.

"We could keep them all," I croak. "Even save them. My parents don't have to be slaughtered. We can give Dervish a stronger heart. Bill-E and Loch needn't die in the cave in Carcery Vale."

"Shark could live to fight another day," Kernel murmurs. "We could let Nadia lead a normal life and spare her the indignity of becoming Juni Swan."

"Bran could enjoy a dignified retirement," Bec muses aloud. "Meera could be spared. Maybe Dervish would finally see sense and fall in love with her."

"We have the power," I whisper. "We need to tinker with things, no matter what. Why not make a few beneficial, personal changes while we're at it?"

"Do we have the right to alter the universe to suit our own desires?" Bec asks.

"Let's call it a perk of the job," I chuckle.

"We should discuss this further," Kernel says.

"A *lot* further," Bec adds.

"Fine," I shrug. "We've got plenty of time. I'm sure we'll sort something out over the next billion years or so." I create a giant pair of knuckles and crack them loudly. "Now let's get this show on the road. Who wants to set the Big Bang in motion?"

"That's your privilege," Bec says. "Everything's in place. Kernel and I can't do any more until you generate the explosion."

"We *can* control it, can't we?" I ask. "The Big Bang I mean. It won't affect any of the other zones?"

"Not this time," Bec says.

"It will all run smoothly," Kernel assures me.

I'm nervous now that the moment has arrived. It's no small thing, creating life, the universe and everything. I'm probably not the best man — hell, best *boy* for the job. But then it's not a perfect universe. You can't hang around waiting for somebody else to pull your strings. Destiny's what you make of it. You have to face whatever life throws at you. And if it throws more than you'd like, more than you think you can handle?

Well, then you have to find heroism within yourself and play out the hand you've been dealt. The universe never sets a challenge that can't be met. You just need to believe in yourself in order to find the strength to face it.

Where to start? I feel like I should say a few words to mark the occasion, but I'm not good at speeches. Perhaps I could borrow from one of the many creation myths that have been – will be – written by others more adept at capturing the spirit of momentous events like this.

I start to ask Bec if she can recommend an appropriate extract. But then I recall something Mum used to read to me when I was young. Mum wasn't especially religious, but she read to Gret and me from a variety of holy books. I don't recall the exact way it went, and I guess my choice won't suit everyone, but what the hell, this is my show, so I'll run it the way I please.

Clearing my throat, to a chorus of good-natured groans from Kernel and Bec, I chant solemnly. "In the beginning Grubbs created the heavens and the earth, and everything was dark. Then Grubbs said, 'Let there be light!'"

And there was light.

Coolio!

THE END

THE DEMONATA
FEBRUARY 6ᵀᴴ 2001 — OCTOBER 1ˢᵀ 2009

Look out for

PALACE OF THE DAMNED

Book 3 in the epic saga
of Larten Crepsley

Damning you all
October 2011

